Thicker Than Blood

Murder, Hide & Go Seek Texas Style

Earl Snort

Barlow Adams Series Book V

TotalRecall Publications, Inc.
1103 Middlecreek
Friendswood, Texas 77546
281-992-3131 Tel
www.totalrecallpress.com

ISBN: 978-1-64883-2567
UPC: 6-43977-42567-6

Library of Congress Control Number: 2023936201

FIRST EDITION
1   2   3   4   5   6   7   8   9   10

Not a speck of this is true. It's all a pack of lies.

Dedication

To my wife of more than 51 years, and to every one of those kind souls who encourage me to keep on writing.

In Memory of Soldier TRT & Lawmen JFM, SWM, & JSH.

Muchas Gracias to JFW.

"Mama, put my guns in the ground. I can't shoot them anymore. That long black cloud is coming down. I feel I'm knocking on heaven's door. Knock, knock, knocking on heaven's door . . . . ."
--Knocking on Heaven's Door - Recorded by Bob Dylan

"I can feel it coming in the air tonight, oh Lord. And I've been waiting for this moment for all my life, oh Lord. Can you feel it coming in the air tonight? Oh Lord, oh Lord. Well, if you told me you were drowning, I would not lend a hand. I've seen your face before, my friend, but I don't know if you know who I am. Well, I was there and I saw what you did. I saw it with my own two eyes. So you can wipe off that grin, I know where you've been. It's all been a pack of lies . . . ."
--In the Air Tonight - Recorded by Phil Collins

"You call me out upon the waters, the great unknown where feet may fail. And there I find You in the mystery in oceans deep. My faith will stand. And I will call upon Your name, and keep my eyes above the waves. When oceans rise, my soul will rest in Your embrace, for I am Yours and You are mine. Your grace abounds in deepest waters. Your sovereign hand will be my guide, where feet may fail and fear surrounds me. You've never failed, and You won't start now . . . . ."
--Oceans (Where Feet May Fail) - Recorded by Hillsong UNITED

Earl Snort - 2023

LIST OF CHARACTERS

MAJOR CHARACTERS - QUAYLE COUNTY

Deputy Sheriff Barlow Adams - Protagonist
Sheriff Solomon Pratt
Chief Deputy Alexander "Alex" Snodgrass
Deputy Sheriff Clarence "Slick" Oldman
Deputy Sheriff Ella Mae Gillespie
Arthur Baker - Rancher - Barlow's Father-in-Law
Clarice Baker - Barlow's Mother-in-Law
Sarah Baker Adams - Barlow's Wife
Cordell Baker - Rancher - Barlow's Brother-in-Law - Victim
Henry "Hank" Baker - Barlow's Brother-in-Law
Bryce R. Garrett - Liquor Store Owner - Victim

MINOR CHARACTERS - QUAYLE COUNTY

Deputy Sheriff Ernie Atwater
Deputy Sheriff Noble "Chunk" Bustamante
Deputy Sheriff Kirk Shoemaker
Deputy Sheriff Randy Meacham
Deputy Sheriff Dewey Carruthers
Sheriff's Administrative Assistant Loretta Youngblood
LaRue Dinkins - President of the Bank - Victim
Judge Maxwell "Maximum Max" Sweeney
District Attorney Able DeWitt
Public Defender Sam Davis
Buck Boyd - Wrecker Driver/Impound Lot Owner
Pete Ricketts - Coroner

MAJOR CHARACTERS - EL PASO COUNTY

Bruce K. "Rocky" Givens - Bandit Leader
Everett M. "Ev" Raymond - Bandit
Rodney A, "Bug Eye" Tinsley - Bandit
Nicholas D. "Nick" Crenshaw - Bandit
Chief Deputy Derrick Hornsby
Captain Stanley Howard
Sergeant Julio Elias

MINOR CHARACTERS - EL PASO COUNTY

Gilbert G. "Texas George" Dinwiddie - Saloon Owner - Informant
Darlene Lynn Underwood - Stripper - Unwitting Informant
Rodolfo Garcia - Manufacturing Plant Night Manager - Informant

Goldie Lassiter - Motel Night Manager - Informant
Mavis H. Crook - Everett Raymond's Sister
Mrs. Lopez - Bruce Given's Elderly Neighbor/Close Friend
Caleb T. Scroggins - Newspaper Reporter
Nancy M. Crenshaw - Nick Crenshaw's Mother
Elaine A. Schmidt - Nick Crenshaw's Grandmother

MINOR CHARACTERS - VAL VERDE COUNTY

Sheriff Will Shive
Captain Jay Ortman
Deputy Sheriff Hiram Snow

MINOR CHARACTERS - CROCKETT COUNTY

Sheriff Enoch P. Larkin
Chief Deputy Calvin Close
Deputy Sheriff Clyde Osborne
Delmont "Bud" Decker - Used Car Lot Owner - Victim

MINOR CHARACTERS - BREWSTER COUNTY

Sheriff Leland Waters - Deputy Ella Mae Gillespie's Uncle
Deputy Sheriff Ambrose Collins
Deputy Sheriff Enos Garvey
Dispatcher Miriam Hanson

MINOR CHARACTERS - WEBB COUNTY

Sheriff Oliver Vincent
Chief Deputy Roland G. Epps
Chief of Laredo Police Linus Merriweather
Jeffrey R. Cooper - Armored Car Guard - Victim
Abraham K. Sipowicz - Armored Car Guard - Victim
Morris L. Yeager - Armored Car Driver - Victim/Witness

MINOR CHARACTERS - DIMMIT COUNTY

Chief Deputy Ethan Heim
Paco Rúiz - Juvenile Car Thief - Witness
Raúl Rúiz - Juvenile Car Thief - Witness
Mr. Gomez - Used Car Dealer

MINOR CHARACTERS - MAVERICK COUNTY

Captain Nathan Bedford Forrest "Captain Reb" Landry
Gavin Greathouse - Juvenile Witness
Times are tough for us!
Be safe friends!

ABOUT THE BOOK

The year is 1973. A four-man crew of stick-up artists has been on a rampage in South Texas along the Rio Grande corridor from El Paso to Laredo.

One day they stick up the bank and liquor store in Mosby in Quayle County, killing one person and severely wounding another. Mosby is a small town in a large county, with only 3,000 souls and very little crime.

The chase is on. No quarter asked or taken by either side. Sheriff Solomon Pratt and his eight-man, two-woman department are committed to bringing the culprits to justice. Deputy Barlow Adams is doubly committed because one of the victims is his brother-in-law. Barlow's bond with his brother-in-law is thicker than blood.

PROLOGUE

The Hard Part is Over

Saturday, March 31, 1945

They did it! They successfully completed their 25th bombing mission! The ground crew was chocking the blocks.

The war wasn't over yet, but aerial combat was over for Arthur G. Baker and the other nine men assigned to the Fanny G.

Arthur was a 20-year-old Technician 5th Grade in the U.S. Army Air Force. For those uninitiated into the hierarchy of World War II U.S. military ranks, a technician 5th grade is a position about a third of the way up the enlisted chain of command, equivalent to a corporal. One who bears such a rank is identified by wearing the same two chevrons as a corporal, except with a "T" underneath the bottom inverted "V" of the two chevrons. In Arthur's case, he received a lofty 50% bump in pay for being on flight status, earning $99 per month, whereas a corporal not on flight pay only earned $66 per month. Consider those amounts to that of a private, the lowest rank, who only received $50 per month. One could posit that Arthur was twice as valuable as a lowly private. Others could posit that his job was twice as dangerous. Take your choice.

Arthur G. Baker and the rest of the 10-man aircrew, including Captain Aubrey D. Clark, pilot and commander of the B-24 Liberator they lovingly named the Fanny G. (for Galore), were all relieved and ecstatic. For the past year and change, they had been assigned to the 44th Bombardment Group (The Flying 8-Balls) in the 8th Army Air Force, headquartered at various airfields in England.

Arthur, one of two waist gunners, and several other crewmen never thought they would live to see this day. Overall, the Fanny

G. had lost two of its aircrew members in combat (one by flack and the other by a German Messerschmitt). Another was maimed (3rd degree burns) and invalided out of the Army. Four other crewmen, still operational, were also awarded Purple Hearts for wounds sustained during combat. That's seven Purple Hearts in one 10-man crew (not including replacements!) Arthur was thankful he wasn't one of them, although he had been awarded the Air Medal for valor. Furthermore, the Flying 8-Balls had lost nearly half of its authorized strength in aircraft and personnel, although Uncle Sam was Johnny-on-the-Spot when it came to getting replacement aircraft and airmen. Sadly, the Brits were not that fortunate, having been at war since June of 1939.

Arthur was ready for this war to end. He had eagerly enlisted a week after graduation from high school in 1943. He completed basic training at Barksdale Field in Louisiana, and aviation gunnery school at Will Rogers Airfield in Oklahoma. Initially, Arthur and other spanking new airmen (referred to as slick sleeves because they were at the bottom of the totem pole and had no stripes on their sleeves) were deployed to begin their warrior duties as bomber crewmen on anti-submarine patrols while stationed at the Army airfield in Savannah, Georgia. (One crew spotted a German sub and sank it.) Then in March, 1944, Arthur embarked on a troop ship to England, where he was assigned to the Fanny G. as a replacement waist gunner (the previous one having been killed). He got his initial taste of aerial combat in Europe within his first two weeks. Before he even changed his bedsheets, the squadron was deployed for a two-month TDY (temporary duty) in Libya for action including the invasion at Anzio. When they returned to England, they resumed bombing raids in Northern Europe.

The only time Arthur hadn't been on operational flying status was when he was hospitalized for pneumonia. There were also times when the Fanny G. was sidelined for repairs and none of the crew flew unless perchance, one of them volunteered to fill in for a sick or wounded airman assigned to another aircraft. Arthur wasn't that crazy. Also, there were times the weather was just too nasty to fly. Those days were usually spent playing cards in the barracks, writing letters home, sleeping, or taking advantage of a pass to let off some steam at a nearby pub.

Arthur was ready to go home. Everyone knew the war was winding down in Europe. Nobody wanted to be the last American casualty. (By in large, they didn't want to be re-deployed to the Pacific theater, either.)

In the beginning, Arthur thought it would be glamorous to be an airman - flying over the wild, blue yonder, sleeping in a barracks between clean sheets, eating hot chow, seeing exotic lands, and not humping a pack for miles and miles on foot while dodging bullets and grenades along the road to victory. He never considered flack, or enemy fighters, or burning to death, or falling 25,000 feet to your death. It wasn't glamorous anymore. It was dreadful, dangerous work. Now all he dreamed about was returning to Texas and marrying his lass, Clarice, (that is, if she would still have him,) ranching like his father before him, rearing a family, and hoping if he had any boys, that they would not have to go to war.

His dreams were modest. He didn't want to be President of the United States, as wealthy as Andrew Carnegie, or an All-Star major league baseball player like Lou Gehrig, and he certainly didn't want a posthumous Purple Heart. He just wanted to ETS (expiration of term of service) and go back home as a PFC (private fucking citizen.)

Arthur was blessed. He got what he wished for. Many didn't.

CHAPTER 1

Plugging Along

Groundhog Day, Friday, February 2, 1973

It was just past midnight. Barlow was back in the saddle at work, sitting at the senior deputy's desk in the Quayle County Sheriff's Office, which was situated on the ground floor in the rear of the courthouse. He was nursing a hot cuppa joe. He liked his coffee black. This was his fifth night alone and he was bored like a deaf mute at a piano recital or a eunuch at a burlesque show. It was too quiet working nights all alone. He wondered how Archie did it for all those years.

Sheriff Sol had thrown Barlow's partner, Ella Mae Gillespie, a bone, assigning her to the afternoon shift this week. Gillespie had been on the job for a little over a year now, performing as well as everyone else in the office and better than some. She deserved Sheriff Sol's consideration. (Both Gillespie and Barlow considered the afternoon shift a huge reward because most of the action occurs on that shift.) After the dust up at the Circle A Ranch last year, where she had been surprised by a gang of illegal alien smugglers and had to shoot it out, nobody had any doubts about her grit or her competence. Gillespie had definitely earned her spurs.

Barlow and Sarah were now in their third semester at Sul Ross State University, still taking twelve hours per. They had two more semesters to go after this one to graduate. Going to night school full-time while working full-time was grueling. Nevertheless, they liked all but one of their professors and the coursework had been interesting.

This semester's course load included American History from 1850 to 1900; the U.S. Legislative Branch; the Rise of Communism; and a Survey of Asian History. Also, for the first time ever, they had Fridays off from school. It felt like they were getting a three-day weekend, even though Fridays were still a workday. They were both counting the weeks until they earned their diplomas and could hang them up on the wall in their office at home. Earning a college degree was worth the effort for both of them, even if it weren't a prerequisite for employment. If nothing else, it added credibility, not to mention pride in the accomplishment. Barlow wished Grandma Bea were still alive so she could see it come to pass.

Sarah's brother, 2nd Lieutenant Henry T. Baker, otherwise known as Hank, was out of the Army now. He completed his year-long tour in Vietnam last March, returning with a Combat Infantryman's Badge, Army Commendation Medal with V-device (for valor), and a Purple Heart, not to mention the standard array of medals all Vietnam veterans were awarded, including the National Defense Service Medal, Vietnam Service Medal, and the Vietnam Campaign Medal (the latter of which was awarded by the Republic of Vietnam.) His military obligation of two years active duty ended in June of 1972. He received an Honorable Discharge. Then he up and surprised everybody. He didn't return home. He had his reasons.

Hank had reported for active duty in June of 1970, two weeks after he graduated as a member of the Corps of Cadets from Texas A&M with a bachelor of arts degree in geography. (He began with a major in agriculture, but switched degree programs his sophomore year.) The first three branches of service on his ROTC wish list for commissioning into the Army Reserve with a two-year active duty obligation, followed by four years in the Individual Ready Reserve (IRR), were Armor, Field Artillery, and Air Defense Artillery. What he got was Infantry, which was number eight out of the twelve choices on the list. What a gut check! Not exactly what he had in mind! Infantry was the same branch a third of all his ROTC classmates got, like it or not.

The Army offered Hank Airborne School as a door prize, with a chance of going to Ranger School afterwards. He respectfully declined both. If he were going to be an infantryman, he would be a leg rather than a paratrooper. He wanted absolutely no part of un-assing a perfectly good airplane while it was still in flight. Furthermore, there were two parachute jumps built into the training at Ranger School, so that also made it a non-starter for him, assuming he were even selected. The bottom line was, one must volunteer to attend either school and Hank was not volunteering. He knew the Army wouldn't be pushing either of those schools if he got one of the first three branches on his wish list. When's the last time the Army dropped a tank out of a C-130?

The Army began twisting his arm. It seems that the Army preferred for all their infantry officers to be airborne. Earning a parachutist badge would be a career enhancer, as would earning a ranger tab. "Get with the program, Lieutenant! You seem like a smart guy."

Hank held his ground. Why wouldn't the Army send him to one of the other branches which don't care one way or the other if their officers are Airborne Ranger qualified, like Armor or Field Artillery, or Air Defense Artillery? Those are all combat branches with important combat roles to play.

Answer - Because brand new butter bar lieutenants don't drive the Army train. Roger that, Lieutenant? They ride the train and obey orders. There's a right way, a wrong way, and the Army way. This is the Army way.

Then, without explanation, the Army suddenly shifted gears. Don't want to wear airborne wings, Lieutenant? Not a problem. The Army respected his wishes and cut his orders to the Infantry Officer Basic Course at Fort Benning, followed by the Motor Officer School, which he hadn't requested, but which was not predicated upon being a volunteer. Upon completion of both, he got two more weeks of leave before embarking on that big silver bird to the Republic of Vietnam as a mechanized infantry platoon leader assigned to the 196th Infantry Brigade operating in Da Nang. The 196th had the distinction of being the last combat brigade to depart Vietnam in June of 1972, but Hank was already back in the world by then.

Returning to the world worked out the same for Hank as it had for Barlow three years earlier. Barlow's unit was still in Vietnam when he departed with six months still remaining on his hitch. The Army transferred him from the 9th Motorized Infantry Division in Vietnam to the 1st Infantry Division in Fort Riley, Kansas, to complete his military obligation.

Hank had three months left and his unit also remained in Vietnam. He had to go somewhere, anywhere in CONUS (military-speak for the continental U.S.) but he was so short, he didn't even cast a shadow, which translated, means that his ETS was nearly up. In other words, it didn't really matter to the Army what billet he was assigned to (so long as it didn't cost the Army money) because he was a short-timer.

Since Hank was from Texas, he requested a transfer to the 36th Infantry Division, which in all actuality, was the Texas Army National Guard. Specifically, he requested an assignment to the 36th's 3rd Brigade, 2nd Battalion, which was headquartered in Austin, Texas, the state capital. No biggie. The Army was happy to fulfill his request. After all, what National Guard unit couldn't use a combat experienced Infantry lieutenant still on active duty for three months? Give other infantrymen who had not been in combat the value of his up-to-date experience.

Hank's commitment only called for him to serve in the IRR upon completion of his active duty time. In reality, all that meant is that he was subject to recall at anytime during those four years if the President declared the country to be in emergency status and he needed all hands on deck like we did after Pearl Harbor was bombed. Otherwise, once Hank received his Honorable Discharge certificate from active duty, he was done, a gone pecan. Adiós amigo. See ya later alligator. That's what his folks thought, anyway.

Hank had other ideas. When he reported for duty in Austin, he told the battalion commander he wanted to join the 36th as a national guardsman upon completion of his active duty service. The Army always has a shortage of lieutenants, especially seasoned ones, so this was a no-brainer for the commander. He even had a platoon of shitbirds in mind. Those jokers needed a buck up by an officer who had seen the elephant, been wounded in combat, and returned a wiser man for it. A lieutenant like that wouldn't tolerate slackers. He would lead from the front.

None of Hank's family understood this - at least initially. Then Hank told them "the rest of the story" as radio personality Paul Harvey would say. Hank was a die-hard Texas A&M Aggie, just like their dear family friend, Judge Maxwell B. Sweeney, who, upon graduation from A&M, enrolled in the University of Texas to attend law school. Setting all differences aside, Hank had been accepted at the University of Texas Graduate School, A&M's sworn enemy in all matters, but especially in football. Hank had applied to UT because it offered advanced degrees in geography and A&M did not. Pragmatism overcame sentiment, just like it did for Judge Sweeney. Hank planned to use his G.I. Bill money to pay for it. The Army National Guard salary would come in handy too, not to mention that he would get promoted to 1st Lieutenant within a year if he stayed in, earning even more money.

Hank had it figured out all along, but he never mentioned it to anybody until it was a done deal. He didn't want to face his family's disappointment by not settling back in Mosby. He also didn't want to put up with the obligatory razzing from all his Aggie buddies until he could no longer put it off. His ultimate career goal was to become a cartographer, or possibly a demographer, but he could always fall back on teaching geography if either of those two fields fell through.

Hank's folks (all except for one) had expected that he would return to the ranch once his commitment in the Army had been fulfilled. Deep down in his heart of hearts, Arthur knew Hank never would from the very moment he switched his major in agriculture for geography. Another of Arthur's concerns had been that Hank would be sent overseas in combat once he enrolled in the ROTC program. (Arthur never confided that fear with Clarice.) Arthur had been right about that, too. Hank's older brother, Cordell, missed combat by enlisting in the Army National Guard. Even then, had Cordell's unit been deployed, at least he was a tanker, not a ground pounder. Setting aside his druthers, Arthur counted his blessings that all his children were happy and successful in their various pursuits. Not only that, the two who married had married well.

Hank was in the middle of his second semester of graduate school. He planned to come home for the last two weeks in June before his Army National Guard unit went to Fort Hood for its annual training. Barlow and the rest of the family could hardly wait. It had been seven years since Hank went off to college, and the family had seen way too little of him since.

The other momentous news in the Baker clan was that Cordell's wife, Darla, was pregnant. She was due to deliver in September. The newborn would be the Baker's first grandchild. Darla and Cordell had just announced it. Since that moment, Clarice had been dropping balloon-sized hints that it sure would be nice if the newborn had a cousin to play with. Since Hank wasn't living in Mosby, plus he didn't even have a full-time girlfriend, it was obvious to whom this heavy-handed hint was directed.

To Barlow's relief, Sarah told her mom that she was only 22 years old with another year left to finish senior college and that she wasn't ready yet to be a mom. Barlow wisely stayed out of this internal, female family discussion. No matter what he opined, he would be on the wrong side of the debate and he knew it. Fortunately, Arthur vocally sided with Sarah, so that topic had been shelved - at least for the next year, but they all knew Clarice would not give up so easily. She loved kids too much. Hopefully by then, she would be too consumed with the bairn, that they could kick this can down the road for another year or so. After all, Darla had just turned 26, and she would be 27 by the time this first grandchild was born.

Barlow's thoughts moved onto other matters. He hoped Sheriff Sol would let him work some day or afternoon shifts while he was out of school for the summer. He knew he was plugged in for a week of in-service POST (Police Officers Standard Training) classes at WTJC (West Texas Junior College) the end of August, the same time as Slick. Also, Sarah and he had planned to take a week off between rodeos at the Quayle County Rodeo Grounds where Sarah worked, sometime this summer to go pay a visit to his sister, Chloe, and her family in Bisbee. That would have to be in July or sometime in August. Sarah had never been to Bisbee, and she had been chomping at the bit to go see it and their nephew, Oliver, who was four years old now. Barlow knew she would fall in love with it, especially with the charm of all the old, historic western buildings, not to mention the array of good eateries.

Barlow had to quit wool gathering. He opted to read a few more chapters in his *Rise of Communism* textbook before giving Asian history a whirl (to reduce the increase in his blood pressure brought on by reading all about the logic, virtues, and humanitarianism of communism). Geez, did Barlow ever hate the commies, especially the true believers! What a bleak way of life for those who were consigned until death in the proletariat! Forcing someone to live in that political system should be a crime against humanity. Wasn't that why we fought in Korea and were still fighting in Vietnam - to stem the tide of encroaching communism?

How was it that Barlow was so convinced that communism was so bad? It was simple. How many capitalists living in democracies run off to the Soviet Union or Red China, renouncing western citizenship to become a good Soviet or Chinese citizen? Answer, virtually no one. That's how he knew! Even a traitor like the assassin Lee Harvey Oswald emigrated from the Soviet Union back to America after his immigration to the utopian Soviet paradise didn't turn out the way he expected it would.

Barlow was all fired up, all his buttons pushed, ready to go fight a faceless enemy again just that quickly! He needed to set communist propaganda aside for the night. Maybe he should just move on to Asian history.

Better yet, maybe he'd get lucky tonight and someone would generate a little police work for him. Give him the opportunity to exercise his law enforcement skills. Keep him razor sharp. Maybe even something usually considered boring and hardly worth his time. Anything!

Perhaps an irate neighbor would call in a barking dog complaint because it was keeping him awake; or maybe some drunks would get into a fight at the Dry Gulch Saloon and need to be tossed out or arrested; or the burglar alarm would go off at the bank (even if it turned out to be a false alarm); or some knuckleheads would start drag racing down Highway 90 and he could get into a high-speed pursuit. That would be the best. Barlow was so desperate for some action, he would even cheerfully respond to a caller who couldn't sleep and was counting sheep, but couldn't remember what number came after a hundred and needed a verbal assist.

Barlow would welcome any call tonight. He was going stir crazy. You know, like a eunuch at a burlesque show.

CHAPTER 2

Living off the Fat of the Land

Thursday, February 8, 1973

They called themselves the Givens Gang. They fancied themselves the modern day version of the Cole Younger Gang, the Jesse James Gang, and the Bob Dalton Gang all rolled into one, only smarter, deadlier, and much better looking.

The reason they were called the Givens Gang is because Bruce K. "Rocky" Givens, at 31 years of age, 6-feet, 2-inches tall, 185 pounds, with sandy hair and hazel eyes was the oldest, toughest, and smartest member, and because he was the only one who claimed to have actually killed somebody, although he never shared any details. Also, he was the only one to have served a prison sentence. He did two hard years for auto theft in the Texas State Penitentiary in Huntsville. He was also a high school graduate with a Bad Conduct Discharge from the Navy for shoplifting a watch from the base exchange for no better reason than because he thought he could get away with it. He didn't need a watch. He already owned two!

The rest of the gang had been in jail but not prison. They weren't convicted felons, convicted being the operative word.

Rodney A. "Bug Eye" Tinsley, 24 years old, 5-feet, 11-inches tall, 175 pounds with black hair and brown eyes, had been arrested in El Paso, the gang's hometown, for drunk and disorderly, simple assault, shoplifting, and drunk driving - all misdemeanors. He never served more than a month for any of those arrests or convictions, but he did lose his driver's license for six months. He had been drafted, but the Military Entrance Processing Station (MEPS) determined that he was IV-F (medically unqualified.) His vision was 20-400. He wore glasses with lenses thicker than the bulletproof glass in an armored limousine. He had quit school in the 10th grade. School was way too boring for a cavalier stud duck such as Bug Eye, who had already knocked up two gullible, mostly innocent fallen angels in his 10th grade class. Besides, Bug Eye already knew that he was smarter than all his teachers. All you had to do was ask him.

Nicholas D. "Nick" Crenshaw, 23 years old, 6-feet tall, 160 pounds, with brown hair and brown eyes, a little on the effeminate-looking side but not queer, got busted one time over in Alpine in Brewster County for possession of marijuana and for carrying a concealed deadly weapon, which just happened to be a switchblade knife he stole from his uncle's bureau drawer. Nick spent a couple of weeks in jail and was sentenced to credit for time served, but this is how that came about. He had a lucky charm in his pocket.

Crenshaw was a mouthy punk. One of the deputies pulling jail duty tuned him up after Nick spit on him. A visitor, who just happened to be a bleeding heart Catholic priest with a fervent dislike for law enforcement, saw it. What the priest didn't see was the precipitating spitting incident. The priest filed a complaint against the deputy. In return for Crenshaw not pursuing formal action against the deputy, the district attorney allowed Crenshaw to plead out to both misdemeanors and take a walk with credit for time served. The deputy was given a verbal reprimand by the sheriff, Leland Waters, Deputy Gillespie's uncle, with a warning to be more careful next time. (Sheriff Waters knew without a doubt the punk had it coming.) Nick had a high school diploma and one year of junior college. He had been drafted and had served two years in the Army Chemical Corps. He was honorably discharged with the military rank of private first class. His civilian rank was asshole first class.

Everett M. "Ev" Raymond, was 29 years old, 5-feet, 9-inches tall, 180 pounds (mostly muscle), with red hair, blue eyes, and lots and lots of freckles. He also sported a tattoo of a black widow spider, one-inch long, on the inside of his left wrist. He had two arrests under his belt. The first, in El Paso, was for public drunkenness and indecent exposure for urinating in a patron's automobile (through an open window) at a strip joint while he was under the influence of alcohol. Ev got tuned up, too, for taking a swing at the arresting officer just outside his jail cell. Being a hard case, Ev never complained. He wore his black eye like the *Red Badge of Courage.* It added street creds. Besides, he knew he had it coming. He spent one night in jail and paid $100 in fines.

The second arrest was far more serious. In fact, technically it was considered a felony. At the time, besides being an up-and-coming, full-time dishwasher at a local greasy spoon on the wrong side of the railroad tracks, his part-time job (and obligation to Uncle Sam and the Governor of Texas) was as a private in C Company, 2nd Battalion, 1st Brigade, 49th Armored Division, Texas Army National Guard, located in Del Rio, which is the same company in which Cordell Baker had served. Raymond considered the National Guard a joke. After all, this wasn't Marine Corps Recon or Army Special Forces. These were weekend warriors, the pretend Army. Not the real deal, even if they all had completed Basic Combat Training and Advanced Individual Training just like the Regular Army. Not only that, some members actually were combat veterans.

Ev had been busted down several times from private first class back to private for habitually being AWOL (away without leave) during summer annual training, not to mention multiple weekend drills. The only reason he enlisted in the National Guard in the first place, so he said, was to avoid the draft, which at that time generally (but not always) meant a one-year tour of duty in the hot, sunny, rainy, and steamy Republic of Vietnam. (Sounds like a Marine Recon's dream vacation, doesn't it?)

After four years of Private Raymond's incorrigible behavior, his company commander, Captain Phillip Ardmore, with endorsements from his battalion and brigade commanders, filed general court martial charges against Private Raymond for dereliction of duty, insubordination, sixteen counts of being AWOL, theft of government property (a barracks mate's issued bayonet), making false statements, and a host of other charges. The court martial board found him guilty on all counts. Private Raymond got off lucky. He was given a dishonorable discharge and a six-month sentence to serve in the Val Verde County Jail (instead of the usual one-to-five years of incarceration in a prison). Everett Raymond was also a high school dropout. He made it through the 9th grade before he was expelled for provoking fights (five times). Everyone at the school was glad to see him go. Ditto for the Texas Army National Guard.

None of these sterling citizens had what one would consider a highly sought-after job. Rocky Givens had the best one. He worked in a factory which made wooden pallets. He earned $1.80 an hour, 20 cents above minimum wage. Bug Eye made minimum wage working as a parking lot attendant. He was the only one to blame if there were an issue during the day shift (since he was the only attendant working days). Nick didn't have a job. He sponged off his widowed mother who was a cashier at the Piggly Wiggly, and his grandmother who drew paltry Social Security retirement benefits. Ev Raymond worked for a company which serviced port-a-potties at construction sites, outdoor event venues, and the like. He was responsible for cleaning the units after the contents had been suctioned out into a tank truck. It was a shit job which also paid minimum wage, but he was well-suited for it. The main reason was, he was nose-blind so he never knew he smelled like the asshole he was when he got off from work before he cleaned up and changed clothes. Ev thought people were just funning him because of his job. Little did he know.

These four troglodytes became compadres after several months in which they had only been casual acquaintances at

Texas George's Saloon where they hung out nearly every night. This was also the same titty bar where Ev Raymond got arrested. They were regulars who fed off each other by laughing at one another's jokes, scaring off other clients they didn't like, screwing the same women, and eventually gang-banging two of them regularly who were more than content to trade a good time for weed or LSD or whatever drug du jour the Givens Gang happened to possess at the time.

One night Rocky suggested that it was high time for them to rake in a few easy bucks. Quit talking like badasses and start being badasses. You know, back up their personas. Right now they were all hat and no cattle. It was high time for them to start acting like a gang if they were going to call themselves a gang. This proposal, which was more of an order than a suggestion, as in put up or shut up, was enthusiastically approved by all.

They piled into Rocky's 1966, midnight blue, Pontiac GTO with pin-striping, white rolled and tucked leather seats, 389 cubic-inch, 360 horsepower engine, four-barrel Holley carburetor, four-speed manual transmission, mag wheels, straight pipes, Cherry Bomb glass packed mufflers, slicks on the back, and a candy apple red, rubber, Rat Fink statue hanging from the rear-view mirror. (The Rat Fink was Rocky's icon. It symbolized arrogance, contempt, meanness, and toughness.)

It was almost 1 a.m. when they parked in an empty A&P parking lot, cut through a dark alley on foot, and watched while drunks staggered out of a bar called Matilda's. Nobody but Rocky knew this was a meat market for queers. Rocky considered this a training mission for his crew.

Before long, an older, balding, pudgy man and a younger, effeminate, blond man with wavy hair strolled out of the bar together arm in arm. They walked over to a late model, white over maroon Cadillac Sedan de Ville, which was parked in the shadows of the building away from the street lights. The older man leaned against the driver's door. The younger man unzipped him and began performing fellatio.

What? These thugs-in-training considered themselves the consummate pussy hounds. They wondered why on Earth Rocky brought them here to watch this insult to their masculinity. This was disgusting! After several minutes, the younger man stood up, dropped his trousers and drawers to his ankles, and bent over the hood. The older man inserted himself and began humping away with fervor to get his rocks off. Both men were in the throes of bliss. Rocky waited a few minutes before he motioned for the crew to follow him over there.

The two rump rangers were too engrossed in their decadent pleasures to notice their encroaching audience. Rocky was in front. He walked up, ripped the older man off his conquest, and slugged him in the mouth. The man fell down to the pavement, and Rocky kicked him twice in the stomach. The man lay still, moaning but not moving. The younger man had started to run away, but Rocky grabbed him by his shirt, spun him around, and slapped him hard three times on his panicked, horrified, pansy face. The man burst out crying.

Rocky was gruff. He said, "Both of you fags hand over all your cash right now or I'll beat the living shit outta both of you. Make it quick before I stomp you both just for kicks."

The younger man was swift and compliant. He opened his wallet and handed Rocky all of his folding money, which only added up to $21.

Rocky said, "Beat it puss, before I change my mind." Puss didn't need to be told twice. He ran off while simultaneously trying to pull up his drawers and fasten his trousers without dropping his empty wallet.

The older man didn't need to be prodded either. Still on the ground, he thrust his wallet up at Rocky. It was thick with cash, credit cards, and photographs of his loving family, especially his wife, who was a well-endowed blonde about 40 years old. (Nice cleavage.) Rocky reached in and took all the cash, which was a whopping $452! He left the credit cards. Then he noticed the wife's photograph. He asked, "This babe really your wife?"

"Yes, sir."

"What's her name?"

"Nadine Jones."

"You divorced?"

"No, sir."

Rocky had the other guys come take a look. They all started panting like horny lizards.

Rocky asked, "Why ain't you home boning her instead of this little twit who just run off?"

"I don't know. Sometimes I just get these terrible urges."

"How about tomorrow night you come back over here and get your jollies while me and the boys go over to your house and show Nadine a good time, just like you was showing the nancy? Whaddaya say, boys? You all wanna give Mrs. Nadine Jones the best time of her fucking life?"

The boys all enthusiastically agreed.

"No, no, no! Please don't even imagine that! Besides, she ain't even a good lay. She just looks good. She don't even like to give it up for me. She'd call the cops on you all for sure. Please, just give me back my wallet and let me go. Keep the cash. I won't say a word. Promise!"

"Your driver's license says you live at 514 Columbine Circle, Mr. Walter C. Jones. That's in a ritzy neighborhood. What kinda work you do?"

"I'm the used car sales manager at Jamison Cadillac. Come in and see me sometime and I'll take good care of you. Can I go now?"

"I just may take you up on that Walter. I could use a new ride, but I think we'd all rather ride your wife instead, maybe while you watched so we could teach you some pointers. Nadine looks like she could use a good horse-fucking to me. Whaddaya say?"

"Please don't. I'm begging you."

"I'll hafta think about it. Nadine sure looks like a good lay to me, and it's obvious she ain't getting no satisfaction from the likes of you. I bet you ain't fucked her in five years, have ya? No, of course not! We know where you live now and what your sexual preference is, and it ain't girls. I bet nobody at your house or Jamison Cadillac even has a clue, do they?"

"No! Heavens, no! Please, just let us be. Please. Don't do this."

"Walter, me and the boys are watching you. Remember that. If you do something that pisses me off, I swear we will come over to your house and fuck Nadine silly until she decides to leave you and run off with us. My guess is you just ain't up to the job of satisfying a woman. Are you gonna piss me off?"

"Oh, no sir! Thank you. I'm leaving now. Can I have my wallet?"

Rocky handed him the wallet and gave him a hand up. He even brushed the dirt off Walter's clothes.

Rocky said, "Tell Walter goodbye, boys."

"Goodbye, Walter."

Walter got in his car and drove away slowly like he was treading on eggshells.

The gang walked back through the alley and headed in the opposite direction. Rocky gave each of them $100 and kept the rest for himself. They drove back to Texas George's Saloon, arriving just in time for closing. They waited outside in the back. Darlene, a big breasted stripper and pole dancer who was just getting off work, stepped outside and lit a cigarette. Darlene was their favorite punch because she was such a lusty nymphomaniac. She could never get enough. They carried her back to Rocky's pad, where they plied her with two, ten-milligram tablets of Valium and four beers. (They didn't know she had already smoked two joints, a gift from a client who really appreciated the blow job she gave him in the bar storeroom.)

They took turns riding her until they were all sated and too tired to stand up. Darlene was satisfied, too. She fell fast asleep with a contented smile on her face. Ev was the only one who went home. He left because he had to be up and at 'em at work at 6 o'clock. The rest of them crashed where they landed.

This was the very first time they actually committed a crime together. They continued rolling queers and drunks, breaking into businesses at night for goods to sell to a fence, big ticket items like TVs, stereos, guns and ammo (which for some reason until later on, they didn't keep for themselves), high-end cowboy boots and hats, etc. This progressed into boosting cars and pickup trucks, taking them across the border where they could sell them without any papers, no questions asked. Anything to make a fast buck. Not as scary as robbing a liquor store, but it oftentimes paid a bigger dividend.

Each success made them feel bulletproof, and they kept getting bolder and bolder. Because they were all-purpose thieves, not just burglars, or armed robbers, or auto thieves, or just targeting queers, they didn't rise to prominence in any of the specialized detective squads, like sex crimes, burglary, robbery/homicide, auto theft, narcotics, etc. They slipped through the cracks of the units which focus on one type of index crime and as a result, become detectives who are accomplished in solving one specific type of crime and in tracking down those types of offenders, but not necessarily the others. (Specialization can have it's unintended consequences.)

Then one day Rocky decided they were ready to step up to the big time and start pulling heists. Be stick-up men. Top of the scumbag food chain in Rocky's mind. Up the ante and the reward simultaneously, but also the penalty if they got busted.

First, they pulled off an armed robbery of a convenience store in the barrio. Piece of cake. No heavy lifting. It was a true adrenaline rush. Like taking candy away from a baby. This was more to their liking. They felt ten feet tall after it was over. Unfortunately, the haul was only $98, and hardly worth the risk.

A few days later, they watched a well-dressed man come out

of a bank counting a wad of cash. Rocky came up behind him and screwed a gun into his ear. Got away with $500 in new twenties. A mugging. Easy peasy, plus it was not a bank robbery which would bring out the FBI. If that happened, they knew they would definitely have problems. They all knew the reputation of J. Edgar Hoover and the highly vaunted G-Men. None of them wanted to be ruthlessly pursued by the legendary FBI who always got their man. You know, like John Dillinger or Pretty Boy Floyd.

Next, they hit a gas station at a busy intersection. This was a huge payday. They got nearly $900! The problem was, the owner came out with a revolver when they were getting into the (stolen) getaway car. Shots were exchanged, but fortunately nobody got hurt, especially them. Even so, the scare didn't prevent Rocky from bragging, "That SOB! I knew I should of plugged him the minute I saw him." The other three tough guys kept their traps shut, thankful that they hadn't been shot. Nick was especially thankful that he didn't shit himself because he nearly did. He would never have lived that down.

This brought them into the attention of the media and to the forefront of the El Paso PD's robbery squad. Wanted posters with written descriptions of everyone in the gang except for Bug Eye, their driver, were disseminated to the newspaper and to every law enforcement agency around El Paso, and maybe even some others, such as Texas DPS. This was the Givens Gang's wake up call. Now if they got caught, they were looking at life in prison.

Fortunately their identities were still unknown. They had to exercise more caution if they wanted to stay out of prison. They had to start sizing up their targets with better planning. No more spur-of-the-moment heists. Time to start wearing a mask. Wear similar clothing to confuse the victims. Something plain and nondescript. Try to mix up their modus operandi. Anything to stay a step ahead of the law.

They decided to lay low in El Paso and start pulling stick-ups in venues where the populace had yet to be alerted to their depredations (or so they supposed). The gang didn't know it yet, but this was the beginning of the end for them; however, the way they saw it, this was just the beginning. Time would tell.

CHAPTER 3

The Crime Spree Begins

Thursday/Tuesday, June 7/12, 1973

For the past week, the Givens Gang had been busy, collectively and individually. Rocky decided it was time to take a road trip, make some fast money, scare some law-abiding citizens, and generate some thrills on the jagged edge. He planned to commit mayhem on boring, unwitting, law-abiding, stupid sheeple throughout the Trans-Pecos, except for El Paso County, of course. No more shitting in their own mess kit.

Rocky told his minions to pack for seven days; to wear jeans, jean jackets, boots, cowboy hats, everyday, nondescript western clothing, nothing bright or unique so as to make it more difficult for them to be singled out or identified, allowing them to blend in with as many other men as possible; to obtain sufficient firepower to withstand a protracted gunfight with multiple cops if it came down to that; to acquire ample beer, tobacco, snacks, gauze, tape, bandages, topical antiseptic, porn magazines, and anything else they might need if they were forced to hole up for a day or two; to steal two muscle cars that would outrun Johnny Law; to bring more cash than they would expect to need, just in case they had a dry spell; to pick up some Texas road maps, including book maps of the big cities; and, to be ready to roll on Monday morning, June 11th.

On Thursday, June 7th, Bug Eye and Nick drove about a hundred miles north of El Paso to Alamogordo, New Mexico, where they found the perfect getaway car. It was a black, 1970 Monte Carlo with red leather seats. It was parked at a strip mall on the main drag. Bug Eye stood watch while Nick hot-wired it.

They were gone inside of five minutes. No one saw a blessed thing.

On Friday night, they burglarized a family-owned gun store in Las Cruces, New Mexico, called Elwood's Shooting Irons. Fortunately for them, it only had a local alarm which Rocky defeated easily. For it's size, the store was well-stocked.

They stole a Remington, Model 870, 12-gauge pump shotgun with a 20-inch slug barrel and rifle sights, and a box of 25 double-aught buckshot shells; two Colt Government Model 1911, .45 ACP caliber pistols with Parkerized finishes, each with one spare magazine, and two 50-round boxes of 230-grain military ball ammo; a 4-inch, blue steel, Smith & Wesson Model 29, .44 Magnum revolver with one 50-round box of 240-grain hollow point ammo; and, two 4-inch, nickel-plated Colt Python, .357 Magnum revolvers and two 50-round boxes of 158-grain, copper-jacketed flat-nose cartridges.

In addition, they stole a zippered, canvas sleeve shotgun case, a belt holster of varying styles for each handgun, a belt-slide, single magazine pouch for each .45 pistol, a gun belt with 12 cartridge loops for a .44, another with 24 cartridge loops for a .357, plus cleaning kits and anything else which struck their fancy, to include a black elastic shotgun butt sleeve with five loops to hold 12-gauge shells, a sheathed Buck Hunter folding knife, a military grade compass, a canvas range bag, and a pair of Bushnell binoculars.

This burglary was pulled off to upgrade their weaponry. Each member of the gang already owned a reliable handgun. Rocky even owned a shotgun, but not as nice as this Remington. They just wanted better guns with the best weapon-related accessories, and this place was a cornucopia for firearms enthusiasts. It was like Christmas Eve for each of them. Even though they had all been naughty, Santa brought them exactly what they wanted.

On Saturday, June 9th, Rocky and Ev spotted a copper-colored, 1972 Oldsmobile 442 at an upscale apartment building out near the airport. It fit the bill perfectly. They made off with it during the wee Sunday morning hours.

All the while, individually, they had been picking up the rest of the supplies a little at a time at a multitude of locations. Rocky bought two Coleman coolers so they could maintain ice cold beer in both vehicles throughout the trip. The idea was to amass everything they needed without raising any eyebrows. It was smart thinking. For example, who buys candy bars by the carton or six cartons of smokes or a dozen cases of beer? Absolutely no one, unless he's a hoarder or a retailer. It might draw some unwanted attention. Fly under the radar. The devil is always in the details.

On Monday morning, they were all antsy and ready to rock and roll. By now, Ev and Nick were wearing a little thin on Rocky. Too much time together in close proximity. All they did was talk trash. Ev talked all the time and Nick never shut up. It was too much. He teamed them up together in the Monte Carlo so he wouldn't have to listen to it. Rocky and Bug Eye took the 442.

Rocky let Ev take the shotgun. Keep him happy. Now each gang member had a new handgun of his own choosing. Rocky and Ev both selected a Colt .45. Nick took the .44. Bug Eye wanted matched Pythons so he stole two. He even stole matched left and right-hand holsters so he could wear them at the same time like Roy Fucking Rogers or the Lone Ranger. When and where he thought he could get away with that and remain inconspicuous was a question nobody bothered to ask. After all, it wasn't as if he could wear them under a long, oiled slicker like mounted men did in the woolly days of the last century. Nevertheless, it was too soon in the adventure to pick an argument just for the sake of arguing. They had to depend on each other to stay alive on this trip. They knew they'd be knocking over hornet nests during this excursion. They needed to stay friendly and focused.

Rocky lead and Ev followed. They drove southeast on US 90.

Rocky took his time. It would be stupid to speed and get stopped by Barney Fife or Deputy Dawg. It could end everything before they even got started. Rocky was on the lookout for someplace easy to pull off a profitable heist with a high probability of an unencumbered escape. No high-speed car chases. Not yet, anyway. He was in no rush. They drove nearly 50 miles just to get to the Hudspeth County line, the first county east of El Paso. There wasn't anything worth stealing in Hudspeth County. Nada. Rocky had been all through it more times than he cared to recall. He didn't entertain anyplace to rob until they arrived in Van Horn, about five miles inside Culberson County, 140 miles and two counties removed from El Paso County. The major north-south intersection was at TX 54, which continued north to Carlsbad Caverns in New Mexico.

Rocky drove north a couple of miles looking for a potential target while also trying to determine whether or not Van Horn had a permanent, competent police presence. (He didn't drive far enough.) Eventually, he came across a small, single-story, ramshackle, flat-roofed adobe building, circa 1870, off to itself on an unfenced, hardpan, half-acre lot, with a weathered, hand-painted, white board sign with black, block letters on the roof which read POLICE. He noticed a one-hole privy in the back. It looked quite a bit newer than the cop shop. He wondered if the privy were still in use, especially by any prisoners in the lockup. Wouldn't that be something - like a violation of the Eighth Amendment prohibiting cruel and unusual punishment? Be a bad place to be stupid enough to get busted.

Parked next to the privy was the rusting hulk of a marked, faded black and white, 1956 Customline Fordor police cruiser without wheels, resting on cement blocks. Rocky observed that there wasn't a terribly great contrast between that relic and the marked, faded black and white, 1965 Ford Custom sedan with a long whip antenna piercing the sky, which did have wheels. It too, had obviously seen a plethora of better days. It was parked in front of the cop shop all by its lonesome.

Fucking pathetic! Each tire was as bald as a cue ball on this presumably operational cop car. This newer fuzz mobile even had the old-style, pair of flat, circular, blinking, red roof-lights, common to those used by police in the early 1950s (and most likely still in use today in enlightened Soviet-block countries like Albania or Bulgaria). Maybe these lights were even cannibalized from the rusted relic. Geez! Nowadays most cops use one modern, cutting edge, domed, oscillating roof light. Heck! Van Horn hadn't even switched from red to blue emergency lights. Weren't they prescribed for all Texas law enforcement vehicles? Did anyone in Van Horn know or even care? Probably not.

Rocky noticed a tall radio antenna on the east side of the building, which meant the base radio probably had miles and miles of coverage, maybe even all the way to Alaska. Something to remember. Even so, Rocky was probably looking at the sorry, sum total of Van Horn's permanent police presence. He could just imagine one wore out old law dog inside, resting his weary, arthritic bones in a rolling, wooden office chair, keeping an eye on an empty jail cell, eating stale doughnuts, bald with a beer belly, wrinkled, armpit-stained uniform, scuffed, heel-worn boots, wearing a disreputable Stetson, armed with a rusty old, single-action Colt revolver which hadn't been fired or cleaned in years, hanging off his hip from a belt with nearly all the cartridge loops empty, pretending to enforce the law in this wore-out old squad car that hadn't been capable of accelerating past 60 since before its first oil change, which it didn't get until it had 60,000 miles on it. A four-year-old ticket book with only three carbon copies of citations written, was laying on the front seat next to the officer's personal roll of toilet paper for his one-hole privy that hopefully nobody but he ever used. What Rocky perceived was a toothless old pit bull guarding an oil-soaked junkyard jam-packed with worthless detritus, protecting the grateful undead. Probably the way it was, the way Rocky imagined it, but maybe not.

Rocky continued to drive through town, up and down US 90 and TX 54, as well as smaller arteries and goat paths throughout this sunbaked patch of redneck heaven. Mostly he saw rundown houses, small businesses, and some scraggly fenced acreage with a few pathetic cows and horses. There were a half-dozen or more parked 18-wheelers in the residential areas. Could be that over-the-road trucking was their primary economic engine here. He couldn't see anything else which would generate much revenue for the local citizenry.

Yes, indeed. Van Horn looked like pretty slim pickings. Then he watched people come and go at the small Piggly Wiggly. It was actually pretty busy. Maybe it would do. He drove in the lot and parked where he could observe the entrance. He told Ev to park across the lot from him in a cluster of other vehicles (for camouflage), and to sit tight.

Rocky studied the map. Assuming they pulled a job, he ruled out traveling east on the new Interstate Highway 10, because it would be flooded with state troopers searching for them. Even so, I-10 would be the fastest getaway. He saw that US 90 continued southeast from Van Horn about 80 miles to a similar-sized town called Marfa, in Presidio County. From there you could take US 67 southwest about 60 miles to the city of Presidio, and cross the border into Ojinaga, Mexico. He definitely did not want to go there. Nobody but the patrones and the bandidos had any dinero in Mexico. You could also take TX 17 from Marfa northeast about 100 miles to Pecos, in Reese County, a larger town known for it's rodeos. He'd been there several times. It was okay. The other option would be to continue east from Marfa on US 90 about 35 miles to another town called Alpine, in Brewster County, where they had a state college.

Rocky lit a Camel cigarette and pondered. Should they knock off the Piggly Wiggly? If they did, which way should they go? How should they do it? Where should they hunker down for the night? He needed a plan.

He decided to case the Piggly Wiggly himself. Once he was inside, picking up a small basket for purchases, he realized that people were both cashing checks and paying utility bills there. The grocery also housed a Western Union window where folks could wire or receive cash. It seemed that the Piggly Wiggly was Van Horn's epicenter of commerce. Who knew? This could be pretty profitable after all.

He purchased a loaf of Bunny bread, a package of Oscar Meyer's bologna, another of Kraft American cheese, a jar of mustard, a bag of Lays potato chips, a bag of Keebler's chocolate chip cookies, and a carton of unfiltered Camel cigarettes. Rocky had seen all he needed to see. He left and walked over to the Monte Carlo. He told Ev and Nick to drive over to the Esso service station on the south side of US 90 and fill up. They would eat lunch under the shade trees behind it while he filled them in on his plan. Then he walked back to the 442 and told Bug Eye the very same thing.

During lunch Rocky told the boys they were going to knock off the Piggly Wiggly. He described the chest-high, walled-in area in the front of the store with teller windows to cash checks, receive utility payments, send/receive money to/from Western Union, take complaints, make refunds on faulty merchandise, etc. He said it housed a safe, and that he had watched the manager, a tall string bean wearing a white, long-sleeve shirt and a black bow tie, open it to put cash inside. He said he would wait to announce the stick-up until he knew for certain the manager was near the safe.

They would park in the same vicinity as they had parked earlier. They would go in separately. He and Ev would do the actual robbery. Nick would take a post just inside the front door to watch for cops. Bug Eye would watch from behind the three check-out lanes, guns concealed, keeping an eye out for heroes with a death wish. Bug Eye's job was to neutralize all heroes.

Ev and Rocky would wait until just before they sprung the

trap to pull up their bandannas to cover their faces. Nick and Bug Eye would not wear masks. Hopefully, no one would snap to the fact that there were actually four robbers instead of two. They had to be in and out in five minutes. They would leave with the natural flow of traffic if at all possible.

Plan A was to take US 90 south about 80 miles to Marfa, where they would take TX 17 northeast about 100 miles to Pecos to lodge for the night. Failing that, if they got separated, Plan B, was to meet up in Alpine which is about 35 miles east on US 90 from Marfa. Find a place near the college and sit tight. Wait until morning. If the other car hadn't showed up by then, you're on your own. If you decide to return to El Paso, be smart about it. Don't retrace your steps unless you just can't wait to get busted. Ditch your wheels someplace out of sight, and grab something nobody's looking for, like an old pickup truck or a granny car. Lay low for a few days. If you see your face on TV, better find a new home at least 500 miles away from El Paso, and never look back. Hang out with the hippies. Get a real job and be a citizen. Join the U.S. Merchant Marine. Whatever you decide, just make sure you don't rat anyone out unless you want to die. He looked each man in the eye, hard for several seconds, to make sure they understood the penalty for snitching.

Nobody had any questions or comments. It was game time.

The cars left separately. The Monte Carlo went first. Rocky waited another five minutes before he and Bug Eye departed. He had Bug Eye park on the south side of the grocery facing east towards the exit. They watched while Ev and Nick walked inside. Rocky went next. Bug Eye followed a minute later.

The manager was still in the office area with his back to the public. He was futzing around with some flyers. The gang was in place. Rocky nodded his head at Ev. Then Rocky turned away and pulled up his mask. He walked over to the half-door of the office area and tried the handle. It was locked. He reached over the top and opened it from the inside. An attractive, forty-ish female teller started to walk over and say something, but she saw his masked face and the .45 in his right hand. She backed up with the palms of both hands facing him chest high. Rocky noticed that she had a well-endowed chest. Nobody else seemed to be paying attention.

Ev was masked, standing in front of the Western Union window. He was pointing a .45 at the teller, who was a young bald man with light blue eyes and a weak chin. His eyes were watering and his chin was quivering. Without a word, he picked up a brown paper grocery bag and began filling it with currency.

Rocky walked up behind the manager and poked him in the back with the barrel of his .45. He whispered softly, "Open the safe and give me all the cash. If you say anything or do anything other than that, your widow will mourn your premature demise. Nod your head if you understand and wish to comply."

Mr. Huffington nodded his head. He stooped down and began dialing in numbers. His hands were shaking but he opened the safe on only his second try. Then he duckwalked to his right, never looking up, to facilitate Rocky's removal of stacks and stacks of currency in which the various denominations were banded together in packs of 100. Rocky found a convenient paper sack and began filling it up.

In the meantime, Ev made his way from the outside of the cage to the other two tellers and waited for them to fill his sack like it was trick-or-treat on Halloween. When they were done, he turned and emptied the cash register drawers of the three grocery checkers. Once that was accomplished, he turned and nodded to Rocky. All during the robbery, Ev never uttered a word.

Bug Eye watched while they emptied all the tills and the safe. He had already begun slowly making his way towards the door. When he arrived, he nodded his head at Nicky, who quietly headed towards the Monte Carlo.

Rocky helped Mr. Huffington to stand. Then Rocky spoke softly to the tellers. "The manager is walking out the door with me. If anyone tries to call the police, he gets it. Understand? I will release him as soon as I've gone. Then wait 10 more minutes before calling the police. You'll be sorry if you disobey me. Everyone understand?"

They all nodded.

Rocky whispered to Mr. Huffington, "Give me your keys. All of them. Your car keys. Your house keys. The store keys."

Mr. Huffington complied. Ev, Mr. Huffington, and Rocky all walked through the store to the front door. Ev waited outside for Rocky to come out. The coast was clear. Rocky looked at Mr. Huffington and asked, "Which key locks this door?"

Mr. Huffington pointed to the correct key.

Rocky said, "Give me your wallet."

He complied.

Rocky opened it and looked at the driver's license on the left side. Then he looked at a family photograph on the right side. He handed the wallet back. Rocky said, "Mr. Marion F. Huffington, Jr., I know your name and that you live at 161 Coffee Street. I know what your wife and kids look like. If you don't do everything exactly like I tell you, I'm going to come back in the middle of the night and hurt you and your family. Capeesh?"

"Yes, Sir."

"Good. I'm going to lock you inside the store. Go back to your office and wait 10 minutes. Then you can call the police. I will leave your keys out here someplace before I go. Do you understand everything I've just told you? I don't want anything bad to happen to you or your family. Are we agreed?"

Mr. Huffington nodded his head.

"Good. As soon as I lock you in, return to your office and tell your staff and customers to wait. Okay?"

"Yes, Sir."

Rocky locked the doors and told Mr. Huffington to get a move on. As soon as Rocky saw he was no longer in sight of the parking lot, both Ev and he walked back to their respective rides. Rocky wiped his prints from the grocery door key and tossed all three key rings along the side of the building towards the rear of the store. Both cars pulled out of the lot and proceeded south on US 90 as if they were hauling fresh eggs on a silver platter. The 442 lead and the Monte Carlo followed. While Bug Eye drove, Rocky counted their ill-gotten gains. They netted $2,814. That was over $700 each! This was their biggest haul ever.

That night they stayed at a Motel 6 in Pecos. They ate at a Mexican cantina. They bought gas and ice at a Sinclair. They recharged their coolers with more bottles of Coors which they drank in their rooms. They had the TV on, waiting for news of the robbery. It did not make the news. What? Maybe the IRA car bombings in Londonderry supplanted the news of their own daring robbery. It was a pity.

On Tuesday morning they took a leisurely drive to Alpine. They checked in at the Palomino Lodge. They rode through town looking for more easy pickings. Rocky decided not to rob anything there because the Brewster County Sheriff's Office was on the main drag and the deputies were too many and too active. He didn't want to flee back west, and there was nothing east until you got to Mosby, 100 miles away. Basically, there was no place to hide and too many cops to outwit. They ate steaks at the Longhorn Emporium. Nick tried to keep a very low profile since he had been arrested here before. They spent the evening in their rooms, swilling more Coors. Tomorrow they would check out Mosby.

CHAPTER 4

A Good Beginning to A Routine Day

Wednesday, June 13, 1973

Barlow was in hog heaven. Sheriff Sol had put him on day shift this week. Gillespie was working the night shift solo. To give each of them a break from working nothing but the midnight shift, Gillespie and Barlow were alternating on midnights to give them both some time on days and afternoons. To ensure that the midnight deputy had backup, the new regulations called for an afternoon shift deputy to assist the midnight deputy on all runs. Since there were so few midnight calls for assistance, this was but a minor imposition. The only drawback was that the midnight shift deputy was like a monk in a monastery who had sworn an oath of silence. No one to talk to. Even so, both Gillespie and Barlow preferred it this way rather than the old way, wherein they seldom had an opportunity to go out on a run. The only deviation from the new procedure occurred if they had a prisoner in jail. Then they both reverted back to the midnight shift.

It was 10 o'clock on a beautiful morning. So far, Barlow had written one non-moving traffic ticket, meaning that no points would be assessed against the violator if he were convicted. Barlow had cited Jasper Elrod for an equipment violation. Specifically, the violation was for operating a motor vehicle on a public right-of-way with a loud (worn out) muffler and a rusted out exhaust pipe which was belching noxious smoke and fumes like an out-of-control funeral pyre.

The offending vehicle was Jasper's derelict, filthy white, 1952, two-ton Dodge stake-bed dually he had been driving west on America Highway. The bed was full to capacity, piled high with metal junk. Jasper pulled over in the parking lot of Bilbo's Auto Parts Store, thoughtlessly blocking the entrance from anyone else who might have business there.

The warning citation Barlow wrote afforded Jasper 30 days to repair the vehicle and bring it to the sheriff's office for inspection. Once an officer verified that the vehicle had been repaired, the offender avoided court, not to mention a fine. Everything was forgiven. No wrongdoing attached. The alternative for not making the timely repairs was that Judge Sweeney would undoubtedly levy at least a $20 fine plus $15 in court costs. Not only that, Jasper would still be subject to an additional ticket each day he got caught driving the smoking, belching truck.

It was kind of ironic. Jasper should have pulled up and parked right outside the front door of Bilbo's, pretending he was headed there to purchase a new muffler system before Barlow flicked on the overhead, oscillating blue light and sounded his siren. No way in Hell Jasper could have been oblivious to all the noise and toxic fumes emanating from of the bowels of his truck. Besides, what other reason would Barlow have to pull him over? He wasn't speeding and Barlow didn't have a reputation for writing chickenshit tickets (like Kirk Shoemaker.) Of course, this ruse would assume that Bilbo's still carried parts for that old dinosaur, and that Jasper actually had the money to pay for them. Both of those assumptions were likely incorrect. Nevertheless, it might have saved Jasper the aggravation of dealing with a ticket. You know. Prevail on Barlow's empathy. It would've been worth a try. Now it was just another lost opportunity in a lifetime of lost opportunities, but then Jasper wasn't known for being an icon in the thinking department. Rather, he was universally known to be off the Richter scale in the dumbass department, as in being almost as smart as an overripe artichoke, except stinkier.

The rest of the story is that this barely mobile piece of automotive antiquity was the vehicle Jasper used to haul discarded junk to the scrap metal enterprise in Alpine, in return for instant cash money to buy fuel and beer and cigarettes among other vital necessities. It was a worthy endeavor, a public service of sorts, removing all the broken washing machines, truck axles, swing sets, tractor parts, radiators, bed springs, and so forth that nobody wanted and/or had abandoned along the roadside in Quayle County in violation of the littering law. This raggedy truck provided both Jasper and his fellow dimwitted neighbor, Jaybird Cadigan, a mostly honest, if modest living. It was mostly honest because Jasper wasn't above making an unauthorized midnight acquisition of an old, rusty, motor vehicle with long-time, expired license plates, which had been abandoned in someone's pasture for the past decade with weeds growing up all around it, not to mention fire ant mounds measured in feet, not inches, if he thought he could get away with it. After all, junk is junk, whether it's on private property or not.

The bottom line was that the citizens of Quayle County needed Jasper and Jaybird, just like swollen hemorrhoids need a proctologist. It was a symbiotic relationship. All parties come out ahead.

Besides being Officer Friendly to Jasper, the only other police duty that Barlow had attended to on this shift besides patrolling the streets, was responding to a call from the anxious, benign widow, Mrs. Demona Turnipseed, regarding a rattlesnake in her flowerbed. The snake was a scary-looking diamondback over six feet long, coiled and threatening to strike. Barlow shot it's head off and threw it's carcass in the empty lot next door for the buzzards to consume. Before that though, he cut off the rattles which had eleven buttons. It was kinda like a trophy, just like deer antlers or alligator teeth, the latter of which Barlow had none.

Around 11:50, as Barlow cruised west on America Avenue, just east of the Rodeo Grounds where it narrows down to two lanes from four, two automobiles in close succession blew past him like they were off to the races. Barlow turned on his blue bubblegum machine and siren, made a U-turn, and joined in hot pursuit. Both vehicles had a quarter-mile lead on him by the time he accelerated to 100 miles per hour, but he was gaining fast. Barlow was driving their newest cruiser, a marked, 1973 Dodge Polara, 4-door sedan, with the 440 cubic-inch, four-barrel carburetor, 370 horsepower engine. It was a model utilized as a pursuit vehicle by many police agencies because it could run 141 miles per hour without any tinkering. This was also Quayle County's second air conditioned, marked unit.

Barlow noticed that the lead car was a black, 1970 or 1971 Chevrolet Monte Carlo. The second car was a copper-brown, 1972 Oldsmobile 442. He didn't have the license plate number on either car, but he expected to get the 442's number once he got a little closer. He called in the chase and requested assistance, particularly from any Val Verde County or Texas DPS unit east of his location. (Barlow knew he was driving the fastest unit in the Quayle County fleet and that nobody could catch up with him unless they were already east of his location.)

Topped out at the top speed of 141 MPH, Barlow caught up with both cars. They were running flat out at 137 MPH. The license plate number on the 442 was Texas RRG-768. He called it in.

Quayle Base responded, "Quayle 6, that license comes back to a 1972 Oldsmobile, brown in color, to a Phillip A. Sneed, 130 Bluebonnet Lane, Apartment 4, El Paso. It's listed stolen as of June 10, 1973. Also DPS is responding from Del Rio westbound on Highway 90. You need to switch to F-2. Base will remain on F-2 until you inform us you've made contact with DPS or Val Verde."

"Roger that. Quayle 6 switching to Frequency 2."

As soon as Barlow changed frequencies, Quayle Base got back on the air. "Quayle 6 from Base. Quayle 1 wants to know how far are you from the Val Verde County line?"

"Tell Quayle 1, I'm about 20 miles west of the county line. We're locked in at 137 miles per hour. I can't see the Monte

Carlo's plate, but both vehicles have a front seat passenger plus the driver."

"10-4. DPS is still at least 50 miles east of you. Val Verde is even farther. We will pass this along."

The passenger in the 442 leaned out his window and fired six shots at Barlow. Three shots penetrated the windshield, one of which was only three inches from Barlow's head. At least one shot penetrated the grill and the radiator. Steam came boiling out, obstructing Barlow's view. He was losing power fast. He pulled over on the shoulder of the road and jumped out, grabbing his .30-30. He fired two rounds into the back glass of the 442 before it was completely out of range. Neither car slowed down.

Barlow returned to his unit and got on the mike. "Quayle Base, this is Quayle 6. Shots fired at the police. I returned fire. My unit is disabled. I'm not injured. Notify DPS and Val Verde the cars are probably nearing the county line. Also, call Buck Boyd and tell him I need a tow."

"10-4, Quayle 6. We'll notify the other agencies. Return to F-1. Wrecker will be there soon."

"10-4."

Barlow stewed while he sat helpless in his disabled unit. "Jiminy Christmas!" He slammed the palm of his hand on the steering wheel. So close, yet so far away. He wondered if he drew blood. He could only hope.

CHAPTER 5

Disaster Strikes

Wednesday, June 13, 1973

Arthur and Cordell left for town about 11 o'clock. They needed to purchase adult beverages to serve about 20 friends and neighbors for Hank's homecoming barbeque scheduled for Saturday. En route, Arthur asked Cordell to drop him off at the courthouse so he could visit with Sheriff Sol. Arthur hoped Sol would join them for lunch at either Betty's Diner or Crabtree's Restaurant. It didn't matter which. (Sheriff Sol and his wife, Joanna, were two of the homecoming barbeque guests.)

Arthur and Sol had been close friends for decades. Their relationship really took off when Arthur, who was in the 12th grade, and Sol who was in the 8th grade, were playing a pickup game of baseball with a dozen or more other boys at the school field. Arthur was the star pitcher on the Quayle County team. Sol was too young to play on the team, but he was a good prospect once he made the 9th grade. Arthur had a wicked curveball. It was his money pitch. Sol was in awe of it and he begged Arthur to teach him how to throw it. Eventually, Arthur relented. He spent many hours teaching Sol, against his better judgment, how to throw it. Sol was really too young to start throwing a curve because his muscles were still developing. He could throw out his arm before his body was mature enough to take the strain. Fortunately, Sol was big for his age so he didn't suffer any injuries.

A few months later, Arthur graduated from high school. He found himself with the Army Air Force in the European-African-Middle Eastern Theater of Operations. Upon his return from the war, he watched with pride as Sol replaced him as Quayle County's star pitcher.

History has a way of repeating itself. Two years after that, Sol found himself assigned to a submarine in the deep waters of the Pacific Ocean, somewhere off the coast of Korea, ready to pounce on any enemy vessels. It was Sol's time to fight for his country, just like it had been Arthur's time before him.

Their bonds continued to grow stronger and stronger. Sol became Sarah Baker Adams' godfather. With only 3,000 residents in Quayle County, the bonds of family and friendship run deep. Today Sol suggested they eat at Crabtree's just as soon as Cordell returned from his errand.

After Cordell dropped Arthur off at the courthouse, he drove four blocks to Bryce Garrett's Desert Rat Liquors, located at 404 East America Avenue. It was about 11:30. When Cordell pulled up in his white, 1970 Dodge 100 pickup, the lot was nearly empty. Old Man Wayne Whitehead was just coming out of the store carrying a pint of Old Crow. He waved at Cordell as he walked to his faded green, 1953 Ford F-100. He drove away just as Cordell entered the store. The only other vehicle in the lot was Bryce Garrett's spotless, olive green, 1972 Mercury Marquis, two-door hardtop, which was parked on the right side of the building in his personal parking space.

At this very same time, Rocky and Bug Eye parked at the Pecos Bank & Trust, cater-cornered across the street from the Quayle County Courthouse (and Sheriff's Office.) Fortunately, no patrons happened to be at the bank when they arrived. Rocky and Bug Eye waltzed into the bank wearing bandannas over their faces with guns in hand. In this instance, Bug Eye had each hand filled with a nickel-plated Colt Python. Once they were inside, Rocky, flipped the sign from open to closed, pulled the window shade down, and locked the door. It was mausoleum quiet in the bank, and the clicking noise of the lock may as well have been the fire alarm going off. Everyone looked up and took notice, even though Rocky and Bug Eye moved as silently as cats on the prowl.

The bank owner, Mr. LaRue Dinkins, looked up through the plate glass window from the desk in his private office. He pressed the silent alarm button under his desk, which rang at the sheriff's office. Then he stood, adjusted his coat and bolo tie, and strolled out to the public foyer like he was meeting a favored client, smug, authoritarian demeanor on his poker face. He faced the bandits along with his clerk who rose from her desk in disbelief. The three tellers watched from their work stations, looks of abject terror chiseled on their faces. There was no doubt in Rocky's mind who was the top dog in this bastion of financial integrity and security.

Rocky spoke softly. "Hands up, all of you. Anyone who tries to trigger an alarm will die, but you, Sir, (pointing his .45 at Mr. Dinkins) I will shoot you dead first.

"The way this works, my colleague here will step behind the counter and empty all the tills. If he picks up a stack with a die pack, I will shoot the teller responsible for whichever drawer it came from. Understand? Upon penalty of death, each teller will be responsible if my colleague gets a die pack. If I have to shoot even one of you, I might as well go ahead and shoot all of you. They can't hang me more than once, so what difference is it to me? Did I make myself crystal clear?"

The silence was palpable.

Mr. Dinkins cleared his throat. "Sir, may I speak?"

"It's your bank. Say whatever you want, but if you piss me off I will shoot you dead."

After a lengthy pause, Mr. Dinkins spoke louder. "Everyone, make sure the die packs are undisturbed. We all want to live."

"Bravo, Sir. Looks like everyone might just live to tell this story after all."

Bug Eye and the tellers made haste emptying all three cash drawers. The die packs were buried at the bottom of the twenties.

The payout from the tellers was decent, but not as decent as what they could get from the vault. That being said, Rocky was anything but stupid. He picked this particular bank because it was not FDIC insured (no sign advertising same stenciled in gold across the door or front window), meaning that the highly vaunted FBI did not have jurisdiction. They were eliminated from the equation; however, the bank was right across the street from the local cop shop. He had noticed two marked units in good condition parked out back. He didn't know how many officers this little burg had, but he knew it had more than Van Horn. His plan for this heist was to take the low-hanging fruit and be in and out inside of two minutes. He expected a speedy police response, but so long as they had a one-minute head start with the muscle cars they had purloined, he believed they could escape unscathed. In less than two minutes after Mr. Dinkins had pushed the alarm button, Rocky and Bug Eye were piling into the Olds with a greedy gleam in their eyes. Rocky sure hoped Ev and Nick were already to bug out, because it was time to disappear like a mule fart in the summer breeze.

In the meantime, back at Desert Rat Liquors, Bryce greeted Cordell warmly. He asked about the family. Cordell reciprocated. They chitchatted for a couple of minutes until Cordell mentioned that he needed to stock up for a little welcome home party they were having for Hank. Bryce told Cordell to take his time and to ask if he couldn't find something. Cordell expressed his thanks. He checked his list and began placing bottles of favorite elixirs on the countertop. Bryce returned to working on his check-sheet for restocking.

Just a few seconds had passed when Cordell heard the bell hanging over the door tinkle, indicating a customer had just entered. He had his back to the door and was standing behind a row of liquor bottles stacked high, so he didn't notice who. Suddenly, he heard Bryce rack a shell in his under-the-counter pump shotgun, and fire a load of buckshot in the vicinity of the front door. This hardly had time to register in Cordell's lizard brain. He was stunned by the loud boom. This was followed a split second later by a series of rapid-fire handgun shots. Cordell saw blood splatter from Bryce's head and shoulders just before he saw him fall down behind the counter.

Cordell was in a state of shock. Without thinking, he turned around and stepped into the center aisle leading from the front door to the counter where the cash register was situated. He saw two masked men holding handguns. Both guns were still smoking. At the same time, the robbers glanced over at him. Cordell raised his hands in submission, but the robber closest to him fired anyway, striking him in the chest. Just as he fired, Cordell noticed that his assailant had a tattoo of a black widow spider on the inside of his left wrist. Then Cordell lost consciousness and fell to the floor on his side.

Nick shouted, "Fuck a duck! What was that all about? The dude had his hands in the air! He surrendered for Christ sake!"

Ev responded calmly. "Once you kill the first guy, it doesn't matter how many you kill after that. You're headed to Death Row if they ever catch you. Best to eliminate all the witnesses. Come on! We gotta hurry up. Rocky will be here any minute!"

Ev and Nick shifted into high gear. They ransacked the cash register, which only had a couple of hundred bucks, all of which Ev put in his jacket pocket before searching for a hidden stash. They found the motherlode in the stockroom, hidden in the bottom drawer of a desk in a small metal box. It contained over $3,000 in small denominations. Ev combined this wad with the other one and handed it to Nick. He said, "Nick, when Rocky asks, I'll say we got a thousand bucks and change. Everything over and beyond that belongs to you and me since we took the biggest risk."

Nick replied, "Rocky'll kill us if he ever finds out."

"Then make sure he doesn't."

They scrambled out of the premises and into the Monte Carlo.

Exactly as planned, they saw Rocky and Bug Eye in the Olds screaming up the highway eastbound towards them. Everett pealed out just ahead of them and took the lead. They were running over 100 miles per hour in a matter of seconds.

While they were screaming down the highway, Nick counted the take. It totaled $3,412. He set $1,012 aside for Rocky, and placed it in the glovebox. He divided the other $2,400 in half. He put $1,200 in his overnight bag and handed Ev the rest, which he jammed into his jean pocket. Done and done.

In the meantime, at the sheriff's office, Miss Loretta Youngblood, the administrative assistant, answered the telephone. It was 11:34. She received a recorded message that the bank was being robbed. This was a first for her in the six years she had been employed there. She was nearly in shock. She hung up and ran over to Sheriff Sol's office. He was drinking a cup of coffee with Arthur. Her voice was breaking. She blurted out, "Sheriff, excuse me, but we just received notice that the bank is being robbed!"

Sheriff Sol jumped up, spilling coffee all over the top of his desk. He shouted, "Chief, Ernie, grab your guns! The bank's being robbed!"

Arthur said, "Sol, loan me a shotgun. I'm coming with."

Ernie handed Arthur an 870 and took the other for himself. He also handed Arthur a bandolier full of shells and said, "It's not loaded."

Arthur paused to load the magazine and chamber a round.

Chief scurried out of the restroom tucking in his shirt.

Sol said, "Chief, you cover the rear. Ernie, you take a position in the courthouse lot so you can go east or west. Arthur and I will take the front door. Wait just a second until I can grab one of the .30-30s."

It only took them three minutes to respond.

Sheriff Sol and Arthur piled into Sol's unmarked, brown, 1969 Plymouth Fury. Chief got into his unmarked, blue, 1967, Jeep

Wagoneer. Ernie got in the nearly new, marked, 1972 Ford LTD, which had air conditioning courtesy of Quayle County Supervisor Archie Willis. Sheriff Sol and Arthur arrived lickity split in the bank's front parking lot. They did not see any other vehicles in the customers' lot. Sheriff Sol waited for Chief and Ernie to report that they were in position. Once they were in place and verified that they hadn't seen any suspicious activity, Sheriff Sol, in uniform, and Arthur walked up to the front door ready to shoot, if necessary. Mr. Dinkins was just pulling up the door window shade. He had already unlocked the door.

"Sheriff, you're a minute or two too late. Two masked men come in with handguns and took all the cash out of the teller drawers. I didn't see what they were driving. No idea which way they went."

"We got here as soon as we could. Did they get anything out of the vault?"

"Nope."

"Did they take a die pack?"

"Nope."

"What?"

"Sheriff, they knew all about the die packs. They threatened to kill us all if they got one, so I ordered the tellers to make sure they didn't."

"Dern. I know you haven't had enough time to make an audit, but can you give me a ballpark figure of how much they got so we'll have some idea what we're looking at?"

"I'd say something in the neighborhood of $2,000. I'll know for sure in an hour."

Sheriff Sol turned to Arthur and asked asked, "Arthur, would you get on the radio and ask Chief to come inside? Tell Ernie to take a swing around town to check for any suspicious vehicles.

"Sure thing."

"This'll be a first. Could you also call Quayle 6 and get his location? I should have had Loretta call him as soon as we got the alarm. I'd prefer not to put the robbery out over the air yet. Too many busybodies with scanners. Just ask if he would head back to town at his earliest convenience and meet up with Quayle 3."

"You got it."

Arthur returned to Sheriff Sol's car. He keyed the mike. Using his posse identifier, he said, "Quayle 2 and Quayle 3. This is Quayle 17."

"This is Quayle 2."

"Quayle 1 wants you to meet him inside."

"Roger that."

"Quayle 17, go for Quayle 3."

"Quayle 1 wants you to take a swing around town looking for any suspicious vehicles. Probably two subjects. No vehicle description or description of the armed subjects. Also, he will have Quayle 6 meet you."

"Roger that."

"Quayle 6. This is Quayle 17. Come in."

He waited a minute, but got no response. He called again. No response.

"Quayle Base. This is Quayle 17. Come in."

"Come in Quayle 17."

"Quayle Base, I'm unable to reach Quayle 6. Could you reach out to him and get his location? Quayle 1 wants him to return to Mosby and meet up with Quayle 3."

"Stand by Quayle 17. He may be out of range for car-to-car, especially if he's on the east side."

Several minutes passed. Arthur never heard Quayle Base send a transmission. He didn't understand why and he was getting antsy. Then he heard, "Quayle 6, that license comes back to a 1972 Oldsmobile, brown in color, to a Phillip A. Sneed, 130 Bluebonnet Lane, Apartment 4, El Paso. It's listed stolen as of June 10, 1973. Also DPS is responding from Del Rio westbound on Highway 90. You need to switch to F-2. Base will remain on F-2 until you inform us you've made contact with DPS or Val Verde."

Arthur switched to F-2. He heard, "Quayle 6 from Base. Quayle 1 wants to know how far you are from the Val Verde County line."

There was another pause. Then "10-4. DPS is still 50 miles east of you. Val Verde is even further. We will pass this along."

Finally, he heard, "10-4, Quayle 6. We will notify the other agencies. Return to F-1. Wrecker will be there soon."

Arthur returned to F-1 just in time. "Quayle 17. This is Base. Tell Quayle 1 to call the office immediately."

"Roger that, Quayle Base. Quayle 17 out."

Arthur locked up and ran inside to the bank. Sol looked up. Arthur walked over and whispered, "You need to call the office ASAP. I think Barlow is in hot pursuit of a stolen, brown, 1972 Olds near the Val Verde County line."

Sol scrambled over to the clerk's phone and called. He was on the phone several minutes. Then he covered the mouthpiece and whispered, "Barlow exchanged shots with the Olds. He's okay. His car is disabled and he's waiting for Boyd to come tow him in."

Sol returned to the phone. He blanched. Then he said, "Be right there." He looked at Arthur and said, "Come on we gotta go." He looked around and said, "Chief, can you handle this by yourself? I'll call you shortly."

"No problem."

Sol got his keys from Arthur and said, "This is bad. Come with me."

They ran to the car. Sol took off like his pants were on fire. He said, "I don't know how to say this. Cordell was shot at the liquor store. He's still alive. Bryce was killed. Loretta called an ambulance. Luckily, one was already at the north end of town. It should arrive very shortly."

Arthur said, "Oh, dear God. Who's with him?"

"Ernie Atwater and Calvin Meeks. Doc Boykin should be there by the time we arrive."

"Does Barlow know?"

"Not yet."

When they arrived, Cordell was on his side. Ernie was using both hands to put pressure on the entry and exit wounds. He said, "The bullet went through his right lung. We need a compress. Bryce is dead. They shot him at least four times. Apparently Bryce shot back, but he missed because there's no blood where his pellets struck. Calvin phoned it in about two minutes ago. Lucky for him, he arrived right after it happened. Nobody saw the getaway car."

Doc Boykin arrived next. He ran over to check Cordell's vitals. Then the ambulance crew showed up. They all watched while the EMTs put an air-tight, foil bandage on Cordell's front and back over the wounds. They secured it as tight as they could with tape. They covered his face with an oxygen mask. Then they placed Cordell on a retractable gurney and wheeled him into the ambulance. One of them said, "His right lung is collapsed. It's full of blood. We're taking him to Baptist Hospital in Del Rio. If one of you officers could lead the way in a marked unit, it might shave five minutes off the trip. That could make all the difference."

Sheriff Sol handed his car keys to Ernie. He said, "Give me your car. Arthur and I will lead. Call Chief over at the bank by phone and get him over here. He's in charge. Then call Loretta and tell her what happened. You all know what to do. I'll call you when we get there. Also, I'll be on F-2, but be as cryptic as you can if you need to contact us. One more thing. Call Clarice. Get someone to take her and Darla to the hospital. Do not let them drive. Send a deputy to notify Constance Garrett. Call out as many deputies as you need, except for the afternoon and midnight shift. I'm counting on you. Copy?"

Ernie croaked nearly imperceptibly. "Yes, Sir."

Quayle 1 and 17 were gone in a flash. The ambulance was right behind. Nevertheless, they would never accelerate faster than the ambulance could go, which was 100 miles per hour tops.

About 20 minutes later, Barlow, who was leaning against the trunk of his unit, arms crossed, waiting for the wrecker, saw a marked unit coming his way Code 3 (emergency light and siren), running traffic interference for an ambulance, also running Code 3. It looked like Sheriff Sol was driving. Barlow got back in his unit and tried to raise Quayle 1 on F-1, but he got no response. He switched to F-2 and tried again. This time he made contact.

Arthur answered. "Quayle 6, this is Quayle 1 and 17. Cordell's been injured. We're taking him to the hospital in Del Rio. Nothing further at this time. Stay off the air. Once Buck takes you back to the jail, talk to Loretta. Then take your POV and pick up Sarah and meet us at the ER. Copy?"

"Quayle 6 copies. Out."

What on Earth? Something wasn't right. There was a reason Sheriff Sol was so cryptic. He hoped Buck would have some answers, but he didn't. Buck had been in the middle of a brake job when he got the call to pick him up. His police scanner was on the fritz. He needed to buy a new one. Son of a gun! Was God teaching him a lesson on patience? It was beginning to look like it.

CHAPTER 6

Covering Your Tracks

Wednesday, June 13, 1973

Rocky knew they had to ditch the Olds muy pronto. The back glass was shattered from the two rifle bullets fired by that county mountie. How did the cops get onto them so fast? He wondered if Ev and Nick had encountered some problems. If so, that might explain it. Probably need to ditch the Monte Carlo too, but first things first. Both bullets exited through the windshield, but at least it was still intact. This had been a close call. Good thing Bug Eye ventilated that county mountie's radiator.

Right now, Rocky's most pressing concern was evading cops coming eastbound to intercept them. It was a foregone conclusion that the law dogs were busting a gut to catch them. His concern was more than justified. It's problematic trying to outrun a police radio. It's like stirring up a nest of hornets. They come fast and furious from every which direction.

Rocky took the bull by the horns and passed Everett at 135 miles per hour. Bug Eye motioned for Ev to follow. Rocky kept the pedal to the metal looking for a road where they could turn off. US 90 might just as well be Interstate 10 in this desolate area. The cops would be swarming on it because there were virtually no alternate routes. The farther east they went, the more antsy he got.

They rocketed into Val Verde County without fanfare. The sign said Langtry was only 20 miles ahead. Hell! Wouldn't that be the shits getting busted in Hanging Judge Roy Bean's little piece of shitbird paradise? They'd have to go down fighting. The alternative was worse (and Rocky didn't even know the half of it yet.)

They slowed down to the speed limit when they approached Langtry. Rocky was sweating bullets. Finally, about two miles east of town, they passed a dirt road going north. They turned around and took it. They slowed up even more to keep the dust down to a low roar. They continued about 20 miles when Rocky finally pulled over. They were in the absolute middle of nowhere. Nothing to see in 360 degrees besides dirt and cacti. Even the jackrabbits had found better digs. Rocky named this site Cactusville.

They all stepped out of the cars to take a leak. They each slammed a couple of beers, tossing the empty bottles to the four winds. Rocky asked, "How'd you all do?"

Ev replied, "We done great. We got over $1,000 bucks. How about you all?"

Bug Eye responded, "We got $1,922."

Rocky said, "That's a huge haul coming from a liquor store on a Wednesday morning in a one-horse, hick town. Nick, you and Bug Eye combine the stashes and divide the take. Should be something over $700 each."

Nick replied, "Will do. It was a big haul. We got more than we imagined, but we almost lost our lives. The owner pulled a scattergun on us. Fortunately for us, he missed. Not for him though. We filled him with lead until he was deader than a door nail. Then Ev here, Dead-Eye Fuckin' Dick, he saw a customer in one of the aisles and blew him to smithereens, even though the poor guy surrendered. Hands in the air. Probably loading his britches. Good thing you all was headed our direction because we had to skedaddle."

Rocky, irked, asked, "What the fuck, Ev? No wonder that county mountie jumped us!"

Ev replied sarcastically, "Maybe. Maybe not. Maybe he chased us because we was running 130 miles per hour. No way that pendejo knew about the liquor store at the time. We was only a couple of miles out of town. Besides, what was we supposed to do? Let the sapsucker shoot us? Wasn't you the one who bragged about living on the ragged edge? Told us to kick up a little dust and have some fun?"

"I did, but you still got to use your head! There's enough of a shitstorm coming our way for killing someone who's shooting at you while you're robbing him. He took his shot and come up short. The law won't look at it that way, but it's still justified to me because you was forced into self-defense. What you done to the guy who's simply in the wrong place at the wrong time was different. Killing an unarmed citizen suggests we're stone-cold killers. Bloodthirsty. That label will prod the cops to shoot first and ask questions later. Savvy? It means we'll have to shoot every fucking cop who looks hard in our direction. With a little luck, we can win all our battles if we get the drop on them first, but the more we kill, the more we have to keep on running. Every cop in West Texas will be primed, looking for us. They'll never stop until we're all six feet under. Get it?"

"Maybe so, but they got no fucking idea who we are. All we got to do is lay low for a couple of days and slip back into El Paso from a northern route. Easy peasy."

"I hope you're right, but did you think of this? Either of you two dickheads leave your fingerprints in that store? They'll dust it, you know. All of us have been arrested. Our prints are on file with DPS and the FBI, or did you all forget that?"

"Fuck! We wasn't wearing no gloves! Me and Nick are screwed! We can't go back to El Paso now. We'll have to split up. Me and Nick got to go to Oklahoma or someplace where they'll never look for us."

"Not so fast. At least now you're head is screwed on straight. Let's think about this first. Don't go off half-cocked or you're done for. Right now we don't know for certain if they got your prints. Listen, the reason I turned off here in the middle of nowhere at Cactusville is to ditch the Olds. We certainly can't tool around in it in public with the windows all shot up.

"Bug Eye, you and Nick get busy. Combine both hauls now and count it out. Divide it into four equal piles. We'll each take our share now. We gotta boogie. Me and Ev will put all our stuff into the Chevy. Soon as we're ready to leave, I'll take an old shirt and dip it into the gas tank. Make a wick. We'll light it and get the fuck out of here. Adiós Cactusville.

"We'll continue north to Ozona. That's about 70 miles from here. We need to get some gas, anyway. We'll look for a place to flop. Tonight, we boost another car, two if possible, and ditch the Chevy. We have several options. If we get two cars, Ev, you and Nick can go wherever you want, or you can stick with us. My idea is to turn back south and go to Eagle Pass down on the border. Lay low there for a couple of days. Decide what to do next. What do you all say?"

Nick said, "I'm in.

Bug Eye said, "Me, too."

Ev said, "I'll think about it on the way to Ozona. Let you know then."

Rocky said, "Fair enough. One last thing. Ev, did you and Nick bring your guns you already had before we robbed that gun store?"

They looked at each other and nodded.

Rocky replied, "It's entirely up to each of you, but if it was me, I'd bury those guns you used in the liquor store right here in two separate holes at least a hundred feet apart. The cops can match the ballistics if they ever get their hands on them guns. Think about it. You really willing to risk that?"

Ev said, "No way. I'm keeping the .45 until I can get me another one. I like it a whole lot better than my grandpa's old Harrington & Richardson .32 caliber revolver, plus I still have nearly a whole box of ammo left for the .45. I only got 14 cartridges for the .32."

Nick said, "Ditto on the 44. My old World War II era .25 caliber Beretta is even more anemic than Ev's .32. The magazine only holds six cartridges and that's all I got anyway. I bought it off a guy last year at Duffy's Tavern for 20 bucks when he lost a bet after the Oakland Athletics beat the Cincinnati Reds in game seven of the World Series. I never really liked it all that much. It's only saving grace is you can stick it in your pocket and nobody knows you got it."

Rocky said, "Suit yourselves. It's your decision, but you better not keep them too long if you value your freedom."

Ev replied, "Right now, I value my life. I'm not so sure we're out of the woods yet. You know that cop got the description of both the cars. The fuzz will stop every Monte Carlo they see within a thousand miles. We might be swapping lead again before the day's over."

Nick concurred.

Rocky responded, "What the fuck, you two? You got your old guns, plus we got a new shotgun. Best thing you could ever have in a shootout. It ain't like you're stripped naked."

Ev replied, "Let me and Nick worry about that. You just lead the way, compadre."

Rocky acceded. "It's your funeral."

In 10 minutes their work was accomplished. Rocky torched the Olds and waited long enough to see that the entire car was being consumed. He drove to Ozona while other three guzzled beer, tossing the empties along the side of the road.

Rocky kept his thoughts to himself as he drove, but he was steamed. Fools! It was as if they were intentionally dropping bread crumbs like Hansel and Gretel. What if the fuzz scoop up the bottles and run them them for prints once they discover the burnt Olds? Look around. There wasn't any other trash lining this skinny little rabbit trail. The land was as undisturbed as the day God created it. It was obvious hardly anyone ever used this road. They might as well just blaze the trail all the way to Ozona. Put up a sign. Bad guys headed this way. Come get us. Double dog dare ya.

He would have to call another audible. He couldn't wait to ditch those two morons riding in the backseat. He and Bug Eye would get a new crew which wasn't so impulsive. Those two assholes were just begging for a six-foot plot in Boot Hill.

CHAPTER 7

The Interminable Time at the Hospital

Wednesday, June 13, 1973

Sarah was almost freaking out. Once she learned that Cordell had been shot during a robbery, she had a flashback to the shooting she was involved in two summers ago during her honeymoon. Ever so often, her body shuddered involuntarily. She was holding Barlow's right hand in a vice grip, silent tears streaming down both cheeks. She was hanging on for dear life.

Barlow was chewing nails as he drove upwards of a hundred miles per hour with just his left hand. Why, Lord, couldn't he have been there? He maybe could have prevented it or at least killed the shooter. The road to Del Rio was endless. It seemed like it was getting longer and longer each mile they went. He was driving his '65 Dodge truck, named Jade after its color, because it could go 30 miles per hour faster than Sarah's VW. He was still in uniform. He hoped the police would extend him professional courtesy if he got pulled over for speeding.

Glory be! In less than a month they finally arrived!

Darla, Clarice, Arthur, Sheriff Sol, Slick, and Captain Jay Ortman of the Val Verde County Sheriff's Office were all huddled up in the waiting room adjacent to the Emergency Department, anxiously expecting an update. All they knew was that Cordell was in critical condition and that he had lost a lot of blood. He was in surgery. He had not regained consciousness from the time Calvin Meeks found him. Clarice had called Pastor Llewellyn from the Methodist Church and he was en route. Pastor Llewellyn had called the church prayer warriors. They also prayed for the Bryce Garrett family. If prayers were Easter eggs, they'd have enough to feed the entire congregation for a year.

The menfolk slipped away from the womenfolk and pooled their knowledge of what had transpired. Since Barlow had jumped two cars, the brown Oldsmobile 442 and a black Monte Carlo, both running in tandem at 130 miles per hour, it would appear that they were operating in concert. As far as the men knew, both vehicles had eluded the Val Verde County Sheriff's Office and the Texas Department of Public Safety. What nobody could understand, was how? It was true that units from both VVCSO and DPS were at least 60 miles east of Barlow's location when he radioed for mutual assistance, but Highway 90 was a straight shot with nowhere to hide. No place to run but east. They should've been intercepted! Captain Ortman was embarrassed, but they were still searching. He had deputies scouring the entire county.

The bank and the liquor store robberies occurred simultaneously. Coincidence? They all thought not! Also, both cars Barlow jumped were high performance vehicles, suggesting that the robbers had planned ahead for the possibility of a high speed pursuit. Furthermore, the Olds had been recently stolen from El Paso. Nobody in this little coffee klatch would take 2-to-1 odds that the Monte Carlo was not stolen. QCSO needed to check with DPS and El Paso SO to see if a black Monte Carlo had also been stolen recently. If so, maybe the bandits were from El Paso. That could narrow down the odds for identifying them.

Bryce Garrett was shot at least four times, three in the torso and once to the head. It was surprising that he fired a blast at the robbers, but not that he missed, even with a shotgun. Everyone knew Bryce was extremely nearsighted. Apparently he hadn't been wearing his glasses unless the robbers took them for some reason. They weren't found on him or near his body. Besides that, Bryce was a gentle soul. He wasn't the hero type. (They all made the assumption the robbers shot first.)

Chief Alex and Gillespie were still processing both crime

scenes the last Sheriff Sol heard. He was in a quandary. He needed to go visit Constance Garrett. He believed that Ernie Atwater had delivered the death notice, but he wasn't sure. The problem was, Sol's best friend's son had been shot and was hanging on by a thread. Loyalty overrode duty. Sol decided to stay at least until they knew whether Cordell would live.

Sheriff Sol excused himself. He located a bank of pay phones in the hallway. He called the jail and spoke with Randy Meacham. They traded information. Randy said Ernie Atwater was still off the air at the Garrett residence. Chief had completed the bank crime scene investigation. He did not recover any latent prints there. The robbers got away with $1922.

Robber #1, whom Chief tagged "The Whisperer," was a white male, approximately 30-35 years of age, over 6-feet tall, 170-180 pounds, with blond or sandy hair. He had an Army model Colt .45 pistol. He did all the talking, except he whispered. It was hard to hear him because he spoke so softly. He threatened to kill all the bank employees if they didn't comply with his instructions. He was exceedingly calm.

Robber #2, whom Chief named "Glasses" was a white male, approximately 20-25 years of age, a little shorter, maybe 6-feet tall, 160-170 pounds, black hair, dark eyes, wearing thick, black-framed glasses. He had two matching, nickel-plated revolvers, maybe Colts. Glasses never spoke. He was jumpy. He made quick, jerky movements.

Both robbers wore a red bandanna to cover their faces. Also, both were dressed alike in jeans, light blue chambray shirt, jean jacket, beige cowboy hat, and boots. They looked like any other ranch hand.

Chief and Gillespie were both still at Desert Rat Liquors. They searched the entire store on their hands and knees looking for trace evidence. They recovered two hollow point, copper-jacketed projectiles, maybe .41 or .44 caliber, and one .45 military ball projectile for certain. Randy hadn't heard if they found anymore projectiles. However, they did recover dozens of latent fingerprints, most of which were probably from customers. The robbers broke into Bryce's desk in the rear of the store. They recovered several nice prints there. Apparently Bryce kept his bank in the desk in a metal lockbox. It was busted wide open. Also, the cash register in the front of the store was open, and its contents were gone except for the coins.

Bryce had been transported by Pete Ricketts to the Val Verde Medical Examiner's Office for an autopsy. Ernie will take Constance Garrett there sometime tonight to view the body just as soon as Bryce is presentable. Chief didn't want Constance to see Bryce at the crime scene because it was too dreadful. Part if his face was missing.

This is everything Randy knew. Sol thanked him and hung up.

When Sheriff Sol returned to the waiting room, Captain Ortman was speaking with one of his deputies named Hiram Snow. He was as black as coal. Sol knew he would never forget this deputy's name due to the radical contrast of his name with his skin tone. Not only that, there were very few blacks in this part of Texas.

After introductions, Deputy Snow said, "Sheriff, my call sign is VV16. I think we've found one of your getaway vehicles. It's a burned out hulk on a dirt road about 20 miles north of Langtry. It's my understanding there isn't much left, but I'm here to take you or one of your deputies up there if you want to see it."

Sheriff Sol replied, "That's great news. How long has it been since you all located it?"

Deputy Snow answered, "Less than five minutes. A patrol unit is standing by to see if you want us to process it as a crime scene. The license plate is missing, and the VIN has been torn off the frame, but it's definitely a 1972 Oldsmobile 442. He said there's lots of footprints."

Captain Ortman spoke up. "Sheriff, we can send our crime

scene unit (CSU) up there. Maybe do a grid search. Deputy Jeters knows how to find the hidden VIN. We can tow it back to our garage if you like."

Sol responded, "That would be great. We would really appreciate it. Would you mind if I sent Deputy Oldman and Deputy Adams up there to get a feel for the crime scene? I know we're running out of daylight, but Deputy Oldman is a tracker. I'd really like to hear his assessment."

"Of course. That would be fine. If you want, Deputy Snow can take them, or they can follow in one of your units.

"Slick, take the unit you're driving. You know what we need.

"Barlow, give Sarah your keys in case you all get back really late.

"Captain, maybe one of your guys could radio your office when they're wrapping up, and your office could call for me here, so I can determine if my guys should return here or go on back to Mosby."

Captain Ortman replied, "Sounds like a plan."

Barlow said his goodbyes to Sarah and her family. Sarah hugged him like he was leaving for Alaska to hunt bears in his birthday suit with nothing but a kitchen knife. Then he and Slick followed Deputy Snow out the door and on up to Cactusville. Barlow was slobbering like a rabid dog to begin the hunt. This was a Black Flag mission.

CHAPTER 8

Picking Up the Thread

Wednesday/Thursday, June 13/14, 1973

Barlow and Slick made a quick stop at the vending machines before they joined Deputy Hiram Snow in the ER parking lot. Barlow hadn't eaten since 11:00 o'clock and he was famished. He bought a dried out bologna and cheese sandwich on rye (he despised rye bread), a package of Hostess Twinkies, and a can of ginger ale. Slick wasn't very hungry, so he settled for a package of Nabs peanut butter crackers and a Barq's root beer.

Hiram had pulled his marked unit around to Slick's marked unit. He was sitting on G and waiting on O. As soon as Slick backed out, Hiram turned on his oscillating rooftop blue light, made his way through the parking lot back to Highway 90, and turned west. Slick followed suit. They were cruising over a hundred miles per hour within a minute. Traffic was light, but they had about 60 miles to get to the one-lane dirt road called Settlers Trail. When they arrived, a VVSO marked unit which was blocking the road waved them in. They had to slow down to a crawl for nearly 20 miles. Then they slowed even further down to 5 miles per hour so they wouldn't smother the VVSO units which were already there. The crime scene unit already had floodlights illuminating the burnt hulk and surrounding area. A wrecker with a flatbed was standing by on the roadside waiting for the go-ahead to remove the vehicle.

Barlow remarked how it would be nice to have so many assets to deploy at a moment's notice. Slick agreed, but said that being a small office, they each had the opportunity to work every aspect of law enforcement without micromanagement, plus they didn't get pigeonholed into just one task, such as patrol, or jailer, or process server, or desk duty. Barlow couldn't argue with that. It was a fair trade-off.

Hiram made the introductions. Then the deputy in charge of CSU, Sergeant Dwayne Bailey, pointed out what they had recovered so far. He said, "This is definitely the stolen Olds. We checked one of the hidden VINs and confirmed it.

"We have four distinct sets of footprints and two sets of car tracks. We'll be taking plaster molds of the set on the north side of the Olds for future identification of the other vehicle, presumed to be the Monte Carlo, not to mention molds of the best footprints from each suspect. Some of those aren't very distinct, but we'll give it a shot anyway.

"It looks like they rendezvoused here for awhile. We also recovered nine cigarette butts, three Camels, one Kool, two Chesterfields, and three Mexican cheroots. They may help identify the culprits when you locate them by what type of smokes they have in their possession.

"The best thing, though, is we recovered eight Coors beer bottles. They're bound to have some latent prints. Whether we get any positive identifications is a horse of a different color. That about sums it up."

Slick asked, "Where does this road go? It doesn't look like it gets much traffic."

Hiram responded, "It doesn't. Frankly, I'm surprised the perps found it, but it explains why we never intercepted them.

"There's a tiny village called Pandale about 20 miles north of here. It's situated a little northeast of the Pecos River, which is just a tiny trickle up there now. Pandale's nothing but a couple or three old run-down ranches. It's only got a dozen or so residents. No amenities. Not even a gas station or convenience store.

"At Pandale, the road parallels a small stream called Howard Draw, which is a branch of the Pecos River. Howard Draw is completely dry now. About 10 miles north of Pandale, Settlers Trail comes to a fork in the road. The western route dead-ends at I-10. Nothing there. Not even a rabbit hutch. The eastern route dead-ends at Ozona, also on I-10, about fifteen miles east of the western terminus. If the assholes are going west, they wind up in Pecos County where the nearest town is Sheffield. I'm thinking they probably went east to Ozona in Crockett County, which is a little bigger than Sheffield, and farther away from Quayle County. Maybe they'll roost there for the night. Maybe they'll just gas up and boogie. It's anyone's guess."

Barlow asked, "What do you think, Slick?"

Slick responded, "Well, if it's okay with Val Verde, I'm thinking you and I could creep along Settlers Trail to see if these yahoos threw out anymore trash such as Coors beer bottles along the route. Maybe we'll get some more prints. Maybe we'll find out if they went to Ozona. You know. Follow the tracks. Hell, they think they're slick and done got clean away. Maybe we'll find the Monte Carlo at a motel or parked outside somebody's house. What says Val Verde?"

Sergeant Bailey said, "CSU is nearly done here. Then we're headed back to the office."

Deputy Snow said, "I'll go with you as far as the county line. Anything you find along the way, I'll take back to CSU so long as you all don't have any heartburn with that. Then I'll call in end of shift. Once we get ready to part ways, I'll radio Captain Ortman and let him know you two bloodhounds are still on the peckerwood trail. He can pass that along to Sheriff Sol. That work for you all?"

Slick smiled and said, "Suits us to a T. Thanks for everything fellas. We'll be in touch."

Hiram lead and Slick followed. They were creeping along like metallic slugs looking for something tasty to eat. Slick shined the spotlight along the right side of the road. They found four more empty Coors bottles by the time they reached the county line. It wasn't marked by a road sign, but Deputy Snow knew exactly where it was.

They stopped. Slick and Barlow waited with Hiram while he radioed his office. The dispatcher responded, telephoned the hospital, and asked Captain Ortman to radio VV16 on F-2. A few minutes later, Hiram received a radio transmission from VV3, who told him to stand by for a transmission from Quayle 1.

Quayle 1 asked, "What do you all have for me?"

Slick responded, "Quayle 10 here. CSU positively identified the burnt vehicle as the stolen Olds. They took plaster molds of the car tracks believed to belong to the Monte Carlo. They also took molds from four distinct sets of boot prints, plus they recovered eight empty beer bottles which they will check for latents.

"VV16, Quayle 6, and I checked the road all the way to the Crockett County line. We recovered four more bottles. VV16 is taking them back to his office. Quayle 6 and I propose to continue along this road, looking for more bottles as far as Ozona where we think they stopped, if for no other reason than to refuel. We'll check in with Crockett SO and scour the area for the Monte Carlo. If we strike out, we'll call the jail before heading back to Mosby. If we hit pay dirt, we'll call in to report our findings. Roger that?"

"Quayle 1 rogers that. FYI, the patient is resting peacefully in ICU. He has not regained consciousness. His wife and mother will remain here for the night. The rest of us are returning to Mosby. VV3 will station a deputy here overnight. I will check in at the jail for your updates. Both of you are on afternoon shift tomorrow. Copy?"

"Quayle 10 and Quayle 6 copy."

"VV16, this is VV3. See me when you return to the office."

"VV16 rogers that. Out."

Hiram Snow, Slick, and Barlow shook hands and agreed to stay in touch. VV16 headed south. Slick and Barlow continued north and east. They found two more empties and three piss holes in the dirt just south of I-10 before they arrived in Ozona. They were on the right track! It was nearly 11 o'clock.

The first stop was at an all-night truck stop called Pedro's. They refueled and emptied their bladders. This time they both bought a hot dog, some Fritos and a Pepsi Cola.

Not surprisingly, the Crockett County Courthouse wasn't too dissimilar to the Quayle County Courthouse, in that they were both built around the same time. Not only that, the population of both counties was 3,000+ souls. Crockett may have had a couple hundred more residents. There were four marked units parked in the courthouse lot. Just as in Quayle County, the entrance to the sheriff's office was in the rear of the building. The single exterior light was lit over the back door.

Both Barlow and Slick stepped inside. The office was manned by a solitary deputy. He walked over, reading their shoulder patches, and said, "Good evening, Deputies. Welcome to Crockett County. I'm Deputy Clyde Osborne. What can I do for you all? It must be really important since you all drove all the way from Quayle County."

Slick said, "Nice to meet you Clyde. I'm Slick Oldman. This here is my partner, Barlow Adams." They all shook hands.

Slick continued, "Clyde, did you all get notified of a bank robbery and a liquor store robbery in Mosby earlier today where we had one victim killed and another one shot?"

"We did. I just read the teletype a few minutes ago when I come on shift. Two cars involved, wasn't it - a brown Olds and black Monte Carlo?"

"That's it. Barlow jumped 'em while they was gettin' away. He traded shots with 'em but they shot out his radiator. Val Verde found the Olds all burnt up on a dirt road south of Pandale. They left a trail of Coors beer bottles from the burn site all the way to here in Ozona. We was hopin' you'd help us look for 'em. Unless they ditched the Monte Carlo, we was hopin' to find 'em holed up here in a motel or maybe at someone's house.

We can't rightly call this hot pursuit but it is a pursuit."

"Dern right I'll help! You want I should call Sheriff Larkin and get some more deputies? What do these fellers look like? Got a plate number on that Monte Carlo? I didn't see that on the teletype."

"How about you don't call unless we spot the car? No need to wake folks up needlessly. We don't have the plate number. We think there's four bandits. The two what robbed the bank was white guys wearing standard cowboy garb. They wore bandannas on their faces. Both was about six feet tall. One was in his 30s and the other'n was about 25. He had on glasses. That's all we know."

"Tell you what. Why don't you fellers jump in my unit with me? I'll drive. Best we don't advertise that Quayle County's nosin' around here on the off-chance one of the bandits notices us before we notice them. Better yet. I'll just take the chief deputy's car. It's unmarked and we just got it back from the garage after a service. He won't miss it until tomorrow morning."

Slick said, "That'll be just peachy. Barlow, would you mind fetching the .30-30? If this morning was any indicator, we may need it."

"You got that right."

They loaded up into a new, 1973 white vinyl over maroon four-door Ford LTD. It looked like a mayor's car. Barlow was in the rear seat. He said, "Wow. This is a lot nicer than our unmarked units."

Clyde replied, "That's 'cause the chief deputy's daddy is on the Board of Supervisors and he owns the Ford dealership in town. Other'n the sheriff's vehicle, the rest of the fleet ain't so nice. The rest if us was lucky just to get air conditioning."

They began cruising in the downtown area. They checked both motels, three taverns, a discreet bordello, and every business parking lot. They drove all through the city residential area. Nada. Next they went to went to Pedro's Truck Stop where they had refueled earlier. Clyde went inside and chatted up the night shift manager, who was a 45-year-old cougar with a nice figure and a perky smile. Then she beckoned for a male employee to come over. Barlow and Slick particularly, watched with increasing interest. Assuming the boss lady was single, she pinged on all of Slick's criteria for quality, part-time, late night, female companionship. He said, "Dern. I knew we shoulda gone in there with him."

Barlow replied, "Isn't Ozona a little out of your range?"

"Was Robstown all the way over in Nueces County out of Archie's range?"

"Touché."

When Clyde returned, he said, "Brenda told me they did have a black Chevrolet matching your description earlier in the evening, like maybe 8 or 9 o'clock. There were four guys in it. She checked with José, the pump attendant, but he didn't recall what they looked like other'n than they was white. All he remembers was the license plate was from out-of-state. New Mexico, he thinks. They filled up and paid with cash.

"José said that while he was pumping gas, cleaning the bugs off the windshield, checking tire pressure, and adding a quart of oil, one of 'em, a young guy, 20 or so, wearing thick black glasses, went inside and brought back a sack full of hamburgers and fries. The other fellas stayed in the car. He figured they was headed west 'cause of the license plate, but instead, they got on I-10 and headed towards Sonora."

Barlow asked, "How far's that?"

Clyde said, "Oh, I 'spect it's about 75 miles. It's in Sutton County. It ain't much bigger'n Ozona."

Barlow replied, "I remember. I spent a night there about a year ago. Nice town."

Clyde said, "Oh yeah! I almost forgot. Maybe it's nothing. The guy wearing glasses asked if José knew where he could buy a good used car. José said both the used car dealers is closed now, but he might want to make a pass by there anyway, just to see if there was anything what interested him. José told him they keep the outside lights on at both locations so you can get a pretty good idea if they have something you might want. You know. Lot of guys like to check out the cars after the dealerships is closed so they won't get pounced on by a salesman if they ain't ready to buy."

Slick said, "I do. Anything else?"

Clyde said, "I'm getting to it. José give him directions. Both car lots is on the east side of town at the next exit at TX Highway 163. It's only two miles down the road. Bud's Used Cars is on the north side of the interchange and Xavier's is on the south. Bud's is a little bigger and has a better selection, but he won't come down much from the price on the windshield. You want we should go check 'em out?"

Slick replied, "Ya think? Hell! They ain't interested in buyin' no car! They're interested in stealin' one! Come on! Let's go! Maybe we'll get lucky and catch 'em in the act!"

Clyde got it in gear and they made a beeline for Bud's Used Cars. They arrived five minutes later. The lot was well illuminated with street lamps. There were at least 40 clean vehicles on the lot, all lined up like toy soldiers, just waiting to be adopted by a new owner. Clyde pulled in and parked directly in the front of the small, white, flat-roofed, concrete building, which faced east. They all bailed out of the car, gun in one hand, flashlight in the other, and began checking the exterior of the building from three different directions.

Clyde checked the front door, which was securely locked. He shined his flashlight through the plate glass windows. The office had been ransacked! He scurried around the north side of the building to get to the rear, which faced west. He saw Barlow, who had just opened the back door. Barlow whispered, "The door was ajar. I think somebody broke in."

Just then, Slick shouted, "I think I found the Monte Carlo parked over here on the south side."

Clyde hollered back, "The building was broke into. Barlow and I are going in through the back door!"

Barlow entered first. He found a light switch and turned it on. The premises consisted of the front lobby, a medium-sized office, a small office, restroom, and storage room. Everything had been tossed. It even looked like something heavy with metal wheels, such as a small safe, had been scooted across the floor from the bigger office. You could tell because there was an empty space along the back wall and parallel scuff marks on the linoleum floor all the way to the back door.

Slick was the last one in. He took one quick look and said, "Clyde, what do you think about getting your detectives over here to process the crime scene before we fuck everything up? We'll need to call the owner too, but it would be best if the crime scene guys arrive first. The owner will go bananas when he sees this. The last thing we need is him accidentally making things worse than they already are. You know, by stepping on footprints, getting fingerprints on top of prints left there by the bad guys. Stuff like that. You agree?"

Clyde swallowed, gulping air like he was drowning. Finally, he said, "Yes. I need to call Sheriff Larkin right away to see what he wants me to do. This is my first burglary. I never done this before since I hired on six year ago."

"That's a great idea, but how about using the phone booth outside at the corner of the building? Stay off the office phones. Here's the dime. Also, I suggest someone check Xavier's car lot just to make sure they didn't break into it, too."

"Oh, Lordy! I never thought of that. Can you dial the phone? My hands are shaking too bad. It's 361-2691."

Slick dialed the phone and handed the receiver to Clyde, who was trembling like a human earthquake about to erupt. Soon as the sheriff answered, Clyde began sputtering like a small engine that was having trouble catching the spark. You couldn't understand a single word he said - all gobbledygook.

Slick whispered, "Clyde, why don't you let me explain the situation. I been on this already for the past 12 hours."

Clyde, with a look of salvation, handed Slick the receiver. He said, "Sheriff Larkin, this is Deputy Slick Oldman from Quayle County. Me and my partner, Barlow Adams, been tracking a four-man, stick-up crew who robbed our bank and liquor store, killed the owner, and shot a customer who's in the hospital hanging on for dear life.

"At Sheriff Solomon Pratt's instructions, we been tracking 'em from Mosby to Langtry, to here. Barlow exchanged shots with 'em this morning, but they shot out his radiator, so our hot pursuit come to a screeching halt.

"They was in two cars. One was stolen out of El Paso. They ditched it in Val Verde County. Now we're at Bud's Used Cars with Deputy Osborne. They done broke in here, and we think they ditched their other car. It's probably stolen too, but we ain't had the time to check. We think they may have stolen a safe from here, not to mention a used car or two.

"Sheriff, we asked Deputy Osborne not to wake anyone up until we was sure there was a reason to. We have a reason now. Could you meet us here, maybe get your detective too? Also, we ain't checked on Xavier's car lot, but there's a chance they robbed him as well."

"Deputy, did you say your first name was Slick?"

"It's really Clarence, but everyone calls me Slick."

"Slick, you all stand by. I'll be there right away. Don't mess around in the crime scene. Bud had a safe, and if it ain't there, they probably stole it. We want these owlhoots just as bad as you do. If you don't mind, assuming it's all clear, why don't you all just wait in the car for me to get there. Savvy?"

"You got it, Sheriff."

Sheriff Enoch P. Larkin responded muy pronto. He rolled up in a spanking new, white Ford F-250 pickup truck. The doors were emblazoned with a two-foot emblem of his agency's silver star, just like the one he wore on his vest. He was an old school western sheriff, about 60 years old, 6-feet tall, 180 pounds, thick gray hair, light blue eyes, Wyatt Earp mustache, large, knotty hands, beige Stetson, dressed in a khaki uniform, wearing a cartridge-filled gun belt with a Colt Peacemaker in a cross-draw holster. He was all gristle and bone and grit.

They shook hands. Slick and Barlow identified themselves. Sheriff Larkin said, "Slick, why don't you come with me to take a gander at the crime scene? Clyde, Calvin and Herman should be here soon. When they arrive, why don't you and Barlow go take a look at Xavier's?"

Clyde responded, "Yes, Sir. Will do."

It only took a minute for Sheriff Larkin to see all he needed to see. They stepped outside and lit a smoke to take the edge off. Slick lit a Lucky Strike. Sheriff Larkin lit a Mexican cheroot. Then they took a look at the black Monte Carlo parked on the west side of the building. The license plate was missing, but they could see a Coors beer bottle on the back seat.

Slick said, "Sheriff, this is definitely the second getaway car. We picked up empty Coors bottles all the way here from Val Verde County. Without a doubt, Bud's got at least one stolen vehicle."

"Probably so. We'll know for sure whenever Bud shows up. I haven't called him yet. We need to complete the crime scene before he does. Assuming they did, what's your next play?"

"I'll call Sheriff Sol. Me and Barlow will probably drive back to Mosby. We're on afternoon shift today (glancing at his watch and seeing that it was already 1:30). I hope he'll let me and Barlow continue to be his bloodhounds. These oxygen thieves shot Barlow's brother-in-law, and we still don't know if he'll live. I've knowed him since he was born. If we find 'em they won't be the first bandits me and Barlow sent to Boot Hill."

"I share your sentiments, exactly. If we find 'em first, we'll take care of business for you, just like I suspect Sheriff Will Shive will do over in Val Verde County.

"Looks like my men are here. I gotta go brief 'em. We'll know before long for certain if this is a getaway car and if Bud had any of his cars stole. Ditto for the safe. After you speak with Sheriff Sol, would you motion to me? I'd like to speak with him. It's been awhile. Too long, in fact. You all are fortunate to have him and I can see he's blessed to have you two."

"Thanks. Sheriff Sol is top shelf. He's admired by one and all in Quayle County. I'll wait a few minutes until I have all the information before I call. I'm sure he'll want to coordinate everything with you, just like we're doing with Val Verde. I'll get out of your way and let you get back to work."

Chief Deputy Calvin Close and Investigator Herman Hobbs arrived in separate marked units. Glancing at Clyde, Chief Close said, "Now I know who copped my ride."

Clyde responded, "Sorry, Chief. Me and Deputy Adams and Deputy Oldman needed an unmarked car so's we wouldn't be noticed by the bandits if they saw us first."

Chief Close cracked a smile and said, "That's okay. Let's switch out now before we get busy."

Introductions were made all around. Clyde and Barlow left to check Xavier's car lot. Slick watched while Herman used a slim jim to unlock the Monte Carlo. The VIN plate was still on the frame. Slick wrote the number down while Herman called it in. It was reported stolen by its owners, Carlos and Dolores Rodriguez, of 623 Camino Way, Alamogordo, New Mexico, on June 7th. It had been wiped clean of all fingerprints. However, the ashtray had plenty of butts. They included Camels, Kools, Chesterfields, and Mexican cheroots. This was definitely the car.

Chief Close conducted the crime scene search within the building. It had plenty of latent prints throughout; however, there were five areas where the countertops and drawer handles had been wiped clean. The bandits obviously knew the areas they had touched. The latent prints were photographed and recovered, and would be checked against employee and customer prints for elimination. Prints of unknown persons would be filed away in hopes of identifying suspect(s) first before sending them as unknown subject latent prints to the state laboratory for comparison with prints within its database. Ditto for the single Coors beer bottle. How quickly do you need your answer? Is six months too long? How about a year? Without a suspect, the search was put on the back burner.

Clyde and Barlow returned. Xavier's lot appeared to be unmolested. The SO would check again after it opened for business at 10 o'clock.

Slick and Barlow watched as Delmont "Bud" Decker and his son, Bradley Decker, arrived in a fully restored, dark metallic green, 1958 Cadillac Fleetwood Sixty Special with a pale green leather interior. Bud was not happy. Bradley waited outside while his dad went into the building to meet with Sheriff Larkin and Chief Close.

They stepped out the front door a few minutes later. Bradley had already counted the vehicles in the lot. There were 45. There should have been 47. It was hard to tell what was missing because not all of the 60 parking spaces had been filled and there was no rhyme nor reason as to the order in which the vehicles were parked. Bud had a clipboard with the inventory list, and they began checking them off. A blue, 1970 Ford Fairlane 500 station wagon, and a white vinyl over pale metallic green, 1972 AMC Matador, two-door, hardtop coupé were missing, as were both sets of keys for both vehicles, which were obviously stolen off the key board. In addition, an unknown number of license plates had been purloined from a stack of discarded plates from the storage room. Most were from Texas, which requires two plates, but a few were from other states, such as New Mexico, which only requires one.

Slick copied the descriptions and VINs from both vehicles. Then he called Sheriff Sol. It was nearly 3 a.m. Sheriff Sol answered on the first ring. Slick reported their findings. Then Sol reported that Cordell had awakened briefly before he was given another sedative. The bullet had missed his heart, but had nicked an artery. It was a .44 or a .45. He had nearly bled out. His lungs were nearly filled with blood. He had been given four pints so far. He was very weak, but was expected to survive so long as he didn't catch an infection. He was still in ICU, and he was not allowed any visitors. Slick said he would tell Barlow. Then Sol told them to come on back home and report for the afternoon shift. They would receive further instructions then. Slick said that Sheriff Larkin was waiting to talk to him.

Sheriff Larkin said, "Sol, I'm sorry to hear what these peckerwoods done in Mosby. You got two dedicated deputies hot on their trail. Glad to have met both of 'em. Look, I won't keep you because we're still sorting out things here. I'll call you before lunchtime to see if we can coordinate with you and Val Verde. This here is a bad bunch and we need to keep the pressure on 'til we smoke 'em out of their holes. They may still be in the wind but I know sooner or later we'll corner 'em and weight 'em down with lead. Hopefully give 'em a dirt sandwich before they can murder somebody else again."

"Enoch, I can't tell you how happy I am that you're on board. Sorry these polecats victimized your county too, but I'm thankful you all are in the hunt. We both know what needs to be done. If I haven't caught up with you by noon, I'll call your office. In the meantime, best regards to Esther and the boys."

"Ditto. Talk to you soon. Adiós."

"Adiós."

Sheriff Larkin hung up the phone. By then Barlow had joined them. They all shook hands again. Sheriff Larkin said, "Hope I see you boys again. You all are welcome anytime in Crockett County. Once this is over, I'd like to buy you all a drink."

Barlow responded, "We'd love that. Nice meeting you, too. Good luck, Sheriff."

Slick and Barlow departed from the courthouse about 3:30.

They arrived in Mosby about 6 o'clock. Slick drove Barlow home before stopping by the jail to pick up his truck.

Sarah was still asleep when Barlow walked in. He stripped off and brushed his teeth. He checked the alarm and turned it off. He tried to slip into bed without waking her, but she was already awake. She snuggled close to him. He started to speak but she put her finger over his lips. She whispered, "No talking."

She hugged him tight. Her scent awoke the formerly dormant muscle in his nether region, which was now throbbing with a screaming, semen headache. It was exactly what she expected and needed. His musky scent and firm body aroused her passion. She pulled up her nightie and straddled him. She squeezed his manhood and inserted it exactly where she wanted it. She leaned closer and held his wrists tightly up over his head. Then she began a slow canter. He got into the rhythm. She began to moan softly. She picked up the pace, so he did too. She started biting his lips and licking his face. It aroused her even more. She began kissing him passionately, unable to stop. He began to gallop. She hung on for dear life and to take full advantage of the sensations coursing through her female receptors. He bucked harder. She gasped for air. She was so wet, she was afraid he'd slip out. He twisted around, getting on top without missing a stroke, and shifted into his fastest, hardest, pile-driving, manic self. Her G-spot became overwhelmed with the intensity. She cried out and collapsed under him. He erupted like Mount Vesuvius. He was completely spent. She was sobbing it felt so good. They lay together like that until their breathing returned to normal. Then she rolled to her side looking at him, resting her cheek in the palm of her hand.

She whispered, "Barlow, I'm so scared for Cordell. This should never have happened to him. He wasn't looking for trouble. Then I thought about you and what a basket case I would be if something ever happened to you. I know you hunt trouble for a living. What would I ever do without you?"

"Sarah, nothing happens in this world that God doesn't foresee or know about. It's all in His plan. If it's meant to be, it will be. It doesn't do any good to worry. I do what I do, hoping to prevent for other folks what happened to Cordell. I don't take crazy chances. I'm good at what I do. I will never leave you unless God takes me first. I hope and pray that won't be for many more years. Until that day, just continue love me like you do. Roll over here so I can hug you."

She snuggled up again, even closer.

He said, "Tell me what's on your agenda today, but before you do, Sheriff Sol said Cordell woke up briefly before they gave him another sedative. He's still in ICU and can't have any visitors. They said he'll be okay so long as he doesn't catch an infection. It's in God's hands. All we can do now is pray for him. Also, Slick and I are still on the afternoon shift."

She replied, "Thank goodness. That's better than I thought. I got the day off. I'm riding over to the hospital with Daddy about 10 o'clock. I expect to be back home before you get off from work. You better be here, Mister!"

"I will if something doesn't shake loose. We tracked the bad guys as far as Ozona, but they were gone before we got there. Sheriff Sol said he would give Slick and me our marching orders when we report back to duty this afternoon.

"Sarah, I pray with all my heart that I'm one of the lawmen who catches up with those scumbags. Cordell is thicker than blood to me. He deserves the best I've got to capture or eradicate those vermin. Truth is, capturing killers isn't really good enough anymore since the Supreme Court ruled the death penalty is off the table until every state applies it exactly the same way. How long will that take? One day the bandits who shot Bryce and Cordell will burn in Hell for what they've done."

"I know. You catching them is what scares me. We all know they're cold-blooded killers. Promise you'll be careful."

"I promise."

CHAPTER 9

Depravity Takes a Pause

Thursday, June 14, 1973

By 9 o'clock Wednesday eve, the gang had selected their new rides, courtesy of the gabby pump jockey at Pedro's Truck Stop. His tip was priceless.

What the gang discovered was nothing less than a pot of gold at the end of a rainbow. Not only did Bud's Car Lot have a wide selection of first-rate, used vehicles, the lack of security measures was astonishing. They must not have any crime at all in Ozona. Zero. Not a thief one. Also, they found a cache of discarded license plates, not to mention an old rolling safe which was undoubtedly stuffed full of cash! The car lot owner, Bud the Unwitting, had provided them with an abundance of Granny Yoakum and Honest John Dimwit motor vehicles from which to choose, plus the means to switch plates back and forth whenever it seemed advisable in furtherance of evading the fuzz. And, as a bonus, there were two sets of keys for both chariots!

Rocky was clever. He selected a faded blue, '70 Ford station wagon with good rubber and only 47,000 miles. It purred like a kitten when he turned on the ignition. It would blend in anywhere. On the other hand, Everett, the moody, deep thinker (not!), selected a showcase, white vinyl over pale metallic green, '72 AMC Matador, 2-door, hardtop coupé because he got his first piece of ass in a Rambler Nash sedan. Did he ever once consider that AMCs are not very common anymore, and thus get noticed and likely remembered? Hell no! Besides, how many white vinyl over pale metallic green automobiles have you seen on the highway lately? Not very many! Ev would probably get busted in the next 24 hours for grand theft auto as a result of his abject hubris. No matter. Rocky was not going down with him. Nick would have to make up his mind very shortly. Who did he trust more to throw in with for leadership and mutual assistance during their crime spree?

A clean getaway being ever-most present in Rocky's mind, he led the way when they departed, heading northbound on TX Highway 163, 180 degrees in the opposite direction from his true destination on the off chance they were noticed by a potential witness. His destination tonight was Eagle Pass on the Rio Grande in Maverick County. Rocky warned Everett to stay at least a hundred yards behind, so it wouldn't look like they were traveling in tandem in the event one of them got pulled over. (Under those circumstances, the other car's job would be to ambush the offending police unit.) Rocky wanted to clear Crockett County just as soon as possible. He also wanted to avoid I-10 or Val Verde County since that was where they ditched the Olds.

They drove about a dozen miles before intersecting with US Highway 190. They turned east and went about 40 miles to El Dorado, in Schleicher County. It had been a very long day, filled with excitement and adrenaline, but tired as they were, they needed to press on before holing up. The very last thing they needed was to wake up when the cops were breaking down the doors of the motel where they crashed.

They continued east another 50 miles to Menard, in Menard County, where they turned south on US Highway 83. They drove 30 more miles before intersecting with I-10 at Junction, in Kimble County, having driven at least 30 miles out of their way just to avoid I-10. They continued south another 100 miles through Real County to Uvalde, in Uvalde County, continuing south another 20 miles to La Pryor, where they picked up US Highway 57. From there, they drove west 50 miles to Eagle Pass. Even then, they didn't stop. Rocky led them all through Eagle Pass, getting the lay of the land before he stopped at the Sundown Inn on the north side of US 57, which also happened to be the main drag.

It was 4:30 Thursday morning. Soon it would be light. Rocky got out of the Ford and strolled over to the Matador. He leaned in the driver's window. Speaking softly, he said, "Me and Bug Eye will check in here. You all go check in across the street at Tom Bodett's Motel 6. I see he "still has the lights on" for you. Get some shut-eye; have a couple of beers; sightsee; hustle up a whore; do whatever, but do it low key. Do not draw any attention to yourselves. Got it? You're just a couple of itinerant cowboys or oil workers or ex-convicts or rodeo clowns. I don't care which. We will meet up at the Denny's down the street for breakfast at 10 a.m. on Saturday.

"Time for you all to decide what you wanna do. Give it some serious thought. I'm not kidding. We can stick together or we can part ways. I'm fine with whatever you all decide. Just understand, if you all get in a dust-up here with the cops, you are on your own. I do not know you, and you do not know me. I swear I will kill you both no matter how long it takes if you drag me or Bug Eye into some unnecessary drama with the cops. Have fun. I mean it. You earned it. See you all Saturday morning. We'll crack the safe after we eat."

Ev retorted with an undertone of sarcasm in his voice. "Whatever you say, Jefe," emphasizing the word Jefe. Then he winked with a straight face. It looked and sounded like a subtle taunt to Rocky. Maybe even a challenge. He decided to ignore it for the time being.

Rocky turned slowly and sauntered back to the Ford, steam roiling out of both ears, his gait belying his rush of anger. The tone in Ev's voice had definitely been taunting, disrespectful. Rocky was livid enough to shoot Ev dead right then, right there. Put eight .45 caliber balls through his sociopathic brainpan before driving away. Let Nick stew in Ev's blood, eyeballs, shattered teeth, and brains. The only reason he didn't - the only reason -

was because he was too exhausted to flee from the police right now. He needed some rest.

Fuck Ev! If he didn't decide to part ways on his own accord, Rocky had decided to force the issue. He would do it after they split the proceeds from the safe, somewhere secluded, out of town, out of sight, and out of earshot. He would have to locate such a place tomorrow.

Rocky was nearly certain the cops would identify Ev from fingerprints he left behind in the liquor store, and he didn't want to be in the same area code as Ev once they did. Ev was on a one-way ascent up to Boot Hill, and all because he was a hothead who acted without considering the consequences. Once the cops do show up, whoever happens to be with Ev would be dragged down with him. Be forced to stand and fight because there would be no time for flight before the air was buzzing with flying lead.

Rocky's mind was made up. He would buy a shovel and a pick tomorrow to bury Ev's body if it became necessary, along with the empty safe once they cracked it.

Saturday would be, "Adiós, pendejo."

CHAPTER 10

The First Major Lead

Thursday, June 14, 1973

Cordell awoke with a start. He had tubes sticking in both of his arms and an oxygen mask on his face. He was groggy, but his mind was pinging. He roused up in bed, eliciting an immediate response from the midnight shift ICU nurse, Rhonda O'Shea.

She asked, "Are you feeling okay, Mr. Baker?"

He replied softly, "Yes. Thank you. What day is it?"

"It's Thursday. Today is June 14th. You arrived yesterday afternoon and have been with us overnight. Are you in pain? Can I get you anything?"

"The pain's okay right now. Some ice water would be nice. What time is it?"

"It's 5:30 in the morning. I'll bring you some water in a few minutes after I take your vitals.

"Is my wife or anyone from my family here now?"

"Your wife, but she can't come in here. You're in ICU. She can wave to you through the window. Shall I go get her?"

"Please. Would you tell her to call the sheriff or the jail if he doesn't answer at home? I need to speak to him right away. It's important. Also, when can I go to a regular room? I'm out of the woods now. I know it. I feel a hundred percent better than I did the last time I woke up."

"That's good to hear. Dr. Ploughman will be making his rounds sometime before 8. You can ask him when he gets here. Now lie still while I take your blood pressure and get your temp. Then I'll fetch your wife and give her your message."

"Thank you. Tell her I love her, too."

Pause.

"Blood pressure is 134/78. Pulse is 66. Temp is 99.0. You're doing great. Let me get you another pillow so you can sit up a little bit. I'll pass your message to your wife while I get you some water."

"Thanks."

*****

Ring. Ring. Ring.

"Hello."

"Sheriff Sol, it's Darla. Sorry to wake you."

"You didn't. I was already up. Is Cordell okay?"

"Yes. Thanks for asking. The nurse said there was a good chance he'd get moved to a regular room this morning. Look. The reason I called is Cordell passed me a message that he needs to talk to you right away. I don't know what it is, but maybe he's remembered something. He said it was important. That's all I know."

"That's great news. Pass along that I'll be there as soon as I can. Hopefully by 8 o'clock. What about you? Are you okay? Have you been home yet?"

"No. Mom's bringing me fresh clothes later today. She's getting Hank's room ready for him. He'll be in sometime tomorrow. What a crummy celebration, huh?"

"I don't think Hank will be in much of a celebratory mood after everything's that's transpired. You know that. He's been in combat. He knows all about bullet wounds. If I know Hank, he'll want to get right to work and pick up Cordell's burden. Do all he can to help. It'll be good to see him."

"I know. My mind is jumping all over the place. Look, if Cordell does get a regular room, I might go home and get some rest. I just think it's important for me to stay over during the nighttime. That's when most of the scary things seem to happen."

"Darla, you know what's best for you. At the same time, once

Cordell returns back home, your job will be to care for him 24/7 until he can take care of himself. Besides, you have a new baby arriving before long. You need to consider that. Listen to me. You have family and friends ready to pitch in at a moment's notice. All you have to do is ask. Okay?"

"I know. You're right. I'm taking good care of myself. If I'm not here when you arrive, you'll know I took your advice. Just so you know, Arthur and Sarah are coming this morning to relieve me."

"Very glad to hear it. I'm sure I'll see you sometime today. Don't fall asleep at the wheel when you drive home. Thanks for calling. Take care."

"Bye."

*****

Sheriff Sol was on his not very merry way by 6:30. Before he departed, he called Chief Alex to inform him about Cordell's condition and his trip to Del Rio.

Alex replied, "That's great. Maybe he'll have something. I hope.

"Look, I'm sending Kirk to El Paso and Alamogordo today to check with the auto theft units in the sheriffs' offices and perhaps the police departments if need be, for whatever he can dig up on the two stolen cars. I also told him to check with their robbery and intelligence units to see if they have any bad boys who come to mind capable enough to pull off simultaneous robberies like ours. I reminded him to interview the auto theft victims too, just to satisfy me that there wasn't any owner collusion. He knows to call here for further instructions before returning home."

Sheriff Sol responded, "Sounds like you've got all the bases covered. When I get back later today we'll have to figure out what we want Slick and Barlow to do when they show up for duty this afternoon. I'll call if Cordell has anything before I head back. Adiós."

Joanna handed Sol a thermos of coffee and a paper sack with

two fried egg and sausage biscuits and a banana as he rushed out the door. She knew he wouldn't take time to stop by a diner in Del Rio before rushing to the hospital. Now all he had to do was avoid spilling any of his breakfast on his clothes while he double-tasked, driving while eating. (Not very likely!)

By the time Sheriff Sol arrived, Cordell had already been transferred to a semi-private room where he could look out the window. He did not have a roommate at this time. Darla was sitting in a straight-back chair at his side, holding his hand. She looked pale and drained. Sol thought Cordell's color looked good, although it was obvious he was weak and in pain.

Sheriff Sol smiled and said, "Hello, you all. Darla, glad I caught you. Joanna said to tell you she's cooking a fried chicken dinner for you all. She'll bring it over this afternoon. Cordell, you look ten times better than you did yesterday. I'm impressed that you managed to wrangle your way into a regular room. That must mean the doctors think you're mending well. Either that or you're a better liar than I thought."

Cordell cracked a weak smile. He croaked an almost inaudible hello.

Darla said, "Sheriff, they just doped him up with a sedative. He's loopy now. He's just about to fall asleep.

"What he wants to tell you is, he's pretty sure he knows the guy who shot him. Both robbers wore red bandannas to cover their faces. The one who shot him is redheaded and has a tattoo of a black widow spider on the inside of his left wrist. Cordell recognized the tattoo. A redheaded soldier he served with in the National Guard has a tattoo just like that. He got a dishonorable discharge. He even served time for it.

"His name is Everett Raymond. He's about 30 years old. He's from El Paso, but he might not live there anymore. It's been a long time since last Cordell saw him. He has no idea why Everett shot him. He had his hands in the air the whole time and he never resisted. In fact, before Everett shot him, Cordell didn't even know it was him, but when he extended his arm, his shirtsleeve slipped back and Cordell could see the tattoo. Then it was lights out. That's all he remembers."

Darla looked back at Cordell and asked, "Is that everything, Honey? Did I forget anything?"

Cordell barely shook his head no. He was beginning to count sheep.

Sheriff Sol replied, "That's a big lead, Cordell. We'll check it out. You go on and get some rest.

"Darla, I need to make a call. I'll be right back. Okay?"

Darla had a Mona Lisa smile. She was watching Cordell drift off into Never Never Land. She replied softly, "I'll be right here."

Sol walked down the hall to the waiting room where they had a bank of pay phones along the back wall. He made a long distance call to the jail. Cost him 35 cents. He would need to get some more change. Ernie Atwater answered. Sol asked him to put Chief Alex on the line. Chief answered promptly.

"Chief, I just spoke with Cordell. He said the men who robbed the liquor store wore red bandannas. The one who shot him was redheaded and had a tattoo of a black widow spider on the inside of his left wrist. Cordell was in the National Guard with a redheaded troop named Everett Raymond, who has a tattoo on his left wrist identical to that. Apparently this guy got a dishonorable discharge and served some time. He was from El Paso originally. He's about 30 years old. Can you run some checks? Also, look to see if Crockett SO put out a BOLO (be on the lookout) on those two stolen cars. I'll call you back in 15 minutes."

"That's great news, Sheriff. Will do. Checking now. Bye."

While Sheriff Sol was waiting for the hourglass to dump 15 minutes worth of sand a second at a time, he got $2 worth of coins from the change machine. He sat down in a hardback chair and lit up a smoke. He tried to relax. He smoked the cigarette down to the filter in less than a minute, so he lit another. He tried to smoke it slowly like it was his last one. His mind was racing. At the 13-minute mark, he stubbed out the butt and walked back to the bank of phones. He stood there staring at his watch like he was mesmerized. It was like holding your breath under water. He lasted two more eternal, infernal minutes before placing the call.

Chief answered on the first ring. "Boss, I think we may have something! Ernie found him in NCIC, NLETS, and DMV! His name is Everett M. Raymond, 29 years of age. Last known address is 916 West Market Street, Apartment 3, El Paso. Convicted in a court-martial by the Texas Army National Guard. Got a dishonorable discharge and served six months in the Val Verde County Jail. Also got arrested in El Paso for drunk in a public place and indecent exposure. Paid a fine on that. He's 5-feet, 9-inches tall, weighs 180 pounds, has red hair and blue eyes. Also Crockett did put out the BOLO."

"Great news. Has Kirk left yet for El Paso?"

"Yep. He just left, but I'm calling him back. I'm going with. Ernie can take care of things here until you return."

"Sounds like a plan. I'll be back in a couple of hours. Call the jail if you all get anything."

"Roger that. Bye."

Chief Alex called out to Miss Loretta, asking her to get Kirk on the radio and tell him to return to the jail. She did. Kirk responded that he would be there in about ten minutes.

Chief checked his Rolodex and found the phone number for Chief Deputy Derrick Hornsby of the El Paso County Sheriff's Office. He picked up on the first ring.

"Chief Hornsby here."

"Derrick, this is Alex Snodgrass from Quayle SO. Hope I didn't catch you at a bad time."

"Alex, how the Hell are ya? It's been awhile."

"I'm doing pretty good. How are you?"

"Finer than frog hair. What can I do for ya?"

"Need some help. We had two armed robberies on Wednesday, pulled off simultaneously. One victim killed and another one in ICU with a bullet hole in his chest. The survivor is Barlow Adams' brother-in-law. You remember Barlow, don't ya?"

"Of course I do. Sounds like these robberies are up close and personal. Tell Barlow I'm sorry to hear about what happened to his kin. I hope he recovers soon."

"Will do. Thanks. Look, we have four doers. One of the getaway cars was stolen from El Paso. The other was stolen in Alamogordo. We tentatively identified one shooter. Name is Everett Raymond. He's got at least one arrest in El Paso. Deputy Kirk Shoemaker and I are leaving shortly to run out some leads in your neck of the woods. Would you all have time to lend us a hand?"

"After everything you all did to help us out when Corporal Orbach got killed? You know we will. I'll get a move on to pull up everything we've got on Raymond. Stop by to see me the minute you all get here. What do you think - about 4 o'clock?"

"Something like that. One last thing before we hang up. How is Deputy Slocum doing?"

"Nice of you to ask. He finally forgave himself for what happened to Corporal Orbach. He's a corporal himself now, assigned to the motor pool. Doing a great job. Sheriff Brady and I are both glad he didn't give up and retire."

"I'm glad to hear it. I could tell he was a dedicated deputy when I met him. Well, thanks for everything in advance. See you all in a little while."

"De nadá. See ya'll soon. Bye."

"Bye."

When Chief Alex hung up, Kirk was standing next to his desk.

"Kirk, thanks for coming back. I just got off the phone with Sheriff Sol and Chief Derrick Hornsby in El Paso. We have one strong suspect. I'll brief you in the car. Did you pack an overnight bag?"

"Nope."

"Me neither. Better call Penny real quick to let her know you may have to spend the night in El Paso. Sorry, but we don't have time to go home and pack. We can pick up a toothbrush at a drugstore once we know for sure. I'll give April a heads up, and then we need to skedaddle. We meet Chief Hornsby at 4. Let's take my unmarked unit so we don't heat up some of the neighborhoods we may be going into."

"Roger that."

It took every bit of six hours to drive to El Paso, including a pit stop along the way to refuel man and metallic beast alike, and to discharge waste.

Chief Hornsby was waiting for them in his office. He had two plainclothes deputies standing by. Chief Hornsby met Alex and Kirk at his door. After shaking hands with the accompanying standard back slaps, Chief Hornsby made the introductions with his subordinates.

"Chief Deputy Alex Snodgrass, Deputy Kirk Shoemaker, this is Captain Stanley Howard and Sergeant Julio Elias. Stan is in charge of CID (Criminal Investigation Division) and Julio is one of the supervisors in the Intelligence Bureau. Stan and Julio, meet Alex and Kirk from Quayle SO. Let's dispense with the titles, at least for today. We're all seasoned lawmen. Call me Derrick." After the second handshaking ritual was complete, everyone took a seat.

Derrick asked, "Alex, can you fill us in on what happened in Mosby? Then we'll tell you what we've discovered."

"Fair enough. By way of background, we haven't had an armed robbery in Mosby for at least five years. Then on Wednesday about 11 o'clock, two robbers held up our bank. They wore red bandannas. No shots were fired. They did not go into the vault. They got away clean with about $2,000 from the teller windows. In and out in two minutes. No further details, other than the robbers were white.

"At the very same time, two different robbers also wearing red bandannas held up our liquor store. They shot and killed the owner, who fired at them once and missed with a shotgun. Don't ask me how. They also shot a customer, Cordell Baker, Deputy Barlow Adam's brother-in-law, who did not offer any resistance. They left him for dead. They cleaned out the till. They also found the store's bank in the storage room. We're guessing they got about $3,000, but don't know for sure. According to the widow, the till would have had about $300, and the stash would have had somewhere between $2,500 to $3,000. Incidentally, we recovered a slew of latent prints from the liquor store, but none from the bank.

"Nobody saw what either pair of bandits was driving or which direction they went, but as you all know, it just about had to be either east or west. As it turned out, Barlow, who was on patrol east of town, jumped two cars headed eastbound, running in tandem at over 100 miles-per-hour. The first car was a late model, black Monte Carlo. Barlow could not get the plate number. The second car was a rust-colored Oldsmobile 442. He called in that plate. It was reported stolen on Monday, June 10th. Owner is a Phillip Sneed from 130 Bluebonnet Lane, Apartment 4, in El Paso. We'd like to talk to Mr. Sneed.

"Before the chase extended into Val Verde County, the passenger in the Olds leaned out the window and fired several rounds at Barlow. Some went through the windshield, but one went through the radiator and disabled our unit. Naturally, Barlow was driving our brand new cruiser. Don't you just love it? Nothing ever happens to the oldest car in the fleet. Anyway, Barlow dismounted with his venerable .30-30 Winchester, which has sent at least eight bad boys to Perdition that I know of. He put two or three rounds through the back glass of the Olds, which kept on running like a striped-ass ape.

"Last night, Val Verde recovered the Olds on a dirt road. It had been torched. Tire tracks indicated that the Olds met with another vehicle, which was most likely the Monte Carlo. The bandits apparently like Coors beer, because they left several empties. Believe it or not, Deputy Slick Oldman - Derrick, I'm sure you remember him. He shot and killed that bucket of pus who murdered Deputy Orbach. Anyway, Slick and Barlow followed the trail of empty Coors bottles all the way to Ozona in Crockett County. They hooked up with Sheriff Enoch Larkin's deputies. Bottom line is, they located a used car lot where the Monte Carlo was ditched. They ran the VIN because the license plate was missing. The car was reported stolen on Friday, June 7th. It belongs to a Carlos and Dolores Rodriguez, of 623 Camino Way, in Alamogordo. We'd like to talk to them, too, but we haven't notified the Otero County Sheriff's Office yet.

"The perps stole two more cars at the used car lot. One is a blue '70 Ford Fairlane station wagon, and the other is a white over green, '72 AMC Matador coupé. Sounds like at least one of them is trying to blend in. They also stole dozens of used license plates, so inputting license plate numbers from cars this crew is stealing, assuming we knew what they were, and expecting to get a stolen car notification is an exercise in futility. At best, all a patrol unit will get is an incorrect registration. It helps, but may not be sufficient to induce the unit to call for backup. Tangling with these assholes will most definitely result in shots fired. It did for Barlow. He was lucky. Nevertheless, Crockett SO entered descriptions and VINs on both vehicles into NCIC. They also put out a BOLO. One more thing. These oxygen thieves stole the office safe from the car lot. No idea how much money it contained. It's doubtful we'll ever find out. My impression is that the dealer might be a little on the shady side, but he cuts a wide swath in Crockett County.

"This morning, Cordell Baker regained consciousness long enough to tell Sheriff Sol that the two bandits in the liquor store wore red bandannas, too. Both were white. The one who shot him has red hair and a tattoo of a black widow spider on the inside of his left wrist. Cordell recalled that a guy he served with in the Army National Guard unit in Val Verde has a tattoo just like it. He said the guy's name is Everett Raymond, originally from El Paso. He also said the guy got a dishonorable discharge from the National Guard.

"And that tale of woe, gentlemen, is what brung us here to historic El Paso on this fine spring day."

Derrick replied, "Alex, it goes without saying that you all never need an excuse to come visit with us. Sounds like you all have done one helluva lot of detective work in very short order. I take it that right now the bandit trail is cold, so you're backtracking."

"You would be correct in your assessment."

"Okay, Stan, what have you got for Alex?"

"Alex, I think you've correctly identified one of the murderers. Everett M. (for Marvin) Raymond is well known to us here in El Paso as a troublemaker and a thug. He grew up in the near east side of downtown, which makes most working class neighborhoods look high class in comparison. Really a tough area. It's been like that since well before my time on the job.

"Everett's father, Leroy A. Raymond, is still serving time in Huntsville for a double murder he did while robbing a liquor store in 1954. Got life without parole. Lucky the state didn't fry him. Supposedly the mother of the two boys he killed told the judge she didn't believe in capital punishment and she begged for mercy. Sound familiar?"

Alex replied, "Yep, unfortunately."

"Continuing, Raymond's mother worked as a waitress in a honky tonk and turned tricks on the side. She died of tuberculosis in 1956.

"Everett has two sisters. They all were sent to St. Rita's Orphanage. That's all I know about them. Don't even know their names.

"Everett quit high school in the 9th grade when he was 16. His juvenile rap sheet shows two arrests for auto theft, four for assault and battery, one for statutory rape, three for drunk and disorderly, and one for breaking and entering. The B&E was two weeks before his 18th birthday. Judge gave him a choice. Get tried as an adult on the B&E, or join the military. It was a no-brainer 'cause he was staring down ten years. He had someone, an aunt I think, in Del Rio, so he joined the Army National Guard unit there. I think he planned to stay with her, but that didn't work out, so he returned to El Paso.

"Dickhead would have been better off if he'd simply asked the Guard for a transfer to one of the units here, but so far as I know, he never did. Anyway, getting back and forth to Del Rio was problematic, and Everett wasn't a righteous citizen anyway, so you know the end result.

"He's had a number of shit jobs over the years, but his current job, so far as we can tell without knocking on doors, really is a shit job. Supposedly, he works at Honey Pot Portable Facilities over on Watkins Road. I'm told he services the latrines. Also, his last known address is at the Desert Arms Motel, Room 11, located at 1108 Tate Street. The address you got from DMV is old. The Desert Arms has a reputation for accommodating a lot of one-hour tenants, but you can rent a room by the week or the month, I suppose, if you are really horny.

"Almost forgot. Raymond supposedly owns a pale blue '65 Ford Falcon, two-door sedan, but I couldn't find anything registered in his name. Probably bought it and left the previous owner's plates on it. That covers what I know. Your turn, Julio."

Julio responded, "I checked around for acquaintances, friends, gang affiliations, places Everett Raymond hangs out at, etc. I couldn't find anyone who claimed to like him, but I did meet some who knew him. He isn't in a gang so far as I know. He was a complete asshole when he attended El Paso Central High. One thing I did learn was, he likes hanging out at strip joints.

"One in particular that was mentioned is Texas George's

Saloon, over on Kirby Street, not too far from where Raymond lives and works. The guys in Intelligence know Texas George's well. Lot of lowlifes hang out there, but we pretty much leave it alone because the owner, Gilbert G. (George) Dinwiddie, currently known as Texas George, formerly known back in the day as "The Texas Tornado" when he was on the professional circuit in the WWWF (World Wide Wrestling Federation), is a rock solid informant. His information is always primo. By the way, he won the WWWF Championship in 1960, so he's a bit of a local celebrity.

"George always wanted to be a cop, but he's too fucking big, as in 7-feet, 2-inches tall, and well over 400 pounds. His mode of transportation is a white, 1970 Dodge 3500, 4x4 dually, because he's absolutely too fucking big to fit into anything else unless it's the back of a paddy wagon or a dump truck. His saloon logo is painted on the doors.

"As we speak, the saloon is open for business but there won't be that many customers there yet. I'd be glad to take one of you all over there if you want to talk with George. I don't believe we all ought to go traipsing over there at the same time. Don't want to draw too much attention to our symbiotic relationship with him. George is a big ass target if someone took a notion to pop a cap at him."

Derrick interceded. He said, "That reminds me. Texas George's Saloon is where Raymond got busted for pissing in another customer's car. Julio, why don't you and Alex go over there, while Stan and Kirk go interview Phillip Sneed. You all can hook up on the radio on the command channel if you develop some new leads. Yay or nay, I suggest checking out the Desert Arms Motel to see if Raymond still has a room there. Might even want to check out Honey Pot Portable Facilities to see if he still has a job, but they probably won't be open until tomorrow."

Alex said, "Sounds good to me."

Derrick interjected again, "Just a couple other things. I

checked our recent armed robberies. About three weeks ago, three armed thugs robbed the Sinclair gas station at the intersection of Garfield and Wells in the city. They were white males. They were not wearing masks. On the way out, they exchanged shots with the owner. Nobody was hit. Guess they all could use some more time on the range. There was a fourth guy, too, the driver, also white. EPPD sent out physical descriptions of the three who went inside. I can't recall what the getaway car was. While you all are gone, I'll check with Major Roberts over at the PD to see if one of the perps matches Raymond's description.

"Also, for what it's worth, on Monday the 10th, two perps, both of whom were white and looked like cowboys, pulled an armed robbery at a grocery store in Van Horn, over in Culberson County. They got away with a couple thousand bucks. Maybe it's connected. I don't know. Might be worth checking out. Don't bother with Van Horn's one-man PD. He's a fucking joke. Check with the SO."

Alex said, "Will do. Thanks to all of you. This has been a big help."

Derrick replied, "De nadá. Talk to you all later. Stan, you and Julio make us proud. If these assholes are from El Paso, we want 'em just as bad as Quayle County, especially since we know they have a penchant for shooting at law enforcement."

CHAPTER 11

Interviewing the Texas Tornado and Other Sources

Thursday, June 14, 1973

Julio and Alex made a beeline to Texas George's Saloon. It was a little after 5 o'clock and the afterwork crowd was just beginning to filter in. Julio and Alex bellied up to the bar and waited for the barkeep to take their order. She was a 30-year-old bleached blonde with all her voluptuous assets barely covered with tiny triangular cloth patches - a sailor's wet dream for certain. She wore an embroidered name tag over her left breast which read "Roxanne." Julio knew her well. He ordered a Coors on draft. Alex ordered an Evan Williams on the rocks. Alex placed a $5 bill on the bar. When Roxanne returned with their drinks, she said, "Julio, tell your sweet sidekick to put that away. You know your money's not any good here."

He replied, "Darlin', my pal is from out-of-town. He don't know our ways, but he does have good manners, don't ya think? By the way, is George here yet?"

"Sure is. Why don't you all grab your drinks and follow me over to his office?"

They took their drinks, but Alex left his contribution to Roxanne's wardrobe fund on the bar anyway. He appreciated being commended as having good manners. Roxanne strolled around the bar, and led them to the rear of the lounge to a door marked "Private". Alex was struggling to avert his eyes from Roxanne's sashaying, tantalizing derrière. She knocked twice before entering. She said, "Mr. George, you got some visitors." Then she backed out and waited for them to walk in. She winked at Julio, licking her lips, before softly closing the door behind her.

Texas George, who was verily bigger than any man Chief had ever seen in the former Republic of Texas, rose from his rolling desk chair and asked, "Julio, how the Hell are you? Who's your friend here?" He extended his ham-sized metacarpus for a pair of brotherly shakes.

Alex took a cursory glance around the room. It was much larger than he thought it would be. Not dirty. Not dingy. Obviously the winning combination of whiskey and pussy makes for a lucrative business. The office was well-appointed, with a large leather divan and a half-dozen overstuffed leather chairs. A floor model color television set the size of a pocket aircraft carrier was situated in the corner. It was turned on (no sound) to a rerun of *I Love Lucy*.

Texas George had just arisen from a rolling chair almost as big as a Wells Fargo stage coach, which was parked behind a well-polished, walnut desk, the size of a Las Vegas Championship billiard table. The desk was sturdy and could definitely bear the full brunt of the Texas Tornado's crushing weight if he elected to sample the wares from any of his young, breathtakingly luscious, all-but-naked employees.

The wall was covered with photographs of the Texas Tornado tying his opponents into painful-looking knots, promotional posters of wrestling matches long since resolved, framed certificates of civic accolades, and huge belts with trophy buckles, to include a 12-inch oval, 1960 World Championship buckle and belt.

Julio introduced Alex. They shook hands all around. Alex felt like a little boy shaking hands with a baldheaded grizzly bear. George's paw was smaller than a catcher's mitt, but not by much. Alex began to wonder how many 9-millimeter slugs it would take at point-blank range to fell the Texas Tornado if he went on a rampage. The reason Alex wondered was because his Browning Hi Power, 9-millimeter pistol only held 14 rounds, including the one in the chamber. Would that be sufficient? He hoped Texas

George was gentle like Dancing Bear on the *Captain Kangaroo* television show. He looked like he probably was. Then they all three took a seat.

"What brings you gentlemen to my humble saloon tonight?"

Julio replied, "George, some bandits pulled a couple of holdups in Quayle County this week. They killed one merchant and shot a customer. We know for sure one of our suspects likes to frequent your saloon. Can't say as I blame him. The eye candy is scrumptious here. Maybe his compadres do, too. Do you know an hombre named Everett Raymond?"

"My gosh! Quayle County's at least two or three hundred miles away from here! This must be serious! Perchance, does this Everett Raymond you're looking for have red hair and a propensity to start fights?"

Alex responded, "Yes, he does."

Texas George exclaimed, "Hell yes! I know this little prick. Thinks he's a certified badass, and he might actually be one if he has a knife or a gun handy. Pissed in one of my better-paying customer's car parked right outside the front door! I called the cops on him. Sure did. They hauled his ass off to jail. I thought about barring him, but the next time he come around, he up and apologized to me and each one of my employees. (Alex, I don't hire no men nor ugly women. I'm cock of the walk in my saloon. What I say goes.) Anyway, never had anymore trouble with Ev after that."

Alex asked, "Does Ev have any friends you know of that he associates with here?"

"Let me think. There's this one guy, good enough lookin' to be a movie star. All my dancers are in love with him. They call him Rocky, but I 'spect that's just a nickname. He and Ev are about the same age. I know! Rocky works at the Acme Pallet Company over on Grover Street. You know where that's at?"

Julio responded, "I do."

"Oh, yeah. Something else. As I recall, Rocky used to be in the

Navy."

Alex said, "That'll be a big help. Can you think of anyone else?"

"Let's see. Well, there's two young fellers, early 20s, a couple of wannabe tough guys, who like to suck up to Rocky. One of 'em wears glasses with heavy black frames. Lenses are thick as the bottom of a RC Cola bottle. They call him Bug Eye. I have no idea what his real name is. The other'n looks like a college kid, a namby-pamby. At first blush, you might think he's a fairy. I think they call him Nick. That's all I know."

Julio asked, "George, are any of these guys doing the horizontal mamba with any of your dancers?"

"Geez, Julio, that's a real tough question. I know all these girls, you know, fuck, some even fuck for free, but I don't keep up with their love lives. Whatever they do off the clock is not any of my business. You all know that."

"We do, but maybe your dancers would know the real names of these guys if they're intimate. Maybe what they drive. Where they live. If they carry a gun. You know the drill."

"They probably would, especially if these guys tip good, but each of them girls has a big mouth. Every last one of 'em would rat you out was you to ask 'em. Ya follow what I'm saying? You sure you wanta risk that?"

"How long's it been since you've seen any of these mutts?"

"Oh, I'd say a week at least, and that's kinda odd. They're all usually here four or five nights a week."

Julio said, "George, you gotta trust me. I'd never blow you in. Just tell me which girls you think they might be screwing and where the girls live. I'll send in someone from Detectives they ain't never seen before to talk with 'em. That is, assuming we can't identify these mutts some other way. I swear the girls will never know where we got the info."

"Well, the only one what comes to mind right off is Darlene. I'm not kidding when I say she's a bonafide nymphomaniac. She brags about fucking three or four guys all at the same time when she's really horny. You absolutely cannot trust her to keep her mouth shut. If you talk to her, them guys will know you're looking for them within 30 minutes."

"Understood. What's Darlene's full name? Point her out to us. Where does she live? We need her telephone number, too."

George checked his payroll files. "Her name is Darlene Lynn Underwood. It ought to be Darlene No Underwear instead of Underwood. Get it? She was born February 4, 1950. She lives at 542 Hampton Place, Apartment 1. Telephone number 854-2319. So far as I know, she ain't married and she ain't got any kids. She claims she began screwing when she was 12 years old. Said by then her titties were bigger'n her momma's. First person she screwed was her momma's live-in boyfriend while her momma was passed out drunk on the floor. She claims she can't never get enough sex. Please don't let her know I told you."

"Thanks, George. I promise you, if we need to interview her, she will never know it was you who mentioned her name. Can you point her out us to us?"

"I don't have to. She's the one with the most bodacious titties of all my girls, and none of 'em have small boobs. She's got long brown hair and brown eyes. Tonight, she's wearing a hot pink sequined outfit with white go-go boots. You can't miss her. Believe me. As soon as you make direct eye contact with her, she'll be reaching for your zipper and promise to drain you dry. Some of 'em call her "Breath of Heaven" and with good reason, too. That's all I can say."

Julio and Alex rose. Alex said, "Very glad I had the opportunity to meet you, George. Thanks for everything."

They went back to Julio's unmarked unit, which was a black, AMC Javelin. He pulled the mike out of the glovebox, keyed it, and spoke, "Car 5 from Car 920. Come in."

"This is Car 5."

"Switch to Channel 8, please."

"10-4."

"Go for 5."

"Sir, did you get any new leads?"

"Negative."

"We did. Could you meet us over at Thompson and Grover at the Conoco station?"

"10-4."

Julio switched back to Channel 4, put the mike back into the glovebox, and closed it. He fired up his muscle car and slowly eased out of the parking lot. He said, "Alex, I should have checked with you first. The Acme Pallet Company runs two shifts. I used to work there when I first got out of the Air Force. In that Rocky works there, but hangs out at George's during the evening, he must be on day shift, which punched out about an hour ago. If you and Stan agree, I thought we might stop by and talk to the night shift manager. I bet they'll be able to identify Rocky for us. We already know he won't be there, especially since he was in Ozona late last night. In fact, he probably already quit his job, but they should have a file on him with his correct name, DOB, and address. You agree?"

"Julio, this is your county. I'm just a guest with my hat in my hand. I like the way you think, and your initiative. I'm 5-by-5 on this. I also appreciate the way you look after your informant. We might need someone to look up Darlene tomorrow morning, but I hope it doesn't come down to that. I'd much prefer we not talk to her. I believe George that she'd blab to everyone in town. Then we'll be looking for fugitives, not just robbers and killers. At the same time, I do accept that it might be the only way we can identify the other two mopes."

"Thank you. Understood."

Ten minutes later both unmarked units were parked at the Conoco. Julio topped off his unit. Stan went inside for a Bubble Up. When he returned, they all met around the corner from the front door.

Stan asked, "What's up?"

Julio said, "We got a solid lead on one of the bandits. Raymond hangs out at George's joint with a guy they call Rocky. Most likely a nickname. He works at the Acme Pallet Company down the street here, probably on day shift. He and Raymond are about the same age. Supposedly, Rocky is a veritable heartthrob. All the strippers want to fuck him. Could be he's a Navy vet.

"You might not know this. I worked at Acme for about a year after I ETSed (expiration of time in service) from the Air Force. I still know a couple of guys there. I thought maybe Alex and I should check with the night shift manager to see what we can dig up.

"Also, Raymond and Rocky have a couple of young wannabe bad boys they party with. One of 'em wears thick glasses and goes by the moniker, Bug Eye. The other one looks like a college kid. They call him Nick. Lastly, it appears that the four of them might be banging the same pole dancer. Her name is Darlene Underwood. George says she would definitely tip them off if we approach her. Alex wants to hold off on that as a last resort and I agree."

"Do your magic, Julio. Kirk and I will wait here."

"Will do. What's the story on Phillip Sneed?"

"A solid citizen. No hanky-panky regarding the theft of his car. He paid $3,200 for the Olds. Had it 13 months. Financed it for 48. He still owes $2,800 with interest. The insurance company paid out $2,500 on his claim. He's $300 in the hole, and no longer owns a set of wheels. This guy is a manager on the early morning shift of Dietzen's Bakery. He goes about 6-feet, 3-inches, and 225 pounds of solid muscle. If he could get his hands on the thief, he'd beat him like a bass drum before he repossessed his own car."

Julio replied, "Couldn't say as I'd blame him. Okay. We'll be back in a few. Depending on what we turn up, you all might want to consider a place to eat supper. My stomach thinks my throat's been cut."

Stan asked, "You all like Mexican? We got a great Mexican restaurant only a mile or so from here. It's called Pancho Villa's."

Kirk replied, "Count me in."

Alex said, "Ditto."

Julio replied, "Good. This shouldn't take too long."

Julio and Alex pulled right up next to the front door of the Acme warehouse in a parking space marked VIP. They went inside and rang a little desk bell on the front counter. An attractive, raven-haired, brown-eyed Latino receptionist about 25 years old rushed into the front office. She smiled and asked, "How may I help you gentlemen?" She had beautiful white teeth and a killer smile. The rest of her wasn't bad, either.

Julio and Alex both pulled out their belt badges and held them up. Julio said, "Sheriff's Office. Is there a manager or someone who can help us? We need to ask a couple of questions."

"Why of course. Let me go fetch Mr. Garcia."

She stepped out of the office again. Two minutes later she returned with a thin, 50-ish, Mexican male with shiny slicked-back hair, who carried himself with great dignity. A smile wasn't going to crack this man's granite mug. He was clothed in khaki trousers, a long sleeve white dress shirt, and a black cotton tie with a tie bar proudly displaying the "Big Red One" emblem (U.S. Army's 1st Infantry Division.) He said, "I'm Mr. Garcia. How may I help you?"

Julio smiled and asked, "Rodolfo Garcia? You used to work on the first shift in C Section?"

"Yes. And you are . . . ?"

The officers showed their badges again. Julio said, "I'm Julio Elias. I used to work in your section. I'm a sergeant on the sheriff's office now."

"Of course. I thought I recognized you (probably lying). Come on back to my office. Rita, would you buzz these gentlemen in?" Julio thought Mr. Garcia might be flexing a little authority since he was closer to the door than Rita. If that thought ever crossed Rita's mind, she didn't show it. She did what she was told and gracefully resumed her seat at the receptionist's desk. What a set of legs!

Julio and Alex traipsed down a long, narrow hallway into the inner sanctum of rank and privilege, where Mr. Garcia's office was (the smaller) one of three. Upon his gesture, they seated themselves.

The office was tight and spartan, furnished with a small desk and roller chair, with two ladder-back chairs for visitors, or perhaps not. Maybe they were there for employees who were summoned, akin to a trip to the principal's office, most likely due to unpleasant or unfortunate circumstances. Probably not for an invitation to receive an attaboy. These digs did not impart an aura of happiness, or smiles, or joy. Furthermore, it was too small, too spartan, too prison-like a venue for the presentation of commendations or promotions. No, sir. It is doubtful that events such as those were ever envisioned for this office, this symbol of prestige and authority over the minions, even more coveted than the posted, up close and personal parking space for the occupant of this office.

All the furniture was solid wood, made of quarter-sawn oak by true craftsmen for a thrifty business owner who values a classic look with enduring quality. Nevertheless, the guest chairs were probably designed for minimal creature comfort, and then only for short periods of occupation. Actually, they were better suited as a platform to rest one's foot while tying his shoe, except Mr. Garcia would never deign to put his foot on any kind of furniture whatsoever. Not in this office. Perish the thought!

At least that is what Julio was thinking. This office brought back bad memories. This is where he turned in his letter of resignation to Old Mr. Ebenezer Buskirk, and where he picked up his final paycheck, also from Old Mr. Buskirk, who was in every sense of the word, a buzzkill. Julio hated every minute while he was at work here, but the only person he ever told was his wife. He had forgotten about the bad times until he returned to this office.

Julio noticed that the only items on the desk were an adding machine, an empty, round, glass ashtray, a wire mesh inbox/outbox, and a five-by-seven-inch silver metal picture frame with sparkling glass protecting a professional portrait taken about ten years earlier of the stoic man himself, his dutiful wife whose eyes looked sad, and four expressionless, scrubbed shiny clean with precision parts in their hair, well-behaved children. Rodolfo Garcia was either a minimalist or he expected to get fired at any moment. He could pack up and be gone inside of a minute.

Mr. Garcia lit a brown Mexican cheroot and offered the packet to his guests. Alex waived him off, but lit a Chesterfield of his own. Julio declined altogether. He already had a dip of Copenhagen working between his lip and lower gum.

Julio inquired, "How is your wife and family, Mr. Garcia? Are they all well?"

Mr. Garcia smiled slightly. He replied, "How kind of you to ask. Everyone is much older than they look in this photograph.

"My wife, Isabelle, is doing very well. Now she is the chief checker at the Winn Dixie. She went to work after the kids grew up.

"The three boys, Geraldo, Eduardo, and Pedro, all joined the armed forces after they graduated from Central. Geraldo and Eduardo both joined the Army. Geraldo is a sergeant now in the 82nd Airborne Infantry Division. Eduardo followed after me. He's a private first class in the 1st Infantry Division. He's a truck driver. Both Geraldo and Eduardo served tours in Vietnam. Fortunately, neither one suffered any injuries. Pedro just joined the Air Force. He's in basic training at Lackland Air Force Base. He's supposed to graduate the beginning of August. He's in training to become a loadmaster on cargo planes.

"And my sweet Rosalita, she just graduated from Central. She got a partial scholarship to UTEP. She wants to be a social worker for the church. She has a part-time job at St. Stephen's Catholic Church as a team leader in the summer camp program for underprivileged children. I've been blessed. How about you, Julio?"

"I'm married, too. My wife, Theresa, is a fourth-grade teacher at St. Angelo's. We have a girl, Alicia, age 7, and a boy, Oswaldo, age 6. Both of them go to St. Angelo's, too. It makes things easier for us. Besides that, since Theresa is a teacher there, both kids get a 50% discount. We've also been blessed."

Mr. Garcia said, "That is good to hear." Then he asked, "How may I be of service?"

Julio said, "Mr. Garcia, do you all have an employee who goes by the name Rocky? I think he's on the first shift."

"We did. He quit about a week ago. He'd been with the company for about five years. He was a good worker. Most likely he will be back when he runs out of money.

"Sergeant Elias, surely you remember how it is here? There is no life or health insurance. No disability insurance, yet we have several serious injuries each year. No retirement plan. None of the hourly workers get vacation days. They get five personal days per year. If an hourly employee needs more than that, he just quits. We hire him back if he is a good worker.

"Management has a little better situation. In addition to the personal days, we get ten days of paid vacation. Even so, sometimes managers quit because they need more time off. When or if they do return, they start back at the bottom rung of the ladder, earning minimum wage, just like everyone else. I have eight more years until I turn 62. Then I will quit and draw Social Security. I will get a part-time job as a school crossing guard. I will tend to my garden and watch baseball on TV. I will think of this place no more."

"That sounds really nice. I do remember. That's why I left. I wish you well.

"Sir, What is Rocky's true name?"

"Bruce K. (for Kermit) Givens."

"Where does he live?"

"Let me go get his file. Be just a minute." (Now anxious to please. He had revealed too much.) He was gone less than that.

Perusing the file, he said, "Rocky lives at 244 Delmont Street. You know where that is? It's only a few blocks from here. I gave him a ride home one time. It's a small, tan adobe house with dark brown trim. It has a wooden, unattached, one-car garage. In that neighborhood, you have to have a garage with a sturdy lock if you don't want your car stolen, and Rocky does own a car. He has a midnight blue, '66 GTO as I recall. A very fine automobile. Once upon a time I had one like it."

"What's Rocky's date of birth?"

"January 6, 1942."

"Do you know if he was ever in the armed forces?"

"Let's see. He was in the Navy, a boatswain's mate. He has a tattoo of Popeye the Sailor on his right upper arm."

"Anything else you can remember about him?"

"He's not married. I know that. His parents are both dead. His house belonged to them. He grew up there. Graduated from high school at Central. He has a brother and sister, I think, but I don't know anymore about his family. Basically, from what I've seen, he's a nice guy. Works hard. Keep's to himself. I think he did some time in prison but I'm not sure. Why are you interested in him?"

"This is confidential. Please don't mention it to anyone. We think he may have been involved in an armed robbery. Not sure yet. Still checking. We need to talk to him. Do you know if he has any friends here at Acme?"

"Not really. He comes and goes by himself. Not sure who he associates with. Want me to call if he does come back to work?"

"You bet. Here's my card. I don't want to cause Rocky any trouble if he's not the guy we're looking for. You know. Innocent until proven guilty."

"I do understand. That is noble of you. Many police are not so considerate. Well, if that's everything, I must get back on the floor. Good seeing you again, Sergeant Elias. Glad you're going places. Lots of guys who earn a living here never go anywhere. Like me. You know that. Let me walk you all to the door."

"Thanks, Mr. Garcia. Glad to see you again, too. Bye."

Julio and Alex met Stan and Kirk back at the Conoco station. They all waited while Julio phoned Derrick with what they had turned up so far. Derrick said he would have the radio room conduct record checks on Bruce "Rocky" Givens. After the call, they all agreed that Stan and Kirk would swing by the Desert Arms Motel to see what they could glean from the night manager about Everett M. Raymond, to include info regarding his mode of transportation. In the meantime, Julio and Alex would check out Givens' house. When they were done, everyone would join Derrick at Pancho Villa's for supper.

The Desert Arms Motel was about what Kirk expected - a circa-1950, single-story, flat-roofed, L-shaped, pink adobe building with 20 rooms, one of which was the manager's. The cacti bordering the front of the motel were grizzled with dead spots the size of baseballs. The macadam pavement was old and cracked, with weeds sprouting up in the fissures. The lines marking the parking spaces were faded almost to non-existence. The motel did have a brilliant blinking blue and red neon sign over the office, identifying this waning urban oasis as the Desert Arms Motel. It indicated that vacancies were currently available. This was in contrast to the pole sign at the entrance, which had long outlived its usefulness. You couldn't read it after dark because it didn't have any lights. Maybe it never did, or maybe some rascally street urchins busted them all out. Either way, it was rusty and faded - a sad sack. A trio of cawing crows perched on top of the sign as if they were hawkers for a peep show at the county fair. One could even say apropos.

There were eleven motor vehicles parked in front of various

rooms. Naturally, the one parked in front of the manager's room was a white, 1971 Cadillac Coupe DeVille. One vehicle not parked by a room was a pale-colored Falcon. Hard to make out if it was powder blue in the dim light and shadows. It was all by itself on the side of the building. The Texas license plates were current. The number was R26-544. Stan radioed for a vehicle registration and wanted check. It came back to a 1964 Ford Falcon, blue in color, registered to one Mavis H. Crook, 322 Delaware Street, El Paso. It was not listed as stolen. Mavis H. Crook was now another person to be interviewed.

Stan and Kirk strolled into the office. They were greeted by a 60-ish white female, hair dyed brighter red than Lucille Ball's and done up in a lacquered beehive hairdo. She was plump, like an overripe melon. She sported garish red lipstick and cobalt blue eye shadow, most likely applied with a tar brush, with long, artificial eyelashes. She was squeezed into a short pink, low-cut, cocktail dress that had seen better days, back when she was thirty years younger and thirty pounds lighter. It was revealing, in that her gargantuan breasts were all but falling out of the top, which was only supported by a quarter-inch strap on each side of her shoulders, both of which looked like they were digging deep into her pale, white flesh. What she really needed was a couple of two-gallon, galvanized steel buckets strapped together by a Mack truck fan belt to contain those puppies. The finishing touch to the ensemble were her fingernails. They were long, curled, glossy red, bird of prey talons. Her entire presentation was just shy of tempting for a man marooned on a desert island all by himself for ten years. She reminded Kirk of a hungry barracuda in a nearly empty fish tank. The only other fish were Stanley and himself. Scary!

She looked up from the Hollywood fashion magazine in which she had been engrossed. She batted her eyes at Kirk and said, "Don't you two look like a pair of stud muffins on the prowl? What can I do for you boys?"

They rolled the gold. Stan smiled and said, "Sheriff's Office. My name is Captain Howard. This is Deputy Shoemaker. What may I ask, is your name?"

"I am Miss Goldie Lassiter. I'm also the night manager. What's on your mind? Looking for some female companionship? I can help you boys out if you are. Ask any of the officers on the police department who work this sector. Call Captain Scarsdale. First name is Ronnie. He'll vouch for me."

Stan smiled again. He replied, "That's good to know, Goldie. Right now we're trying to locate someone who lives here. Name is Everett Raymond. What can you tell us about him?"

She asked, "Says who? I don't recall his name right off the top of my head."

"A little birdie told me. Maybe you could check your register. I'm sure he's in there."

"Maybe he is. Maybe he ain't. What's in it for me? People expect me to respect their privacy, and that's what they get when they rent a room here. I ain't no rat."

"No ma'am. I never once imagined that you were. If you just answer our questions and respect my privacy for asking, as in keep it to yourself, we'll get along just fine. I know Ronnie Scarsdale, too. I bet he wouldn't appreciate you throwing his name around at the drop of a hat. Wanna be friends, or do you want me to call in the county vice detectives? Remember, the city sits smack dab in the middle of the county. We own it, too. All of it. If you're doing anything shady, I promise we'll get down to the bottom of it. I'll even call Ronnie Scarsdale and ask him to assist while we confirm there's nothing going on here to interest the district attorney. By the way, he's in my Rolodex too, same as yours, I bet."

"Gosh, Captain, I was just having a little fun with you. Didn't mean to twist your panties in a wad. I'm sorry if I pissed you off, and yes, we do have a long-term tenant named Everett Raymond, but he may not be the onliest Everett Raymond in all of El Paso.

How old is the one you're looking for? What's he look like?"

"He's about 30, approximately 5-feet, 9-inches tall, 180 pounds, with red hair and blue eyes. That sound like your tenant?"

"Sure does. What's he done? Must be something bad if a captain of detectives is out at night looking for him."

"Captains are still lawmen, Miss Lassiter. We like to work the streets, too. I'm not certain Everett Raymond's done anything wrong. I just need to talk to him. If you're asking if there's paper out on him, the answer is no. What else can you tell me about him? Where's he work, for instance. What kind of car does he drive? Does he have a wife or a girlfriend? Does he have any close friends that you know of? Stuff like that."

"Well, I ain't sure anyone likes Ev all that much. Besides being touchy, he can be a mite uppity. He's lived here for two or three years now. He's got unit 11. Pays his rent on time each month. Haven't had no problems with Ev. I've never seen him hanging out with anyone, male or female, but that don't mean he's a fag. I've seen him talking to some of the working girls once in awhile. Not sure where he works, but it's a company that sells and services port-a-potties. That's everything I can think of."

"How about a car?"

"He's got a light blue Falcon. It's several years old. Think he bought it from his sister or aunt or someone. He parks it on the side of the building. He told me one time it has a lot of miles on it, but still runs good. Doesn't burn no oil or nothing."

"Okay. How long has it been since you've seen him?"

"Not for certain. Maybe four or five days."

"Is that unusual?"

"Maybe a little bit. I can't recall him ever being gone for more'n a week. Don't hold me to that, though."

"Any idea where he would go? Who would've taken him if he didn't drive his car?"

"No idea. Ev's not much of a talker unless he's trying to get a discount when he's looking for a good time. Maybe across the border to Juarez where both the booze and the fancy girls don't cost as much? You got me."

"Do you know if he carries a gun?"

"I'm pretty sure he has one. What man in Texas don't? Never seen him with one, though. I know dern well he wouldn't leave no gun in his room. A six-year-old could break into these rooms. They ain't got that many hidey-holes. He might carry one in his car, but I doubt he'd stash it there overnight. I really don't know. Sorry."

"That's quite all right. You've been most helpful. I'll say kind things about you the next time Ronnie and I get together. Here's my business card. Would you give me a call next time you see Ev? I'd really appreciate it."

"Sure will, and mum's the word. Nice meeting you, Captain. You too, Deputy."

It didn't take as much time for Julio and Alex to check out Bruce Givens' digs. Small lot. Well maintained farm fence all around it. Old, well-maintained, tan, single-story adobe house. Sturdy, wooden, one-car garage at the back of the driveway. Enormous padlock on the garage door. Elderly, Latina, across-the-street neighbor lady smoking a brown cheroot and rocking in her chair on the shaded and unlit front verandah, keeping a watchful eye on things. Probably had a cannon under her lap blanket, cocked and ready to fire. Julio bet the old gal knew everything that had ever happened on this street in the past 40 years. He briefly considered chatting her up, but decided against it. Save it for another time if it became necessary. Time to boogie so they wouldn't heat up the street.

*****

They were all seated in a large booth at Pancho Villa's before 8 o'clock. They shared a half-gallon pitcher full of potent, frozen margaritas. Then another. And another. They saved business until after they supped. The food was scrumptious. Everyone arrived famished. They gorged until they were all ready to burst.

When they were done and all who smoked lit up, Derrick said, "Alex, you all are definitely on the right track. Bruce K. Givens is a sleeper, but I'd bet a dollar to a doughnut hole, he's the ringleader of the crew which wreaked havoc in Mosby. So far as I know, he's only been popped twice. Born and raised here in El Paso. Graduated from Central High School in 1960. Joined the Navy. Served three years before he got a Bad Conduct Discharge for felony theft. Prior to that, it appears he was a good sailor. He was a third-class petty officer when got busted back down to seaman recruit.

"In 1964, EPPD popped him for auto theft. Served two years at Huntsville on a five-year beef. Completed his parole in 1969.

"Two years ago, EPPD Homicide picked him up on suspicion of murder. He got in a row with a guy named Roger "The Rooster" Eldridge. Actually, it was worse than a row. He and Rooster tangled assholes over a stripper named Cherry Bell Goodness at her apartment.

"Apparently they were both boffing her, but on alternating days. Neither one snapped to the other until Rooster stopped by for a little nookie a day early, except Rocky was already banging away in the saddle. It was a short but violent fight according to Cherry and confirmed by the photographs taken by EPPD when they were called to the scene. The Rooster stood about four inches taller and thirty pounds heavier than Rocky, so Rocky got the worst of it. Besides, he was taken by complete surprise when it all commenced. Nobody wanted to press charges - not Rocky, not the Rooster, and certainly not Cherry, whose apartment got turned upside down. The boys went separate directions and the girl stayed home to clean up the mess. This was 10 or 11 o'clock on a Monday evening.

"About three hours later, EPPD got an anonymous call regarding a dead man in a car in an alley about two blocks away from where the Rooster lived. The vehicle was still running. The driver side window was rolled down. Rooster was sitting behind the wheel, face contorted into a look of terror, torso a bloody fucking mess due to perforations caused by nine .33 caliber lead balls from a single, 12-gauge, double-aught buck shotgun blast to the chest. The assailant couldn't have been more than three feet away when he pulled the trigger because the shot pattern was so tight. No witnesses to the shooting, of course.

"Homicide went straight to Rocky's apartment and dragged his ass out of bed. They tossed his house and his car. No guns, no ammo. No blood-spattered clothes. They swabbed him for gunpowder residue, but the test came back negative. No blood alcohol in Rocky's system.

"They sweated Rocky off and on for several days but he never copped. They couldn't prove it so he was never charged. It went down as an unsolved. Everyone was certain Rocky did it, but he's real smart. Definitely smart enough to plan and pull off two robberies at the same time. Now all we gotta do is find him or Raymond.

"Also, I spoke with Major Roberts over at the PD regarding that armed robbery at the Sinclair gas station. The descriptions of two of the robbers sort of match Raymond and Givens. Givens is 6-feet, 2-inches tall, goes about 180 pounds, has sandy hair and hazel eyes. One of the robbers was tall like that. Another one was about the same build as Raymond, but they didn't get his hair color. They got away in a blue Chevrolet Impala, probably a '70 or '71. Didn't get a license plate number. We'll mark this robbery down as a strong maybe for Givens and Raymond as two of the perps. Keep them in our sights.

"Raymond's a complete Neanderthal. He'd probably shoot it out with the cops if he were rousted. Rocky's smart. If you don't make him by latent prints, eyewitnesses, or in possession of a firearm or swag, he'll take you to court and most likely win."

Alex said, "I bet you're right, but don't forget there are two other suspects. If we can ID Nick and Bug Eye, maybe one of them will roll. Big George said they were wannabes. Maybe we could find them first. Also, now that I know the FBI and DPS have prints on file for Givens, I might get lucky with the latent prints I recovered at the liquor store.

"What about this? It's late and it's been a long day. What say we knock off for the night? Also, what I was thinking, maybe tomorrow morning Kirk could drop me off at your office. He could go to Alamogordo and see what he can learn about the stolen Monte Carlo. In the meantime, maybe one of you could take me to talk with Mavis Crook to get the lowdown on that blue Falcon.

"Also, if we can identify the port-a-potty company, maybe we could see if they have some information on Everett Raymond. Plus, I hate to do it, but we need to interview Darlene Underwood. We'll think up a ruse so she won't get too alarmed. We really need to ID Nick and Bug Eye and I think she can do it for us.

"One last thing. Kirk and I will check the SO in Culberson County on our way back home to see what we can learn about the robbery there. Once we're down for the night, I'll call my office and see if we have any new information."

Julio asked, "Could we talk some more tomorrow about interviewing Darlene?"

Alex replied, "Sure." Then, looking over at Derrick, he said, "Kirk and I need to get a room for the night. Any suggestions?"

Stan said, "There's a swanky place called the Desert Arms Motel over on Tate Street. You might want to stay there. Probably get laid if you get the deluxe package."

Alex smiled. His response was swift and caught Stan by surprise. "No thanks, Stan. Maybe next time, but not until you try it out first. I heard Miss Goldie was kinda sweet on you. Why don't you take her out for a rodeo ride? Try her on for size. I bet you'd like it. You know what they say. The bigger the cushion, the better the pushin'. Besides, everyone here can see you're in serious need of getting your ashes hauled. I defy you to say it ain't so."

That cracked up everyone, because they all read Chief as being too strait-laced to crack a joke about sex.

After the laugh, Derrick said, "Let me make a call. We can usually book rooms at the Best Western Downtown for $11 a night if they have any vacancies. Besides, it's close to the office. They have a great breakfast there too, for a buck-fifty."

Kirk replied, "That sounds great. Do you know of an open drugstore along the way? We didn't bring a change of clothes or a shaving kit. Actually, we'd be happy if we could just buy a toothbrush and some toothpaste."

Derrick replied, "Not to worry. The hotel will give them to you for free if you ask when you check in."

*****

It was after 9 o'clock by the time Chief Alex called Sheriff Sol at home. He told the sheriff everything they had learned and what their plans were for Friday.

Sheriff Sol was impressed. He said, "I figured it was something significant when I hadn't heard from you by 7. Sounds like Chief Hornsby is taking real good care of you all."

"He is. What have you got Slick and Barlow doing tonight?"

"Well, I hated to put my two bloodhounds on the desk instead of out on the street ferreting out evildoers, but I had no choice. Nothing's popped yet. I looked at the map of Texas, and marked off all the southern and western-most counties closest to us. I think I counted 38, but maybe it was 40, but no need for them to call us or Crockett or El Paso. I gave each one of them half the list. Their job is to call each SO within this area to see if anyone else has had an armed robbery recently, or if they've seen the stolen Matador or station wagon. If we get wind of one which sounds similar, or a sighting of the Matador being that it's pretty unique, they have my blessing to go run out the lead. I had them pack an overnight case for just such an event.

"That brings us up to next week. I'm keeping Slick and Barlow nominally on the afternoon shift, although if they're chasing leads out of Quayle County, they'll be working both night and day. Gillespie will go on afternoons too, but she'll stay in Mosby. Dewey will work midnights, as much as I hate to do it. If we clear this matter up next week, Barlow will go back on mids the following week."

"I guess that means no new developments east of Mosby."

"Not yet."

"Too bad Gillespie is on mids now. Making the calls would be a perfect job for her. When she finished, you'd know everything that's happened in all those counties for the past month."

"True enough. If Slick and Barlow aren't done by shift change, I'll have her make the rest of the calls. Give me a shout before you all head back home tomorrow."

"Will do."

CHAPTER 12

More Mischief

Friday, June 15, 1973

It was nearly 8 o'clock. Nick was still sawing logs. His exhalations practically shook the drapes. Ev rose and sat in his underwear on the side of his bed, scratching his balls. He lit up a Mexican cheroot and inhaled. He needed to clear out the fog and the cobwebs (including the spiders) cavorting in his mind, so he popped the cap off his first beer of the day and took a slug.

Besides being hungover, Ev was bored to distraction. He was also agitated. His jaws ached from clamping them shut and gritting his teeth in his sleep. He resented Rocky making all the decisions. Ev was still pissed that Rocky was in possession of the safe instead of him. Ev always did have authority issues, and they were flaring up like surface-to-air missiles. It probably really was time to part ways before he and Rocky murdered each other.

Ev and Nick had slept and drunk away Thursday, June 14, 1973, in The Year of Our Lord. It was gone now, never to return. Ev was done sitting on his ass. He was rolling in dough. He'd never had this much money at one time in his entire life. Nevertheless, robbing people was a *"Rocky Mountain High"* as John Denver would sing. Ev was jonesing for the rush. He was like a hungry leopard. Today he would satisfy his craving without clueing in Rocky. They would do it in a different county. He was almost certain Nick would passively go along. Nick was the kind of person who would follow anyone smart enough and strong enough to take the lead. Ev was the Cisco Kid and Nick was his Pancho. Pancho's role was to be agreeable and to do whatever he was told. Nick did that pretty fucking well.

Decision made. Ev stubbed out his butt, stripped, and headed for the shower.

By the time Ev had cleaned up, Nick was ready to jump in. When Nick was done, he noticed that Ev was cleaning his .45.

Nick asked, "What's up?"

"I decided to do a little sightseeing, being as we ain't supposed to get together with Rocky and Bug Eye 'til tomorrow. Thought I'd take me a little jaunt over to Carrizo Springs in Dimmit County. Ain't never been there before. Then maybe head down to Laredo over in Webb County. Ain't never been there neither. Interested?"

"What's over there?"

"What the fuck do I know? That's why I'm going, 'possum brain. You in or out?"

"How far is it?"

"From what I can tell from the map, maybe 130 miles - each way that is, not including the miles just cruising around to sightsee. We ain't got nothing better to do. Last time I'm asking. You in or out?"

"I'm in. Why you cleaning your gun? Plan on using it today?"

"Well, that's the $64,000 question, ain't it? The answer is, I don't fucking know. What I do know is the National Guard was mostly wasted time, but one thing they emphasized was always having a clean, fully-operational gun. What we had in the Armor was the .30 caliber M-1 carbine and the Colt .45 pistol, same as this one, only this one ain't been rode hard and put up wet like some of the Army pistols. The National Guard was where I shot a handgun for the first time. I got a thing for it. Qualified Sharpshooter the first time we shot for record and that's why I'm cleaning it. Satisfied?"

"Yep. Think I ought to clean my .44 before we go?"

"I do, if you can get 'er done and be ready to roll in 30 minutes. I'm hungry and I wanna eat someplace different today."

*****

It was 45 miles down the road and well after 10 o'clock before Ev pulled into a diner called Cosmo's in Carrizo Springs. He didn't stop to eat in Eagle Pass because he wanted to avoid Rocky. Nick was still clueless, so far as Ev knew, but he grossly underestimated Nick. Nick wasn't stupid - anything but. He just wanted to please his sidekick. He was also intuitive. He had surreptitiously put a bandanna in his hip pocket and a pair of leather work gloves in his inside jacket pockets just in case.

Breakfast was plentiful and tasty - pancakes with maple syrup, scrambled eggs, pork sausage links, biscuits, and coffee. No grits today. No room on the plate or in their stomachs. They were as full as a couple of blood-engorged ticks on a furry scrotum bulging at the seams stuffed like a blivet with a massive pair of sperm-saturated hog testicles.

After their gluttony, Ev cruised around town looking for a potential robbery target. He saw a couple of possibles, including a credit union and an A&P grocery, but he decided to pass. Maybe Carrizo Springs was too close to Eagle Pass. What if the robbery was covered on the 6 o'clock news and Rocky saw it on TV, assuming of course, that both towns had the same media outlets?

Ev drove another 80 miles to Laredo, which was a little bigger city than Carrizo Springs. Ev kinda liked it. There were a number of dives where a person could get both hammered and laid all before noon. It was tempting. Ev was certainly horny, but he needed to do what he came to do without leaving a trail of squawking witnesses. He focused his attention, and began honing in for a soft business target ripe for the picking.

While they were tooling around, Ev spotted a Brinks armored car making a stop at a jewelry store in a strip mall. His little gray cells kicked into overdrive. He parked and watched while two guards exited the vehicle - one from the passenger door, who came around and unlocked the rear door to let out the other guard. Did that leave just the driver, or was a fourth guard still in the back with a submachine gun? Ev didn't know. Both guards were wearing revolvers in gun belts. One guard rolled a dolly with a substantial metal box of some sort into the shop. The unoccupied guard pulled out his revolver and held it down by his leg. His head was on a swivel. They remained inside the store for eight minutes. When they came out, they reversed the process, except the unoccupied guard assisted the one with the dolly in loading the box into the back of the truck.

Ev followed the truck from a safe distance. Nick sat up straight. He choked on his spit and queried, "What are you thinking, Ev? Are you out of your fucking mind? They probably got a guard in the back with a Thompson submachine gun! This is insanity!"

Ev replied, "Shut the fuck up, Nick. This is the fucking Holy Grail. Get the shotgun out of the gun case. Make sure it's fully loaded and chambered with a round. Leave the safety off. When they stop, I'll find a place to park. I'll make sure we have a clear getaway path. Then I'll get out of the car and take up a vantage point that works to my advantage. I won't do anything if I see a cop. I'll take 'em when they come out of the store. So long as the one holding his gun throws it down, I won't shoot. If he doesn't, he's a dead duck and so is his partner. I'll grab the loot from the dolly and run back to the car. Your job is to cover me with the shotgun. Soon as I jump in the car, you take off. I'll tell you which way we need to go if you can't remember. Everything we get in this haul we split 50-50. Can you do this or are you chicken?"

"Christ on a crutch! I can't believe I'm saying this. I'm in! We'll know if they got a guy in the back with a machine gun because he'll open up on you if he's in there. That truck has a gun port in the left back door. You can see it. If I see a gun barrel or hear a shot fired from inside the truck, I'll focus on shooting at the gun port. Maybe it will make the inside guard have second thoughts and he'll stop shooting, but Ev, I'll be doing this from behind the driver's car door where I have cover. If you go down, I'm a gone pecan. I won't be hanging around. You gotta get back to the car on your own. Are we clear on that?"

"Not only crystal clear, we're in complete agreement. I knew you had a set of balls on you Nicky Boy, from the moment you blasted that liquor store dude. "Yahoo! Mountain Dew!""

They followed the Brinks truck loosely for a couple of miles. Then it pulled into a large, downtown corner lot, which was home to the very impressive Texas Sovereign Bank & Trust (which did not have any subsidiary branches, which is why very few people outside of Webb County had ever heard of it). The edifice was Greek Revivalist, and consisted of three massive, chiseled and polished granite stories which bespoke of pride, security, and power, all of which emanated from owners who had beaucoup bucks, thousands of acres of real property, and each owner being a blood relative. No outside investors.

The bank had been in existence since Reconstruction. The founding fathers, being former Confederate soldiers, loathed the Yankees and the entire Yankee government. (All Presidents from Ulysses S. Grant through William McKinley were former Yankee generals.) Therefore, the bank was not affiliated in any way with the Federal Deposit Insurance Corporation (FDIC), created in 1933, to insure deposit holders against bank closures (think 1929 and the Great Depression) or losses due to bank robbers (think John Dillinger, Pretty Boy Floyd, Machine Gun Kelly, and Bonnie and Clyde, among others), all of which is to say that the FBI had no jurisdiction whatsoever to investigate robbers who victimized this bank. It didn't preclude state or local law enforcement (think Texas Rangers or the Webb County Sheriff's Office) from doing so, but the descendants of founders Colonel Rutherford W. Farnsworth and Major Woodrow C. Farnsworth, Confederate States of America, were just fine with that. Of course, neither Ev nor Nick knew any of this. They just wanted to rob the armored car guards once they left the bank building while they were bringing the loot back to the truck. Why would anyone other than the local yokels give a hoot about a bank not being FDIC insured, or the FBI having no jurisdiction to investigate crimes committed against the bank? It wouldn't have made any sense to them.

The guards entered through a side entrance on the west side of the building. Ev found a parking space on the street only 50 feet away behind the truck where they could see everything. Ev got out of the car, bandanna around his neck. His .45 was in a cross-draw holster under his blue jean jacket. He was wearing dark sunglasses and an Astros baseball cap instead of his Stetson. It had been two minutes. He strolled towards the side entrance to the bank and squatted down behind a parked car like he was tying his shoe, only he was wearing cowboy boots. It didn't matter. He only saw three pedestrians in the lot and none of them even noticed him.

Nick slid over behind the steering wheel. The shotgun was on the seat next to him. His .44 was in a shoulder holster under his jacket. The engine was running but he could barely hear it, even with the windows rolled all the way down. This Matador was the nicest automobile he had ever driven. It had air conditioning, power steering, AM/FM radio, and comfy seats. He was watching for the cops or another guard getting out of the truck, but all was clear and remained clear, even as the armored car guards exited the bank. A bank guard held the door open for them, but he turned around and went back inside and closed the door.

Ev stood, pulled up his bandanna, and began cutting through the parking lot behind the guards like a hungry shark cruising a crowded beach on a summer day. They never once saw him. The armored car guard whose head was supposed to be on a swivel must have been daydreaming because he never looked behind him. Just as they approached the back of the truck and the guard with the dolly put his key in the door and started to open it, the guard who was asleep at the switch finally turned around and saw Ev, who was standing six feet behind him pointing a .45 caliber pistol directly at his heart. The surprised guard's eyes opened wide with disbelief, jumpstarting his lizard brain. Ev could see the exact nanosecond the guard's lizard brain triggered the reaction to shoot. The rest of the guard's body screamed "no" but a lizard brain always trumps common sense. Ev shouted "stop!" but the guard raised his gun anyway. Ev shot him twice in the chest, and he collapsed face up into the afterlife.

The guard with the dolly, also unwitting, had the door wide open by now. He didn't comprehend the "stop!" but his lizard brain processed the sound of gunshots. He spun around, slapping leather for his own gun before he even looked. Ev never thought twice. He blasted him in the chest twice, too. Both visible flesh and blood obstacles were now eliminated.

Nick had pulled his mask up when he saw Ev pull up his. Nick crouched down behind the open driver's door of the Matador, aiming the shotgun through the window towards the open door of the armored truck. Ev ran to the armored car door and peeked inside, prepared to shoot the guard with the submachine gun if one existed. He didn't.

The driver was sitting behind bulletproof glass and a steel barrier. He was frozen in shock, looking through the bulletproof window over his shoulder at Ev. Ev saw the strongbox, plus six money bags on the floor. The strong box was too heavy, but he grabbed all the bags. The driver came to life suddenly and began getting the truck in gear to move out but he was a day late and a dollar short. Ev was already a bad memory, like a nightmare. He had six money bags from inside plus three from the outside. He holstered his gun and ran back to the Matador as fast as his legs would carry him. He threw the sacks in the back seat, picked up the shotgun, and slid in the front seat.

Nick eased out of the lot and proceeded north in a leisurely manner just like they were in a Mardi Gras parade, especially after he saw that the armored truck was headed lickity-split eastbound (with the back door flopping back and forth like a broken leg on a galloping horse.)

Ev's head was on a swivel looking for cops or heroes or witnesses. He saw a few witnesses but they were all too far away to pose a serious threat. Once Nick put a couple more blocks behind them, they untied their bandannas and stuffed them in their jacket pockets. Ev tossed his Astros hat in the back of a pickup truck which was parked next to the curb. Then he replaced it with his Stetson.

Five minutes later and ten blocks away, they saw a marked police unit going Code 3 (lights and siren) towards the bank. They picked up US 83 and continued northbound to Carrizo Springs. They stopped at a small, vacant roadside rest area (two dusty cement picnic tables and a 55-gallon metal waste drum with no lid but lots and lots of flies) but no restroom. (Where were visitors supposed to take a leak?) They popped the trunk, stashing the cotton money sacks containing the swag, and the shotgun, and anything else they didn't want visible. Ev changed into a different shirt. It was a Los Angeles Dodgers tee shirt. Nick took both his jacket and shirt off, wearing only his tee shirt. He took off his holster and put it in the trunk, too. He placed his .44 under the front passenger seat. Then they returned to the car and continued northbound. It was 3:30.

Ev said they needed to find another chariot. As nice as this one was, some witness must have copped the make and model, not to mention the distinctive color combination of white vinyl over metallic mint green. They definitely needed to find something else muy pronto.

On the southern outskirts of Carrizo Springs, they spotted a small used car lot. It looked a little on the seedy side. Nick suggested, "Why don't we just buy a fucking car? We have the dough. Pull in here at the Mexican restaurant and wait for me. I'll walk back and buy one. Put it in an alias name. I'll tell the guy I'm tired of riding the Greyhound bus. I'll meet you back here soon as I get us a different set of wheels.

"While I'm doing that, see if you can find something to wipe off our prints. We can drop this shit magnet at a sketchy location. Leave the keys in the ignition. We'll hit the dusty trail like a pair of cow turds and let the new car thieves get busted instead of us. What a hoot! Whattaya say?"

Ev grinned and replied, "You're a shifty character. You know that? Got enough cash on you to buy a car?"

"I do. I'll take it out of the armored car proceeds once we get back to the motel."

"Good deal. I'll buy you a couple of burritos and a cold drink while I'm here. Don't take too much time. No telling how long before the cop grapevine starts buzzing down here."

"Gotcha."

Nick began his half-mile trek back to Gómez's Auto Sales. When he arrived, a wiry Mexican about 50 years old wearing a well-worn, brown western suit with a white shirt and bolo tie, brown Stetson, and cheap, dusty brown, pointy-toed cowboy boots stepped out of the tiny office. He said, "Hola. Can I help you with anything, Señor?"

"Maybe. I'm tired of riding the Trailways bus whenever I have to go someplace. I thought I might look around to see if you have anything I like and can afford."

"Sí, sí. What are you looking for? I might have something which would meet your needs."

Nick didn't respond. He was too busy checking out the inventory.

"Look around. I'll be right here if you have any questions. All the cars have the price on the windshield. Take your time, Mr…? I'm sorry. My name is Gómez. I didn't catch yours."

"Aaron. Aaron White."

"Nice to meet you, Señor White. Take your time. I bet I have something nice which will interest you."

"Thanks."

Nick was looking for a nondescript van which ran good and had good tires. He saw several. Finally, he spotted a white Dodge A100, maybe a '66 or a '67. He asked, "What can you tell me about this van?"

"You have a good eye, Señor. It is a 1967. A one-owner vehicle. Has a Slant-Six engine. 87,000 actual miles. This one has air conditioning and an AM radio. The tires are almost new. Manual 3-speed transmission. 145 horsepower. The previous owner was Roger Godfrey. He owns the Burger King. It runs very well. Would you like to take a test drive, Señor White?"

"Maybe. Do you know how long since it's been serviced?"

"I do. This one was serviced by me when I bought it about two months ago. The brakes are good. All the electronics work. New wiper blades. New belts. I flushed and replaced the antifreeze in the radiator. The transmission had been serviced not long before I purchased it. It runs really well. The front end alignment it good. No shimmy. You'll see. Let me go get the keys so we can take it out."

"Thank you."

Mr. Gómez returned with a key ring which had two sets of keys. He handed them to Nick. Nick turned south on US 83 and drove it about four miles before turning around. It did run well. It had been well-maintained. He said, "I see you're asking $750. Is that your final price?"

"Tell you what. If you purchase it today, I will sell it to you for $700.

"Deal. I think I can swing that."

They returned to the lot. Mr. Gómez went back in his office and returned with two blank bills of sale and a set of Texas license plates which wouldn't expire until the end if the year. He said, "These are the plates that were on the van when I purchased it. Of course you will need to register the van and get a new title from the state, but this should work until you do. This van should serve you well for years to come."

Nick counted out $700 in twenties and tens and fives and handed them to Mr. Gómez.

Mr. Gómez was busy filling out two copies of the bill of sale. He handed them to Nick and said, "Now all you have to do is sign both copies. The second copy is for you. My son will notarize mine after he gets off from work. Thank you for doing business with me. Vaya con Dios, Señor White."

"Vaya con Dios, Mr. Gómez."

Nick drove back to the Mexican restaurant. Ev handed him a sack of burritos and an Orange Crush in a large paper cup. Nick retrieved his .44 from under the seat of the Matador.

Ev said, "Follow me. I'm looking for a good place to ditch the Matador. It's a shame. I'm going to miss it. This has been a great ride."

They drove slowly to the north end of town. They stopped at a park in a Latino neighborhood. Nick took everything out of the car and put it in the van. They left the front windows of the Matador all the way down. Nick wiped down the entire car for prints, inside and out, because he didn't trust Ev to have done it right. That took longer than he expected, but he was meticulous. They hooked both sets of keys together and put them in plain sight on the floorboard. Then they drove away in the van. Before they had even traversed the street, they saw two teenage boys walk over and check out their old set of wheels. Ev and Nick didn't hang around, but they felt certain the AMC had already been boosted. Nick wondered how long it would be before the new thieves got busted. He chuckled to himself.

When they got back to the motel, they counted their haul. They had $22,688 in cash and another $11,000+ in checks, which they quickly tore up. They split the proceeds after Nick recouped the cost of the van. Then they went to a Ponderosa Steak House. They noticed an old oil drum in the back of the building which was filled with burning trash. They retrieved the cotton bank sacks, two of which contained the torn-up checks, and fed them into the fire two bags at a time. They hung around like arsonists with a sexual fetish until the sacks were fully consumed. Then they went inside the restaurant and ate like ravenous carnivores.

After dinner, they bought four cases of Coors and two bags of ice at a package store. They returned to the motel and turned on the boob tube. They watched the 10 o'clock news to see if the armored car robbery made the headlines. They were watching a local station. It wasn't on the air. This was twice now they went unnoticed. They were a little disappointed.

They continued drinking until they could hold no more. Not even one drop. They both pissed like men taking turns washing off a gas station parking lot with a pressure hose. Then it was lights out before midnight. This was the best day ever for both of these unscrupulous, sociopathic predators.

CHAPTER 13

Hank Finally Returns Home

Friday, June 15, 1973

It had been way too long and Hank knew it. He was ashamed for staying gone for so many months. He had departed his family's home in March of 1971, when he shipped off to Vietnam. By then he had been gone for four years in college plus six months of Army training. During those four-and-a-half years, he only came home for a week or so during semester breaks. He always enjoyed coming home, but he knew even then that he wanted to strike out on his own. Live somewhere else. Pursue a different occupation than sheep ranching. He just didn't have the heart to tell his folks.

He declined to take any leave a year later when he returned from Vietnam. He waited three months until June of 1972, shortly after he finally came clean with his family. The truth was, they were sorrowful he decided to live elsewhere to pursue his dreams, but they were not disappointed in him. Au contraire. They were all bursting with pride over the man he had become and for all of his accomplishments. They understood. They wanted him to flourish, but he was too wracked with guilt to understand that.

Now it had been another year. Time to make amends.

It was nearly noon when he arrived. He pulled up to the ranch house in his new, yellow, 1973 Dodge Adventurer, D200, standard cab pickup truck with a 5.2 liter V-8 engine, automatic transmission, AM/FM radio, air conditioning, and a white aluminum topper. His folks had never seen this truck before, so if they looked out the window while he was pulling up, they might think it was someone else. He was surprised to see his mother's Imperial pulled up near the back door because she usually parked it in the barn lot. She was picky about the yard looking like a used car lot.

He left his bag in the back of the truck and entered through the kitchen door. The house was tidy and neat like always, but something was amiss. When his mother heard him come in, she ran down the stairs and hugged him with an intensity that completely overwhelmed him. She wept heavily on his shoulder as she clung to him for dear life. Finally, she composed herself, dried her tears with a tissue she pulled out of the pocket of her house dress, and told him how glad she was that he was home. She asked if he wanted some iced tea or something to eat. He said he didn't.

She took a seat in her rocker, wringing her hands, and asked him to sit down. He chose a seat in the recliner that his dad normally sat in.

Clarice said, "I have some very bad news. I didn't want to tell you until you got home. Wednesday, Cordell was shot by a bandit holding up Bryce Garrett's liquor store. There were two robbers and they shot and killed Bryce. Cordell's been in the hospital over in Del Rio. He's going to be okay, but we were really worried for awhile. They shot him in the chest, and he was unconscious when Calvin Meeks found him. Cordell knows the person who shot him. We just brought him home today. Your dad and sister are over there right now. We . . . ."

"Momma, why didn't you tell me? I'd have dropped everything and left Austin like a flash of lightning. I could have been here Wednesday evening!"

"I know, Honey. I would've called if the doctors thought he wasn't going to make it. Why don't we go over there right now so you can see him? He'll be tickled to death to see you. Before I forget, Bryce's funeral is on Tuesday. I hope you brought a dress uniform."

"I did, Momma."

This was unbelievable! Shot in Mosby? It rocked his universe. Hank was in disbelief.

He put on his Stetson and helped his mother out the door. When she saw his new truck, she paused and said, "Oh my goodness! When did you get this gorgeous new truck? I love the color."

He replied, "Just last week. The old Ford finally just gave up the ghost. I needed something reliable so I bought this. I love it. Come on. I'll drive you over there in my fancy new buckboard. By the way, where's Marisa and her kids?"

"Oh. I forgot to tell you. I've had so much on my mind. It's been about three weeks now. Marisa asked if it was okay if she went back to Mexico to visit her family. Of course we said yes. She said she wanted to go for the summer if she could. That about broke my heart because I've grown so attached to all of them. She's such a big help, and Guillermo and Angela are perfect little dears. Your father even helped Marisa get a driver's license and sometimes she runs errands for me. Anyway, we drove them to Del Rio, and your dad bought them Trailways bus tickets to Agua Dulce with open returns. They have to be back by Labor Day because Guillermo starts the first grade when school picks up again. Can you believe it? In a way, I suppose this worked out for the best after what happened to Cordell. Guillermo is Cordell's shadow. Follows him everywhere. Cordell got him a pony named Taco, and he already thinks he's a vaquero. It would've been really hard for him to see Cordell all laid up."

"Gosh, Mom, I guess I've been so wrapped up in my own little world that I've lost track of everything that's going on here. I'm so sorry. I promise to stay closer in touch."

"I'm holding you to that, Hank. You better call me every week from here on out. Sunday afternoons would be nice. I only need ten minutes to know you're okay. Maybe twenty on my birthday if you don't home come to see me. Okay?"

"I promise."

"Good. Before we get there, I need to know. Do you have a girlfriend yet?"

"Not exactly. I've been seeing a girl from Austin that I met at A&M. She's a nurse."

"What's her name?"

"Jasmine. Jasmine Oakley. She's two years younger than me. Her mom's a kindergarten teacher and her dad's a rodeo clown."

"What?"

Hank guffawed, beside himself with his joke, and relief because his homecoming was a thousand times better than he thought it would be. He said, "Just part-time, Mom, but it's the job he loves most. The rest of the time he's a heating and air conditioning contractor. He owns his own business."

"You rascal! You got me all stirred up. Is she pretty?"

"No, Mom. She's beautiful. Let me show you her picture." He pulled out a wallet photo of her in a Texas A&M cheerleader's outfit. She had blond hair, blue eyes, and a peaches and cream complexion.

Clarice said, "She's stunning. Does she have any brothers or sisters?"

"She does. Her younger sister, Audrey, is a sophomore at A&M. Her older brother, Boyd, is a state trooper stationed in San Antonio."

"Are you serious about this girl?"

"I really like her, Mom, but our relationship hasn't gotten there yet. We dated some when I was at A&M, but neither of us were ready to take the next step. We corresponded a few times when I was in 'Nam, and then I called her when I got back. We've been going out ever since. You never know. She might be the one. We have a lot of common beliefs and interests and we get along fabulously. We'll see."

"Hank, you better treat this girl the way your daddy treats me. Bring her home so we can meet her. Okay?"

"Okay. How's Labor Day weekend sound? If we're still going strong, I'll bring her then."

"That would be perfect."

Two minutes later, they pulled up in Cordell's driveway. He and Darla owned a red brick ranch house with white trim and a hip roof with charcoal-colored asphalt shingles, similar to the hundreds of thousands of houses one sees in suburban neighborhoods throughout the nation. It was situated on a 160-acre plot two miles west of the family homestead. The house was about 1,600 square feet with three bedrooms, two baths, dining room, screened-in covered patio in the rear, and an unattached two-car garage.

When they entered, Cordell was resting in his recliner. Darla was waiting on him hand and foot. Her pregnancy was beginning to show. Arthur and Sarah jumped up off the couch to greet and hug Hank like they hadn't seen him for a year. Then Hank hugged Darla and shook Cordell's hand. He looked mighty good for a guy who had been shot in the chest only a few days earlier.

Cordell smiled and said, "Hank, you look like you could drink a beer. Honey, would you fetch him one?"

"Coming right up."

Hank replied, "Thanks, Big Brother. You look a whole lot better than I expected. Thanks to the Lord for that. Is it true you know the lowlife who shot you?"

Cordell responded, "Thanks right back at you. You look pretty good yourself, Little Brother, especially for a man with a Purple Heart. Are you hale and hearty? They didn't blow off your thingamajig, did they? Still got all your parts, do ya?"

"Yep. They tried, but they missed. Who is this peckerwood that shot you? Dad and I will round up Barlow and we'll end his evil ways."

"I appreciate the sentiment. I really do, but I think Sheriff Sol already has it under control. His name is Everett Raymond. We served in the same platoon in the National Guard. He was your basic gold brick. A total slacker. Got a dishonorable discharge. Served some time over it. Slick and Barlow tracked him as far as Ozona, then lost the scent, but I'm not worried. I know Sheriff Sol and his deputies will find him."

"Okay, then. Sarah, where is Barlow? I'd love to see him."

"He's anxious to see you, too. I expect he's getting ready for work about now. He's been putting in a lot of long hours. Sheriff Sol has him and Slick ready to roll just as soon as they get a new lead on those outlaws. If he's still home tomorrow, maybe he can see you then. Just so you know, we're planning a barbeque at Mom's for tomorrow afternoon. It's in honor of your return. You better not run off back to Austin. You better be there, Buster."

"I will. I absolutely will, the Good Lord willing and the Creek (Indians) don't rise."

It was a merry reunion for everyone who could make it. Too bad Barlow wasn't one of them.

CHAPTER 14

Running Out the String
in West Texas & Southern New Mexico

Friday, June 15, 1973

Kirk dropped off Chief Alex at 8 o'clock at the El Paso County Sheriff's Office. Then he beat feet for the Otero County Sheriff's Office in Alamogordo, New Mexico, his quest being to look up Carlos and Dolores Rodriguez of 623 Camino Way, owners of the stolen, black 1970 Monte Carlo. It was a pleasant, traffic-free trip north on US 54 after he navigated his way through the congestion in El Paso. It took about an hour-and-a-half. Alamogordo was a city of about 20,000 souls, not including Holloman Air Force Base on the southwest side of town.

The Otero County Sheriff's Office was centrally located in the six or eight block area which comprised the downtown. He met with Sergeant Larry Finch of the Detective Bureau, who teamed him up with Deputy Alfonso Gutiérrez, the detective who investigated the auto theft.

After introductions, Kirk explained why Chief Alex sent him to personally interview the victims. He said they had interviewed the owner of the other stolen car with El Paso SO yesterday. Just like they expected, it was a straightforward auto theft.

Detective Gutiérrez said, "I'll be happy to take you over to see them. The Rodriguez' are hardworking people. Carlos is 25 percent owner of the Auto Zone on White Sands Boulevard. His wife should be at home now. Does your boss want you to interview both of them, or would interviewing the husband be sufficient?"

"Not sure yet. Do you know if they have two cars?"

"No. Just the one. The thing is, Carlos had liability insurance on the Monte Carlo, but not comprehensive. He dropped the comprehensive after he paid the car off because it was so darn expensive. Now they are without any transportation, so they borrowed Dolores' brother's old Chevy pickup, which is a 1958 model, all rusty and shit, holes in the bed and floorboard, engine sounds like a cement mixer out of balance and all that, because they can't afford to do anything else. You'll see. I'll show you."

"What're the details regarding the theft?"

"Dolores took Carlos to work that morning so she could do the shopping. She was parked at the Sears & Roebuck, which is also on White Sands Boulevard, to buy her son, Jesús, a new pair of jeans. She knows she locked the car. I asked because many people don't around here. Carlos and Dolores do, because the car is so nice and because they don't have comprehensive insurance.

"She was in the store about 30 minutes because she got to talking to her friend, Belinda Sánchez, who works there. When Dolores came out, the car was gone, simple as that. I interviewed everybody I could find who had been in the area about the time the car was stolen. Nada. We figured the car would be in Juárez by now, driven by some lackey on the alcalde's staff. But hey, I guess you heard there's a happy ending. Did you know they found the car in Ozona, Texas?"

"I did not. Have they gone to pick it up yet?"

"Nope. The last I heard, Carlos was waiting until Saturday to take the Greyhound bus over there to go get it. Money is tight for them now, and he doesn't want to miss any work. He's off on weekends. The Crockett County Sheriff's Office said for him to get off the bus in front of the courthouse and walk around back to the sheriff's office. A deputy is always on duty and he would have the tow lot release the car anytime, night or day. No charge for storage. Ain't that something?"

"You bet. They're good folks over there in Crockett. Did they say if the car is running all right?"

"They said it was. Carlos is taking some tools with him just in case."

"I'm happy for his family. Well, let's go see what he has to say. Sounds like it's just what it appears to be. Don't mention it to him yet, but we have a couple of suspects. Problem is, we don't know where they are. We're pretty sure this crew is the one which killed a resident in our county and shot another one, so when we find 'em, they'll have bigger problems than just grand theft auto to deal with."

"Sure thing. Follow me. We'll take two cars. When we're done, you can be on your way and I can go back to trying to identify some chicken thieves up in High Rolls."

It turned out to be just like Deputy Gutiérrez said. Kirk was rolling en route to El Paso by 10:30.

In the meantime, Chief Alex and Captain Stan Howard went to the Mavis H. Crook residence, 322 Delaware Street, El Paso, the registered owner of the light blue, 1964 Ford Falcon driven by Everett Raymond. It was a tidy little dwelling in a lower, middle class neighborhood where most of the houses looked sad and in need of some TLC, but not hers. Mavis Crook answered the door. She looked to be in her mid-30s. She was wearing a gingham house dress covered by an apron. She was also wearing a cotton scarf over her hair. She appeared to be knee deep into housecleaning.

She smiled politely and asked, "What's the matter, officers?" Being plainclothes detectives in an unmarked unit didn't confuse her even a little bit. Her only mistake was in assuming they were El Paso PD.

Stan asked, "Are you Mrs. Mavis Crook?"

"I am."

Stan flashed his star and said, "Mrs. Crook, I'm Stan Howard and this is Alex Snodgrass with the sheriff's department. Do you own a light blue Ford Falcon?"

"Well, I used to. My husband bought us a new Plymouth Satellite. It drives like a dream, so my husband convinced me to sell the Falcon. It had some age on it, and was starting to get a little cantankerous. Truth is, we didn't need a second car so I sold it to my brother for $300, who really was in need of some cheap transportation. That was several months ago. What's the matter? Oh Lordy! Didn't he buy liability insurance for it?"

"Who's your brother, ma'am?"

"Everett Raymond. What's he done now?"

"Well, he parked the car in a tow away zone and left it for at least two days. We saw the registration is still in your name. The car still has your license plates on it, which lead us to believe the car was yours - maybe even stolen, but not reported as such yet. Now from what you said, I'm pretty sure your brother did neglect to purchase insurance because he hasn't registered the car or transferred the title to himself."

"It figures. What do I need to do?"

"Do you still have your bill of sale?"

"Oh Hell, yeah! Ev never follows through with anything. I let him keep the plates until he had the money to register the car in his name but I should've known better. My husband will be furious when he finds out about this."

"Do you know where your brother lives?"

"Yeah. The seedy Desert Arms Motel over on Tate Street. Room 11."

"Do you know if he has a job?"

"Sure do. Honey Pot Portable Facilities over on Watkins Road. He cleans and services port-a-potties. It's the perfect job for him because he doesn't have much of a sense of smell. Besides, nobody else wants to hire him. He aggravates the dickens out of me, but officer, we had a rough time growing up. I still love him and try to take care of him, but truthfully, he's so hotheaded, I'm afraid one day he'll wind up in prison serving life without parole just like our daddy."

"We'll check to see if he's at home or work. If we don't find him there, do you have any idea where he might be?"

"Not really. It's not like his job comes with a vacation package. If he wasn't such a turd, he could get on with Standard Oil like my Duncan and make some real money with a complete benefits package. You know. Time-and-a-half for overtime, health insurance, $10,000 life insurance policy, pension plan with survivor benefits, two-weeks paid vacation, etc. The whole enchilada."

"Very nice. Sounds like your husband is really doing well for himself."

"You can say that again."

"Do you know if Everett has any close friends he runs around with?"

"Not really. Ev's kinda hard to get along with. I know he used to be drinking buddies with a guy named Nick Something-or-Other. A young guy, nice-looking, used to be in the Army. Something like Crankshaft or Crankshaw but that ain't it. I only saw him one time. White, of course. About six feet tall. That's all I remember."

"Well okay. You've been most helpful. Listen, you need to go to the courthouse and talk to someone in the motor vehicle licensing division. Show them your bill of sale. They'll take the Falcon out of your name. Show them your brother is the new owner. Most likely they'll ding him for failure to do what he was supposed to do. Make him pay a penalty or something. At least the monkey will be off your back. Besides, if he gets drunk and totals the car after he runs over a pedestrian and kills him, at least you won't be the one getting sued."

"Oh my goodness! I never considered that."

"It could happen. Well, I reckon that's about everything. Thanks for all your cooperation."

"No problem. I'll straighten out the title first thing Monday morning."

Next, they drove over to Honey Pot Portable Facilities. They met with the owner, Delbert Baxter. Captain Howard said they would like to speak to Everett Raymond. Mr. Baxter wanted to know what this was about. Captain Howard used the tow away zone violation and failure to register his vehicle as the nexus.

Mr. Baxter said Ev had taken a leave of absence. Said he had a number of things he needed to take care of and that he would probably be gone for a week. Maybe more. Mr. Baxter was sorry he left because Ev was absolutely the best worker he had ever hired for servicing the portable latrines. That being said, he thought Ev was also the biggest asshole he had ever met. All the other employees literally hate his guts.

When queried, Mr. Baxter said he didn't know where Ev went, or what was so important that he would willing give up his paycheck for at least a week. He promised to call Captain Howard when Ev came back.

When they returned to Captain Howard's unmarked unit, Chief Alex said he thought it had become necessary to interview Darlene Underwood discreetly at her apartment while no one else was around. Captain Howard concurred. He contacted the radio room and told the dispatcher to locate Car 920 and have him reach out for Car 5 on Channel 8.

A couple of minutes later, Channel 8 came to life. "Car 5, this is 920. Come in please."

"920, have you heard back from Deputy Shoemaker yet?"

"Roger that. He's with me now."

"10-4. Could you bring him to the Pizza Hut at Carmichael and 36th?"

"Roger that. See you in about 20 minutes."

"Roger that. Car 5 switching back to Channel 4."

When Julio and Kirk arrived, the four of them went inside to have lunch. During the meal, Kirk discussed his foray into New Mexico - another lead put solidly to rest. Then Captain Howard discussed the interviews with Ev Raymond's sister and his employer. The only new lead was that Ev has a pal named Nick Something-or-Other, last name similar to Crankshaw or Crankshaft, but not either one, all of which which marries up with what Texas George had told them.

Chief Alex picked up the thread from there. He said, "Julio, I had hoped it wouldn't come down to this, but it has. We need to identify Bug Eye and Nick Something-or-Other. I think Darlene Underwood can do that for us.

"What I propose is this. Darlene doesn't know Stan or Kirk. They do a ruse interview with her. Best to let her assume Kirk also works for EPSO. They spin a yarn something like this. You all got a missing persons report on Everett. His sister thinks he may have been kidnapped or even killed. He's disappeared and this is highly unusual for him. She said he mentioned being very good friends with Darlene and a guy named Nick and some other guys, but he never mentioned their names. He's been incommunicado for a week. Does she have any idea where he might have gone or who he was with? His car is parked at his apartment building, but no one has seen him there for at least a week, either.

"I know you've been against interviewing her from the get-go, and I was too, but circumstances have changed. What say you now?"

"I'm on board. I think this is a good plan and it might work."

Captain Howard said, "Good. Let's go do it. You and Chief wait for us at the Lion King parking lot at Garfield and Wellington. It's near her apartment complex over on Hampton. Kirk and I will meet you over there when we get done."

It was a little past 1 o'clock when Stan and Kirk parked one space down from Apartment 1. A red Mustang convertible was parked directly in front of it. Captain Howard called in the plate number and confirmed that it belonged to Darlene L. (No Underwear) Underwood.

Captain Howard had to knock on the door three times.

Finally, the door opened about six inches. Darlene was barefoot, wearing a pink terrycloth bathrobe. You could see the cleavage of her luscious melons. Her hair was tussled. You could smell the faint scent of her perfume. It smelled like lavender. She exuded unadulterated, raw sex. She softly wiped sleepy dirt from her eyes.

She asked alluringly, "Yes?"

Stan displayed his buzzer. He said, "Ma'am, I'm Captain Howard from the sheriff's office. This is Deputy Shoemaker. Sorry to bother you. Are you Darlene Underwood?"

Looking a little startled, she replied, "Yes."

"Ma'am, may we step inside? We'd like to talk with you. It won't take long. Sorry, we woke you up."

"Of course. Come on in." She opened the door wide so they could enter.

After she closed and locked the door, she turned around and offered them seats on the divan. She started to sit in a recliner. Her robe wasn't tied securely, and both men got a full body glimpse of the goddess Venus in the flesh. She smiled and opened her robe wide open for several seconds so they could have a better view before tying it around her again. She sat and crossed her legs, such that the skirt of her robe barely covered her nether region. The only hair on her body was on her head. She said, "I hope I didn't embarrass you, officers. Whenever I'm around handsome men such as yourselves, my clothes just seem to fall right off of me. Hope you didn't mind."

Stan replied, "No ma'am. It's been a long time since I've seen such a beautiful woman in the nude."

She licked her lips and said, "Please, call me Darlene. I work at Texas George's Saloon. I'm a pole dancer. No. I'm Texas George's best pole dancer. You fellas should stop by and see me perform sometime at work. Trust me. You won't be disappointed.

"By the way, what did you all want to talk to me about?" She winked and said, "If the cat's got your tongue, I would be more than happy to show you some of my routine. I guarantee you won't be bored but you will be stiff, that is of course, assuming you like girls."

Stan smiled, rubbed his hands on the top of his thighs to dry the perspiration, and said, "Darlene, we can both see that you are at the top of your tradecraft. I almost did forget why we came. That might be a poor choice of words under the circumstances.

"We got a missing persons report on a guy named Everett Raymond. I believe he goes by Ev. Has red hair and blue eyes. About 30 years old. His sister said he's disappeared. He's not at home, but his car is parked there. Neither his boss nor his landlord have seen him for at least a week. His sister said he's never been gone for this long in the past. She's afraid he's been kidnapped or maybe even been killed. She said he mentioned you as a very close personal friend, and also a guy named Nick. We were wondering if you could tell us anything."

"Oh my gosh! I haven't seen Ev in about a week, either. He comes to George's three or four nights every week. I'm flattered that he told his sister that we were good friends. I always assumed our relationship was casual, if you know what I mean. Maybe it's a little more than that and I just didn't know it. It's not like we have an exclusive relationship. He knows I date other men. See, I love men and they love me back. Heck, even from here I can see that both you heartthrobs would like to date me too, unless of course, you each have a cucumber stuffed in your pants down where your joystick camps out."

She wasn't wrong either, and they both knew it.

Stan replied, "Darlene, you've got us dead to rights. I'm awfully distracted right now, but I gotta do my job first. Getting back to Ev, do you know who he runs with, where he might have gone, if he's in any trouble, stuff like that?"

"Well, he's real close to this guy, Nick Crenshaw. Also, he cuts up with these other two guys. One is Rocky. I think his last name is Givens. He's an absolute hunk, and he has this beautifully restored GTO, I think it is. Dark blue with a scrumptious white leather interior. He's real particular about it. Keeps a towel in the trunk so he won't get any spots on the back seat when he pleasures the girls. (She winked.) I know all about that.

"Then there's this guy, a funny-looking character, but he's got this enormous salami if you get my meaning. A huge, beautiful instrument. The biggest I've ever seen, and I've seen more than a few. A magic wand, and he definitely has the magic. Makes me wet just thinking about it. He wears thick black glasses. Kind of dorky. They call him Bug Eye, but I call him Donk because of his delicious donkey dick (excuse my French), but his real name is Rodney Tinsley.

"That's all I can think of. There's probably others he hangs out with that I don't know. And seriously, I have no idea if he was in some sort of trouble, but I don't believe so. Wait! I haven't seen any of those guys for at least a week! Maybe they all went on vacation together."

"Can you tell us anymore about Nick Crenshaw or Rodney Tinsley - how old they are, where they work, what kind of cars they drive, where they live - that sort of thing?"

"Nick and Donk, I mean Bug Eye, are both about 23 or 24. Ev and Rocky are about 30. I know Ev has a blue Falcon. I've only seen it once or twice. I don't know what Bug Eye drives, but I think he said he has a Ford pickup, but he might have lost his license for drunk driving. Nick doesn't have a car. He usually drives this cute little Corvair convertible, white with a blue ragtop. He said it's his mother's. I don't know where any of them live except for Rocky. He lives on Delmont Street but I don't know the number. That's all I can think of. I hope they're okay."

"Darlene, you've been a tremendous help. Thanks for everything. Maybe I will stop by your show one night."

"Well, if you really want to thank me, I could use a good ride in the sack right now. I'd love to do you both at the same time. That's sort of a specialty of mine. I'm up for anything you hunks can imagine. I do it all. I mean ev-er-y-thing. I can see what both of you are trying to conceal from me, and I'd love to ease your painful throbbing by milking you both bone dry. Whattaya say, guys? I'm really, really horny and I need some relief."

She stood and dropped her robe to the floor. She turned around and bent over the recliner and wiggled her derrière. "Come on, guys. Just a quickie. I'm begging you. Please."

They both stood. Kirk walked stiff-legged to the door and unlocked it. Stan went over and rubbed his hands all over Darlene's heavenly body. With every last vestige of willpower he possessed, he finally let go. He was harder than Chinese arithmetic. Then he walked to the door beside Kirk and said, "Darlene, this is about the hardest thing I've had to do in years. I gotta go because the sheriff is impatiently waiting for me. Give me a raincheck. Please. I'll come back. Promise."

She replied, "The thing is, I know just how hard it is. I'd really love to relax that throbbing woman-pleaser right now. 'Bye 'bye, Handsome."

Stan drove them out of there as fast as he could before he changed his mind. He asked, "Have you ever seen anything that scrumptious in your life and then just walked away?"

"Nope."

"Me neither."

To save some time, Kirk got in Julio's car and Chief got into Stan's so they could debrief en route to the Detective Bureau. They couldn't get there fast enough with all the new leads they had. They provided an analyst named Beverly Walcott with the two new suspect names so she could start running record checks. While they were cooling their heels, Captain Kirk called Chief Hornsby's office to see if he had time to stop by. He did.

Darlene's information paid off. Rodney A. "Bug Eye" Tinsley, age 24, of 1611 Elm Street, in El Paso, had four misdemeanor arrests on file, including drunk driving. Nicholas D. Crenshaw, age 23, of 808 Douglas Avenue, El Paso, had one arrest in Brewster County. Beverly pulled up rap sheets on all four suspects. She also pulled up a set of fingerprints and mugshots on Everett M. Raymond, Rocky K. Givens, and Rodney A. Tinsley, all of which she provided to Chief Alex.

Chief Derrick asked, "What's your next move now, Alex?"

"Well, I gotta call Sheriff Sol first to touch base. I can tell you this, though. Unless Sheriff Sol instructs me otherwise, we will make a stop in Van Horn on the way home just to satisfy ourselves that this crew was not the one to knock off their grocery. Then we'll stop by Brewster County for a set of prints and a mugshot on Nick Crenshaw. It's 3:30 now, so this will be another long day for us. I was wondering, "Would you all mind stopping by the Tinsley and Crenshaw domiciles to see what you can pick up? I think the missing Raymond ruse would be the best way so as not to tip our hand."

Chief Derrick said, "Consider it done. If we get something juicy, we'll call it into your duty deputy tonight. Otherwise, we'll call you all tomorrow."

"'Preciate it."

Chief Alex found an empty desk and telephoned the office. Miss Loretta picked up on the third ring. After the customary pleasantries, she switched the call to Sheriff Sol's office.

"Hey, Chief! You all still in El Paso?"

"We are. In the interest of saving time, I'll make this short so we can start rolling eastbound.

"Both stolen vehicles were righteous auto thefts. We are 99 percent sure our other two robbers are Nicholas D. Crenshaw, age 23, and Rodney A. "Bug Eye" Tinsley, age 24. Both reside in El Paso, same as Everett M. Raymond and Bruce K. "Rocky" Givens. All but Crenshaw have arrest records here in El Paso, so we picked up copies of their rap sheets, mugshots, and fingerprints. Crenshaw has a record in Brewster County, so we're stopping by Alpine on our way home to get copies of his prints and mugshot.

"Before that, though, we're stopping by Van Horn to check

with Culberson County SO on the armed robbery at a grocery there on Monday that I mentioned yesterday. Apparently it was only a two-man job, but so were both of ours. The timeline fits, anyway.

"Also, EPSO will check out the LKAs (last known addresses) for Tinsley and Crenshaw. We've already checked the others. No one has seen any of these mutts for a week or so. That's all we have. Anything popping there?"

"Maybe. We just got wind of a holdup of an armored car in Laredo in which two guards were killed. Two bandits, both white males wearing jeans, jean jackets, one with a Stetson and one with a baseball hat, and red bandannas. For sure, one was carrying an Army Colt .45. Not certain, but the getaway vehicle might have been a white over green Matador. A car matching that description was headed northbound out of Laredo shortly after the holdup. Slick and Barlow are ready to head over there as we speak. They'll hook up with the Webb County Sheriff's Office and the Laredo Police Department, and run out whatever leads turn up if they think the robbers are our doers. I told them to call me for any updates before they check in at Webb SO. I don't expect to hear anything after that until tomorrow morning unless they shoot somebody. You can never tell with those two."

"That's very true. Those two are not at all shy about spilling some blood if it needs to be spilt. Okay, then. Very good. I'll see you sometime tomorrow. Probably won't be until noon. I'm bushed and so is Kirk. He's still off tomorrow, isn't he?"

"Correctomundo. Speak to you sometime tomorrow if I don't see you. Oh yeah, before you go home tonight, check your desk for any last minute updates or instructions. Don't forget."

"You got it, Boss. Adiós."

Chief and Kirk hit the dusty trail just as soon as their departure would not be considered an act of rudeness. Besides, it was Friday afternoon and Chief was certain their hosts wanted to call it a week just as soon as they could.

Their second stop, after first making a pit stop at the Sinclair service station on US 54 just north of I-10 for fuel (and bladder relief), was at Culberson County's new, hideous, state-of-the-art jail about five miles north of downtown. It looked like it had been designed by an angry, psychotic architect in the Soviet Union with an axe to grind.

The Sheriff's Office was the only entity to have relocated. Every other county office, employee, and especially the courtroom itself remained in the old, but classically designed courthouse in downtown Van Horn, which just happened to be undergoing renovations (to divvy up the sheriff's former space and to make some luxury offices for the county supervisors).

The county's official position on this matter was not that they relocated the jail way out in the tulies because the county supervisors wanted more space, but because they were doing the sheriff a solid - providing him with more space. There was no room for him to expand in the courthouse. The county board of supervisors had pure, altruistic intentions for everybody concerned, to include the inmates.

Make no mistake about it. Everyone in Van Horn knew first and foremost that the banishment was done because the supervisors did not like the very popular incumbent sheriff, who drew a significantly greater percentage of votes in the past two elections than any of the supervisors, not to mention that he was a blackhearted Republican. Then, the move was subsequently presented as a faux concern for the public's safety as a result of two jailbreaks they had suffered within the past two years. One escapee was serving six months for non-support. He walked off during a garbage run and drove straight to a tavern to have a beer (which the bartender gave him on the house, saying it was well-deserved). The other was a trusty serving three months as a result of his twelfth conviction for public drunkenness. (Think Otis on the *Andy of Mayberry* television series.) He was assigned to wash county motor vehicles at the Spic & Span Automatic Car Wash.

One afternoon he took an unauthorized hiatus to sneak home and copulate with his wife. (Even a drunk needs a little loving, too.) Both escapees surrendered peacefully and without incident. How's that for putting lipstick on a pig? Don't you just love politicians?

Chief Alex and Kirk entered through the front door of Culberson County's new Stalag 13 (the new one, not the *Hogan's Heroes* TV version), and displayed their badges through a bulletproof window to a uniformed receptionist. Chief said they would like to speak to an investigator if one were available. A few minutes later they were welcomed into the secure office area by Sergeant Haywood Epperson.

Haywood Epperson was an ex-Army MP. He was also a 32-year-old, 5-feet, 7-inch, 140 pound, muscular, brown-eyed, brown-haired, clean-shaven, military-style burr haircut, country-looking man with large knotty fingers, big feet, and elephant ears. He was wearing the standard Texas lawman's uniform consisting of khaki trousers and a khaki long-sleeve shirt, which in Haywood's case looked to be hand-me-downs from his much bigger brother, in that the trouser legs were at least an inch too long and the shirt was so baggy he could have fit in there twice. He was wearing the modern-style, plain brown leather gun belt with a pair of six-round, dump bullet pouches instead of cartridge loops, nightstick loop holder, and a handcuff case instead of a handcuff strap. His sidearm was a satin finish, blue steel, Smith & Wesson Model 28 Highway Patrolman, .357 Magnum revolver with a 3-1/2-inch barrel. His brown, pointy-towed cowboy boots were dusty and scuffed with traces of dried horse shit all around the soles.

He smiled and shook hands vigorously. He told them to call him Haywood. Then he offered them coffee which they gladly accepted, before escorting them back to his office. He asked, "What brings you boys to come see us from all the way over in Quayle County?"

Chief replied, "We're working a murder and robbery case. It's one and the same. We believe the bandits, and there are four altogether, are a crew out of El Paso. We just left EPSO after running down a number of leads with them. Chief Derrick Hornsby mentioned that you all had an armed robbery of a grocery store here on Monday. We thought we would stop by on our way back home and check to see if your robbers might also possibly be our robbers."

"Hot damn! I certainly hope so, then you can catch 'em and save us the trouble of hanging 'em here, except so far as we know, we only had the two robbers."

Chief replied, "Our robberies occurred on Wednesday, two days after yours. Our robbers split up into twos. One pair robbed our bank and the other pair robbed the liquor store. The ones in the liquor store shot and killed the store owner and a customer they left for dead, except he lived. The robberies occurred simultaneously. Both pairs fled in tandem eastbound on US 90 in two stolen cars. One was a rust-colored, 1972 Oldsmobile 442, and the other was a black, 1970 Chevrolet Monte Carlo. One of our deputies jumped 'em and exchanged shots with 'em. Unfortunately, they blew out his radiator and got away. They fled from Quayle County to Val Verde County, and from there north to Crockett County, where they stole two more cars. Right now they're in the wind. We've identified one of the shooters for sure, and we have strong probables on the other three. Can you tell us what happened here?"

"Dang! This here is a real bad bunch, ain't they? What we know is two white cowboy-lookin' fellers wearing red bandannas robbed the Piggly Wiggly just after lunch. They was both thin. One was over six feet tall and the other'n was a little shorter. The taller one was the only one who spoke, but all he done was whisper. Scared the livin' shit out of ever' one there. Both robbers was carrying an Army .45. No shots was fired, but the taller one threatened to kill the manager's family if he didn't comply 100 percent. Even examined his driver's license and memorized his address. They cleaned out the safe and all the cashiers' drawers. Got away with somewhere between $2,200 and $2,500. We got no idea what kind of cars they was drivin'. This sound like your bandits?"

"I believe so. Do you think any of your witnesses could identify either of the robbers?

"Well, they was both wearing Stetsons besides masks. The taller one had light-colored hair, not exactly blond, maybe a dishwater blond. The other'n coulda had red hair, but he mighta been a dirty blond, too. No idea what color eyes they had. The taller one was definitely the boss. He took the manager's keys and locked everyone inside the store. We found the keys in the parking lot."

"One of our shooters has red hair. I think this is them. Could you give me a copy of your incident report and any witness statements that were helpful? Tomorrow I'll make copies of some mugshots we have. I'll put 'em in the mail to you on Monday or Tuesday. Maybe you could make up some photo arrays and see if any of your witnesses can identify them."

"Sounds good to me."

"One other thing. El Paso likes this crew for an armed robbery of a gas station a couple of weeks ago where they traded shots with the manager. You might want to talk with Chief Hornsby at the SO. It occurred within the city limits. I don't have all the details."

"I'll run this by my chief. He might want to make the call hisself."

Ten minutes later, Chief Alex had the reports and they were on their way. They stopped at a diner called The Country Kitchen before they left town. Chief had meatloaf and mashed potatoes with gravy, green beans, a house salad with honey mustard dressing, apple pie, and coffee. Kirk had spaghetti and meatballs, a house salad with Italian dressing, garlic toast, tapioca pudding, and iced tea. Now they were both ready to crash, but as Robert Frost penned, "But I have promises to keep, and miles to go before I sleep. Miles to go before I sleep."

It was 8:30 when they arrived in Alpine. As soon as Jeremy Logan, the duty deputy, met with Chief Alex and Kirk, he called Sheriff Leland Waters, knowing about the close relationship he had with Quayle County. Sheriff Waters responded within ten minutes.

"Alex, Kirk, so happy to see you all. What on Earth is so important in Mosby that you're here on my doorstep this late on a Friday night?"

"Sheriff, I had supposed that Sheriff Sol would have given you all a heads up. You heard about the robberies of our bank and the liquor store, didn't you?"

"Of course. Is that what this is about? How can we help? I'm so sorry to hear about Bryce Garrett getting murdered and Cordell getting shot. How's he doing?"

"Believe it or not, he's already at home. He seems to be mending well but he's got a ways to go yet.

"The reason we're here is we're headed home from El Paso, Alamogordo, and Van Horn, running out leads. We've positively IDed one bandit, Everett M. Raymond, as one of the shooters. He's from El Paso. We think we've IDed the other three, but it's not a lock yet. They're also from El Paso. These suspects are Bruce K. Givens, Rodney A. Tinsley, and Nicholas D. Crenshaw, age 23. All of these malevolent souls have arrests in El Paso, except for Crenshaw, who has one arrest here. I need to get a set of prints and a mugshot of him. We've recovered some latents from the liquor store and we need to make some comparisons."

"Of course. Jeremy, can you take care of that? Also get a copy of the incident report."

"Yes sir, Sheriff."

Sheriff Waters continued, "Normally I might not remember an arrest, but I remember this one well.

"Crenshaw is a wiseass punk with a big mouth. I think he got caught for possession of some weed. Not really that big a deal. Oh yeah! He also had a switchblade on him that he stole from his uncle's bureau drawer. It was a World War II trophy from Italy, not to mention being illegal to carry on your person here in Texas. Can you believe that? Stole it from his own uncle? What a lowlife! This was his first arrest as I recall, so he wasn't looking at more'n a month or two in the clink.

"That's not what happened, though. He was in jail pending trial. What he did was spit on one of my jailers when he was being escorted back from a court hearing, and my man tuned him up a little bit. Didn't draw any blood or require any stitches. (I can assure you that he woulda got a worse ass-kicking than that from me if he'd 'ave spit in my face.) Anyway, our resident do-gooder, the left-wing, police-hating, dick-sucking, activist, San Francisco, California Catholic priest who hides behind his robes and stirs up dissent everywhere he treads, just happened to walk by when my deputy unloaded on Crenshaw.

"Father Ignatius McSwain made a big stink about it. Said he was going to file a suit against the deputy, the jail, me, everyone who ever toted a badge or a gun, John Wayne, America-at-large, that sort of thing. Our bulldog district attorney, Bradford Delaney, you know him, stepped up to the plate and put the kibosh on it, thank the Lord. Brad agreed to release Crenshaw with credit for time served, if he pleaded guilty to both charges and signed an agreement not to pursue any civil or criminal action against anyone in Brewster County. This really pissed off the self-righteous Father Ignatius "Joseph Stalin" McSwain, but Crenshaw knew a good deal when he saw it, plus he also understood now that he irked us, he was looking at two years at hard labor if he didn't take the deal. Him being such a pretty boy and all, he knew the booty bandits would turn him into a wide receiver from a tight end by the time he completed a serve out. In the end, he wound up serving two weeks and beat feet out of

Brewster County just as fast as his momma could drive.

"So you really think that punk, girly man Nicholas Crenshaw is one of your doers?"

Jeremy returned and handed Chief a packet with prints and mugshots, etc.

"I'm pretty sure, but what I don't know yet, is if he was one of the guys who shot Bryce Garrett. Maybe God will smile on me, and I'll make a match on him with some of the latents from the liquor store."

"I certainly hope so. Look, if you all need anything else from us, and I mean anything, don't hesitate to call. Give Sol my regards. Gotta go. Babysitting grandkids. Take care. 'Bye."

"Thanks for everything, Sheriff. Adiós."

Chief drove the final hundred miles back home to Mosby. He was dragging ass. He parked in his reserved spot at the jail. The Baptist church bells were ringing. It was 11 o'clock. Kirk said goodbye and fired up his personally-owned vehicle (POV), a canary yellow, 1970 Dodge Dart, to make a beeline for home.

It had been a long couple of days, albeit extremely fruitful. Chief was more than ready for his evening nightcap - a gin and tonic with a twist of lime. Tonight he might even drink two, but first he had to check his desk to see if Sheriff Sol left anything for him which required immediate attention. No rest for the weary and the wicked don't need none, as the saying goes. Kirk's ambition was much more modest. He just wanted to crawl into his bed next to his sweet wife.

Chief Alex dropped his recently obtained files with all the mugshots, rap sheets, confession, and incident reports on top of his desk. He picked up a cryptic note from Sheriff Sol. It read, "Derrick H. called. Tinsley lives in boarding house, 1611 Elm St., # 3. Landlady said gone several days. Pays rent monthly. Due July 1. Parking lot attendant near courthouse. Quit/fired. Last known job at unk gas station. No wheels. Walks/rides bus. Crenshaw 808 Douglas Ave. Mother's house. No job. No wheels.

Broke. Rode w/friend to get hwy construction job north of EP near NM. Empl. provides housing/meals. Not called home yet. EPSO spot checking on both."

It was about what Chief had expected, except sooner. He put it all aside. Tomorrow, with all its promise and strife, would be here soon enough.

CHAPTER 15

Picking up the Trail Again

Friday, June 15, 1973

Sheriff Sol received a call from Sheriff Enoch Larkin in Crockett County. Sheriff Larkin had received a call from Sheriff Oliver Vincent in Webb County. He wanted to know if the white over green Matador on the BOLO had been recovered yet. The answer was no.

Sheriff Vincent said a car matching that description might have been used in the armed robbery and murder of two armored car guards in Laredo earlier in the day.

Sheriff Larkin said he would pass this along to Quayle County Sheriff Solomon Pratt because Quayle County was working two holdups and the murder of one victim by persons driving and/or riding in that stolen vehicle and the blue Ford station wagon also listed in the BOLO. Crockett County's primary interest was in the recovery of the two vehicles and a stolen safe. They would, of course, vigorously prosecute the thieves if they were ever positively identified and/or apprehended.

Sheriff Vincent said to tell Sheriff Pratt to contact his office if he thought these robberies were connected. Sheriff Larkin agreed to do just that.

Sheriff Sol called Sheriff Vincent. During the conversation it became obvious that Sheriff Oliver Vincent was a fish out of water. He was completely beholden to and under the control of Rutherford W. Farnsworth III and all his next-of-kin, who happened to be the most prominent (meaning filthy rich) family in all of Webb County. They were also the sole proprietors of the Texas Sovereign Bank & Trust, on whose property the armored car heist had taken place.

Sheriff Vincent said he was under tremendous pressure to make some arrests, even though the robbery and murders occurred within the city limits of Laredo. Unfortunately, Chief of Police Linus Merriweather and he don't gee haw very well because Sheriff Vincent defeated Chief Merriweather in the election. Merriweather was career law enforcement, but had insufficient political backing to get elected (meaning at a minimum, that the Farnsworth family didn't back him). Thus, Sheriff Vincent had no idea what Chief Merriweather's officers had uncovered so far. In fact, it had been almost open warfare between the city cops and the county deputies since the election.

Sheriff Vincent went on to explain that his family owned the only mortuary in Webb County and until he was elected sheriff last November, he had never been involved in law enforcement. He only ran for office because R.W. (Mr. Farnsworth) insisted. He wished now that Linus Merriweather would have beaten him. This armored car job and double murder was the biggest disaster Sheriff Vincent had encountered since taking over in January. Honestly, he didn't know where to turn next.

Sheriff Sol knew it was shameful, but all this drama was music to his ears. He told Sheriff Vincent that the bandits were probably the same crew who robbed two businesses and murdered one person in Quayle County. He said his men were tracking this crew to the ends of the Earth. He also said the crew was probably long gone, unlikely to ever return to Laredo again. Nevertheless, he was sending two of his deputies to see if they could pick up the trail. They would arrive around nightfall. Sheriff Sol thought they would be able to trade information with the PD, which they would pass along to Sheriff Vincent or to whomever he designated. Sheriff Sol promised that if his deputies did locate and arrest the robbers, they would give credit to the Webb County Sheriff's Office and him for all their assistance.

That was music to Sheriff Vincent's ears. He would be waiting for Slick and Barlow in his office. The gates to Webb County were wide open.

Sheriff Sol briefed Slick and Barlow about the Webb County saga at the same time he passed his car keys over to them (so they could travel in an unmarked unit). He also filled them in with Chief's latest update. Finally, he told Slick to call him at his house before they laid their heads to rest tonight.

Slick and Barlow were lickety-split like Ricochet Rabbit out the door before Sheriff Sol could even collect his thoughts, and why not? Laredo was 300 miles east and south of Mosby. They had a long drive ahead of them. No matter. Picking up the tracks of the bandit trail again was akin to the scent of blood in the water to a pair of starving sharks.

Next, Sheriff Sol called Gillespie and woke her up. He asked if she were ready for a special assignment. What? You bet she was! In fact, the adrenaline was already flowing and she didn't even know what the assignment was.

Sheriff Sol said her midnight shift tonight would end at 4 am. Switch the phones to the answering service. Go back home and get some shut-eye. He expected that Chief and Kirk would roll in about midnight. Chief would have some mugshots which need to be assembled into photo arrays (sometimes referred to as six-packs because each array has six mugshots of similar looking persons). Gillespie was to search their mugshot files for as many photographs as she could find of men who resemble the three new suspects, Bruce K. Givens, Rodney A. Tinsley, and Nicolas D. Crenshaw. Chief would make the final selections. (No need to make one for Everett M. Raymond because Cordell had already identified him as one of the bandits at the liquor store.)

Gillespie was instructed to report back for duty at noon to assist Chief in assembling the six-packs and anything else he needed, to include participating with him when he interviewed Mr. Dinkins and his entire bank staff Saturday afternoon.

Whenever Chief was done for the day, she was done. She would report back to duty on Monday and work the afternoon shift all next week. Did she have any questions? What? Did Joe DiMaggio have any questions when he stepped up to the plate? Hell no! He just waited for the first fastball to come flying across the strike zone to send it sailing out of the park.

Finally, Sheriff Sol called Mr. Dinkins at the bank. Sheriff Sol was dreading this call. Mr. LaRue Dinkins was a real stinker. Sheriff Sol caught him just before the bank closed for the weekend. He told Mr. Dinkins that he and all his staff need to expect a visit from Chief Alex and Gillespie at their respective homes Saturday afternoon. Each of them would be shown several photo arrays in an effort to determine if they could identify any of the photographs as likenesses of the bank robbers. Mr. Dinkins was not happy about having his weekend interrupted! Couldn't this wait until Monday during regular business hours?

This is exactly what Sheriff Sol had expected and it ticked him off! He replied rather tersely. "LaRue, (Sol called him by his first name to cut him down to his true diminutive size) my deputies have been working 12- and 16-hours a day with no overtime to figure out who held up your bank, not to mention who killed Bryce and shot Cordell. We're close to solving both robberies and we could really use your cooperation. Under the circumstances, since the bandits have absconded to places unknown, we need to get arrest warrants filed on them so other law enforcement agencies will arrest them if they locate them before we do. Understand? We're hoping to get this done first thing Monday morning. Two deputies have been gone two days now running down leads in El Paso, and two more are en route to Laredo to do the same thing. LaRue, for the love of God, can you bring yourself to sacrifice just an hour of your time tomorrow afternoon to help us pursue justice for you and your bank?"

"Sheriff Pratt, I prefer to be called Mr. Dinkins. You should know that by now. Yes. My staff and I will make ourselves available tomorrow for interviews. Honestly, I didn't know the lengths the sheriff's office was going to in order to catch the villains. Bravo! Good day, Sir."

What a surprise! LaRue Dinkins was actually acting like a regular joe - almost. Don't ever forget to call him by his title - Mister. Familiarity breeds contempt, you know.

Sheriff Sol collected what he needed and bade the duty deputy, Randy Meacham, good night. Then he checked out the keys to the second newest marked unit and drove home. It was time for a frosty cold Miller High Life. No! Ezra Brooks 7-year-old Kentucky bourbon on the rocks.

Slick and Barlow made it to Laredo in record time, to include having stopped to eat and refuel. It was dusk when they parked in a space marked "Visitor" at the Webb County Courthouse. They were surprised to learn that the sheriff's personal office, distinct from the jail and administrative portions of the agency, was located on the second floor. There was more activity ongoing in the courthouse than they had expected this late at night. Sure enough, Sheriff Oliver Vincent and Chief Investigator Roland Epps were waiting for them.

Sheriff Vincent was a tall drink of water. He was about 38 years of age. He stood 6-feet, 4-inches tall and tipped the scales at a maximum of a buck-fifty. He had perfectly combed black hair slicked down, and combed back with Brylcreem hair pomade or something similar like the 1920s movie star, Rudy Valentino. He was clean shaven. He had piercing, sunken, black eyes. His nose and his fingers were long, and his ears and Adam's apple were prominent. He was wearing a well-tailored black suit, a white dress shirt with French cuffs, and a bolo tie with a sterling silver, handmade clasp in the shape of an oval. The stone was jade. The clasp matched his cufflinks. He was wearing a simple gold band wedding ring on his left hand and a gold domed ring with a black onyx on his right. He wore highly polished, black, lizard skin, pointy-toed Tony Lama cowboy boots. He had a black leather fold-over in the breast pocket of his suit jacket displaying his highly polished, six-point, silver star emblazoned with "Webb County Texas" in small block letters around the periphery and "Sheriff" in larger block letters centered across the middle. If he were carrying a sidearm, it was well-concealed.

Barlow glanced around the office. The floors were polished hardwood. The first thing that caught his attention was a classic, double-barreled, Parker 12-gauge shotgun resting on a gun rack made of bull horns above the door. Then he noticed the coat tree behind the desk with a leather bandolier full of shotgun shells on a hook. The sheriff's black Stetson was perched on the top. Centered on the wall behind the desk was the gold leaf framed State of Texas certificate with the governor's signature and the Great Seal proclaiming Oliver H. Vincent as Webb County Sheriff effective January 1, 1973.

Across the room from the desk was a splendid, large window with a fabulous view of downtown Laredo, the Rio Grande, and Old Mexico. Barlow also saw an antique, framed map print of Webb County along a side wall. Then he checked out the desk. It was moderate-sized and made of oak. A rectangular jade potted dish of miniature cacti was centered on the front, next to a small, bronze Frederic Remington statue of a mounted, well-dressed cowboy. The sheriff's chair was also oak, as were six other matching chairs strategically placed around the room. This was a classic, modest but at the same time auspicious, chief executive's office. Barlow had to confess, if he ever became a sheriff, this is exactly what he would want his office to look like.

Chief Investigator Roland Epps was pretty much everything Sheriff Vincent was not. First, he appeared to be about 60. He was completely bald with just a little gray fringe around the back and sides. His face was weathered without looking craggy. It was a comforting face. Strong. Friendly. Steady. He looked like someone's grandpa, maybe because he was.

He had a bushy, gray walrus mustache. His eyes were a

captivating pale blue. He was burly, and stood about 5-feet, 10-inches tall, and he was probably carrying 210 pounds of muscle, bone, and fat. He was big-boned with thick arms and short, thick, blunt fingers.

He was wearing the standard issue khaki trousers, except his were pleated, a long-sleeved white shirt, mostly crumpled, open at the throat, a well-worn beige Stetson, dusty brown, slightly scuffed, round-toed, low-heeled Justin cowboy boots, and a thick brown basketweave gun belt with a large, silver, oval belt buckle of the Great Seal of Texas, a cross-draw holster with a parkerized Colt, Government Model 1911, .45 ACP (Automatic Colt Pistol) caliber, and a single magazine pouch with extra ammo. He also wore a plain gold wedding ring. His star was sterling silver, too, but his was weathered and a little tarnished. If it really mattered to him, he could have put some silver polish on it and buffed it out. Another difference from Sheriff Vincent's badge was that Roland Epps' badge read "Deputy Sheriff."

Barlow thought Sheriff Vincent looked formal, serious, aloof. He thought Chief Investigator Epps looked friendly, happy, at ease. Barlow was correct on both counts.

After introductions were made, Sheriff Vincent asked, "Why are Sheriff Pratt and you all so convinced that our robbers and your robbers are the same crew?"

Slick replied, "We can't be absolutely certain until we gather a little more information. What we do know is this. The crew we're after has four men; however, not all four men have been involved in every robbery.

"First, four men robbed a gas station in El Paso, which, by the way, is where this crew originates. The descriptions of two gas station robbers match the same two robbers who hit a grocery in Van Horn next.

"Two days after Van Horn, in Mosby, both at the same time, two robbers hit our bank and two hit our liquor store. We positively identified one of the shooters, because one of the victims, who just happens to be my partner's brother-in-law, knew him. They shot the liquor store owner dead, and they shot Barlow's brother-in-law in the chest. They left him for dead.

"They escaped in two cars in a running high speed gun battle with Barlow. They shot out his radiator, or I know Barlow woulda smoked at least two of 'em. One car was stolen from El Paso. It was found by Val Verde SO all burned up. Barlow and me tracked the second car to Ozona, in Crockett County. It was stolen in Alamogordo, just north of El Paso. In Ozona they stole two more cars - the white over green AMC and a blue Ford station wagon. In the meantime, we have tentatively identified the other three robbers.

"What can you tell us about the robbery here?"

Sheriff Vincent replied, "Tell 'em what you know, Roland."

Roland cleared his throat and replied, "You may or may not know about some of the problems going on here between us and Laredo PD. We don't always get along, but we are getting along better on this heist. My son is a patrolman on LPD. What I know I got from him."

Slick interrupted, "Sorry, but Sheriff Pratt's gonna ask me. What's your son's name?"

"Junior."

"You mean like Roland Epps, Jr.?"

"Yep, Roland G. (for Gilman) Epps, Jr. Gilman was my mother's maiden name."

"Gotcha. Thanks."

"So Junior was on patrol north of town when the heist went down. When the call went out, he headed south to the bank. At the time, he didn't pay any attention to it, but he passed a white over green Matador with two men in the front seat going north. All he knows is they were white. Traffic was fairly heavy and this car was just one of many going north, but he remembered it because it was a classy-looking ride.

"Junior was the first to arrive on the scene. The armored car was not there. In fact, he never saw it until much later. Nevertheless, there were two dead guards in the parking lot. Both had been shot twice in the chest. The first was Abraham K. Sipowicz, 28, a Marine vet with a Purple Heart he received in Vietnam. He was lying face down by the dolly they use to pick up their packages. The other was Jeffrey R. Cooper, 44, an Air Force vet from the Korean War. He was face up. His unfired revolver was by his side. Sipowicz's gun was still in his holster, but the strap had been unsnapped like he was drawing it.

"Inside of ten minutes, darn near every city officer on duty was at the crime scene. They canvassed 19 people who were anywhere near the bank. Six never saw a thing. Some denied hearing any shots. Nine reported seeing a white over green car depart the curbside parking area right after they heard the shots, but that's it. Four said the robbers were white males in jeans and jean jackets. One had on a baseball cap. The other was wearing a beige cowboy hat. They both were wearing red bandannas.

"One witness observed the shooting itself. He said the robber in the baseball cap came up on the guards from behind. Cooper turned around and saw him, and extended his weapon as if to fire. The robber yelled "stop" and then shot Cooper twice and he went down. Sipowicz was unlocking the back door. When he turned around, the same robber shot him. Then the robber ran up to the back of the truck and got inside. A few seconds later he exited, and the truck sped off with the back door flapping like clean sheets on a clothesline on a windy day. That robber had a bunch of money sacks in his arms. Maybe eight or ten. He got in the white over green car, and the other robber who had the shotgun drove away slowly like this never even happened.

"The armored car driver, Morris L. Yeager, 64, a IV-F military reject from the Army during World War II due to nearsightedness, but who has been employed by the armored car company as a guard for 44 years, and who had been shot once before in an armored car robbery, drove to police headquarters and reported the incident. The company stated that Yeager followed company procedures and he was cleared of any dereliction of duty. Anyway, Yeager said the robber who got in the truck was wearing an Astros baseball cap. He said the robber had blue eyes and red hair, and had it not been for the bulletproof glass, he would've ended up a dead duck, too. I believe that's everything. Does it fit?"

Slick responded, "Oh Hell, yeah. It fits like an opera glove. Sheriff, I have to ask before I say anything else, how do you plan to proceed on this investigation? Will you share info with the PD? Do you trust them to be square with you, and Quayle County, and El Paso County, and Culberson County, and Crockett County? We all have a dog in this fight."

"In the past, I would have said no. However, Chief Merriweather agreed to share everything Roland just told you. I think we are patching things up. In other words, I feel comfortable stating that the PD is playing ball with all of us."

"Good, because we want this crew in the worst way. There would be bad blood forever if somebody decided to cut us out of the picture."

"Understood, and I wouldn't blame you all. What else do you have?"

"You all might want to take some notes. After doing your own checks, you could call Chief Merriweather and maybe make an ally for life.

"Your shooter is Everett M. Raymond, about 30 years old, red hair and blue eyes, a dishonorably discharged vet. He's one of our shooters at the liquor store.

"I forgot to ask. Did your driver wear glasses? Did anyone mention it?"

Roland said, "Nobody said anything about glasses. My guess is no."

"Okay. Your driver is probably Nicholas D. Crenshaw, age 23, with one arrest in Alpine in Brewster County. The other possibility is Rodney A. Tinsley, age 24. They call him Bug-Eye because he wears thick, black frame grasses with Coke bottle lenses. The glasses are the first thing everyone notices about Tinsley, so he is probably not your guy. The leader of this group is Bruce K. Givens, 32, I think, with at least one trip to Huntsville under his belt. Givens is really smart. He doesn't leave many breadcrumbs. Everyone except for Crenshaw has an arrest record in El Paso.

"Right now, we don't know where these owlhoots are, but they always skedaddle someplace other than where they commit their crimes. Most likely, they're somewhere north of here. They gotta ditch that Matador, so they'll need some new wheels. Put an updated BOLO on the Matador and tie it in to your armored car robbery and you'll probably generate some interest. Don't forget to tie the stolen blue Ford station wagon to the Matador.

"Once you get mugshots on Raymond and Crenshaw, I bet some of your witnesses might ID them from a six-pack, especially the driver, Mr. Yeager, with respect to Raymond.

"Any lawman who comes into contact with any of these bandits better be prepared to pull the trigger. They are not afraid to kill and they will shoot first.

"That's what I know. You probably want to make a personal call to any adjacent counties tonight. You might get lucky.

"Sheriff, Barlow and I need lodging for tonight. You all have any places who give a police discount?"

Sheriff Vincent said, "Sorry, I forgot to mention it. After I spoke with Sheriff Pratt, I made you all reservations at the Red Roof Inn. It's about six blocks down the street. You probably saw it on your way in. Your rooms are on us tonight.

"Roland and I have some calls to make. What say you all check in with us about 8:30 tomorrow morning. If anything breaks, we know where to find you. Also, if you're hungry, Armando's Cantina next door to the motel has outstanding food. It doesn't close until 10. They're also open for breakfast at 6."

"Thanks, Sheriff, Chief. If you all don't call us first, we'll see you all in the morning. Adiós."

"Adiós."

The sheriff reserved a room for each of them with a king-size bed. Not only that, their money was no good at Armando's. How's that for Texas hospitality?

CHAPTER 16

"Man Plans. God Laughs"

Saturday, June 16, 1973

It was 9:45 when Rocky and Bug Eye walked into the Denny's restaurant. Ev and Nick were waiting in a booth, sipping on coffee. After Rocky and Bug Eye slid into the booth, Rocky said, "Good morning, girls. We didn't think you all were here yet. We didn't see the Matador."

Ev replied, "That's a long story. I'll tell you all about it after we place our orders."

Rocky had already smelled a rat but he smiled benignly, and ordered pancakes and sausage links when it was his turn.

Once the waitress left, Ev looked up and said, "You was right, Rocky. That Matador was just too flashy. It was drawing too many smiling looks. We took your advice and swapped it out for a van in a plain white wrapper so as not to draw any attention to ourselves. We done it over in Carrizo Springs to keep it outta Eagle Pass, just like you said. In other words, we didn't shit in our mess kit. You should be real proud of us."

Rocky knew there was more to the story than that, but he nodded in affirmation and let it slide for the moment. He asked, "What else you all been up to besides switching your wheels since we saw you last?"

Nick quickly responded, "Well, we got drunk and slept all day Thursday. Friday we went walkabout checking out Carrizo Springs then then down into Laredo just to see what was going on over there. Interesting place. Looked like a target-rich environment if you want to get laid."

Rocky caught Ev's bone-chilling look at Nick. If Ev had been an orc, the look would have transformed Nick into an ice sculpture of a plump elf ready for consumption. The look wasn't lost on Nick, either. He looked down and shifted gears. "Not much there to see in Laredo, actually. You probably already knew that, so we made a U-B (U-turn) and went back and got us the van in Carrizo Springs. Then we ate a steak dinner here at the Ponderosa and bought more beer and got drunk again and now here we are. What did you ladies do?"

Bug Eye said, "We bought some tools to take care of that little chore we need to do after breakfast, plus we found the perfect place north of town far away from prying eyes."

Ev smirked and said, "Well ain't you all the clever ones?"

The waitress brought their meals and left again. Then Rocky asked, "You all have any excitement over in Laredo? See anything worth mentioning, being that it's such an interesting place?"

Ev replied, "I don't think so. Did you, Nick?"

Nick replied, "Not that I can recall. Why do you ask?"

Rocky responded, "Oh, no reason. You all must have missed it. I was watching the news on TV this morning. The reporter said an armored car had been robbed in Laredo and two guards were shot and killed. Lucky you all weren't there when it went down. The fuzz are all stirred up about it, looking for scalps to hang up on the wall. The Chief of Police said they were running out leads and that they expected to catch the robbers very soon. Being an armed robber myself, it made me shudder just to think about it. Geez, I wonder what the take would be from a job like that. I bet it's a bundle."

Ev replied, "No doubt."

Rocky knew they were lying, so he threw a knuckleball to see if they could hit it. Since it sounded like they hadn't seen the news, he lied and said, "They're looking for a green over white AMC. Wouldn't you call that an exceptionally rare coincidence, especially since you all were over there and ditched the one you were driving?"

Bug Eye gave Rocky a quizzical look. He had seen the news too, and they never said that. Then he looked over at Ev.

Ev was getting all fidgety. He threw down the gauntlet, snapping, "It's starting to sound like you all think we done it."

Rocky replied casually, but the point had already been scored. "Nope. If you say it wasn't you, it wasn't you."

From that moment forward, nobody uttered a word until they were all done eating. Then Ev said he needed to use the restroom. He got up and left. Once he was gone, Nick whispered, "Rocky, Ev's on a tear. His fuse is already lit. Watch yourself, or you could be sorry."

Rocky replied, "Nick, after we split the loot, you're gonna have to decide what you wanna do. We're done with Ev. It will be time to split up. You can go with Ev or stay with us. If you decide to stay, you better keep an eye on Ev your own self."

When Ev returned, they paid their checks and got up to leave. Rocky said, "You all follow us. It's not very far. We'll see what we got in our Easter basket. Then it'll be time to fish or cut bait. Talk it over amongst yourselves."

It took them about 30 minutes to get to the abandoned farm. Part of that was due to their decision to top off their gas tanks first.

When they arrived, Rocky led them to the back side of the barn so their vehicles would not be noticed if someone drove down the dirt road past the farm. Rocky backed up within six feet of the rear barn door. Ev parked farther away, nose facing out towards the dirt driveway. Rocky didn't say anything, but it made him wonder if Ev were preparing for a fast getaway. They all got out and stretched. Rocky let down the tailgate of the station wagon, and lifted up a tarp. The safe and tools were hidden underneath.

Rocky said, "Bug, get the tools and open up the barn. Nick, you and Ev help me get the safe out. We'll bust it open in there. I bought a chisel and a sledgehammer to open the safe, and a pick and shovel so we can bury it after we're done. We do not want to leave any clues for the cops. There'll be enough hay inside to cover up the dig site. Let's dig the hole first. That way we can vamoose as soon as we're done."

Ev retorted, "Who fucking died and made you boss? There ain't no reason to waste time digging no fucking hole to bury it in. Get a life! No one's gonna find it here. Even if they do, so what? Ain't no one who's gonna know where it come from."

Rocky measured his words carefully before he responded. He stood erect facing Ev, jacket pushed back, hand on the grip of his .45. His eyes were blazing. Showdown time. He said, "Ev, start digging now, or hit the road without your share. I could give a shit less. Either way, when we're done, you are on your own. If Nick wants to go with you, that's fine by me. It's for damn sure you and I can no longer work together. Best if we stay out of each other's way unless you want to commence dancing right now."

Nick piped up. "Come on, Ev. We already talked about splitting up. Let's get our share before we go. You take the shovel, and I'll take the pick. Then in 15 minutes, we can trade places with Rocky and Bug Eye and let them sweat for awhile. No need for us to go away all pissed off and empty-handed."

Ev was still glaring at Rocky, but he said, "Fine, but this is the last time I'm gonna go along just because Rocky says so. He ain't the boss of me. Besides, we don't even know if the safe has any money in it, period."

Rocky tersely replied, "Then the joke's on us. How many people have you heard of who buy a safe just to store their fucking toilet paper? Either dig, hit the fucking road, or slap leather!"

Ev begrudgingly, and Nick hastily, started digging. Rocky and Bug Eve watched before relieving them when it became obvious they needed a rest. This continued for the better part of two hours before Rocky was satisfied that the hole was both big enough and deep enough.

They took a 20-minute beer break to rehydrate. They were all sweating like boxers after going 15 rounds. Break over, Bug Eye held the chisel while Rocky pounded it with the sledgehammer into the seam of the door and combination lock to break it off. Even after the lock broke off, they still had to keep chiseling away in the seam of the door to loosen the three deadbolts. It was harder than Rocky thought it would be. Heck! In the old cowboy movies they just shot the lock off. Finally, the door swung open. What they found were titles, insurance documents, sales records, a five-shot .38 Special Smith & Wesson snub-nose revolver, and cash. Lots and lots of cash, mostly in 20s. They sequestered the bills by denomination and began counting, and counting, and counting again and again until they all came up with the same exact amount. What they scored was $38,560, or $9,640 apiece!

After the split, Rocky said he needed to go get a fresh pack of smokes. He strode out of the barn, got in the Ford, pulled forward and turned it around 180 degrees. He moved it 20 feet or so from the barn and parked. Now it was out of their way. He got out and began to walk back to the barn. He remembered the smokes, so he turned and went back to the car. He opened the front passenger door, leaned in bent over at the waist, popped open the glove box, looking for his Camels instead of Bug Eye's Chesterfields. He heard someone shout, but he couldn't make out what was said. He sensed something wasn't right. He drew his .45 and waited to see who would come running out. In his heart of hearts, he already knew.

As soon as Rocky walked out of the barn, Ev perked up and listened intently. When Rocky turned off the ignition, Ev bounced up from the box he was sitting on and drew his .45. He trotted towards the door, apparently looking to ambush Rocky.

Bug Eye, who had been on pins and needles all morning over the tension between Rocky and Ev, watched as Ev drew his gun. A second later, Bug Eye jumped up and followed Ev. He took no chances. He filled both hands with his matched, nickel-plated .357s.

Nick, who had been absorbed counting his stolen lucre, finally realized what Ev was up to. He looked up in horror, and yelled "no!" Then he ran after Bug Eye, but his .44 remained holstered.

Rocky had anticipated a showdown between Ev and himself sooner or later. This was one reason he had picked this site to divvy up the loot. No external witnesses. He was mentally prepared. This was it. He just wanted Ev to show his hand first. As soon as Ev cleared the barn door with gun in hand, Rocky stood up from behind the open car door, which he used for cover. Seeing Ev before Ev saw him, Rocky had time to take careful aim with his own .45. He drilled Ev twice in the 10-ring, rapid fire. Boom! Boom!

This turn of events caught Ev completely by surprise. Ev thought he had taken Rocky by surprise, but he hadn't. He was dead wrong. It wasn't supposed to go down this way! Even so, Ev managed to squeeze off one hasty shot in Rocky's general direction a microsecond after Rocky fired. The distance to target was seven and-one-half yards.

This was the story of Ev's life. The sum total. Ev was always a day late and a dollar short, or in the legendary words of Gordon Lightfoot in his ballad, *Sundown*, "Sometimes I think it's a sin when I feel like I'm winning when I'm losing again." Bingo!

Ev's shot sailed wide right past Rocky's right ear like an angry, buzzing hornet, and on into oblivion. It would have taken a metal detector and the patience of Job to find Ev's spent projectile, but at the moment, both were in short supply. Nevertheless, in that very instant, Ev was knocked backwards by the sledgehammer force of two, 230-grain, copper-jacketed, lead round-nose slugs, traveling at 800-feet per second, expending all their energy and mushrooming to almost twice their size on contact, landing somewhere in the barn, or perhaps not. Perhaps they blasted right through the deteriorating, wooden barn walls and came to rest on a pair of toadstools side-by-side out by the pond. Either way, Ev was still dead on arrival when he landed three feet backwards on terra firma, face up, eyes staring blindly in wonder at the passing clouds in the sky. In contrast to Ev's errant, wasted shot, both of Rocky's shots turned Ev's heart into mincemeat. In fact, there was bloody confetti and mist everywhere. To say it was gratifying to Rocky would have been a gross understatement.

The report of the three shots had hardly died when Rocky pivoted slightly right, aiming his .45 center of mass at Nick's worthless, chickenshit heart. Nick stopped on a dime and jammed his empty hands high in the air as far as they could go like he was silently singing *"Hallelujah"* to God at a church revival. Maybe he was in his mind; however, for the second time in a minute, he shouted "no!" Thankfully for Nick, it was just in the nick of time. Rocky held his fire, but he did not lower his gun. It was still cocked and trained on Nick's racing heart. Instead of firing his pistol, Rocky fired off a question. He screamed, "Nick, did you know this son of a bitch was going to do this?"

Nick had never been closer to death in his miserable short life, and he knew it. He said, "No! On my mother's grave, I didn't know! I swear! I even warned you as soon as I saw him pull his gun."

Bug Eye watched in horror. His own pals were now killing each other. He interjected, "Rocky, it's true. I heard him. That's why I drew both of my guns and ran out as soon as I heard him. It was obvious that Ev was out for blood. Truly. Nick's telling the truth. I swear. Look, Nick never drew his gun. He's innocent."

"Innocent, huh? We'll see about that! Tell me right now, Nick. Tell me straight, like your miserable life depends on it. You all robbed that armored car and killed those two guards, didn't you? You both lied to me with a straight face!"

"Yes! Yes! We robbed that armored car! I didn't shoot anyone. Ev killed 'em both. I had no idea he was going to do it until the very last minute. All I did was drive. Honest! Count my bullets.

Look! I shot twice at the liquor store dude, and that's it. Not sure whether I killed him or if it was Ev, but I fired twice. I've still got 48 bullets left out of that box of 50. I'll show you."

"Tell you what, Nick. You want to redeem yourself? You walk over to Ev right now. I want you to fire two rounds into his conniving, double-crossing, weasel brain. You better not fucking miss either if you want to live!"

Nick did just what he was told. Ev's head looked like a pumpkin that had been run over by a tractor. Then he holstered his revolver and held his hands halfway in the air, palms showing.

Rocky said, "Your turn, Bug. Put two rounds from both revolvers into Ev's chest, right where I shot. Shoot right into his black, traitorous, murdering heart!"

Bug Eye complied without objection and reholstered.

Rocky finally holstered his gun. He said, "Okay. If anyone ever finds Ev's carcass, they won't be able to determine who killed him. He's riddled with .45, .44, and .357 caliber bullets - all kill shots. You all know what that means? It means if we get caught, we'll all be blamed. If anyone rats, he's ratting out himself. Got it? You better carry this little secret with you to your fucking grave.

"Nick, where did you all steal that van?"

"We didn't steal it. I bought it for $700 at a used car lot in Carrizo Springs after we robbed the armored car."

"You got a bill of sale in your name? Who do the plates come back to?"

"No. I gave him a phony name. Told him I was Aaron White. I got a bill of sale. The plates are registered to a dude named Roger Godfrey. He owns the BK in Carrizo Springs. They're still good for another couple of months."

"How's it run?"

"Like it's brand fucking new. Not kidding."

"Okay. How much did you all clear from the armored car heist?"

"$22,688 in cash. We burned all the checks and bags."

"That means you both got $11,344. Divide that by two and you get to keep $5,672. You give Bug Eye $5,672 from your stash and I will take $5,672 from Ev's."

"Yes, except for I paid myself back for the van first. The actual split was $10,994."

"Not anymore. You own the van outright, so pony up or make your stand. What'll it be?"

Nick knew he was pushing his luck but he was greedy. He whined, "But you all weren't even involved in that robbery."

"And for all intent and purposes, you and Bug Eye weren't actively involved the grocery store robbery but nevertheless the split was divided four ways. Likewise, we pooled the take from the bank and liquor store robberies, even though you all didn't rob the bank and we didn't rob the liquor store. This was our agreement from the very beginning. Also, you all concealed the armored car robbery from us, and you know I would never have sanctioned it. Too fucking risky. You all got lucky, but the heat from the fuzz is scorching all of us. Make up your mind. Pony up or slap leather."

Rocky backed up several steps and squared off. His eyes were as bright as fanned coals. He started pulling his .45 out of its holster. Nick had a sudden change of heart. He knew he was holding a losing hand and that Rocky was about to kill him right there where he stood. He also knew that even if he got lucky and managed to shoot Rocky first, which had less than a one percent probability, Bug Eye had Rocky's back. Either way, Nick was a dead man standing. Besides, he was never what one would call brave or fearless. He shuddered as a little stream of pee ran down his leg. His body started to shake like he had a sudden chill and he thought he was about to shit his pants. What on Earth was he thinking?

Nick reached for the sky to demonstrate peaceful intent for the third time in the past ten minutes. "Okay. Okay. Consider it a done deal. I'll make the split. I'm sorry. I know better."

"Glad you finally had an epiphany and come to Jesus. I won't tolerate a liar or a weasel. You ever pull a stunt like this again, I will shoot you dead no matter if it's in the middle of Times Square with a thousand people watching. Savvy?"

"Savvy."

After a pregnant pause, Rocky said, "Okay. This is what we're going to do. First, I want to see every last thing that belongs to Ev; his bag, his clothes, his guns, and all his money. Everything."

"His .45 goes in the grave with him. The cops probably have spent bullets from it in Mosby and Laredo. Anyone caught with that gun would probably wind up taking the fall for both of them. Savvy?"

Both Bug Eye and Nick nodded.

Rocky continued. "I'm the only one of us with a .45. I want all his ammo and his spare magazine. Also, if there are no objections, I'll take the snub-nose .38 revolver from the safe. Any problems with that?"

Both men shook their heads no.

"Nick, if Ev brought his other gun, it now belongs to you. Bug, you get to keep the shotgun. Take the box of shells. After I get my cut of the armored car robbery from Ev's poke, we'll divide the rest of his stash three ways. Does anyone have an objection? If so, speak up now."

Bug Eye said, "I'm satisfied."

Nick said, "Me, too."

Rocky smiled and said, "That's settled then. Next order of business is to count all of Ev's money, but first we got to drag this piece of shit inside and dump him in the grave."

They set to it with vigor. Then they commenced to count Ev's stash. Rocky collected his $5,672 first. That left $19,011. Split three ways, they each got $6,337.

Accounting complete, Rocky said, "Put all of the rest of Ev's stuff into the grave with him and his gun. Dump the documents from the safe in there too. Once Ev's planted, we'll cover up the grave with straw. We also gotta find a spot to hide the safe.

"The last order of business is this. We gotta find a secluded spot away from here to ditch the Ford. I'm thinking Del Rio someplace close to the river in a Mexican neighborhood. We definitely don't want to leave it here in Maverick County. Nick, the way you all ditched the Matador was a good idea. Let some Mexican gangbanger get caught with it. Hopefully, the Ford will end up in Mexico and never be found by the cops.

"Boys, we're headed for home. We'll take US 90 all the way. It'll take us a couple or three days. No more robberies on the way back. Run silent. Run deep. No more drama. We all have more money than we've ever had in our entire lives. In fact, none of us will have to work for at least two years so long as we don't start acting like we're high rollers and blow it all on booze and whores.

"Nick, you keep the truck. Now you've got your own set of wheels.

"Once we get back to El Paso, we'll split up. We will not associate with each other for at least 30 days. It's the only way. This is why. If the cops are onto us, we don't want to lead them to each other. Savvy? We'll designate a neutral site we've never been to. Pick a day and time to meet. We'll decide on the way back. If someone doesn't show, that's okay. The others will figure the no-show got himself a new life. I'm thinking someplace like Alamogordo, but it could be anywhere so long as it's at least 20 miles from our old neighborhood. We do not want to run into someone who knows us. Savvy?

"Do not go back to your old address except to pick up the rest of your gear. Got it? If the cops are looking for you, they'll be watching your digs.

"Nick, that might be problematic for you, but you gotta come up with a convincing story for your mom.

"Bug, I know it won't be a big deal for you. Wherever you do decide to go, stay the Hell away from your past haunts. Move across town or out of town altogether. Get a job - or don't. Do something you always wanted to do. Get a commercial driver's license. Join a bowling league. Learn how to swim. Buy a laundromat and let people pay you for the privilege of washing their dirty laundry. Above all, do not go back to Texas George's unless you are itching to go to prison. Ever! Nick, that especially means you. I am not kidding.

"Also, remember this. Tattoo it on your arm if need be. Rats die a painful death. Any questions?"

There were none.

"Okay, let's get this done and get outta here. I'm sorry it had to end this way."

Chapter 17

The Grunt Work Is Paying Off

Saturday, June 16, 1973

Gillespie almost made herself blind searching the mugshot file for perps who resembled Bruce K. "Rocky" Givens, Rodney A. "Bug Eye" Tinsley, and Nicholas D. "Nick" Crenshaw. She went through hundreds of photographs, some of which originated in Quayle County, but the lion's share of which originated in other, mostly nearby counties. The fact was, Quayle County didn't generate a sufficient number of arrests to provide a large enough sampling. Some years past, Chief Alex prevailed upon the chief deputies of every department within a 300-mile radius to send him as many mugshots as they were willing.

To make a six-pack properly, the mugshot pool needs photographs of Caucasian, Negro, Latino, Asian, and Native American men and women. One needs the entire gamut of mankind - old, young, thin, fat, long-haired, short-haired, bald, with facial hair, no facial hair, attractive, ugly, not to mention dozens who look similar to many other perpetrators. This includes some mugshots even taken with the perp wearing glasses.

For Quayle County's specific demographics, they needed mostly white males, followed next by Latino males. They didn't have any mid-Eastern, Asian, or Chinese triad gangsters. To put a fine point on it, an array would be tossed out in court if it had Stanley Laurel's photo next to Oliver Hardy's photo next to Cassius Clay's (Mohammad Ali's) photo next to Lucille Ball's photo, or Ricky Ricardo's, or Kojak's (Telly Savalas'), or the Lone Ranger's, or Tonto's, or Mahatma Gandhi's, or Ho Chi Minh's.

All the photos in the same array need to bear some resemblance to each of the others. For Gillespie, the good news was, every sheriff's department in this neck of the woods still took black and white mugshots. That eliminated the contrast between redheads and blonds, as an example.

Gillespie's biggest headache was finding look-a-likes for Rodney A. Tinsley. His photographs all showed him wearing what they referred to as FREDs in the Army. (The military provides glasses to servicemen who need them. Most of the glasses they issue are referred to as TEDs, which is the military acronym for Tactical Eye Devices. Not great looking glasses, but not bad enough to guarantee you'll never get laid again if a woman sees you wearing them. Unfortunately, sometimes for special needs, the glasses are uglier than homemade sin. These are referred to as FREDs, the soldier's acronym for Fucking Ridiculous Eye Devices. Rodney "Bug Eye" Tinsley wore FREDs and he had never even been in military service.)

Gillespie could only find mugshots of five young, white males with hair, no beards or mustaches, wearing FREDs. She was beside herself. She had failed in her mission! Chief made it all mo' better when he told her all the robbers were wearing cowboy hats. The witnesses wouldn't know if Bug Eye were bald or not. This widened her parameters and she found three more possibles.

Their first stop was at Mr. LaRue Dinkins' domicile. He had the biggest, most pretentious house in all of Mosby. His wife, Eunice, showed them in. Mr. Dinkins was in his study smoking a pipe, studying a chessboard. He was pondering his next move in a long distance game he played by mail. He greeted them warmly and offered them coffee or iced tea. They declined politely. One by one by one they handed him a photo array. He selected Bruce Givens' mugshot as a highly probable for the leader. He said if he could hear that man speak, he thought he could firm up his selection. Then he looked at the second array with Nick

Crenshaw's mugshot. None of them looked familiar. Finally, he looked at the array with Bug Eye's photograph. He exclaimed, "That's the other scoundrel! I'd recognize him anyplace!" They thanked him and left. At least Mr. Dinkins finally understood that this inconvenience was not an exercise in futility.

Next they went to Brenda Llewellyn's house. Brenda was the bank's only clerk. She was also the Methodist minister's sister-in-law. In the words of Yogi Berra, the New York Yankees Hall of Fame catcher, "It's like deja vu all over again." Brenda nearly recited Mr. Dinkins' comments verbatim.

Third, they went to Percival Larrick's house. He was the chief teller. He positively identified Bug Eye. He said he didn't look very closely at the robber calling all the shots because he scared the bejesus out of him.

Fourth, they went to teller Harmon Aristede's house. He also identified Bug Eye. He said Bruce Givens was a maybe. It could be him, but he didn't want to accuse the wrong man.

Lastly, they went to Melissa Johnson's house. She was the newest and youngest teller. She said Bug Eye looked like the one who took the money from her. This was probably the same guy, but she wasn't sure; however, she pointed to Bruce Given's photograph and said she was almost certain he was the leader. He spoke softly even though he threatened to kill them all. She could see in his eyes that he meant it. If she saw him in person, she would know for sure. He was scary evil.

Both Chief Alex and Gillespie were ecstatic. They returned to the jail to work on the next phase. They got busy, pecking away on two of the office's three manual Remington typewriters. One was a fixture on Chief's desk. One was a fixture on Miss Loretta's, the office manager's desk. The other one sprouted legs and traveled between the two deputy desks and the jail desk.

Gillespie typed reports of interview for all five witnesses. Chief typed complaints on Bruce K. Givens and Rodney A. Tinsley for armed robbery. He also typed a complaint on Everett

M. Raymond for murder, aggravated assault, and armed robbery. Finally, he typed up the arrest warrants for all three. Chief said they didn't have enough on Nicholas D. Crenshaw, unless a latent print examination (which had not even been requested yet) placed him in the liquor store.

Chief said he would take the complaints to District Attorney Able DeWitt and get him to approve them first thing Monday morning. Then he would swear to and sign the complaints before Judge Maxwell B. Sweeney, who would affix his signature and seal. The complaints and accompanying arrest warrants (signed only by Judge Sweeney) would be filed at the clerk's office, allowing Chief to input them into NCIC (the FBI's National Crime Information Center) and NLETS (the National Law Enforcement Communications System), which is controlled by the various states. In essence these are electronic wanted posters attached to the BOLOs, alerting law enforcement agencies in Texas and the four contiguous states - Louisiana, Arkansas, Oklahoma, and New Mexico, which were the most likely states where Chief Alex expected the bandits would be located.

Chief Alex explained that he didn't want to testify before the grand jury in an effort to obtain indictments because the cases were not strong enough to secure a guilty verdict in a trial - yet. They needed more proof, such as identifying suspect latent prints from a crime scene, a ballistics examination if they recovered the firearms used against Bryce Garrett and Cordell, identifications made by witnesses in a physical lineup, confessions, a co-defendant rolling over on another defendant, etc. In essence, a complaint is a written testimony alleging specific criminal violation(s) against a specific person, sworn to under oath under penalty of perjury. A complaint is generally sufficient for law enforcement officers across the nation to make an arrest for another jurisdiction.

After the party named in the complaint is arrested, he is taken before the nearest magistrate or judge and given an initial appearance. This might not occur for a day or two. In the meantime, the defendant would cool his heels in jail unless the warrant comes with a pre-set bond that he can afford to post. That usually only occurs for misdemeanors - things like traffic offenses, shoplifting, disorderly conduct, public indecency, etc.

At the initial appearance, the defendant is advised of the charge(s) filed against him. He also has an opportunity for a bond hearing. The judge would schedule the defendant for a preliminary (probable cause) hearing to take place in just a matter of days. This is an opportunity for the defense to get discovery - to see how much irrefutable evidence the prosecution has against the defendant. Is the case weak or strong? The prosecution normally hates to tip its hand this early in the legal process, so if at all possible, the prosecution will seek to obtain an indictment against the defendant prior to the preliminary hearing. If that occurs, the preliminary hearing would be cancelled, and the defendant would be arraigned.

At an arraignment, a formal reading of the indictment would take place, and a trial date would be set. Also, if the defendant posts bond at any juncture, he is released on bail pending a dismissal of all charges, or a guilty, or not guilty verdict. Failure to appear in court for any appearance usually results in voiding the bond by the judge, and the issuance of a new arrest warrant. Sometimes this is referred to as a bench warrant. Also, additional charges could be filed against the defendant - bond jumping, contempt of court, fugitive from justice, etc. Chief said it is much easier to dismiss a complaint than it is to quash a warrant if the case fell apart, and that these particular cases would definitely fall apart without more evidence.

Gillespie's head was spinning. This was so much more complex than her previous cases had been when she testified before the grand jury or in a court hearing. Apparently it was a lot more difficult if the suspect were not already in custody, especially if he had cut a chogy. Now she understood why an outside agency would not make an arrest on a case they hadn't worked without an arrest warrant on file. If the case fell through, the arresting agency was much more likely to be sued for false arrest. It would even be a hundred times worse if they had to use force on the suspect while making a probable cause (PC) arrest with nothing stronger than the word of an officer from a different jurisdiction that PC actually existed.

Chief and Gillespie worked like rented mules until 7:30. Being a criminal investigator was a paper-intensive job. Gillespie began to understand why some officers preferred being patrol officers. They were usually done at end-of-shift. Not so for a detective.

CHAPTER **18**

Explosive New Developments

Saturday, June 16, 1973

In the meantime, in Laredo, 300 miles away, Barlow and Slick began reaping what they had sown. They met Sheriff Oliver Vincent and Chief Deputy Roland Epps back at the Webb County Sheriff's Office at 8:30 as agreed. Both were smiling like the cat who ate the canary. After the customary greetings and small talk, Sheriff Vincent said, "Fellas, last night after you all left, Roland and I started working the phones and we hit pay dirt. Tell 'em, Roland."

"About 2:30 this morning, I got a call from Ethan Heim, Chief Deputy at the Dimmit County Sheriff's Office up in Carrizo Springs. They located the Matador stolen from Crockett County. They caught four local Mexicans joyriding in it. They're all juveniles. In fact the oldest is only 16 and the youngest is 12. The boys claimed they found the car abandoned in a neighborhood park. They said the keys were in it, and being that the oldest boy was in possession of both sets, it's probably true. Dimmit dusted the car for latents, but every legible print they got belonged to the boys. Ethan agreed to hold them until we get up there, so long as we get there by noon. Otherwise, they're going to release them to their parents or take them to the regional juvenile detention center up in Crystal City in Zavala County."

Slick replied, "That's great news. Do you know if Dimmit County called Crockett?"

"They did. Crockett notified the owner, Bud Something-or-Other, and he's going to send someone to pick up the car on Monday."

"Sounds good. Are you all going up there? Barlow and I are ready to roll if you all are."

Chief Epps replied, "I am. Junior's waiting for me downstairs at the lockup. He'll represent Laredo PD. Take some photos, etc., for their files. Nobody thinks we'll get much more than we already have as it relates to the car, but who knows?"

Slick said, "Agreed, but it's on our way home anyway. Maybe we'll get lucky. Stranger things have happened.

"Sheriff Vincent, we are much obliged for your hospitality. We'll keep you informed of any new developments."

"Same here. Chief Merriweather and I believe the skells you mentioned are most likely our bandits. As soon as we collect enough evidence to file charges on 'em, either the PD or we will do so. That could be sooner rather than later, once we get their photographs. Happy hunting. I pray you all catch this crew."

"Us too."

Before they left, Slick made a short call to Sheriff Sol to fill him in. He also said they expected to be home that afternoon unless something popped. Sheriff Sol said he would pass this along to Sarah.

It was about 80 miles from Laredo to Carrizo Springs. Chief Epps and Junior lead the way in a marked WCSO cruiser. They arrived about 10. Chief Ethan Heim was waiting.

All four boys had been thoroughly interrogated, but Chief Epps and Slick gave it another shot. Junior, Barlow, and Ethan watched through the one-way glass while each boy was questioned independently. The only additional information they gleaned was from the oldest boy, Paco Rúiz, and his brother, the youngest boy, Raúl. They were together when they saw two Anglos ditch the car. They drove away in an old, white van - a Dodge, they both thought. The boys only saw the men from a distance. One of them had red hair. The other had black or dark brown hair. That's all they could see.

Slick asked if the man with dark hair was wearing glasses.

Both boys said "no." That was enough for both Slick and Roland to conclude that Nick Crenshaw was probably the second man.

It was about noon when they wrapped up. They decided to break bread together with Ethan at a small diner called Cosmo's before heading their separate ways. Towards the end of the meal, the owner came over to the table and whispered something in Ethan's ear. Ethan said, "Excuse me for a moment. I have to take a call."

He was gone for about 15 minutes. When he returned, he said, "You fellas won't believe this. Maverick County SO just put out a BOLO. You know that blue Ford station wagon stolen in Crockett? A car like that and a white van were involved in a shooting about five miles north of Eagle Pass off US Highway 277. They think both vehicles took a powder northbound but they ain't for sure."

Chief Epps asked, "How long ago was this?"

"The witness reported it about an hour ago, but wait! The main thing is, they have a dead body!"

Slick asked, "Do you know the exact location of the homicide?"

"Yes and no. I've never been there. Deputy Harry Hamm of Maverick County said it's off an unmarked, dead-end, dirt road that runs east off US 277, just north of a billboard advertising the Sunset Inn in Eagle Pass. The locals call it Avery Pickett Road, but there's no sign. Naturally, it's not on the state map, either.

"Hamm said Avery Pickett Road meanders, but runs generally northeast until it dead ends. There's an abandoned homestead about three miles down the road on the left side. It's an old, dilapidated, weather-beaten house with some other rundown buildings. Oh, yeah. He said it also has an old Aermotor windmill that's no longer operational. From what he told me, you can't miss it. Famous last words, right? Anyway, that's where the shooting occurred.

"As I understand it, a neighbor boy who was supposed to be

in school but decided to play hooky instead, witnessed it. Once the shooters left, he ran home and called his mom who was at work. She was livid when she found out her kid wasn't in school. He flunked 9th grade English and has to pass this remedial course in summer school if he wants to be classified as a 10th-grader come September. Anyway, she called the SO, and they had the boy and his mama lead them to the farm. As I understand it, they're still there working the crime scene."

Chief Epps asked, "Are you sending anyone or going yourself?"

"Don't think so. Right now we don't have a crime to investigate. What about you all?"

"Junior and me are on our way right now Code 3. Those guys sound like our killers. How about you, Slick?"

"We'll be hard on your heels. How far would you say it is?"

Chief Epps said, "Oh, I'd say 40, maybe 50 miles. Let's settle our bills and roll. Ethan, can I ask a favor?"

"Sure. What is it?"

"Would you call Sheriff Vincent and let him know what's going on, and that Junior and I are rolling?"

"You bet."

Slick asked, "While you're at it, would you ask Sheriff Vincent to call our sheriff and tell him the same thing?"

"No problem."

The officers examined their checks, figured generous tips, and left dinero on the table. Both Epps and Slick were laying rubber by the time they exited the parking lot. It took them 40 minutes, to include the slow crawl down the dirt road. The directions were surprisingly accurate.

When they arrived, they were greeted by Deputy Ted Newman out by the front gate, who was screening traffic (universally understood by all cops to mean keeping the gawkers and untrustworthy press out of everyone's hair). Deputy Newman was a familiar face to Chief Epps.

Roland asked, "What you all got here, Ted?"

"Not for sure yet. We're just getting into it. A neighbor boy roaming the woods saw a strange white van and a blue Ford station wagon parked up near the barn. It captured his interest since they didn't belong, so he popped a squat behind some scrub brush to see who it was. This farm has been vacant for two or three years now. The owner, Old Man Leonard Turner, passed away. The property belongs to his daughter, Lisa Morrison. Her and her husband live up in Dallas. The farm's over 180 acres, but she don't want to sell it. She grew up here. She decided to keep it as a sort of long-term investment.

"Anyway, the kid . . ."

Roland interrupted, "What's the kid's name?"

"Gavin Greathouse. He's only 15. Like I said, he hid in the woods and watched to see who it was. He saw two white guys square off. Then they both pulled a gun and started blasting away at each other. One got shot and went down. The other was still standing. Then two more guys come running out from the barn, and the guy who wasn't shot drew down on one of them. They argued for awhile. Then the other two dudes walked over and shot the shit out of the guy who was already shot. Then they dragged the body into the barn. The kid was afraid they'd kill him if they saw him, so he waited for as long as it took - maybe an hour. Then the three guys come out of the barn. The shooter and the guy not involved in the argument got in the station wagon and the other guy got in the van. They left together back towards 277."

"Was the kid able to describe any of these men?"

"Not that I know of, except they was all Anglos. You'd have to ask Captain Landry. He's still up at the barn."

"Is Gavin Greathouse still up there, too?"

"Oh, Hell no! His momma, Belinda Greathouse, was freaking out. She's Hell on Wheels, you know, like General Patton's 2nd Armored Division in World War II. She's a screaming maniac.

Always has been. That's why she can't hang onto a man. A person can only take so much shit no matter how good that nu-nu is. Know what I mean? Deputy Maxwell had to run 'em both back home. Better him than me."

"You know, Ted, these men are most likely the guys who robbed the armored car yesterday in Laredo and killed the two guards. Ditto for robbing a bank and liquor store in Quayle County Wednesday where they killed a guy there. That's where the two deputies behind me in that brown Plymouth is from. They been tracking the robbers ever since then. Anything we can get out of this would be a great help to me and to them."

"Dern. Well, you all go on in and talk to Captain Nathan Bedford Forest Landry. He goes by Captain Reb as in Rebel. He's in charge. He's the grizzly old guy with the white hair. Looks a little bit like that movie star Lee Marvin. Just be mindful of the crime scene. He's old school and don't tolerate no sloppy work nor interference. Maybe you all will get lucky and the dead guy is one of your perps."

"That would be nice, but I never get that lucky except on my birthday and Christmas when my old lady gives it up. Thanks, buddy."

Chief Epps waved his hand for Slick to follow. Then he proceeded through the gate, closer to the crime scene. Slick followed on his heels. They parked well back from the two marked, Maverick County units and the crime scene van. They got out of their cars and waited to be recognized. Even though he was all alone, Captain Landry stood out like a matador in an arena full of bulls. Looked like he was taking a smoke break. He glanced up at the newcomers and waved them over. When they got up close, he stared for the longest time with his piercing blue, bird-of-prey eyes, sizing up Chief Epps. Finally, he asked, "Don't I know you?"

Roland extended his hand and said, "Captain Landry, nice to make your acquaintance. Maybe you do. I'm Chief Deputy

Roland Epps with Webb County. I been to a few regional law enforcement conferences. Maybe we crossed paths at one of them. This here is my son, Patrolman Junior Epps with Laredo PD. This feller here is Deputy Slick Oldman, and that'n there is Deputy Barlow Adams. They're both from Quayle County. They been tracking a gang of armed robbers since Wednesday."

They all shook hands with firm grips, sizing each other up. Captain Landry looked to be about 60 or 65. He stood 5-feet, 10-inches tall, tipping the scales at 180 pounds of bone, gristle, and muscle. He had a linebacker's build. His hair, besides being alabaster white, was thick and straight and just a mite shaggy. His face was weathered like tanned leather - craggy and clean-shaven. He was still a very handsome man. He was dressed in the Texas lawman's standard khaki uniform, plain brown Tony Lama boots, and beige Stetson. His choice of sidearm was a blue steel, .45 caliber Long Colt Peacemaker with a 5-1/2-inch barrel and stag grips in a well-worn, brown leather, cross-draw holster secured on a cartridge-filled gun belt.

Captain Landry started the ball rolling. He said, "Most folks call me Captain Reb. That's what I prefer to be called. If you didn't know, I was named after a Confederate general."

Studying Slick and Barlow like they were insects under a microscope, he observed, "I can pretty well guess why you all are here. You're still chasing that blue Ford station wagon stolen in Crockett County by the assholes who robbed your bank and liquor store in Mosby and kilt a man, most likely a friend.

"Ditto for you Chief, because it's probably the same crew that robbed the armored car in Laredo. You're all getting close and you each can smell blood. I see it in your eyes. You all want these sidewinders real bad and I don't blame you. It's personal, and ain't a one of you will stop until you've planted each one of them bad boys six feet under, unless of course, they lose their nerve and surrender, although I can tell you all from my experience, that ain't never going to happen. In fact, I'd bet a dollar to a doughnut hole that you two (pointing the first two fingers on his right hand at Slick and Barlow) have more than just a little experience in doing just that. I can tell by the way you two carry yourselves - seasoned and confident. Also, one of your perps is a dude named Everett Marvin Raymond from El Paso. How'm I doing so far?"

Slick responded, "Right as rain."

"Thought so. Everett M. Raymond has transcended from our mortal coil. He is no longer our problem. His soul belongs to the devil now for all of Eternity. His own momma wouldn't recognize what's left of him. His pards really did a number on him. I only know his name from the driver's license in his wallet. He must've really pissed them boys off."

Slick asked, "Does he have red hair and a tattoo of a black widow spider on his left wrist?"

"He does."

"Can we see the body?"

"You can in just a few minutes. Tell me though, who are the other three dick wads what shot him and got away?"

Barlow responded first. "The leader, and most likely the guy who traded shots with Ev Raymond, is Bruce K. Givens, age 31 or 32, over 6-feet tall with sandy hair. They call him Rocky. They say he's as handsome as a movie star. I haven't seen his picture yet, so I don't know for sure. He's an ex-con.

"Another one is Nicholas D. Crenshaw, about 23 or 24. He's the weak link. The most inexperienced criminal, we believe.

"The last one is a nearsighted dude with thick black glasses named Rodney A. Tinsley, also about 23. They call him "Bug Eye" for obvious reasons. They're all from El Paso, same as Raymond."

"Sounds like you boys done your homework. Where do you think they're headed to now?"

Slick replied, "No idea, other than north. Someplace to hole up until the heat dies down. Maybe go back to El Paso, but I doubt it. They pulled off some other robberies there and in Van Horn. El Paso knows who they are and is scouring the Earth for 'em, too. Besides, they're flush with stolen money, so they can afford to take a breather - at least that's what I would do. I expect they'll probably dump the Ford and the van and steal something else. It's curious though, that we ain't heard a peep about a white van being stolen in Carrizo Springs around the time they ditched the AMC. Anyway, we'll more'n likely pick up the trail when they steal some more wheels."

"You don't think they'll camp out in Old Mexico?"

"Well, being from El Paso, I'm sure they're at least somewhat conversant in Mex, but they'd stub their toes down there along the way and have to fight the whole dern Mexican Army. They know that. They wouldn't blend in. You know what it's like across the border and so do they. Besides, they ain't about to go down there without their hardware. Not only that, the Mexican police are bigger robbers and more skillful at it than they are, plus everyone knows Mexican jails suck. You know, it would be like Butch Cassidy and the Sundance Kid in Bolivia. I can't see them going that route, but I could be wrong."

"No. I think you're right. Okay, let's walk over to the barn. You all can take a look at the body. Maybe my guys have picked up some new evidence while I've been out here having a smoke. It makes 'em nervous if I hover over 'em for too long. I expect 'em to do the job right, so I give 'em some space."

They walked over towards the barn. They could see a large pool of blood on the ground as they approached the rear entrance. Captain Reb pointed it out and said, "Mr. Raymond was standing right about here, facing towards the woods when it all went down. Our witness was hiding behind those bushes over there by that rusty Farmall tractor. The Ford had been backed in right there up next to the barn. You can tell because these divots here closest to the barn are deeper than those where the front end was. Remember, they was hauling a safe and the rear shocks was probably shot.

"Just prior to the shooting, Mr. Givens, assuming you boys are correct, came out of the barn alone. He got in the Ford and drove over here and parked it. I'm not sure why. You can see the tire tracks and divots where it was parked both times. Besides, that's where our witness said it was. Mr. Givens got out of the Ford and started walking back to the barn. Then he turned around and went back to the car. He opened the front passenger door and leaned in. He was lost from sight for about a minute.

"The van was parked out there facing that direction, so it did not afford any cover when the shooting took place. We checked ourselves, and the witness had a clear line of sight for the shooting, but it's 84 yards away. Note that Mr. Givens had some cover but Mr. Raymond did not.

"The witness said, the way it went down, Mr. Raymond ran out of the barn with a gun in right his hand. He paused briefly, apparently looking for Mr. Givens, who then stood up straight, extended his right arm, paused, and fired two shots. Mr. Raymond returned fire with a snap shot, but he never paused long enough to aim good. Just raised his gun and fired.

"The witness heard "Boom! Boom! Boom!" Just like that. No further spacing between shots. Mr. Raymond fell backwards and landed tits up right here where all the blood is. We found one spent .45 shell casing belonging to him there at that little yellow marker, and two more .45 casings belonging to Mr. Givens at those yellow markers over there to the right of where the Ford had been parked.

"Right after the shooting, a third guy ran out of the barn. He was wearing black glasses. He had a nickel-plated revolver in each hand. He stopped just as soon as he saw Mr. Raymond's body. Number three was standing somewhere over here in this area. Then a fourth dude come running out. The first shooter aimed at him. When he did, number four raised his hands up high like he was under arrest. He was wearing a blue steel revolver which was still in its holster.

"The first shooter and number four exchanged heated words, but our wit couldn't make out what they was saying. Next thing you know, number four walked over to Mr. Raymond's body, pulled his gun, and shot him twice. Then number three went over and fired two shots from each of his revolvers into the body. Not sure why they done that unless it was some rite of initiation."

Slick opined, "Probably because the killer didn't want them to be able to rat him out."

"Maybe so. I never considered that. Okay. Let's go take a look inside. Watch you don't step on any evidence. We'll examine the body and anything else they've turned up."

Ev's body was lying on a makeshift bed of old weathered barn boards. He was a bloody mess. His head was essentially missing from his lower jawbone up. Nevertheless, you could readily tell that he had red hair. Barlow pulled up Ev's left sleeve and confirmed the spider tattoo. Ev's gun, a blue steel, Colt Government Model .45, had been placed next to him. The slide was locked open, and an empty magazine and seven .45 caliber rounds were laying next to it. Barlow copied the serial number of the gun.

Slick said, "Captain, this is probably the same gun he used to kill Bryce Garrett in Mosby and the two guards in Laredo. Would you have a problem if Webb County and we piggybacked on your lab request to DPS, asking them to compare spent .45 rounds and casings we recovered at our crime scenes, and any .45 rounds and the casings you recover here with this gun? We can even sweeten the deal. The state senator from our county is chairman of the legislative committee which oversees funding for anything related to law enforcement. We use him to grease the skids at the lab so we get the results quicker - sometimes in just a day or two."

Chief Epps spoke approvingly, "That would be fantastic."

Captain Reb responded, "Done deal. In fact, Roland, why

don't you have someone bring me your evidence and lab request? I'll have a deputy deliver yours and ours to Quayle County. Slick, will your sheriff send a deputy to the lab as soon as he has all three requests?"

"You can count on it. We do it all the time on stuff as critical as this. In fact, the last time, Sheriff Sol told our deputy who was the courier to wait at the lab until everything was complete. Then he called the jail with the results before he come back home with the evidence and the reports. If you all can get us your packets on Monday, I believe Sheriff Sol will send a courier on Tuesday. We should have a verbal response by Thursday or Friday at the latest."

Chief Epps said, "I'll ask Sheriff Vincent to call Sheriff Sol today."

Captain Reb said, "I'll ask Sheriff Semmes to do the same thing."

Barlow asked, "Did you all find anything else?"

Captain Reb replied, "Yep, but it ain't of any consequence to Quayle or Webb County. We recovered the busted safe from Crockett County. We also have some documents from the safe. We'll get with Crockett on that."

Barlow said, "It's just a thought. There's a real good chance there are latent prints on those documents. Since all four of our suspects have fingerprints on file, once the latents are lifted, it should be easy for the lab to make comparisons. If we get real lucky, we could tie all four of our suspects to the burglary of the car lot in Crockett, especially the three suspects who hauled ass from your homicide here. Even if you don't recover any spent slugs, it could still help prove they were all here at the time of the shooting. Might be important if you all wind up going to trial."

"You're a smart cookie, young man. Good idea. I'll get our fingerprint specialist on it today to see if we can come up with some identifiable latents. However, unless you all sneak up on these bastards while they're fast asleep, there won't be any trial.

You know that as well as I do. The only thing you'll have is a coroner's inquest.

"Anything else you all can think of?"

Slick replied, "Not from us. We're fixing to head back home. Chief Epps, Junior, Captain Reb, it's been a pleasure working with all of you. If you all need anything from Quayle County, don't hesitate to call. If Sheriff Sol isn't in, ask for Chief Deputy Alex Snodgrass or Barlow or me. We'll do everything we can to assist."

Chief Epps said, "Same here."

Captain Reb replied, "Ditto. We'll be in touch."

Slick and Barlow left Maverick County at 4:30. When they stopped to refuel, Slick called Sheriff Sol and Barlow called Sarah.

Slick provided a quick update on everything they had discovered since his call Friday evening. Sheriff Sol replied, "Good job to both you all. We'll gladly take care of the lab requests for Webb and Maverick, especially while we still can. It's to our benefit. You never know if Darnell Sweeney will get even more ambitious than he already is and decide to make a run for Congress. Then, being as small as we are, we'd lose most of our clout with the state. The more allies we make, the better off we are.

"Also, I'll tell Chief Alex to forget swearing out a complaint for Everett Raymond since his parking meter's expired. Isn't that just a crying shame? I know Barlow's disappointed because he made no bones about wanting to be the one to punch his ticket. I don't blame him, being kin and all to Cordell, but it's probably better this way. Now no one can claim Everett Raymond's demise is an unjustified law enforcement slaying. Besides, he got what was coming to him.

"Oh yeah. One more thing. You're on days next week, Saturday and Sunday off. Tell Barlow he's back on mids, Sunday and Monday off. I'm sure he expected it, but it's still a bass-ackwards way to reward someone doing a good job."

Barlow's call to Sarah was short and sweet. She said for Barlow to wake her up if she were asleep. She casually mentioned that she had an itch which needed to be scratched with a blunt instrument. Probably need a thousand strokes to assuage it. He replied that unfortunately he had his tool kit with him. Her answer to that was, "Then hurry home, Cowboy. I miss you and you know what I need."

Slick had a lady friend lined up too, so they made haste. By disregarding the speed limit and not stopping to eat, they arrived in Mosby about 7:30. It was much earlier than Sarah had expected and she was thrilled. Now she expected to be thrilled again and again and again.

Barlow walked through the front door and hung is hat and gun belt on the coat tree. Sarah was lying on the couch in one of his old Army T-shirts. He could see enough to confirm that she wasn't wearing anything underneath it.

The radio was tuned in to an easy listening station. There were two empty Miller High Life bottles and another half-full one on the end table. She had been reading a paperback girly romance novel. The cover had a picture of a long-haired, redheaded, voluptuous bombshell attired in white, Victorian undies, exposing lots of cleavage, in her boudoir, with outstretched hands reaching to a formally-attired, Clark Gable-looking character. A pussycat was sitting in the window looking on. The only reason the novel wasn't X-rated and the drugstore sold this genre of book, was because the front cover had the only picture in it. You know. A picture is worth a thousand words, as in a *Playboy* magazine. The book had thousands of titillating, descriptive words, but no other pictures. It flew under the radar of the impure thoughts book censorship police.

Sarah looked up and said, "Barlow, my naughty alter ego has been lusting and waiting for you from the moment you left for work yesterday afternoon. Why don't you shuck those dirty clothes and let me see your birthday suit? I'd love to find out if you have any swollen muscles. I bet you do. I know you work so hard. Oh my! Did I say hard? I can't believe I actually said that. I'm not even lit yet. (She took another sip of beer. Then she polished the rest of the bottle off, smacking her lips.)

"Hard has been on my mind. You know, hard as steel, hard to resist, hard to walk away from, hard not to think about it, hard to satisfy, hard on my mind. That's it. Hard on. Why don't you show me?"

Sarah shifted her position on the couch, causing the T-shirt to ride up and expose her nether region. She batted her eyes, licked and pursed her lips, and rubbed her forefinger gently over them. The eroticism of a beautiful naked woman softly stroking her wet lips was having the desired effect on Barlow, who was sweaty and stinky and thought he should probably shower first.

She rose up from the couch and shucked the T-shirt, dropping it on the floor. She said, "Oh my. Clumsy me." Then, facing away from him, she spread her feet wide apart like she was going to do left-right, toe-touch exercises. She bent over to retrieve the shirt, exposing her sweet spot. After a full, five-second pause, she undulated her fanny a half-dozen times before picking up the shirt. Then she slowly sashayed down the hall to the bedroom, turned down the cover and top sheet, and lay on her back and stretched. She spread her legs and drew them up, sliding the soles of her feet on the bed until her heels were touching her bottom. She arched her back and whimpered, "Barlow, can you help me work out my kinks? I could really use your magic touch."

Barlow had followed her into the bedroom, pulling off his boots and socks, and all the rest of his garments along the way. Roscoe was standing at complete attention, as tight as a fiddle string, as hard as quantum physics. He throbbed like a bass drum being beaten in a parade with a high school marching band, or perhaps more like a fucking migraine headache, only in a good way so long as adequate relief was forthcoming forthwith. He said (Barlow, not Roscoe), "Um, I was going to take a shower first. I'm pretty sweaty after the day I've had."

Sarah replied, "Barlow, hush up. Do you really think you won't be sweating like a thoroughbred in the Kentucky Derby after the paces I plan to put you through? I cannot wait one more minute. You better bring on your A-game Buster, because I'm ready to rodeo all night long."

He replied, "That's perfect then, you bewitching, naughty woman, because I'm hornier than a triple-peckered billygoat." Then he mounted her and took her all the way up to Mount Everest and back three times.

She squealed. She moaned. She squeezed. She lost control. She cried. She scratched. She French kissed. She bit. She begged. She panted. She exhorted. She bucked. She thrust. She rolled over on her hands and knees to do it a different way. She told him not to stop. To do it just like that. To speed up. To slow down. She got on top. She controlled the pace and the rhythm. She was a tigress in heat, and then she wasn't. She collapsed on the crumpled, sweat-soaked sheets. Eventually her breathing slowed down to normal. She whispered, "Barlow, I love you so much."

He whispered back, "I love you more."

It was sensational.

Sarah was finally sated. She fell fast asleep. A five-bell fire alarm could not have awakened her. All this energy had been pent up for days, and now it had evaporated. She was completely spent.

Barlow was out of breath. He was spent, too, but his satisfaction had a short half-life. He hoped he didn't over-satisfy her, because he wanted some more in the morning after he'd had some shuteye.

He was not disappointed.

CHAPTER 19

The Givens Gang Goes on Sabbatical

Saturday/Sunday, June 16/17, 1973

They got a late start Saturday on their long journey home. It had been a tense day for each of them. Every single one of their collective millions of nerve endings were on the ragged edge. Some were pinging intermittently with little bolts of electricity. Paranoia was running amok.

Rocky no longer trusted Nick.

Nick no longer trusted Rocky or Bug Eye.

Bug Eye was a loyal minion to Rocky, but he thought Rocky had been way to hard on Nick. Nick was essentially a good guy, but he was too easily swayed by anyone older and more experienced than he. Ergo, Ev took advantage of Nick and almost dragged him down into the pits of Hell with him once Rocky confirmed their treachery. Bug Eye figured that once they got home, neither he nor Rocky would see nor hear from Nick again. Maybe that was for the best.

Once Bug Eye and Rocky got situated in the station wagon, Rocky said, "Bug, you got a piece of paper and something to write with?"

"Yeah, why?"

"I want you to write something down for me."

Bug Eye retrieved a small pocket notebook and a pen. "Shoot."

"Write this down. My neighbor lady is an old woman. Her name is Mrs. López. She's kinda like a grandmother to me. She keeps an eye on things. Her phone number is 654-2771. Write that down. If something comes up before our meet and you need to get a message to me, call her. She will pass it along to me. I'll call you back as soon as I can. Got it?"

"Yep. Mrs. Lopez, 654-2771."

"Good. Tear that page out and stick it in your wallet. Don't lose it. Next, I need you to write down the name and number for someone you trust that will do the same for you."

Bug Eye thought for a minute and said, "I got a sister I don't see very often. Her name is Rosa McGillicuddy. She lives at 330 Burton Avenue. Her number is 239-0147. I just wrote it all down for you." He tore out the page, folded it into quarters, and passed it to Rocky.

Rocky put it in his shirt pocket. "Okay, this just in case of emergency. Otherwise, we'll meet wherever we all decide before we split up."

"Gotcha."

They only drove 150 miles that day. Rocky and Bug Eye lead in the station wagon. Nick followed in the van with all their gear. They continued north on US 277 to Del Rio, where they found a bustling Mexican cantina named El Gordo's a stone's throw from the Río Grande in the oldest part of the city. Nick copped a parking space fairly close to the entrance. Rocky deliberately parked the Ford closer to the street where there was virtually no lighting. It was the kind of parking space human predators favor. The weather was still sweltering, and they left the windows completely rolled down. They accidentally-on-purpose forgot and left the keys in the ignition when they went inside to eat. The only thing they didn't do was place a blinking neon light on the roof which said, "Steal me."

They took their old sweet time during supper, making an effort to relax and smooth things over with Nick. They each wolfed down the house special, the humongous El Gran Buffet de Muestras, otherwise known to gringos as the plentiful sampler buffet. They split two large pitchers of frosty cold Dos Equis. By the time they walked out the door an hour-and-a-half later, the parking lot was half-empty and the blue Ford station wagon was a gone pecan. Mission accomplished.

They all piled into the van and pressed on to Sonora. Nick drove. Rocky sat in the right front seat. Bug Eye sat on the back bench seat. Rocky was impressed. The Dodge rode a whole lot better than he expected, and it ran like a striped-ass ape. They found overnight lodging in a Holiday Inn. This time they each had their own room. They were up on the second floor.

Sunday morning they drove all the way back to El Paso on I-10. It was roughly 400 miles. Having air conditioning in the van made a monumental difference. En route, they all agreed to meet on Wednesday, July 18th at 11 o'clock for lunch at a place they had all been to once before - the Jack's hamburger joint on US 54 and Hondo Pass Drive on the north side of El Paso near Fort Bliss.

By all outward appearances, it seemed that their differences had been resolved. Everyone was in high spirits. Ev was no longer a bone of contention. They all had been silently making plans as to where they would go, and what they would do during the next 30 days.

Nick dropped off Bug Eye first at his boarding house. He was relieved that his landlady, Mrs. Albertson, had the closed sign posted on her suite door. It was 4:15. That meant he had time to clear out without being accosted. Bug Eye knew she would be cloistered until at least 6 o'clock, maybe even later. It all depended on Mr. Simpson.

It was the worst kept secret on all of Elm Street. Mrs. A. always entertained her star boarder, Mr. Antoine Simpson, on Sunday afternoon, and once in awhile on Monday afternoon. Mr. Simpson was a barber, very fastidious, a natty dresser, and those were his days off. It's also when he got off, like Old Faithful. It's always hot in El Paso, and most folks have their windows wide open if they are at home. The window fans in Mahoney's Boarding House were loud, but not loud enough to muffle the sounds of satisfaction emanating from Mrs. A's suite. Mr.

Simpson always tried to sneak in when no one was in the hallway. Without fail, he brought a fifth of Jim Beam and a Whitman's Sampler box of assorted chocolates. It was thoughtful of him, but it didn't really matter. The walls were thin and uninsulated, and Mrs. A was a vociferous squealer.

Mr. Simpson must have had the stamina of three satyrs. You could hear Mrs. A a half block away, begging him not to stop, and squealing with delight as the cast iron bed banged up against the wall at least a dozen times a minute, off and on for two or more hours. It was truly amazing because Mrs. A was 5-feet, 10-inches tall, and went about 200 pounds, half of which were titties. Mr. Simpson stood 5-feet, 7-inches tall, and went about a buck forty soaking wet. Bug Eye always said Mr. Simpson really weighed 135 pounds plus five pounds of dick.

Bug Eye slipped into his room unnoticed. He crammed all his stuff into an Army surplus duffle bag. He picked up all his belongings, consisting of travel bag, sheathed shotgun, and duffle bag. He locked up his room, and sneaked out the back door. He walked through the alley to 11th Street, turned right, and stopped at a bodega where the local taxi drivers congregated, drinking coffee and smoking, while waiting to be dispatched on a run. Many times they were hired by walk-up customers.

Bug Eye got lucky because it was Sunday and two cabs were standing by. One was a Yellow cab and the other was a Checker. The cabbies, both Latino, were sharing a small outside table, whiling away the time by chewing the fat. He walked up and said, "I need to go to Fabens. Can one of you take me?"

One cabbie said, "Señor, Fabens is 25 miles away, almost to Hudspeth County. The fare would be $25."

The other cabbie replied, "Sí, but it's on my way. I will do it for $20 if you pay me up front."

Bug Eye quickly responded, "Deal." He opened his wallet and handed the cabbie a $20 bill. A minute later he was riding in the back seat of a bright orange, 1965 Ford Galaxie, 4-door sedan with red leatherette seats, now protected by a thick, clear plastic cover. Obviously this car had been another color in a previous life. Nobody puts red seats in an orange car. He wondered why yellow cabs were painted orange instead of yellow. At least this one was spotless. There weren't even any dusty footprints on the black vinyl floor.

The cabbie, Enrico Trevino, according to the taxi driver's license attached to the sun visor, asked, "Where in Fabens do you wish to go, Señor?"

"Downtown. Do you know of a clean place where I can rent a room which won't cost me an arm and a leg? Somewhere I won't have to worry about getting mugged?"

"Señor, who would be crazy enough to mug you? You have that great big gun."

"Yes, my shotgun. Right now it's unloaded, but I can't carry it with me everywhere I go. It was my daddy's gun. When he died it was bequeathed to me."

"Oh, sí sí. My condolences.

"I know of the perfect place for you, Señor. The Fabens Arms Hotel. It is on Broadway and 2nd. My cousin works there as the front desk clerk on the afternoon shift. His name is Humberto Rivera. You can't miss him. Muy gordo. Siempre feliz. You know. Very fat and always happy. In fact, he is working right now. How long will you be staying?"

"At least a month."

"I can get you a very good deal. For one month it will be $125. It is very clean. You will see. No trouble at all."

"Okay. Let's go there. If I like it, I will give you a $10 tip."

"Gracias. I think you will like it. Why do you go to Fabens, Señor?"

"Well, two reasons. First, I quit my job. My boss was an asshole. He pissed me off so bad, I just have to get far away. Otherwise, if I ran into him on the street, I'd probably beat the living shit out of him. Then I'd get arrested and go to jail. I hate him worse than dog shit on the sole of my shoe!"

"Where did you work?"

"The big parking garage by the courthouse. I was an attendant there for more than a year. Nearly every week he made me work extra hours without paying me more money. He screamed at me if someone parked over the line, like it was my fault. He called me shithead in front of customers all the time. If it wasn't one damn thing it was another. I just couldn't take it anymore. Someday, someone will clean his clock really good, but it won't be me. I'm adiós amigo. I do hope to hear about it though, after it happens, and I'm sure it will. Then I will celebrate. Joy to the world!"

"Ah, chihuahua. He must be a very big prick.

"What is the second reason, Señor?"

"Well, when I was a kid, once in awhile, my mother would take me and my little sister on the train to Fabens to see my Uncle Ned. He was her big brother. That's where he lived. He lost an eye in the Korean War. Got hit with shrapnel. Fucked up his left leg, too. He walked with a limp the rest of his life. They gave him a Purple Heart. He was only 19 years old when it happened. The Army gave him a full medical discharge like he had been in for 20 years even though he had only been in for one. He got a check every month, but he was only a private. The higher your rank, the more you get. His check was peanuts, so he found a job as a janitor at the train station in Fabens. He walked to work everyday. He rented a room from an old widow woman who lived near there. Her husband had been an engineer on a train. I don't know which railroad company, but I think it was the Santa Fe. She was very kind. She always fixed us lemonade and made us cookies when we came to visit. Uncle Ned was my hero. He is dead now. He died from diabetes four years ago. I always enjoyed going to Fabens to see him. That is the second reason."

Humberto did right by Bug Eye. He gave him a corner room on the third floor, which was the top floor. Room number 316.

That particular room had a locking closet. He could secure his shotgun and other valuables. It had two windows, so he could catch a cross breeze. It also had a nice view of the city. He liked to sit in the padded chair with the windows wide open and smoke and drink beer. It was the best place he had lived since he was a young boy.

Before Bug Eye had even cleared out of his boarding house, Nick had dropped off Rocky at the corner of 15th and Elmwood, two blocks away from his house on Delmont. Rocky was a little more paranoid about the cops looking for him than either Bug Eye or Nick, so he took more precautions. He'd already done a couple of years in the joint and he didn't want to return for a repeat performance. He cut through the alleyways and approached Mrs. López' house from the rear.

He didn't open the unlocked, back farm fence gate because of her three yapping chihuahuas that were jumping around like popcorn bouncing off a hot stove. They guarded her house like it was Fort Knox. Besides, she carried her 16-gauge, double-barreled shotgun around the house with her everywhere she went - even to the john - especially to the john! The world was full of rapists and she had no intention of letting anyone rape her. She hadn't given up a slice since her husband died, and that was over 20 years ago. Mrs. López was spry, blessed with eagle vision, and she maintained situational awareness at all times.

Mrs. López was a little hard of hearing though, and that's why she had Pepe, Miranda, and Toto. They listened for her, and yapped anytime a bird farted or a mouse blinked his eyes. Sometimes Pepe sneaked off the clock and wasn't there to sound off. He was a veritable horn dog, always slipping through the fence to bang one of the neighborhood bitches who was in heat, of which there were more than just a few. Hell, there were at least a half-dozen times more chihuahuas residing in this neighborhood than homo sapiens.

Pepe should have been named George Washington. He was

most definitely the Canine Father of Delmont Street for a radius of twelve houses in any direction. Mrs. López was well aware of Pepe's proclivity for practicing indiscriminate, unsafe sex, and doing his part in repopulating the chihuahua dog world, and that's why she had three furry, four-legged alarm systems instead of just one. She believed in a redundant security alarm system.

As soon as her alarm systems went off, Mrs. López pulled back the curtains of a kitchen window and looked out to see if there were a potential threat which merited her attention. Anyone looking in her direction could see the twin barrels of her airborne home self defense system. Upon sounding the alarm, it progressed from Defcon 5 to Defcon 4. At least a hundred BBs were poised to launch simultaneously at the twitch of her trigger finger. Then she saw Rocky smiling at her outside the fence. She put her fingers in her mouth and let loose with a shrill whistle. That was the signal for the alarm system to stand down and it did - suddenly, as if the yapping had just been in your imagination all along.

She hollered, "The coast is clear. Come on in."

Rocky opened the gate and followed the sidewalk to her back porch. She had opened the door for him to enter. Mrs. López had already benched her hardware and was reaching into the cupboard next to the sink for two recycled (from the 1940s and 1950s like nearly everything else she owned), four-ounce glass jelly jars with colorful cartoon characters depicted on the outside. The glass she handed Rocky had Bugs Bunny on it. Then she selected her favorite glass for herself. It had a picture of Elmer Fudd with his trusty shotgun.

She also retrieved a nearly full quart bottle of Mexico's cheapest brand of tequila. It was called Escupidura de Lagarto, or Lizard Spit to the uninformed gringos, not that the translation would have mattered one whit to them. Escupidura de Lagarto was extremely popular with the working classes because it was

100-proof, got the job done quickly, and didn't break the bank. Taste was a distant fourth to them in their hierarchy of needs. The label had a picture of a lizard, perched on a Saguaro cactus out in the baking desert, tongue fully extended with a green bottle fly on the very tip, a split second away from consumption. She got it for two bucks a quart over in Juárez. She bought two bottles every week. She knew they sold it to the locals for 24 pesos, or the equivalent of a buck twenty-five. At least they threw in the dead worm for absolutely free, whether you were a local or a rich American. Even though she had been born in Ciudad Juárez, now that she was a naturalized American citizen, she was considered rich. As such, all the merchants knew she could well afford the bump in price. After awhile, she gave up and just quit bitching about it.

Rocky and Mrs. López sat at a hundred-year-old, handmade (out of poplar by her grandfather), kitchen table. The four ladder-back chairs were also made of poplar by him. Mrs. López poured them each a cartoon jelly glass full of distilled lightning, edged with razor wire, and aged in battery acid.

Rocky offered Mrs. López an unfiltered Camel cigarette. She declined, pulling out a packet of Mexican cheroots and a small box of Diamond brand, wooden matches out of her apron pocket. Rocky already knew she would decline because Camels were tame in comparison to her aromatic brown, iguana turds, and didn't contain nearly enough nicotine. He was just being polite. They both lit up, took a deep drag, exhaled, clicked their cartoon characters in a salute to each other, and slammed a half-glass of lizard spit. It mule-kicked Rocky in the gut, a real double whammy, causing a profusion of tears to cascade down his cheeks, but not like a waterfall. More like an equatorial summer squall at sea. His stomach rebelled violently like a bad case of seasickness, and it was all he could do to not blow beads everywhere.

Mrs. López cackled like an old hen. She said, "I'm sorry,

Rocky. You do this every time. The look on your face is priceless. When are you going to learn to drink like a man?"

He responded in a coarse voice, "Probably never. When are you going to buy a beverage not distilled by Satan, himself? I swear I don't know how you've lived this long drinking this swill."

"I'll be 81 on the 10th day of August. I've lived this long because I'm una cucaracha. Even an atom bomb can't kill a cockroach. I will outlive you by 50 years! Just how old are you anyway, Rocky?"

"I'm 31."

"Drink up or you won't live to be 32, Gumdrop."

She slammed the rest of her drink and poured another. Rocked slammed his, too. This time it was only half as awful as the first slug. She refilled his glass.

She asked, "Rocky, what have you been up to this past week? I know it wasn't anything good."

"What makes you so sure? Maybe I'm just dodging a loanshark."

"Do loansharks drive unmarked fuzz mobiles and make a half-dozen passes a day by your house? Wouldn't they just throw a brick through your front window or leave a dead horse head on your front porch?"

"Well, it wouldn't be the first time the cops thought I did something but I didn't."

"Yeah, but if they nab you, it could be a long time before you walk the streets a free man again. Besides, you know you did a lotta shit over the years and they didn't get you for it. Maybe it's your karma. How bad is it this time?"

"I'm not sure. I wish I knew. You're right. Even a little beef could be bad for me. I've already done a two-year stint, plus three years of probation. I'm a free man now. A while back they brung me in for killing a dude that I had a fight with earlier that day. They put me through the wringer, but they didn't have anything, and finally cut me loose."

"I remember that. I was worried for you, but I know you done it. Did you even hear yourself? You didn't say you didn't do it. You said they didn't have anything on you. Did you do something as bad as that?"

"I can't say for sure. Maybe. I've done a couple of things lately that could get me sent up the river if they could prove it, but I think I'm clear of all that. But there is a guy who could make some trouble for me if he turned rat. I don't think he would because it would implicate himself, too. Of course, they might give him a pass to rat me out if they want me worser than him. Think I need to go take a vacation somewhere far away from here to get my head screwed on straight, and give it time for the dust to settle."

"Since when you have money to go on vacation? Travel costs dinero. Besides, you already been gone a whole week."

"I put a little away in a passbook savings account. It's just sitting there earning five percent. Also, let's just say I made a few bucks while I was out of town."

"What about your job, your house?"

"I quit my job a week ago because they wouldn't give me any time off. I can always find another job as shitty as that one.

"My yard is xeriscape. Don't need to cut any grass. Ain't really got anything in my house worth stealing.

"You get my mail for me. I'll pay ahead on any bills that come in. I'll leave some extra here with you in case I do have to stay away for longer than just a couple of weeks. You could pay my bills for me. You've done it before.

"If the cops quit buzzing around, I'll come back home. If I knew what they wanted, I might stick around, but I don't. Also, if you haven't seen them knock on my door, that's significant. It means they aim to bushwhack me."

He reached into his pocket and pulled out five $100 bills. He folded them in half and handed them to her. He said, "I better go pack a few things and be off."

She counted the bills and said, "Rocky, this much money could last me a year or more paying every one of your bills. You ain't got that many. Fifty bucks a month would more than cover 'em."

"Mrs. López, I love you like you're my own flesh and blood. I ain't got any next of kin. You're all I got. Use some of that money to buy a better grade of tequila or get your dogs fixed. It's all the same to me."

"Rocky, a dog that won't fuck won't fight. I like my dogs with both their balls and ovaries. I also like my Escupidura de Lagarto. It suits me just fine. I already got a sack full of shotgun shells, like 62 to be exact. My Ford runs like it's new, even if it is a 1950 model. It's old just like me. I take good care of it - like myself. Nobody wants to steal a car that old. I ain't spending none of your money on me. Just on you. Please don't stay gone too long. I've gotten used to having you around. Savvy?"

"Savvy. I'll be back just as soon as it's safe. One last thing. I haven't decided where I'm going yet, but it will definitely be out of state. I will call you next Sunday around noon to see if the coast is really clear. I gave a friend your name and phone number. I told him to leave me a message here with you if something pops. His name is Rodney Tinsley, but he goes by Bug Eye. Not sure which name he would use. If he calls, it will be an emergency, okay?"

"Okay. Before you leave, check first to make sure there ain't no suspicious cars parked down the street. Then hurry back home soon as the heat's off."

Rocky looked, then darted across the street like a little leaguer chasing a ground ball. His house was sweltering, having been buttoned up for so long. Good thing he didn't own any potted plants or pets. He packed what he needed, loaded his flashy, pristine, midnight blue '66 GTO with the custom rolled and tucked white leather interior, and departed forthwith. First stop was at an enormous gun store called the El Paso Armory, where he purchased a box of Remington .38 Special, 158-grain, round-nose lead bullets, a copper .38 caliber bore brush, a leather inside-the-waist holster for an S&W Chief Special, and a sturdy leather money belt with a nickel-plated, oval belt buckle depicting the Alamo under siege. Then he hopped back into his stunning muscle car and jumped up onto I-25 northbound to Albuquerque, where he spent the night at a Howard Johnson's Motor Lodge.

Last but not least, after dropping off both Bug Eye and Rocky, Nick tooled westbound on I-10 en route to Tucson, 260 miles away, a place he had never seen, but had always wanted to visit. He had no idea where he would finally wind up. All he knew was he couldn't go home and that he needed to put some miles between himself and El Paso.

How in the world did he ever allow things to get so fucked up? He never felt so awfully alone in his entire life, even when he was conscripted into the Army going through basic training. At least in the Army, he never had any major screw-ups. He did his hitch, got his discharge, and caught a Greyhound bus back home as quickly as he could.

Nick had been lucky. They never sent him to Vietnam. Thank goodness for that. Instead, he served his tour at Fort Knox putting new recruits through the paces in the chemical warfare tent. Taught them how to put on their gas masks in the dark after the tear gas had been released. He got a certain degree of satisfaction watching them panic while their skin and eyes were on fire, but at least he never seriously hurt anyone. Now, he might have killed a guy he didn't even know, simply because he panicked. What would his mother think if she knew? She raised him better than that. Everything he did after he graduated from high school, good or bad, was all on him. It was solely his responsibility. Momma did her job. She was blameless.

Guilt overtook him in a rush like a stampede of buffaloes being chased by the Sioux. He made an unplanned stop in Las Cruces and went to a WalMart that had a Western Union window. He bought a $200 money order, a packet of envelopes, and a book of stamps. He went back to his van and wrote a letter to his mother.

He wrote: "Dear Momma, Me and my friend got a good paying job for a construction company in New Mexico building houses. The job will probably last two or three months. We're staying in a cheap motel now, but we are looking for better accommodations. I'm sending you this money to help ends meet. I'm sorry I didn't do this sooner instead of sponging off you and Grandma. I will send some more when I can. See you when the job is done. Your loving son, Nick."

He drove to a post office and deposited his letter into an inside mailbox. If the cops were looking for him and they squeezed his mom and she cracked, or thought she was proving that he couldn't have done whatever they said he did, this letter would send them on a wild goose chase trying to find him. He would mail the next letter from here too, only maybe from a post office with a different zip code.

Mission accomplished, he pressed on to Tucson. He didn't arrive until the wee hours. It was a beautiful city from what he could see. Very clean looking and prosperous. He loved it. He rented a room for a week at the Roadrunner Motor Court. Tomorrow, if he wasn't too fagged out, he would take a day trip to Tombstone. It was only 80 miles away. He'd check out the legend of Wyatt Earp and the Gunfight at the OK Corral. Maybe he would pick up a gunfighter's trade secret that could save his life one day. Maybe not. Maybe he would always be a loser.

Geez, he had to quit thinking like that. He had plenty of dough. He was free. He had his whole life ahead of him. What he really needed to do was pick a trade that interested him and then sign on somewhere as an apprentice. Make something of himself. That was the ticket. Maybe he could learn to be a commercial, over-the-road truck driver. See America. Earn the big bucks. Maybe even own his own rig someday. He started feeling better already.

Sunday evening found Bug Eye looking for a job within walking distance from the Fabens Arms Hotel. He had circled some Help Wanted advertisements in El Paso's newspaper, *The Bugle*. The one he hoped to secure was at the Gulf service station a block away. He walked by it before it closed. It looked clean and prosperous. Lots of customers. They advertised for a pump jockey on the afternoon shift. The next best option was at a warehouse four blocks away. They needed some men to load tractor trailers. That would be ball-busting work, but it paid well. There were other jobs he had circled too, if neither of those panned out. Time to be Joe-Fucking-Citizen again instead of a bandit. Less pay, but more longevity, and certainly not wasting any of it in a prison cell.

Rocky was too wound up Sunday night to sleep. He cleaned the .38 he appropriated from the safe twice, just to insure it didn't have a speck of dust or any fingerprints on it. He dry-fired it through several five-shot cycles to confirm that it functioned properly. Five shots in five seconds. Again and again. He needed to take it out in the desert and put a few rounds through it to see if he could hit anything with it. A two-inch barrel couldn't possibly be very accurate from more than five or six yards away. It was basically just a belly gun, but it was small and concealable, something he could carry with him everywhere he went.

His next task was also gravely important. He spread out all his take accumulated from their crime spree. He counted $9,726 in all denominations, more than $200 of which was in $1 bills. Only one old $2 bill. He couldn't hide all this pile of dough in his new money belt. He divided the bills into stacks of $1,000, mixing the denominations in each stack to avoid suspicion. He put $726 into his wallet. Tomorrow he would go to nine different banks to trade his currency for uncirculated $100 bills.

He was worried that trying to conceal this much money in his money belt might be more than it was designed for. That's why he bought the wider 1-1/2-inch belt. Even so, it still might bulge too much for complete concealment. Because of this, uncirculated currency was important. It was thinner than well-used bills. Nevertheless, a bulging belt was better than carrying all that cash around in a valise. Once he switched out the bills, he would take I-40 westbound to Kingman, Arizona. He'd figure out the rest tomorrow.

CHAPTER 20

Catching Up at Home

Sunday, June 17, 1973

Barlow awoke at 9:10. Sarah was still asleep. They were too late. Church had already started. He tiptoed to the bathroom in an effort not to awaken her. It didn't work. In midstream, relieving pressure from his bladder like a steam valve, he heard her say, "Barlow, we missed church! Momma's gonna be upset with me."

He finished up, gargled, washed his face and hands, and walked back to the bedroom. She was sitting straight up in bed, still in her fabulous birthday suit. God had fashioned her into the most beautiful, erotic, fascinating creature he had ever seen. Her hair was mussed, just like she had made love all night. She was wiping sleepy dirt from her eyes with a look of exasperation on her lovely face.

He crawled in beside her and said, "Just tell her you were busy banging your lights out trying to make babies."

She replied, "Hush! I wasn't trying to make any babies. I don't want any babies right now. I was just trying to pacify some intense physical urges."

"Right-o, but doesn't she want you to make a baby? Just tell her you were busy practicing on how to make one. That ought to shut her up."

"Barlow, you're incorrigible! It would make things worse! She would put even more pressure on me. Why don't I just tell her I fucked all night long? How about I say I just can't get enough of your peter? How about telling her I get wet thinking about you whenever you're not here?"

"That too. You always turn me on when you talk dirty, but she'd still probably be upset. Besides, I hope you get wet when I am here, like right now with Roscoe raging like the untamed savage beast that he is."

"You know what I mean. Thinking about you keeps me in a constant state of wetness."

"Good. That's my girl. Why don't you lay back down and let me see if I can relieve some of your tension?"

"You're a wily, smooth-talking, horn-dog Mr. Adams. What do I get if I do?"

"How about another trip to Nirvana? Maybe even two trips."

"You're on. Let me go pee first and brush my teeth. Then we'll see if you're really as good as you think you are. I have my doubts, Peter Man."

*****

It was after 10. Church would wrap up and let out any minute now, and they'd begin ringing the steeple bell. Sarah's faux doubts about Barlow's virility were put to rest, at least for the time being. All she wanted to do now was lie in bed and glisten and glow. Barlow, on the other hand, was famished. He asked, "What would you think about breakfast?"

"It's a great tradition, but Betty's and Crabtree's are closed on Sunday. Your wife is worn out from having so many climaxes. I couldn't even rustle up a bowl of Frosted Flakes right now. Anyway, I think Tony the Tiger gets Sunday off, too. Now that I think about it, I hope he gets off on Sundays too, just like I did."

"Now who's incorrigible?"

"Touché."

"All right. I'll cook you breakfast. How about scrambled eggs, sausage patties, grits, toast, and orange juice? As you know, my biscuits suck, and besides they take too long to make, especially for a guy who hasn't had a bite in nearly 24 hours. First though, I'll rustle us up some coffee."

"What? You never ate dinner last night? How come?"

"That's why. You asked me to come home fast so I could make you come, so I did. We ate lunch around noon. Time was of the essence for both me and Slick. He needed to get back too, so he could satisfy the erotic needs of one of our neighbors."

"Who?"

"He never said, but I know it was someone here in town. I bet she didn't make it to church, either. Probably walking all bowlegged this morning after Slick was done pile-driving her."

"I certainly hope so. I'm thankful that you rushed home and took care of me. That was sweet of you. In fact, so sweet that I've decided to get up anyway and make your breakfast, provided you'll strip the bed and put on some clean sheets. We don't have much time, so it'll only be a fried egg and bacon sandwich. Momma expects us to be over there about noon for lunch about 1, so don't fill up. She's fixing a beef roast with all the trimmings, biscuits, salad, and lemon meringue pie."

"I can't wait. Besides, I still haven't seen Hank yet."

"Speaking of Hank, he said for us to bring our guns. He wants to ride down to the river and go shooting. He brought a couple of new guns he said you hadn't seen."

"What about your dad and Cordell?"

"Well, you know Dad's not a big shooter unless a rattlesnake or a coyote needs killing. A box of bullets lasts him about five years, and Cordell's not up for it yet. It'll just be us three."

"Which gun are you gonna take?"

"My .22 revolver. It has a longer range, and .22s don't cost as much as .25s. What about you?"

"My trusty .30-30, of course, and my .41. I need the practice on both. My .38 gets the day off."

"Okay. By the way, what shift are you on this week?"

"Mids. Today and tomorrow are my days off."

"Maybe you could stop by tomorrow at the rodeo grounds and pick me up for lunch. We could go to Crabtree's."

"Good idea. Maybe we'll even have time for a nooner."

"Shut up, you incorrigible old horn-dog! Get a move on, Buster. Quit jawboning. Daylight's a-wasting. We both got work to do."

*****

Happy got to go with on this trip. He was excited and gave the truck seat a sound thrashing with his tail. He loved playing with Arthur's dogs.

With the turn of events during the past week, everyone was glad to see Barlow. They all knew why he had been absent. They all wanted to know if the sheriff's office were any closer to catching the bandits who killed Bryce and shot Cordell. They knew he knew. They also knew he would get around to telling them at the right time.

Clarice was grateful for this day. She did not mention church or babies. She knew exactly why Sarah and Barlow weren't in church this morning. The subtle smile on Sarah's face was always a dead giveaway, but Sarah didn't know that and no one ever told her.

It was a warm, happy get together.

Cordell was mending well.

Darla was blooming. No problems with her pregnancy.

Arthur was thrilled to have Hank home, even if it were just for a couple of weeks.

His boys were both the same and they were both different. They were handsome, strong, centered, forthright, kind.

Cordell was quiet, steadfast, content, a team player, reliable as the sun rising in the morn and setting in the eve. He joined the National Guard to fulfill his military obligation and to stay close to home.

Hank was independent, incisive, intense, jocular at times, full of wanderlust. He enrolled in ROTC in college, knowing it was almost a guaranteed ticket to Vietnam. He didn't care. He needed to see what it was all about.

Both boys the same. Both very different.

And then there was Sarah. Fathers love their daughters differently than their sons. Daughters need more protection. They steal your heart. They can be confusing, bewildering. Letting them spread their wings and fly is far more difficult than for sons. Daughters will be your refuge in old age if you treat them right. Fathers pray fervently that their daughters will choose the right man for matrimony. Sarah did.

If the Good Lord called Arthur home today, he would be at peace. With Clarice at his side and his children at home, he had all a man could ever ask for. Besides, soon he would be a grandpa.

Today was not a holiday on anyone's calendar, but it was a "Kodak moment" type of day for Arthur that he etched in his mind for all of Eternity.

Days like this cannot be planned, anymore than one can plan a cosmic event. If the stars are in perfect alignment, if one is at peace with the world, if God is pleased and happens to glance down upon you when the time is right, then a day such as this can occur. You never know when it will happen. It just does. Carpe diem. You may never have another.

Over dessert, Barlow told everyone what had transpired on his trip to Laredo, then to Carrizo Springs, and finally to Eagle Pass. He sidestepped the gory details of Everett Raymond's demise, but it had to be mentioned if for no other reason than to give Cordell and Darla some closure. Now they could go on with their lives and plan for the future. The boogeyman was alive no more. Nightmares could be set aside.

Barlow said the other three bandits had been identified but they had fled to parts unknown. Law enforcement agencies throughout the region were looking for them. In the meantime, forensic examinations were underway to strengthen the cases against them. Whenever they surfaced, wherever they surfaced, singly or together, the sheriff's office would respond rapidly. In the meantime, Barlow was back to his summer schedule of rotating midnight shifts with Gillespie.

After lunch, Barlow saddled Boyo. It was the first time he had ridden in two weeks. Shame on him. Sarah saddled Rita. Hank saddled Hobo. They brought their hardware and a tote full of empty cans and bottles and jugs. It was a beautiful day with clear blue skies and a slight breeze out of the west. They hobbled the horses fifty yards behind them because Boyo was the only horse who did not shy away from gunfire, and it had been quite awhile since even he had been exposed to it.

Hank was wearing a Colt Government Model .45. He bought it before he deployed to Vietnam. He said officers were allowed to carry their own sidearms in combat. He bought his own because it was new and tighter than many of the Army issue .45s, some of which had seen service in World War I and World War II. He also unsheathed a brand new Colt AR-15, which is the semi-automatic version of the fully automatic M-16. He said he became a full-blown disciple of the M-16 during his tour in Vietnam.

They all took turns firing at targets they tossed into the river. It was both shallow and sluggish today, providing multiple opportunities to obliterate and sink the targets before they floated away. They tried out each other's weapons. Hank had 400 rounds of .223 for the AR-15, and 100 rounds of .45 ammo. He said they always had plenty left over whenever they qualified. Some might consider this purloining, but he looked at it as cleaning up the leftovers. Besides, proficiency in both weapons was a must for him in the National Guard too, and he shot as often as he could to maintain an expert rating with both weapons.

By the end of the day, each of them had fired every single cartridge they brought with, except for Barlow. He packed his gun everyday as part of his job, on or off duty, so he held back twelve .41 rounds to get him back home, just in case. Neither Sarah nor Hank expected any less from him.

They returned to the ranch about 4 o'clock. Cordell and Darla had already gone home. First, they groomed and fed the horses. Then they sat under the shade trees and drank several frosty beers while they cleaned their weapons. Clarice fixed them a supper from leftovers. Barlow gobbled down the last slice of lemon meringue pie. Then Sarah and Happy and Barlow returned home about 7:30.

Darla had been the only one who remembered to take photographs. Sometimes Kodak moments are only preserved in your memory.

CHAPTER 21

Cleaning Up Loose Ends

Monday June 18, 1973

Gillespie was assigned day shift this week to shadow Chief Alex. She was his man Friday. He was her Robinson Crusoe. They got busy putting together their laboratory requests, along with all the evidence they had recovered from Bryce Garrett's Desert Rat Liquor Store. They had recovered three spent .45 caliber projectiles and two .44s, but they did not have a gun to compare the .44s with, but they could still be compared with two .44 projectiles from Maverick County. They also had three .45 ACP shell casings, and 52 latent prints recovered from throughout the store.

Chief had a number of calls to make, so he told Gillespie to take the complaints and warrants upstairs to the DA's office.

She said, "But you wrote them. Is this kosher?"

He replied, "Yes, of course it is. I wrote them but you read them. You interviewed the witnesses with me and wrote the reports of interview. Can you swear that the information within the four corners of each complaint is true and correct to the best of your knowledge?"

"Yes. Of course I can."

"Then hubba hubba, Deputy Gillespie. Mr. DeWitt is waiting. Make us proud. Make sure they get filed with the clerk before you return. We gotta get them entered into NCIC and NLETS pronto, because I gotta call Chief Deputy Hornsby in El Paso as soon as I can. Those irredeemable malefactors may have already returned home by now. EPSO needs the warrants on file to arrest Rocky and Bug Eye if they ever locate them. Savvy?"

"Savvy, but what about Nick?"

"Like I said Saturday, unless we recovered his latent prints from the liquor store, about all anyone can do is haul him in for an interview. Unless he cops, they'll hafta kick him loose, and then by the time we do have enough evidence, he'll be long gone, hiding in East Roosterfart, Wisconsin or Timbuktu. It sucks, but that's the way it is unless we get more evidence.

"Off with you! Hurry back, and don't forget to bring us a copy of everything after its been signed.

"Also, tomorrow bring an overnight bag with you when you come to work. You're the designated courier to go to the lab. The drive to Austin is about 350 miles. The lab is open 8 to 5, Monday through Friday. If you hustle, you can be there in time to sign in the evidence. Otherwise, you'll hafta do it first thing Wednesday morning. You'll probably have to spend two nights there, but it may well morph into three.

"This may sound like a lackey job, but it's not. We have to maintain a chain of custody on all the evidence. Deputy A finds the evidence. Deputy B confirms. They both sign the chain of custody log. Deputy A secures it in the evidence room. Deputy C signs it out and takes it to the lab. Lab rat D signs it in and examines it. When he's done, he signs it over back to Deputy C, who puts it back in the evidence room, and so forth and so on. If the defense can show that anywhere along the line, someone who had possession of the evidence didn't sign for it, thus breaking the chain, the evidence is tainted and gets thrown out, the concept being that the person who didn't sign for it failed to do so for nefarious reasons. It may not sound like it, but being a courier is a critical job. Most of us here have been the courier at one time or another.

"Have some fun. Take some time to sightsee while you're cooling your heels. There's a clean Best Western about two miles from the lab. It's reasonable, $12 a night, but you don't have to stay there. You can stay wherever you want. Tom Bodett only charges $6 at Motel 6, but it's farther away and not as nice.

"Take one of the marked units and wear your uniform. It'll make things a whole lot easier for you at the lab. After you get back from Judge Sweeney's chambers, go see Loretta. She'll give you an advance of funds to cover your expenses. She'll also show you how to do your travel voucher when you come back. Also, save all your receipts. If you have any questions, Loretta can get you squared away.

"I almost forgot to tell you. Take a book. Take two if you're a fast reader.

"What are you waiting for, Deputy? That "peachy" Mr. DeWitt you mentioned after your first encounter with him isn't getting any younger."

Gillespie flushed bright scarlet from head to toe. She picked up the documents and rushed out the door. That stinker Barlow ratted her out! She said that a year ago when she first started the job. How else would Chief know? She'd have to think hard about how she could return the favor. The snot!

CHAPTER 22

A Tribute to Bryce Garrett

Tuesday, June 19, 1973

Bryce Garrett's funeral was conducted at St. Paul's Methodist Church in Mosby on Tuesday. He was 53 years old when he died. He was beloved by nearly everyone in town. The local weekly newspaper, *The Trail's End,* published a two-page (out of six total pages) obituary with Bryce's life history on Monday before his funeral. Even though nearly every Quayle County resident knew Bryce, few knew much about his past. The esteem in which he was held mushroomed exponentially once his friends and neighbors knew "the rest of the story," as Paul Harvey was wont to say.

Bryce Royce Garrett was born in 1920, and reared in Galveston, Texas. He graduated from Galveston County High School in 1938, where he was a two-year letterman on the football team. He also sang in the Glee Club. Upon graduation, he obtained a license, otherwise known as a ticket, from the U.S. Coast Guard to work as an ordinary seaman (deck hand) in the U.S. Merchant Marine. After two years, he was promoted to able body (AB) seaman. He served on nine different U.S. flagged commercial vessels between 1938 and 1945.

The merchant marine sailors did not wear uniforms. They wore the same work clothes that they wore at home. However, all the captains on the vessels Bryce was on wore a white billed hat like the ones Navy officers wear, with the exception that the hat badge had the fouled anchor on it instead of the Navy badge with the crossed anchors superimposed with the American stars and stripes shield. Sometimes the hats were navy blue, especially during the cold weather months. Some of the other officers wore these hats too. Other than that, it was impossible to determine the rank of a merchant seaman.

During World War II, Bryce was wounded twice when the commercial ships he served on as an AB seaman were torpedoed by German submarines. Both times he survived the sinking of his vessel. Many merchant sailors were less fortunate and perished. For each combat injury, he was awarded the Merchant Marine Mariner's Medal. The second award was a gold star which was pinned in the middle of the ribbon. This medal is equivalent to the Purple Heart.

Likewise, for both events, he was awarded the Merchant Marine Combat Bar. The second award was a silver star pinned in the middle of the ribbon. This award is equivalent to the Combat Action Ribbon awarded by the Department of the Navy to Navy, Marine Corps, and Coast Guard personnel who served in combat.

He was also awarded the Merchant Marine Defense Bar for service in the Merchant Marine between September 8, 1939, and December 7, 1941. (World War II began in Europe on September 1, 1939, when Germany invaded Poland. On December 7, 1941, the Japanese attacked Pearl Harbor.) This medal is equivalent to the American Defense Medal awarded by the Department of Defense to armed forces personnel who served on active duty between the same dates.

In addition, he was awarded the Merchant Marine Atlantic War Zone Medal and the Merchant Marine Mediterranean - Middle East War Zone Medal for serving in both theaters. For military personnel, both zones were combined into one award named the European-African-Middle Eastern Campaign Medal.

Finally, he was awarded the Merchant Marine World War II Victory Medal. This is equivalent to the World War II Victory Medal issued by the Department of Defense to armed forces personnel who served during World War II.

Bryce met his wife, Constance Marie (neé Hammond) Garrett of Mosby, in November of 1944. She graduated from Quayle County School that May, and she wanted desperately to support the war effort. Her parents reluctantly allowed her to go to Galveston to live with her aunt and uncle, while working as a bookkeeper for the Gilbertson Shipping Company in the Port of Galveston. This was the same company where her uncle worked as an assistant office manager.

Constance met Bryce in July while the vessel he was assigned to was briefly docked for some repairs. He asked her out for a date. After eight months, six more cruises, and numerous dates, he proposed. She accepted, with the understanding that she wanted to reside in Mosby. He agreed, stating that after seven years at sea with two ships sunk out from under him, he had had quite enough of the life of Barnacle Bill the Sailor.

In September of 1945, they packed their belongings and took the train to Mosby, where they were married on September 29, 1945, in the same church that is holding Bryce's funeral services. They have two children, Harvey, age 25, and Beverly, age 20.

In October of 1945, Bryce went to work as a stock clerk at the local IGA grocery. It didn't take long, now residing in a community of 3,000 after having grown up in a city of 80,000, for him to discover that a small town does not offer many goods and services which are otherwise readily available in a bigger city.

In Mosby, the residents had three options if they wanted to purchase something not available for sale locally:

1 - Order things through the mail, predominately from Sears & Roebuck or Montgomery Ward, or JC Penney's, among others;

2 - Drive 100 miles east to Del Rio, population 19,600, or 300 miles west to El Paso, population 175,000;

3 - Do without.

Bryce hated doing without. He selected option 2 - driving to Del Rio for most things. On one occasion, later on, he broke down and took the train to El Paso.

Initially, he only went to Del Rio once a month. He paid his daddy-in-law $5 in rent to borrow his 1934 Model A Ford sedan. He paid for all the gas and any repairs, such as oil changes, flat tires, broken fan belts, new points and spark plugs, filters, burned out headlights, etc. In fact, before making his very first trip, he had to purchase a complete set of tires, to include a spare. He would set out early in the morning and return late at night.

Before long, he discovered that if folks knew he was making a trip, they'd pay him to pick up something for them. He'd charge them 20 percent of the price of the merchandise to recover his costs and they had to pay up front. No COD (cash on delivery.) Folks were more than willing to do it. He always gave them the receipt so they would know he wasn't cheating them.

Constance was an experienced bookkeeper. She purchased a ledger, and meticulously recorded the date, name, address, and phone number of each client, specific items purchased (including brand names and sizes), cost, mark-up, name and address of the merchant, and any miscellaneous comments. Within three months Bryce was making two trips a month. Two months after that, he went once a week. During all this time, he learned where just about any type of merchandise could be purchased in Del Rio, saving him time searching, plus he made friends with most of the merchants.

The things most in demand were automotive parts, kitchen utensils, toys, bicycles, hard-to-find tools, unusual colors of paint, wallpaper, fans, radios, household devices, such as vacuum cleaners, electric mixers, irons, etc., and last but not least, distilled spirits. Just about everyone wanted distilled spirits.

The IGA was only licensed to sell beer and wine. Quayle County was not a dry county. You could buy distilled beverages to drink in the Dry Gulch Saloon, but no carry-out. Nobody in the entire county sold distilled spirits by the bottle. It became apparent to Bryce within a few months, that distilled spirits were his number one requested item. Within a year, distilled spirits were 90 percent of his business.

Bryce started buying the most popular brands by the case out of his own pocket. Buying it by the case netted a 10 percent discount, which he did not pass along to his customers. Within a year, he was making twice as much money as a part-time deliveryman than he made by working at the IGA. He saved every last penny he could.

In 1946, he made his only trip to El Paso to make a purchase. The only client was himself. He bought a brand new, snot green, 1946 Dodge panel truck. It cost $1,450, and he paid in cash. The only other available color option at the dealership, unless he wanted to wait for one to be ordered, was black. He didn't want to wait. Bryce wanted something snazzy, something that stood out from the crowd. Snot green wasn't his first choice, but it served his purpose well. Bryce was the only person in Mosby with a snot green vehicle.

The following week he put in his two weeks notice at the IGA. He had decided to work for himself as a deliveryman. He began making pickups and deliveries Monday through Friday. He was averaging 1,200 miles a week in the Snot Rod, his name for the new Dodge.

One day, Mr. Silverstein, owner of Abe's Package Store, asked Bryce if he were afraid of being arrested for bootlegging. Bryce replied, "So far as I know, bootlegging is running alcoholic beverages from one place where it's legal to another place where it ain't. Alcohol ain't illegal in Quayle County, although the Baptist church might wish it so. I'm just running errands back and forth from Mosby to Del Rio, delivering a commodity what's legal in both places. Not only that, I'm not in competition with anyone because nobody sells distilled spirits in Mosby.

Abe replied, "You ever consider getting your own retail liquor license from ABC (Alcohol Beverage Control) and setting up your own package store? Once you get licensed, you could begin buying from wholesalers. Make more money, and at the same time, reduce the cost to your customers. It's a win-win situation. I could help you with the paperwork and introduce you to my suppliers. If you stick to just selling distilled spirits, you won't be taking away business from those who sell only beer or wine. In other words, you won't be making any enemies. Do you have enough money to lease or purchase a building to set up shop?"

That's how Desert Rat Liquors came to be. The original location was on US 90 across from the entrance to the Quayle County Rodeo Grounds. Bryce bought an old, small, weathered, ramshackle, clapboard building which had belonged to an ancient saddle maker/leather repair artisan by the name of Boniface Cortéz. He was known locally as the Desert Rat due to his diminutive size and lifetime of living off the land in the Chihuahuan Desert before he became civilized.

Mr. Cortéz was a mysterious man, alleged to have ridden with Pancho Villa at the turn of the century. He had also been a professional saddle bronc rodeo man of some repute before he got busted up. Mr. Cortéz had passed away intestate at age 85 a year ago, and no heirs had surfaced to claim his property. As such, Bryce was able to purchase it at a sheriff's auction for $50, plus $14.22 in back taxes and administrative fees. It cost thrice that amount to fix it up. It was still a fire sale bargain. The building came with two acres, including a 200-foot right of way on US 90. Desert Rat Liquors remained on this site until 1967, when Bryce built his new store. Now the old building is open as Desert Rat Ice Cream & Sodas, operated jointly by his son and daughter.

After Sheriff Sol read the tribute by Phineas Rumsfeldt, owner/editor of the newspaper, he took immediate action. He told his entire staff and everyone else with whom he had some influence, that although it was not the custom in Mosby for veterans to wear their uniforms at funerals for non-vets, he was asking them to do so. If their uniforms didn't fit, or if they no longer owned one, he asked that they wear their rack of ribbons, or even the actual medals, to include all badges, on their civilian clothes or law enforcement uniforms, in honor of Bryce. Sheriff Sol was incensed that a man who had given so much in service to his country as a merchant mariner during the war was not considered a veteran, especially since the government awarded him decorations equivalent to the ones they awarded to military personnel.

This slight by the government irritated him so much he did some research. He found that the U.S. Merchant Marine had a higher percentage of casualties in World War II than any of the uniformed branches of service. According to the War Shipping Administration Press Release 2514, dated January 1, 1946, the Merchant Marine had 243,000 sailors who served during World II. Casualties of war totaled 9,521 war dead, which encompassed "killed at sea, POW killed, or died ashore from wounds." That is a 1 in 26 death ratio, or 3.9%.

Another shocking statistic he found was this. The U.S. Merchant Marine Academy was established in 1943, largely as a result of World War II. Part of the curriculum includes sea duty for months on end while enrolled as a student. During the war, 142 cadets lost their lives at sea and many more were wounded. As a result, of the five federal service academies, the Merchant Marine Academy is the only one authorized to carry a battle standard as part of its color guard.

Sheriff Sol called Lane Barnes, commander of the local American Legion post. He asked, "Lane, did you read the article about Bryce Garrett?"

"Sure did. He got more decorations than me and I was in the Infantry during the war, to include D-Day. I was thinking about making him an honorary posthumous member of our post. Get the honor guard to give him a 21-gun salute and present Constance with a flag."

"What if the state or national headquarters finds out about it and get their panties in a wad? It could cause you some trouble."

"What are they going to do - take my birthday away from me? You know it's easier to beg for forgiveness than to ask for permission. If they bust me back to regular member status, so be it. Our first vice commander will inherit my headaches, and I'll just be another stiff in the rank and file. Been there. Done that. Tell you the truth though, I think they'll punt. No right thinking person could believe Bryce doesn't deserve veteran status."

"You're probably right. I'm going to make some calls and ask our vets to wear their uniforms or medals."

"Good idea. I'll do the same thing here. I think we'll have a good turn out."

Every veteran Sheriff Sol spoke to was in concurrence. There were eight vets on the SO including himself.

For the first time since he was honorably discharged, Sheriff Sol wore his silver dolphins (Submarine Warfare Insignia awarded by the Navy) above his Korean War rack of four ribbons.

Chief Alex wore his pewter Coast Guard Coxswain Badge above his Purple Heart Medal. He didn't wear his other three World War II medals. The Purple Heart was his biggie.

Deputy Ernie Atwater, an Army vet from the Transportation Corps, wore his rack of three Korean War ribbons and his Driver W (Wheeled) Badge. (He couldn't find his Rifle Marksman Badge.)

Deputy Noble "Chunk" Bustamante had been in the Field Artillery in the Army National Guard. He didn't have any ribbons, but he wore his Rifle Marksman Badge.

Deputy Kirk Shoemaker served four years in the Air Force in the Security Police. Now he was a staff sergeant in the Air Force Reserve. He wore his uniform and his rack of three ribbons.

Deputy Barlow Adams served a two-year hitch in the Field Artillery. He wore his Army uniform with his rack of five

Vietnam War ribbons and his Rifle Expert Badge.

Deputy Dewey Carruthers did a three-year tour in the Army Finance Corps. Now he was a first sergeant in the Army Reserves. He wore his uniform with his rack of three ribbons and Rifle Sharpshooter Badge.

Deputy Clarence "Slick" Oldman was a Marine Corps vet. He wore his two World War II medals, his Combat Action Ribbon, and his Expert Rifleman Badge.

Deputy Archibald Willis (Retired) wore his World War I Victory Medal with Silver Citation Star and three campaign clasps, and his World War I Honorable Service Lapel Button, euphemistically referred to as a ruptured duck.

Judge Maxwell B. Sweeney served as a major in the Army Quartermaster Corps in World War II. He wore his uniform, amazingly well preserved, with his rack of three ribbons, his Rifle Sharpshooter Badge, and his Pistol Marksman Badge for the first time in nearly 30 years. He also wore the World War II version of the ruptured duck.

Arthur Baker wore his silver Army Aviation Crewman Wings over his four World War II medals.

1st Lieutenant Henry "Hank" Baker wore his Army uniform with his Combat Infantryman's Badge over his rack of five Vietnam War ribbons and Expert Badge with Rifle and Pistol Qualification Bars.

Cordell Baker had been in the Army National Guard. He didn't have any ribbons but he wore his Rifle Sharpshooter Badge, which he finally found at the bottom of his jewelry box after a lengthy search.

Both Hilary M. Gossett and his wife, Beverly, were World War II vets. Hilary was bald, short, and stocky. He was in the Army Adjutant General Corps. Beverly was a tall beanpole with short hair. She was in the Women's Army Corps (WACs.) They met when they were both assigned to Fort Benjamin Harrison in Indianapolis. Hilary's extended waistline prevented him from wearing his uniform, but he wore his Good Conduct Medal, American Theater Campaign Medal, World War II Victory Medal, and his Rifle Marksman Badge on his suit. Beverly could still wear her uniform, so she wore it with her WAC Service Medal, American Theater Campaign Medal, and World War II Victory Medal. Most folks never knew she had been a WAC so she made quite a splash.

There were dozens of other veterans wearing uniforms or medals, including Bryce's own son Harvey, who was currently a specialist (E-4) in the Field Artillery in the Army National Guard. He wore his uniform with his Rifle Marksman Badge.

Those men who were not veterans and all of the women were gussied up in honor of Bryce.

The community gave Bryce a first class send off. He had been one of them for 28 years. He was a happy, cheerful, considerate neighbor and businessman. He had favorably impacted the lives of everyone who lived there. They were comforted knowing that one of his killers had been slain, probably by his fellow bandits if the rumors were true. They hoped the other three bandits who victimized their community, particularly the other shooter, would be killed or arrested soon.

"An eye for an eye and a tooth for a tooth . . . ."

*****

Author's Note

World War II merchant marine sailors were not awarded veteran status by the United States until Congress passed the Merchant Marine Service Act in 2019, and it was signed into law by President Trump in 2020, long after most World War II merchant marines had since passed away.

CHAPTER 23

Plodding Along - No Target in Sight

Tuesday/Wednesday, June 19/July 4, 1973

On Tuesday, Gillespie took the evidence collected by Webb, Maverick, and Quayle Counties to the state laboratory. She was eager to do it to learn more about being a criminal investigator, although she regretted missing Bryce's funeral. On the plus side, she made some new contacts and some were even excited to show her how they conducted their examinations. She stored all of this in her memory bank for future reference.

On Thursday, she got the results. The Cliff Notes version which she phoned in to Chief Alex was this:

> 1 - The .45 caliber Colt pistol recovered next to Everett M. Raymond's body was used in the shooting of both Abraham K. Sipowicz and Jeffery R. Cooper, the two armored car guards, at the Texas Sovereign Bank & Trust parking lot in Laredo.

> 2 - It was also one of two handguns used in the shooting of Bryce R. Garrett, owner of Desert Rat Liquors in Mosby. The other handgun was a .44 Magnum Smith & Wesson revolver. The latter was determined by two recovered projectiles at Desert Rat Liquors which have identical lands and grooves with two .44 caliber projectiles recovered from the shooting of Everett M. Raymond.

> 3 - Four .45 caliber shell casings recovered in Laredo in the bank parking lot were fired by Everett Raymond's Colt .45.

4 - Two .45 caliber shell casings recovered at Desert Rat Liquors were fired by this same Colt .45.

5 - One .45 caliber shell casing recovered outside the barn in Maverick County was fired by this same weapon.

6 - One latent fingerprint belonging to Everett M. Raymond was recovered from a .45 caliber shell casing found in Laredo in the bank parking lot.

7 - Six latent fingerprints belonging to Everett M. Raymond were recovered from Desert Rat Liquors in Mosby.

8 - Two latent fingerprints belonging to Nicholas D. Crenshaw were recovered from Desert Rat Liquors.

9 - Three latent fingerprints belonging to Bruce K. Givens were recovered from documents from the safe in the barn in Maverick County.

10 - Nine latent fingerprints belonging to Rodney A. Tinsley were recovered from documents from the safe in the barn in Maverick County.

11 - One latent fingerprint belonging to Everett M. Raymond was recovered from a document from the safe in the barn in Maverick County.

12 - Two latent fingerprints belonging to Nicholas D. Crenshaw were recovered from documents from the safe in the barn in Maverick County.

Chief Alex was elated. He scribbled notes as fast as he could. He told Gillespie that the Colt .45 found in Raymond's grave had been stolen from a mom and pop gun store in Las Cruces, New Mexico, called Elwood's Shooting Irons. A second .Colt 45, two Colt Python .357s, one Remington 12-gauge shotgun, and one .44 Magnum Smith & Wesson were also stolen in the same burglary.

He exclaimed, "That stolen .44 Magnum will be the one Crenshaw used to kill Bryce! I just know it! Also, today I just learned from the coroner that both mortal wounds were inflicted by a .44, not a .45, although the .45s were contributing factors. We find that .44, and we own Nicholas Crenshaw for murder! Get on your steed and hurry back home! I have work for you to do." (What he had planned was for her to write the criminal complaint and arrest warrant for Nick Crenshaw and get them signed. Get promoted from the 2nd grade to the 3rd grade in criminal investigations.)

Even though Gillespie's 8-hour shift was nearly over, she split a gut returning to Mosby, arriving at 11 o'clock. She didn't want to miss whatever Chief Alex had planned for her on Friday. Besides, she knew she would return to the midnight shift the following week.

Chief was pumped. He started working the phones. He called Chief Deputy Roland Epps at Webb County SO first, because his murders were now resolved. His only pending issue would be making a prosecutable case against the getaway driver, who had to have been Nicholas Crenshaw. All they had so far were a couple of iffy identifications from photo spread arrays, and that was simply not enough.

Next, Chief called Captain Nathan Bedford Forrest "Captain Reb" Landry at Maverick County SO. The first thing Captain Reb said was, "Chief Alex, you all are a wonder. We only dropped off our evidence to you all on Monday, and now three days later we have the results. Normally that would be a 60-day turnaround for us. Not only that, it was your Deputy Adams who suggested we dust for latents on the documents. I really thought that would be a waste of time. Sure enough, we caught every single one of the perps just by doing that. We ain't got enough for murder yet, but we got enough for RSP (receiving stolen property.) That's a 5-year felony. We'll file the complaints and warrants tomorrow. BOLOs will go out NLT (not later than) COB (close of business) Friday."

Chief Alex replied, "Captain Reb, we were happy to do it. As long as Darnell Sweeney remains a Texas state senator, we can get speedy results. Just so you know, El Paso County is doing multiple checks everyday on the perps' last known addresses. I'll let them know to expect three more warrants and BOLOs by Friday night. That will help us tremendously, because until now, nobody had enough to obtain a warrant for Nick Crenshaw."

Next, Chief Alex called Chief Deputy Calvin Close at Crockett County. Chief Alex gave him a complete update on the Givens Gang investigation. Then he asked, "Are you all going to draft any complaints regarding the two stolen vehicles and the stolen safe?"

Chief Close replied, "Even though we know those yahoos stole the cars, we can't really prove it beyond a reasonable doubt. Besides, Bud Decker got the Matador back and it wasn't any the worse for wear. He only had $550 invested in the Ford, so it wasn't a tremendous loss. He'll just write that off. However, with the scumbags' latent prints recovered on the contents of his safe, we can definitely take some action. Bud said he had nearly $40,000 in cash in it, but he only has proof of $35,400. At least his insurance is covering most of his losses. We'll file complaints on the three living bandits for burglary and grand larceny. Can you send me a copy of the lab report?"

"Putting it in the mail today."

"Okay, we'll get the complaints and warrants filed not later than tomorrow. How's that sound?"

"Perfect. We think the assholes went back to El Paso. EPSO has been doing drive-bys at their last known residences several time a day. I truly believe we're close to finding them. Coupled with Maverick County's warrants and ours, we've got them stitched up like a bug in a rug."

"Sounds good. If you don't see our warrants and BOLOs on NLETS by COB tomorrow, give me a call. I'll sort it out, and Alex, thanks for the call. We really appreciate what you all have done on this case."

Finally, Alex called Chief Deputy Derrick Hornsby at El Paso

SO. Chief Alex gave him the most recent update on the investigation, especially with arrest warrants being issued for Nick Crenshaw for murder and armed robbery in Quayle County, receiving stolen property in Webb County, and burglary and grand larceny in Crockett County.

Chief Alex knew the murder charge was flimsy without the murder weapon, but felony murder did apply. Felony murder occurs whenever any party dies during the commission of a felony without regards to the means. As an example, if the victim of an armed robbery dies of a heart attack, and there were three armed robbers, all three can be convicted of felony murder. Likewise, if one of the robbers accidentally shoots and kills himself, his two partners could be convicted of felony murder.

Chief Hornsby thanked Chief Alex, and said EPSO would ratchet up their search for Rocky, Bug Eye, and Nick. He promised to call the moment they had anything new. He also said that Culberson County had positive eyewitness identifications from photo arrays on Bruce Givens and Everett Raymond. They plan to indict Bruce Givens in the next couple of days.

*****

Barlow was scheduled to work the midnight shift all this week, and the week of July 1/7. He was scheduled to work the afternoon shift the weeks of June 24/30, and July 8/14. Gillespie was on the opposite schedule. The midnight shifts had been agonizingly slow for both of them. The afternoon shifts had received a modicum of routine calls - nothing noteworthy, but still it was something. Something is better than nothing. All leads on the Givens Gang had dried up. It was frustrating for everyone, but it was also a time to catch up with family and hobbies.

All of life can't be an adrenaline rush, no matter how much the adrenaline junkies want it to be. Barlow and Gillespie were both bored to distraction. They weren't the only unhappy campers, either. Sheriff Sol and Chief Alex were both chewing nails. The investigation and resolution of two of the biggest crimes to occur in Quayle County for more than a decade were hanging in limbo. No one could believe these three thugs were so clever that they could evade capture for so long, especially with so many officers looking for them.

Then on Wednesday, July 4th, they finally got a lead. Everyone was euphoric. Static electricity was crackling throughout the Trans Pecos like humming telephone lines, but Barlow was sick. He was benched by being on the midnight shift! He kept telling himself it wasn't about him. That's what the best batters at any level of baseball tell themselves during the bottom of the ninth inning when they're down a run with three weaker batters slated to step up to the plate before them - that is, assuming they don't go three up, three down. It's a team effort. You gotta keep that in mind.

"Swing batter, batter! Swing! The noise in the ballpark was deafening. Same-same in Barlow's head. Tick tock.

CHAPTER 24

It was Bound to Happen

Wednesday/Thursday, July 4/5, 1973

Bug Eye had settled down into a slow, peaceful rhythm. He worked five nights a week, one time six, to include a few intermittent hours of overtime at the Gulf service station in Fabens. He liked his boss and his co-workers. For the first time in years he had harmony in his life. If he was off, he usually went to the Saturday matinee at the movies. Two weeks ago he saw *High Plains Drifter* with Clint Eastwood. Last week he saw *American Graffiti*. This week he planned to watch James Bond defeat the forces of international evil in *Live and Let Die*. Life was good.

He started thinking that he would not meet with the other guys on Wednesday, July 18th. He was happy. He was making a decent salary and his overhead was next to zero. He hadn't spent the first dime out of his ill-gotten gains since Nick had dropped him off. He didn't want to get mixed up in all that drama again. He realized Rocky might drag him into the pits of Hell like Ev nearly did to Nick. Bug Eye was free. He was pretty certain he would not go back.

In the meantime, Rocky had driven from Albuquerque to to Kingman, Arizona on I-40. Then he picked up US 93 to Las Vegas, Nevada. He secured lodging at the Sands Hotel & Casino. He wasn't a big gambler. He did play some quarter-ante blackjack. Generally he was about even, which was all anyone could hope for and he knew that. Very few ever beat the house odds for any extended period of time.

He also got laid a couple of times by show girls who picked up a little extra jingle on the side turning tricks. Darlene

Underwood was definitely wasting her time at Texas George's Saloon. She could easily make $50,000 a year here with her looks and witchy woman talent, so long as she stayed sober and didn't get hooked on smack which was a hot commodity here.

He also did a little sightseeing, driving across the Hoover Dam and taking the tour, learning how it was built. It really was an astonishing feat. One day he drove to a campground with fishing access on Lake Meade. He paid to reel in a few nice rainbow trout, which the cook at the camp cafe cleaned and fried for him.

He called Mrs. López on Sunday, June 24th, and again on Sunday, July 1st. Nothing much going on back in El Paso, except the cops were still doing drive-bys past his house. What the fuck? What did they know? He never got made on any of the robberies he pulled. Even if they found Ev's body, why would they suspect him? Up until the very last minute, they were both buds. It just didn't add up. Besides, Mrs. López said the fuzz had been cruising by his house even before Ev got his just desserts. That was even scarier because it was baffling.

With respect to Nick, it only took two weeks before he was bored shitless. He just couldn't stay away from Texas George's Saloon, attracted like a moth to light, or probably more like a rutting buck chasing a doe in heat. He drove back to El Paso, but being ever so clever, he stayed in a Days Inn on the northern outskirts of town. He just wanted his old life back. He missed hanging out at Texas George's. He missed banging Darlene and Wanda and Vivian and some of the others. He knew it would be risky going back there, assuming the cops were actually looking for him.

He pondered the situation carefully, looking at it from every which way he could think of. His greatest exposure was the armored car job. There were at least a dozen potential witnesses, but he had been wearing a mask, and besides they weren't standing right on top of him. He didn't see how the cops would ever suspect him of being the getaway driver. Ev was dead and buried out in the middle of nowhere. Nobody was there to witness it when everything turned to shit. The farm was deserted. There would be no reason for the cops to be looking for him. Nevertheless, Rocky had warned him several times not to go back to Texas George's unless he was just begging to go to prison.

What did Rocky know? Absolutely nothing! That's what. Rocky was just a paranoid, bossy prick. No wonder Ev hated him so much. Rocky saw ghosts in all the shadows. Nick was a big boy. He decided to go anyway. Besides, he was long overdue for some puss. He hadn't gotten laid since the last time he had been at Texas George's House of Prime Vagine, as he and the boys lovingly called it.

He went big time. He splurged, purchasing a fifth of primo Jose Cuervo. Cost him eight bucks. He had a little taste or two. Smooth. Worth every penny. He was patient, waiting until 1 a.m. to drive over there. Hell, now it was already the Fourth of July! Happy birthday, America! Home of the Free and Land of the Brave because of veterans such as himself who had sacrificed so much. Made him want to parade around wearing his dress greens with his National Defense Service Medal, and his Rifle Marksman Badge. He paid his dues.

At least Nick did have enough presence of mind not to step inside the joint, just in case Rocky was right. He smoked and listened to the radio while he waited in his van, which he wisely parked in the shadows in the back of the building like Rocky used to do. He waited for 2 o'clock closing time to see which girls did not have a hook-up.

It was 2:10 when Gloria came out all alone. She was the last dancer to walk out of the building. He drove up closer and stopped. He said, "Hey, Gloria! Long time no see. How ya doing?"

She looked up and gave him a big smile. She asked, "How's it hanging, Nick?"

"Like a fucking tentpole, pointing straight up in the air. Harder than Mickey Mantle's baseball bat. It keeps bumping into the steering wheel, even all zipped up in my trousers. If it had a hand, I'd let it steer. That's how."

"Hmmm. Sounds tantalizing, like it needs a woman's touch. If you're looking for a good time, I can take care of you all night long for twenty bucks. Of course you gotta provide the booze."

He reached into his wallet and handed her a twenty. Then he held up the nearly full bottle of Jose's premium elixir and shook it so she could see that there was still plenty left.

Her smile got even wider. She used her tongue to poke her cheek several times like she was giving head. Then she took the twenty and stuffed it into her bra. She said, "Follow me, Big Boy. I'm so horny I've soaked my panties twice tonight. You better give me a good ride, or I'll kick you out and go find me someone who will."

He replied, "Gloria, when I get done with you, you won't be able to stand up. Your pussy will be whistling Dixie. Your legs will feel like rubber."

"My kinda man, Nick. Just follow that car (pointing to a 1970 Ford Maverick two-door sedan, white with baby blue accents on the hood and rocker panels.) It ain't far."

He followed her home to her third floor apartment. Nothing could convince him now that he should have stayed away. That's because he didn't see Texas George, who looked out the back door before he locked up (and departed through the front) just to make sure all of his employees got out safely. Everyone was gone except for Gloria, who was talking to a man in a white van. George did a double-take. Glory be! It was none other than Nick Crenshaw in the flesh himself. The detectives were quietly looking for him on a murder beef. Texas George decided to wait until later in the day to report this to Sergeant Julio Elias. If this didn't earn him some major league good will with the sheriff's office, nothing ever would, especially if they caught Nick because of his tip.

Nick quietly slipped out of Gloria's apartment like a wraith around 5 a.m. He drove back to his room at the Days Inn up near Fort Bliss to crash. He had another date set up with her for tonight after she got off from work. He decided Gloria was the absolute best piece of ass he had ever had. He deliberately stayed sober while she consumed most of the tequila to give himself more staying power. He knocked the bottom out of it three times before she passed out. Then he did her a fourth time while she slept. When he was all done, he was thoroughly satisfied in addition to being drained dry.

George waited until 3:30 that afternoon to call the SO. Sergeant Elias was not in because it was a holiday. George asked the detective in the Intelligence Bureau to have Sergeant Elias call him as soon as possible. He said it was important. Later, when George's girls began showing up for work, he cornered Gloria while she was by herself getting ready.

He said, "Gloria, I was a little worried about you after we closed last night. I always check the back parking lot after you all punch out, just to make sure none of you are being harassed by our clientele. When I looked, you were talking to someone in a white van I hadn't seen before."

"Thanks, Boss. That is so sweet of you. No, I was okay. That was just Nick, you know, the college boy that hangs out with Rocky and that crowd? We were just catching up. I hadn't seen him for a couple of weeks. We made a date for tonight. That was it. Everything's peachy."

"Well okay then, just so long as you weren't having any trouble. All righty, I'll get out of your hair so you can finish getting ready. Knock 'em dead tonight, Sweetie."

At 4:30, Sergeant Elias returned the call. He asked, "What's up, George. Your call had me worried."

"Thanks for getting back to me so fast. Hey, are you all still looking for that kid, Nick Crenshaw?"

"We are. How did you find out?"

"I try to stay tuned in on things which could have a negative impact on my business. You know I appreciate you all, and everything you all do. Anyway, I thought I saw Nick in a white van last night right after closing. I checked with Gloria Reed, one of my dancers. That's who he was talking to. She said he was coming back tonight after her shift to take her out on a date. If I had to guess, he's planning to get his ashes hauled. If you still want him, now you know where he'll be at 2 o'clock tomorrow morning."

"Thanks. You bet we do. Yes, we'll definitely be there. Do you know what type of van he was in?"

"Well, it was an old, white van, probably a mid-60s model, maybe a Dodge. I know it wasn't a Chevy. I didn't get that good a look at it. I only saw it for a couple of seconds, same as with Nick."

"Do you happen to know where the rest of that crew he hangs out with has crashed?"

"Nope. That's all I know."

"Well, okay George. I owe you a big one. We'll pick him up quietly in the parking lot if he lets us, and do everything we can to keep your saloon out of the limelight. Thanks once again. Adiós."

Sergeant Elias called Captain Stan Howard. He called his crew and told them to meet him at the Denny's on Lee Boulevard at 10 o'clock. Then he called Chief Hornsby, who called Chief Alex. Chief Alex called Sheriff Sol.

Sheriff Sol asked, "Who you taking with?"

"Gillespie, of course, assuming she wants to roll. She's earned it. I've been putting her through the paces."

"You know she will. You all better skedaddle if you want to make that 10 o'clock rendezvous."

"En route. Keep you posted."

"Barlow's on the desk tonight. Call him when you know

something, unless it's urgent. Then call me."

"Roger that. See ya later alligator."

Chief Alex called Gillespie. He told her to wear soft clothes and meet him at the jail ASAP.

Gillespie was already in soft clothes. (It should be noted that since this was a holiday, those on duty were expected to spend a little time in the jail, but otherwise, they switched the phones to the answering service and went about their own personal business. They didn't wear their uniforms so they could participate in any festivities, minus the alcohol, of course.) She grabbed her kit, and beat Chief Alex to the jail by five minutes. They were pressed for time and she was a better driver than he, so he let her drive, telling her to step on it, meaning drive Code 2 minus the blue light and siren. He briefed her along the way.

Gillespie was thrilled that Chief chose her for this potentially dangerous takedown assignment over the senior deputies, especially Barlow and Slick. That's who they always went to if shots might be fired. She had a little experience in that arena herself, but in her heart of hearts, she knew she would also pick them over her in this type of situation. Of course, EPSO would be there as well, and it was their county even though they were executing Quayle County's warrant. She probably wouldn't do much more than unholster her revolver and hold it down by her leg for the takedown. Even so, she was included. That was the main thing.

Chief Alex and Gillespie were only five minutes late for the briefing. They hadn't even ordered a meal yet. The consensus was breakfast all the way around.

Captain Howard made the introductions for those officers who were meeting for the first time. Gillespie met Sergeant Julio Elias, Detective Dave Marshall, and Detective Conrad Standing Bear, all from the SO. She also met Lieutenant Willard Rosenthal, Patrolman Leonard Harkrader, and Patrolman Luis Aparicio, all from EPPD. Everyone of them seemed like nice guys. Nobody made any catty remarks about female officers. She was quietly thrilled.

She didn't know it, but Chief Alex had long ago clued in both Chief Hornsby and Captain Howard about Gillespie's gunfight with the Mexican alien smugglers at the Circle A last year. They might have already read about it in the paper or seen it on TV shortly after it occurred, not knowing who she was. The press feasted on this because a female deputy was the hero(ine.) Most likely however, Captain Howard had clued in these officers before Chief Alex and she arrived. Most of them had never shot anyone in the line of duty, especially four gang members at the same time, so she was greatly elevated in their eyes.

Captain Howard passed around Nick's mugshot for all to study. Then he passed around Rocky's and Bug Eye's on the off chance one of them might be with Nick.

Chief Alex detailed the armed robberies in Quayle and Webb Counties, where four victims were shot, three of them fatally. He also mentioned the murder of their partner, Everett Raymond, in Maverick County by Nick and the other two of them still on the loose. This was where they cracked the safe they stole from the car lot in Crockett County. He also mentioned the armed robbery in Van Horn, the high speed chase with shots fired in Quayle County, and the car thefts in El Paso, Alamogordo, and Crockett County. He said at this time, there were felony warrants on file for all three suspects from Quayle, Maverick, and Crockett Counties.

Lieutenant Rosenthal mentioned the armed robbery and shootout at the Sinclair service station at the corner of Garfield and Wells, to bring it all back home. Every officer present was loaded for bear and primed for the takedown by the end of the gang's crime spree narrative.

Captain Howard laid out a hand drawn map of Texas George's Saloon, the parking lot, and surrounding environs. Everyone except for Gillespie was familiar with it. He passed out assignments, telling everyone to put their radios on channel F-2.

He said he wanted the marked unit with Leonard Harkrader and Luis Aparicio to hang way back out of sight. When it was time for the takedown, he would call for them to be the first to approach the van, waiting until the last second to turn on their blue light. He wanted Nick to know without a doubt this was a law enforcement bust in case they had to punch his ticket.

Captain Howard and Chief Alex would set up in the strip mall parking lot adjacent to George's.

Lieutenant Rosenthal and Detective Marshall would take up a position in the back lot in their undercover Mustang, mixed in with the employee vehicles to give them the eyeball.

Sergeant Elias, Detective Standing Bear, and Deputy Gillespie would set up in Chief Alex's Jeep Wagoneer to cover the front parking lot in the event Nick didn't park in the rear like he did last night.

All units were to converge at the takedown signal.

Captain Howard's plan, besides covering all the exits, was to blend personnel insomuch as it made sense. He didn't want any agency to feel slighted. Besides, he called up way more officers than he would have under normal circumstances to arrest just one man. He was acting just like a Fed with all this overkill. It was just that, if all three murderers showed up, he knew without a doubt shots would be fired. Better safe than sorry. He'd gladly take the ribbing.

*****

Nick waited a little later than yesterday before leaving for Texas George's. He could hardly wait. He even ate two servings of spinach when he dined for lunch at the Cracker Barrel, because he was told in junior high school it gave men more stamina in the bedroom. In fact, he believed eating something as vile as spinach was the subliminal joke in the Popeye the Sailor cartoons. Popeye gobbled it up cold right out of the can in order to pleasure Olive Oyl whenever they hooked up, whereas Wimpy always ate hamburgers and he never got any nookie. The spinach obviously worked because Popeye knocked up Olive Oyl and they had a baby named Junior. Nick thought spinach blew beads, but he scarfed it down anyway because he needed the extra umph after all his copulating last night.

Nick set up in exactly the same location as the night before, engine off, windows down. It was 1:45. He lit up a smoke and was juking out to Merle Haggard's platinum song, *"Mama Tried"* on the radio. Nick sang along, " . . . . Despite all my Sunday learnin' towards the bad I kept on turnin' 'til Mama couldn't hold me anymore, and I TURNED 21 IN PRISON DOIN' LIFE WITHOUT PAROLE . . . . " and then the shit hit the proverbial fan.

Lieutenant Rosenthal had confirmed Nick's identity. Said it looked like he was all alone. Captain Howard ordered the takedown. Patrolmen Harkrader and Aparicio kicked it in high gear. Nick was too busy belting out the song at the top of his lungs to even notice if the sky was falling. At the very last moment, Harkrader flipped on the blue overhead bubblegum machine. Captain Howard converged from the rear of Nick's van, blue dashboard teardrop light oscillating. Gillespie blasted in behind the marked unit with her dashboard light on, too.

Nick looked up five seconds too late. Without thinking, he reached under the seat for his .44, and had just gotten ahold of it when Harkrader jammed his .38 hard enough into Nick's left ear to cause it to bleed. Harkrader shouted, "Drop the gun motherfucker, or you're a dead duck!" Nick looked up and saw cops with guns pointed at him from everywhere. He pissed his pants torrentially, leaving a two-feet in diameter puddle. He dropped the gun on the floorboard in the piss, and raised both hands, palms out. His stomach was turning vicious summersaults.

Aparicio jerked open the driver's door and ripped Nick out of the seat, like he was a 160-pound sack of shit. He shoved Nick face down into the pavement and stomped his size 12 boot hard into the small of Nick's back, almost knocking the wind out of him. He handcuffed Nick's hands behind his back, and yanked him up onto his feet. Nick burst out in tears. Then his bowels released their contents and he soiled himself.

Harkrader choked on the smell and yelled, "Jiminy Christmas! For a coldblooded murderer, this guy sure is an asshole! I can't believe he just shit himself! Hell's bells!"

Captain Howard choked and tried to suppress his laughter. He said, "Good job, fellas."

Lieutenant Rosenthal said, "Leonard, now that you scared the living shit out of this asshole, you and Luis have the privilege of transporting him to County CID (Criminal Investigation Division.) Take him to the jail first and see to it that he cleans himself up real good. Have the jailers get him a red and white striped outfit, extra fucking large, so the next time he shits himself, the turd can slide all the way out of his pants leg and save us some of the mess. We'll meet you at CID as soon as we give this van a quick toss. We won't be long.

"Everyone, please turn off the blues. Let's try to get out of here before the girls punch out and see what just transpired."

Captain Howard said, "Detectives Marshall and Standing Bear, you all call a wrecker and follow it back to the garage. Get CSI (Crime Scene Investigation) to dust it for prints. Then meet us back at the office. Before you do though, bag his gun and give it to me."

Detective Standing Bear started to pick up the gun when he saw the puddle. "For the love of God! He dropped the gun in a pool of piss! Someone get me a napkin or something so I can pick it up."

That time Captain Howard couldn't hold it back. He laughed so hard, tears were streaming down his face.

Before they left, Lieutenant Rosenthal said, "Stan, you and Alex need to see this." He held up a cheap red and yellow plastic gym bag. The zipper was open. It was filled with cash of all denominations mixed together. He said, "It looks to be $20,000 or more. What do you want me to do with it?"

"Chief Alex said, "Sign the evidence form and give everything to me. We'll count it at CID. I'm going to seize it as proceeds of the robberies and the safe. We'll let the judges determine which victims get what. I can tell you for damn sure that none of it is going into Nick's canteen account."

Two minutes later, everyone was gone except for Gillespie, Marshall, and Standing Bear. Five minutes after that, the wrecker hooked up the car and departed with Gillespie and crew close behind. Then the first two pole dancers stepped out of the building, totally oblivious. The entire operation was flawless except for Nick shitting himself. The CIA couldn't have executed Nick's disappearing act any better than this.

CHAPTER 25

More Answers

Thursday/Friday, July 5/6, 1973

Chief Alex called the jail. It was 2:25, and the only call Barlow had received all night. He picked up on the second ring. "Quayle County Sheriff's Office. Deputy Adams speaking. How may I help you?"

"Barlow, this is Chief Alex. Are you ready to copy?"

"Of course. Shoot."

"Here's what I want you to do. We busted Nick without incident. He had the .44 Magnum Smith & Wesson on him that was stolen from Elwood's Shooting Irons in Las Cruces. I checked. The serial number matches. That serial number is N-Nora 23544. Copy?" (The phonetic letter for N was cited so there would be no mistake. It could be disastrous regarding chain of evidence if Barlow thought he said M23544 instead of N23544.)

"N-Nora 23544. Copy."

"Roger that. Get in the evidence locker. There are two different evidence envelopes in this case I need you to find - one by me and one by Captain Reb in Maverick County, each of which contain two .44 caliber slugs. The lab has already matched them as having been fired from the same unknown .44. Get them and prepare a lab request to have those four slugs compared with this .44 Magnum.

"An EPSO deputy is driving Gillespie back tonight with the gun and a gym bag filled with cash - $21,067, to be exact. You or your replacement need to count it again with Gillespie to make sure we didn't make a mistake. Then to log it in as evidence.

"Is Atwater working the desk this morning?"

"Nope. It's Chunk."

"Okay. Call Chunk and tell him to pack a bag. He's the designated courier for the bullets and the gun. I want him on the road to the lab as soon as he checks in this morning. If for some reason he can't do it, call Dewey. Any questions?"

"A couple. Has Nick copped?"

"We haven't interviewed him yet. He probably will, because he filled his trousers when we busted him. When I know, I'll call Sheriff Sol. What's the other question?"

"You just answered it."

"Okay. Listen up. Nick is being arraigned on all three counties' warrants this morning. If at all possible, meaning if the judge says so, I will transport Nick back to Mosby right after court. If the judge punts, I'll probably come home anyway. I'm giving you a heads up in the event we need a hurry-up indictment on Nick this morning. You might have to do it. We do not want to go through a preliminary hearing here in El Paso. Besides, I know the other two counties couldn't get it done by then. Copy?"

"Copy. Whatever you need. Just let me know. Good luck on the interview."

"Thanks. I'll be in touch. If for some reason you need to track me down, call and ask for me at EPSO CID. Somebody here will pick up."

"Roger that. Bye."

"Bye."

Barlow was back in the saddle again, but it was indoors. It was like riding a child's electric hobby horse in the supermarket or kissing your sister. Not much of a thrill. Still, he couldn't complain. He went from being benched, riding the plank as it were, to pinch hitter. That was something. At least he was back in the game. If this dragged out until next week, he might even have a shot at the starting lineup again.

*****

Captain Stanley Howard decided to conduct the interview of Nick in an interview room in the jail. The ambiance just outside a cellblock with clanging doors and other scary sounds of things that go bump in the night should aid in bringing a scaredy cat like Nick back home to Jesus. He also decided to lay in the weeds, keep his mouth shut, and let Chief Alex conduct the dialogue. After Alex was through, he'd pick up the ball if there were any loose ends.

Captain Howard called Lieutenant J.B. Guthrie, the supervisor during the midnight shift in charge of the jail and its 500+ inmates. Lieutenant Guthrie said Nick would be waiting in an interview room whenever Captain Howard arrived.

When Chief Alex and Captain Howard entered the spartan, concrete floor, pale green concrete-block-walled room, (the only things missing were blood splatters and instruments of torture), Nick was wearing thick red and white horizontally striped pajamas reserved for murderers and other dangerous offenders, and flip flops. His arms were shackled on the top of a metal table bolted to the floor. A six-year-old could see Nick was scared shitless. Chief Alex was thankful Nick had voided his bowels earlier.

Captain Howard and Chief Alex sat in metal chairs across from Nick. Chief Alex said. "This is Captain Stanley Howard from the El Paso Sheriff's Office. My name is Chief Deputy Alexander Snodgrass from the Quayle County Sheriff's Office."

Chief Alex opened his valise and pulled out a manila file folder with blank copies of the Miranda Warning. He pulled out one and read it slowly. He asked if Nick understood his rights. Nick nodded "yes" so Chief passed him a pen and asked him to sign it. Afterwards, Chief Alex wrote in the date, time, and location. He signed it and passed it to Captain Howard for his signature. Then he put the document back in the folder and returned it to the valise. He retrieved a half-inch thick manila file folder with Nick's name on the tab, and a blank 8-inch by 11-inch yellow pad of notepaper. He made sure Nick saw his name had been typed on the white label. It was an indicator that this file had been assembled with care for quite some time just because of him. It's as if to say, "We know all about you, Mr. Crenshaw."

Chief Alex opened the file and read from selected documents. "Let's see here. Nicholas D. Crenshaw, white male, DOB January 6, 1950, POB El Paso, Texas, resides at 808 Douglas Avenue in El Paso, with his mother, Nancy M. Crenshaw, age 44, and grandmother, Elaine A. Schmidt, age 66. One arrest in Alpine, Brewster County, Texas, for possession of marijuana and an illegal switchblade knife, resulting in two misdemeanor convictions. Sentenced to serve two weeks of incarceration. No automobile registered in his name, to include the van he was driving, which is registered to a Roger V. Godfrey in Carrizo Springs, Dimmit County, Texas. Bill of sale found in the glovebox shows the vehicle was recently purchased by one Aaron White, of 120 Florida Avenue in Laredo, Webb County, Texas. Dern! The Laredo Police Department says there is no such address in Laredo, and no such Aaron White on record there anywhere. Huh!

"Nick, can I call you Nick?"

Nick nodded.

"Nick, I don't know your place of employment, or previous employment history, how far you got in school, if you ever served in the armed forces, belong to any organizations, pay your taxes, are registered to vote, look at dirty magazines, ever been married or divorced, have any kids, legitimate or illegitimate, if you like chocolate ice cream, what your favorite color is, and so on and so forth. That is to say, I don't really know who you are. Understand?

"What I do know for certain is this. You robbed Desert Rat Liquors in Mosby, Quayle County, Texas, with one Everett M. Raymond. You shot and killed the owner, Bryce R. Garrett, with the .44 Magnum Smith & Wesson revolver found in your possession. Mr. Garrett was an honorable man, a highly decorated veteran of World War II, devoted to his wife and family, beloved by nearly everyone who ever knew him.

That .44 Magnum was stolen from Elwood's Shooting Irons in Las Cruces, Doña Ana County, New Mexico, along with several other firearms, to include the .45 caliber Colt Government Model pistol found in a hidden grave in a deserted barn near Eagle Pass, Maverick County, Texas, where we found the body of your partner, Everett M. Raymond, who also happened to be shot with the .44 Magnum found in your possession. Whew! Do I need to repeat myself?"

Nick shook his head, "no".

"Continuing, four other firearms - another Colt .45, two Colt .357s, and a Remington 12-gauge shotgun were also stolen the same night from that same gun store.

"Furthermore, the documents recovered in Raymond's grave were taken from a safe which had been stolen from Bud's Used Cars in Ozona, Crockett County, Texas. The safe was also recovered at Raymond's grave site. The documents were covered with latent fingerprints belonging to Everett M. Raymond, Bruce K. Givens, Rodney A. Tinsley, and you. Hmmm.

"Latent prints we recovered at Desert Rat Liquors also belong to you. Wow! Things are really piling up against you, Nicky Boy.

"I'm 99 percent sure you were the driver of the white over green Matador stolen from Bud's Used Car Lot in Ozona, Crockett County, Texas, same place where the safe was stolen, and used as the getaway vehicle in the armed robbery and vicious murder of two armored car guards, Abraham K. Sipowicz, and Jeffrey R. Cooper, by Everett M. Raymond, in Laredo, Webb County, Texas. Just so you know, both of these men were war veterans. Lucky for you, at least for the time being, you have only been charged with burglary and grand larceny in Crockett County, receiving stolen property in Maverick County, and armed robbery and murder in Quayle County. Since murder takes precedence over all other charges, you will be tried first in Quayle County.

"As you already know, Quayle is a rural county. What you don't know is, we only have one judge, Maxwell B. Sweeney, otherwise known by lawmen and court-watchers far and wide as "Maximum Max." Unfortunately for you, the U.S. Supreme Court struck down the death penalty last year shortly after Maximum Max sentenced another heinous murderer to death. I guarantee the death penalty is what you would have been looking at a year ago. Today, however, you are facing life without parole in Mosby County, and I expect that charge will be superseded with murder of Everett M. Raymond in Maverick County and felony murder of the Abraham K. Sipowicz and Jeffrey R. Cooper in Webb County. Everything else, even armed robbery, is small potatoes compared to murder.

"The reason I say that it's unfortunate for you that you aren't facing the death penalty is this. You are a very pretty young man. It won't be long before the predators in Huntsville break you down like a shotgun and pump you full of baby juice. They will take turns mating with you, every day, every night, over and over again. You will either start to enjoy it and become a queer bitch, or you will end up hanging yourself in your cell.

"Say their names. Memorize their names - Bryce R. Garrett, Abraham K. Sipowicz, Jeffrey R. Cooper, Everett M. Raymond. You bear responsibility for the murders of all four men, plus the nearly fatal shooting of Cordell F. Baker by Everett M. Raymond in Quayle County.

"I just wanted you to know what your future holds. I'll see you in court in a few short hours. If the judge so orders, I will transport you back to Quayle County post haste. First though, I will stop by your house and tell your momma and grandma what you've been up to. They'll cry their hearts out every night, but there's nothing they can do to save you. Basically, you're fucked, Mr. Crenshaw, no pun intended.

"Anything you want to say before we leave?"

Nick had been quietly weeping and shaking like he was freezing cold, but he broke down in howls and staccato sobs, unable to catch his breath. After a minute or so, when Chief Alex and Captain Howard stood up to leave, Nick whispered hoarsely. "Tell me what I can do to save myself. I am so so sorry. I would take every bit of it back if I could."

Chief asked, "Do you want a lawyer?"

Nick replied, "What for? My life is over. I'll do whatever I can to help myself. Please tell them to put me in solitary confinement. I already been raped twice in jail in Alpine. Please, I'll tell you everything."

Chief Alex and Captain Howard sat back down. Chief said, "Start from the beginning. Tell me everything you all did. Tell me where your partners are hiding. I need to know every last detail if you expect to get some mercy."

Nick told them about his entire life of crime, beginning with the strong-arm robberies of Walter Jones and his homosexual boyfriend in the parking lot back in February. He laid it all out, including the rendezvous scheduled for 11 o'clock, Wednesday, July 18th at Jack's Hamburgers, located at US 54 and Hondo Pass. Captain Howard and Chief Alex took copious notes. Then Chief hand-wrote an 11-page confession for Nick, deliberately making six mistakes for him to find, correct, and initial, proving that he read his confession word for word before he swore to it and signed it. Finally, Nick stated everything was 100 percent accurate. Then Chief swore him to it. Nick confirmed the veracity of his statement once more before he signed it. Then Captain Howard and Chief Alex signed as witnesses.

While Chief Alex had been busy writing out the confession, Captain Howard stepped out of the room to order a meal for Nick. Breakfast would not be served for another two or three hours, but a trusty made two fried bologna and cheese sandwiches with mustard on white bread, served on a paper plate with potato chips, and a couple pickle slices. He also brought a cup of black coffee in a paper cup. After all Nick's angst, he had finally calmed down, like he was glad he got all his crimes off his chest. Confession is good for the soul. He ate like a starving buzzard feeding on a two-day-old roadkill of rotten, stinky 'possum.

It was 5:30 when they wrapped up. In the presence of Nick, Captain Howard instructed Lieutenant Guthrie to maintain Nick in solitary confinement. He said they would. Captain Howard told Nick he and Chief Alex would see him in the courtroom when it convened at 10 o'clock.

Afterwards, Captain Howard and Chief Alex drove to Belle's Diner for a second full breakfast, to include a half-gallon of black coffee. In a manner of speaking, they finished off the rest of the roadkill that Nick had devoured. It was satisfying and delicious after the night they just had.

After eating, Chief called Sheriff Sol. Then he called Barlow at the jail. He told Barlow it would not be necessary to testify before the grand jury since Nick Crenshaw had signed a confession. He said he hoped Nick would be a temporary guest in their jail by late this afternoon.

Barlow thought to himself, "Great Scott! Gillespie and I will have to babysit Nick until he goes to prison, or one of the other SOs picks him up for additional judicial action. What a paradox! Good news is really bad news for Gillespie and me. I'm supposed to be ecstatic, but not so much."

*****

It was almost noon before El Paso County Circuit Court Judge Lawrence Ernhardt called Nick's case. The bailiff read all the charges filed against him in Quayle, Crockett, and Maverick Counties. His court-appointed attorney, Judith Carr, told the judge that Nick was ready to be transported to Quayle County to face his charges there. The judge asked Nick, and he confirmed. This was a no-brainer - a blessing for a conscientious judge with an over abundant docket. He remanded Nick to the custody of Chief Alex and the Quayle County Circuit Court.

Captain Howard had really come to admire Chief Alex, having worked with him three times now. He had the opportunity, so he did Chief Alex a solid. He tasked the transportation supervisor, Sergeant Dorance Hobgood, with assigning two deputies to transport Nick to Mosby in a jail paddy wagon forthwith. Captain Howard knew Chief had been up-and-at-'em for a day-and-a-half, and it would be too dangerous for him to make the 300-mile trip with a prisoner all alone, especially without any rest. He tried to talk Chief Alex into remaining overnight, but Chief said he really needed to get back. He thanked Stan profusely, but insisted that he would be okay following the paddy wagon and keeping his Jeep between the ditches on the way back home. It was a win-win for everyone, except for Barlow and Gillespie. It definitely was a win-win for the two deputies making the transport. They were thrilled to take on the assignment because they were getting paid ten hours of overtime at time-and-a-half.

Nick Crenshaw's arrest without incident (shitting himself doesn't count), coupled with his confession where he also ratted out Rocky and Bug Eye, put the good guys two giant steps closer towards wrapping up the entire case. Captain Howard and Chief Alex had already made rough plans to set up on Jack's hamburger joint on July 18th, but unbeknownst to them, there was a fat, shiny, green bottle fly in the ointment.

Caleb T. Scroggins, veteran police beat reporter for the El Paso *Bugle* newspaper, was where he always was at 10 o'clock, Monday through Friday mornings. He was in district circuit court. The hearing on Nicholas D. Crenshaw was out of the ordinary. Besides being charged with murder, the mother of all crimes, charges against him were filed in three different counties, none of which was El Paso County. Mr. Crenshaw was whisked out of the courtroom before Mr. Scroggins even had a chance to try to ask a question. All he had to go on were the three warrants, a copy of which were on file at the El Paso Circuit Court Clerk's Office. None of his sources at the SO claimed to know anything about it. How was it that three counties which weren't even near one another, managed to coordinate the filing of these warrants?

What was going on here? There was so much more happening behind the scenes than met the eye. Mr. Scroggins decided to nose around some, but first he had a deadline to meet. He wrote his bread-and-butter article, including Mr. Crenshaw's arrest and the charges filed against him in three different counties, being only one of 42 miscreants who also had initial appearances in district court today. Mr. Scroggins would circle around later to get the skinny on Mr. Crenshaw.

Mr. Scroggins' daily article appeared on page 8 of section 1 on Friday's *Bugle*.

Bug Eye had been reading the local newspaper since he quit high school. Besides following sports and reading the comic strips, he was an avid reader of articles about crime, especially murders. Over time, he'd seen more than a few of his friends and acquaintances named in the daily arrest docket article. Friday morning he was shocked to see a familiar name, not to mention the list of charges from three different counties. How did the cops get onto Nick so fast? Did he squeal? Bug Eye didn't have the answer to his first question, but he was convinced that he did on the second. Both he and Rocky were in great peril!

He checked his wallet for Mrs. López' telephone number. He went down to the bank of four pay phones on the first floor of the hotel. He put in his dime and dialed.

"Hello."

"Hello. Is this Mrs. López?"

"What are you - some kind of idiot? Did you just make a call and not know who the number belongs to?"

"Ma'am. My name is Bug Eye. I need to get a message to Rocky. He gave me this number and your name. Do I have the right person?"

"What dipshit christened you Bug Eye? Is that really your given name?"

"My given name is Rodney Tinsley. That name ring a bell?"

"Yes. It does. Rocky's not here. What do you want, Rodney?"

"Do you get the *Bugle* Mrs. López?"

"Of course I do. What's it to you, Bug Eye?"

"Please, would you open up today's paper in section 1 and turn to page 8? Check out the article called Police Beat. Look at the 9th name on the list."

"Hold on. Let me check. (One minute pause.)

"Found it. Which number?"

"Number 9."

"Let me see. Nicholas D. Crenshaw, murder and armed robbery in Quayle County, burglary and grand larceny in Crockett County, receiving stolen property in Maverick County. So what? Why should I care about Nicholas D. Crenshaw? What's he to me?"

"You need to ask Rocky the next time you talk to him. When do you think that will be?"

"Sunday. He always calls on Sunday morning."

"Mrs. López, please listen to me. If you really are like a grandma to Rocky, you need to read this article to him. Then ask him to call me, Bug Eye. I have two new numbers to give you. Will you write them down?"

"Hold on. Let me get something to write with. Okay. What are the numbers?"

"The first one is where I live. It's a hotel. I'm in room 316. The number is 776-4999. I'm off on Sundays. I'll wait in my room for his call. If he can't call until Monday through Saturday, ask him to call 777-2121. That's my job. I'm on the 4-to-12 shift. Have him ask for Rodney at either location. That's how they know me. Did you get that?"

"What do you think? Do I sound like I'm a deaf nitwit to you?

I'll tell him. Most likely he'll call on Sunday about noon, so hang around your room. Savvy, Bug Eye?"

"I do. Thank you. This is really important. Goodbye."

"Goodbye."

Mrs. López was really worried now. What had Rocky done? Was Nicholas Crenshaw the rat he was concerned about who would blow himself out of the water if he ratted out Rocky? She wondered. Dern.

Bug Eye would camp out in his room on Sunday morning by 11 o'clock, fully fed, with plenty of cold beer and smokes to await Rocky's call. What should they do? Where should they go? He thought he was free and clear. He wasn't planning to go to the rendezvous. He had shucked off that old snakeskin and had a shiny, new outfit now. No choice now, really. He had to disappear far away from his birthplace in El Paso or he was doomed - a dead duck! If he stayed, sooner or later the cops would find him. This was exactly what Rocky predicted would happen. Fuck Nick Crenshaw and the horse he rode in on!

CHAPTER 26

Two Robbers Down - Two To Go

Saturday/Sunday/Monday, July 7/8/9, 1973

Nick arrived at the Quayle County Jail late Friday afternoon. Dewey Carruthers was the welcoming committee. So this was the robber who killed Bryce Garrett. He didn't look scary or act scary. Easy to deal with. No complaints. No wisecracks. Compliant. Looked about five years younger than his 23 years. Virtually no beard to speak of. Boy, this fella is swimming in deep waters. Dewey despised Nick for what he did to Bryce, but otherwise he felt sorry for him. A year from now he'd either be singing soprano or slitting his wrists with a shank.

Just before midnight on Friday, both Gillespie and Barlow reported for duty. Dewey went home. He said they would have a quiet night as he walked out the door. Barlow had been on mids for the past week anyway, so he was wide awake. Gillespie was trying to suppress a yawn. They smiled at each other with looks which bespoke of a lot of midnight shifts pulled together, resulting in a strong bond between them.

Gillespie said, "Barlow, it's déjà vu all over again. It seems just like my first day at work here after I completed the POST academy, speaking of which, thanks a lot amigo, for ratting me out to Chief Alex for saying Mr. DeWitt was peachy after my very first time testifying in court. Some friend you are! Nevertheless, in spite of your awful betrayal, and although I'd much rather work days and afternoons, I've really missed working with you. You helped me so much to learn the job. I owe most of what I know about the craft and the mores of law enforcement to you. In fact, as we speak, I'm reminded of some wisdom you conveyed which is probably the best advice anyone ever gave me."

"Thanks, Gillespie. Sorry about mentioning the peachy comment to Chief. I just thought it was funny at the time. You didn't understand how a comment like that goes over in a macho man society. I've missed you too. What piece of sage advice do you recall right now?"

"No matter what, never bitch. Suck it up. Nobody wants to hear it. Ever."

They both broke out into near hysterical laughter because neither one of them wanted to pull another midnight shift, but also remembering Gillespie's first midnight shift on jail duty guarding Polecat and Jaybird. When they finally caught their breath, Barlow replied, "Thanks, Partner. I really needed that tonight. I'll take the first push in the lockup with our new guest, but before I go, fill me in on what you've been up to this summer. It's already halfway over."

"I know . . . . ."

Old times, good friends, pleasant company. The midnight hours passed before they knew it.

*****

Saturday afternoon, Quayle County's only public defender, Sam Davis, came to the jail and met with his new client. Chief Alex had already given Sam full discovery on what he had. The only portion of the case that was still incomplete was a ballistics examination of the .44 revolver. Chief expected a verbal report from the lab on Monday. It wasn't absolutely necessary, because of the felony murder rule, but it would put the icing on the cake. Besides, Nick had already signed a full confession. Chief Alex had told Sam that he would take Nick's case before the grand jury to secure an indictment on Monday morning.

Sam was floored when Nick said he wanted to plead guilty straight up to everything. Nick said he was guilty and he just wanted to get it over with, knowing full well he was staring life without parole square in the eye. If Quayle County didn't put him away for the rest of his natural life, Webb County surely would, or perhaps even Maverick County, although Nick knew for certain that Ev was already dead when he blew Ev's head into smithereens at Rocky's insistence, all the while he was pointing a cocked .45 at him. What else could he do? Sam told Nick he needed to do some checking on case law and that he would be back in a couple of hours.

Sam knew he could write up a bill of information, in which Nick waived indictment by the grand jury, but he wasn't certain it would hold up in a capital murder case like this one, even though Nick was in no danger of being executed (due to the new Supreme Court ruling). Sam called a law school classmate in Dallas with a sterling record as a criminal defense attorney. The classmate told Sam the bill of information would hold up in an appeal or an incompetent counsel review, but he strongly advised against it. He said it would make Sam appear lazy. Make the prosecution dot all the Is and cross all the Ts.

Sam called District Attorney Able DeWitt and ran it by him. Able said he was all for streamlining the case, but it wasn't necessary. He said he had the grand jury scheduled for 9 o'clock Monday morning. Judge Sweeney had a short docket that day. Able planned to arraign Nick after all the other stuff was done. He expected everything would be wrapped up by 11 o'clock. If Judge Sweeney held true to form, Nick would be scheduled for a plea on Tuesday or Wednesday, at which time Nick would be sentenced and turned over to the next jurisdiction who had dibs on him. He said Nick would be a bad memory in Mosby by Friday, except of course, for Bryce's family and the officers working on this case.

Sam asked if there were any way Nick could just be sentenced to life instead of life without parole, especially due to his youth and nearly clean record.

Able said, "Probably not. You know Judge Sweeney, but I'll tell you what I will do. You go see Constance Garrett. If she and her two adult children agree to that and they come see me and sign an affidavit saying so, I will not oppose your plea for mercy. Then Judge Sweeney will have to decide. He may actually agree since at least two other jurisdictions have a shot at sentencing him to life without parole or stacking their sentences, making it a moot point."

Sam said, "Fair enough. Thanks."

Sam went straight over to the Bryce Garrett residence. Constance and Beverly were both at home. They listened quietly as Sam made his pitch. Constance said, "Sam, I don't honestly know how I feel about that. I know you need an answer soon. I'll call Pastor Llewellyn to see if he can stop by to talk with Harvey and Bev and me. We'll pray on it. If we are not all three in agreement, the answer is no. I'll call you tomorrow after church and give you our answer."

Sam thanked her and said he would wait for her call. He went back to the jail and told Nick that he would appear before Judge Sweeney Monday morning. He would have his initial appearance and arraignment then. If he still wanted to plead guilty to all three counts, he could do so at that time. Otherwise, the judge would most likely schedule him for trial later in the week. Assuming he was convicted, he would probably be on his way to Webb County by Friday.

Before Sam left, Nick said, "One last thing. My mother and grandma don't know where I am yet. I haven't called them because I'm so ashamed. Would you ask the sheriff if it would be possible to receive a visit from them tomorrow? Then, either way, would you call them? The number is 773-7564. Tell them everything. Maybe they could come to court on Monday, too. It could well be the last time I ever see them."

Sam said he would get back to him once he had some answers.

Sam called Sheriff Sol, who said under the circumstances, Nick's family could meet with Nick anytime on Sunday, as well as on Monday after court.

Then Sam made the dreaded call. He had to call twice before someone answered the phone. It was answered by Nick's mother, Nancy Crenshaw. His grandmother, Elaine Schmidt, was listening. At first, Mrs. Crenshaw maintained that this was a mistake, that Nick was working a construction job in New Mexico. Then Sam asked, "Ma'am, do you take the El Paso newspaper?"

"Yes. What's that got to do with it?"

"Look in yesterday's paper in the first section. Check the page with the article on who all was arrested. I'll wait."

Mrs. Schmidt said she still had the paper, but part of it was used to line the bottom of the bird cage. She would find it. He waited several minutes. Finally, someone said, "Found it!" It was deathly quiet for a couple of minutes. Then he heard the receiver drop to the floor, and Mrs. Crenshaw blurt out, "Oh, dear Lord!" before she began sobbing uncontrollably. She never stopped. Finally Mrs. Schmidt got on the phone. She asked, "Can we come see him?"

"Yes. The sheriff said you can see him anytime on Sunday, night or day, and after court on Monday, which will probably be after noon. Do you all have reliable transportation?"

"Yes."

"Do you know where Mosby is?"

"Not exactly. I know it's east of here."

"Yes. It's 300 miles east of you on Highway 90, a straight shot from El Paso. You need a full tank of gas. The only place to get gas in between, is Alpine, which is about 200 miles east of El Paso.

"There's a small motor court on the west side of Mosby called the Travelers' Rest. They have 12 little cottages. Cost you about ten bucks a night. If you want, I can make you a reservation, although you probably won't need it, or I can give you the number and you could call them yourself. Betty's Diner is almost next door, but it's closed on Sundays so you might want to bring some sandwiches or something if you want to eat before 6 o'clock, Monday morning."

"What will they do in court on Monday?"

"Court starts at 10 o'clock. It's in the courthouse on US 90, smack dab in the middle of town up on the second floor. The sheriff's office is on the first floor in the back of the building. The jail is in there.

"Anyway, Nick will get an initial appearance, followed by an arraignment. That's when he will be asked if he's pleading guilty or not guilty. You have to prepare yourself. Nick says he's pleading guilty. If he pleads guilty, the judge will probably sentence him right then on the spot. If he pleads not guilty, he will probably get a trial on Tuesday or Wednesday. Understand, Judge Sweeney runs a tight ship. He won't tolerate loud sobbing or theatrics. You must brace yourself.

"Also, I have to tell you, the evidence against Nick is overwhelming, not to mention he signed an 11-page confession after he got arrested in El Paso. Nick admits that he shot and killed the owner of a liquor store here in Mosby with a gun he stole in a burglary in Las Cruces. He's facing life in prison. That's another reason you have to prepare yourself.

"Nick will be transported within a day after sentencing, or maybe even the same day from here to Laredo, in Maverick County, 300 miles east of Mosby, for two counts of murder and one count of armed robbery. His situation is bleak. You may not have an opportunity to visit him again until he begins serving his prison sentence at the Texas State Penitentiary in Huntsville, which is somewhere up north of Houston.

"Mrs. Schmidt, what do you all want me to tell him?"

"Tell him we will see him tomorrow afternoon sometime. Should we bring him something for him to wear in court?"

"Yes. Bring a suit if he has one, or dress slacks and a dress shirt, and a change of underwear with some shoes and socks. No tie. If he has some loafers, bring them. He's not allowed to have shoe laces. Otherwise, he will be wearing the jail outfit consisting of a black and white striped shirt and trousers and shower clogs. Anything else?"

"No. Thanks for calling, Mr. Davis. We will see you soon. Good day."

"Good day."

*****

At noon Sunday morning, just like clockwork, Rocky called Mrs. López. She answered on the first ring. Just as she put the phone up next to her mouth, a loud burp slipped out. She said, "Oops. Excuse me. Is that you?"

"It's me. You hitting the Lizard Spit early today?"

"What of it? When you get as old as me you can do it too, whenever you want to, but remember what I told you? You ain't never going to grow as old as me.

"Sweetie, you done screwed the pooch. I love ya and it kills me to say it, but it's probably curtains for you, and if it is, it might as well be curtains for me. In case you ain't noticed, just like I'm all you got, you're all I got."

"What happened? The cops sitting in my driveway waiting for me to come home? What?"

"I got that call you said I might get from Rodney, who prefers to be called Bug Eye. He told me to read an article in Friday's paper. I read the part he mentioned which said, listen to this. Nicholas D. Crenshaw, arrested and charged with murder and armed robbery in Quayle County, burglary and grand larceny in Crockett County, and receiving stolen property in Maverick County.

"So I says, "So what?" and Rodney says, "Just be sure and read this to Rocky." Also, he said he has two new numbers. The first is his hotel where he's staying at in room 316, 776-4999. He's waiting for a call there right now. Otherwise, call 777-2121 Monday through Saturday between 4 and midnight. That's where he works at. Said to ask for Rodney at either location.

"What is this all about, Rocky? There, I said it. I wasn't going to say your name in case they bugged my phone, but it slipped out anyway."

"Okay. I shot and killed a man in Maverick County who drew down on me. Nick Crenshaw was there and he saw it. I drew down on Nick and almost shot him too, because they was both holding out on me on some jobs we pulled together. We were pals but they both ripped me off big time, in fact, for thousands of dollars. Bug Eye was there, too. He witnessed everything. He saw Ev, the guy I shot, draw down and shoot at me first. He knows Ev had it coming because they double dealt him, too.

"I finally decided to let Nick live. I thought about it real hard though, because I figured he'd get caught doing something else later on and trade me in for a better deal, like a reduced sentence or even a pass. The only reason - the only reason - I let Nick go was because he wouldn't draw down on me, although he considered it real hard for nearly a minute. At that point, shooting him really would have been just plain murder. I should've waxed him anyway, because now the cops are looking for me for murdering Ev, only it was in self defense."

"If that's the case, why don't you take it to trial? You said Bug Eye could verify this."

"Because we were all living a life of crime! We pulled some jobs together. I would wind up in jail anyway on something else. Everything would come unravelled. You see? Nick had to have squealed. That's the bottom line. I'll wind up in prison for the rest of my life if they ever catch me. Same as Bug Eye."

"Oh, Rocky. (Silently weeping.) Everything's ruint now. I ain't been in St. Rita's in forty years now, but I'm marching right over after we hang up. I'll go to confession, ask the priest to say some prayers for you. Call me when you can. I'll be looking for your call this time next Sunday. Promise me."

"Promise. Bye, Grandma. I love you."

"Adiós, Niño."

Rocky called Bug Eye next.

"Hello."

"Bug, it's me."

"You heard."

"Yep. Sorry now we didn't plant Nick with Ev."

"What do you want to do now?"

"Not sure. I'm in Vegas now, but it's not my kinda town. Everyone here has his hand in your pocket. They only got two types of people here - suckers and grifters. Besides, this place is all mobbed up. A guy on his own here doesn't stand a Chinaman's chance. What about you?"

"Well, I thought we were in the clear, but now we're not. I like it a lot here in Fabens. The people are nice and I like my pad and my new job. I work the afternoon shift at a Gulf station. Life is good, but I know now I can't stay much longer. I never got my driver's license back after it was suspended, and now I can't because if they run my name, they'll probably discover I got outstanding felony warrants. Not just saying this, but I'd shoot Nick right between his lying eyes right now if I had the chance."

"Know how come he got busted?"

"No, but I bet that fucker went back to Texas George's. He just couldn't stay away from that easy pussy."

"That's what I think, too. I warned him twice. You heard me."

"I know. Water under the bridge now."

"You wanta go on your own, take a bus to New Orleans or someplace like that where the livin' is easy, or you want to go together?"

"Together. Life alone as a fugitive is a whole lot harder. Nobody's got your back."

"I agree. Look, it's about 800 miles from Vegas to Fabens. I need to get my car serviced. I can leave sometime tomorrow. Be there Tuesday night or Wednesday. We can head east the next day. Where are you staying?"

"At the Fabens Arms Hotel. It's in the CBD (central business district.) They got plenty of vacancies. I'm in room 316. I'll quit my job Tuesday night when I get off. If I don't see you Tuesday night, I'll see you Wednesday sometime. We can head out either then or Thursday."

"Sounds like a plan, see ya when I get there. Adiós."

"Adiós."

*****

It was almost 3 o'clock Sunday afternoon when Momma and Grandma arrived at the sheriff's office. They were greeted by Chief Alex, who was catching up on Nick's case file, and Deputy Randall Meacham, who was on jail duty. The looks on the ladies' horrified faces said it all. It was as if they had just stepped into Dante Alighieri's *Inferno* in his *Divine Comedy.* Neither of these ladies had ever set foot in a sheriff's office before, let alone a jail. Both Chief and Randy treated them kindly and with respect. Chief offered them coffee but they both declined. Randy took custody of Nick's suit for court. He searched both of their purses with tender loving care. He extracted the two Mars candy bars out of Grandma's purse, but upon receiving a slight nod of approval from Chief, he handed them back. He said they would have to leave their purses on the desk in the jail while they visited with Nick, but they could give him the candy bars.

Randy escorted the ladies through the three sets of doors before they even got to the cellblock. The rattling and clanking of the two steel doors scared Grandma so much that she had to be escorted to the jailer's restroom in the very back of the jail before she could even visit. (They didn't have Depends in those days. At least they did have toilet tissue, paper towels, soap, and warm running water.)

After Grandma composed herself, Randy unlocked Nick's cell door and let the ladies enter for their visit. Even though Randy shut the door softly, the sound of the lock engaging after they were inside almost created another accident for Grandma. She burst into tears. Randy said, "Sheriff Pratt said you all could take as much time as you want. I'll be in the back office where the restroom is. Give me a holler when you ladies are ready to leave."

Randy skedaddled as fast as he could because the real moaning commenced and the tears began flowing like Niagara Falls. He turned on the radio to help drown out the mournful commotion. The Cubs-Astros baseball game was only in the 3rd inning. He wondered if the ladies would be ready to go by the time the game was over.

*****

Monday started off like always at the stroke of midnight. A new day with new problems and new opportunities quietly emerged in the quiet of the darkness.

Sheriff Sol unexpectedly showed up at the jail at 6:30, not long after Gillespie pushed off Barlow in the lockup. He poured himself a cup of java and asked Barlow to grab a seat in his office. Barlow brought his coffee and followed Sheriff Sol in. He told Barlow to shut the door.

Barlow asked, "What's up?" (Sheriff Sol seldom ever shut his door.)

He said, "I've been meaning to talk to you for several days now. First, I want to say how much I appreciate everything you've done recently, especially in light of our murder case and how many uncompensated hours you've worked, including extra days on the midnight shift. I'm going to share some things that you must keep to yourself, not so dissimilar to our conversation before I hired Gillespie. A lot of this you can't even mention to Sarah. Savvy?"

"Savvy. You have my word."

"Good. These are all personnel issues. I'll start at the top of the roster.

"Chief is now our senior citizen since Archie retired. He's even older than Slick by a couple of years. He's the glue that holds things together. He works untold unpaid hours as both our chief deputy and our investigator. We would be in a soup sandwich here if anything ever happened to him. Recently, he's been having some health issues. Soon as Mr. Crenshaw gets transferred to Webb County, at my behest, Chief's taking some time off. He's under the care of a cardiologist over in Del Rio and he's scheduled to take some tests. I don't want to get ahead of myself, but he might need surgery. Even if he doesn't, he's taking some time off anyway. He's exhausted and he needs to rest. Hopefully, he'll get a clean bill of health and be back to work in a week or two. This is extremely personal for him, so keep it to yourself.

"Next is Ernie. He's got in-service training coming up. He's out for a week.

"Saturday, Chunk's mother-in-law, his sister-in-law, and her four kids showed up unexpectedly from Columbus, New Mexico. There's some kind if drama with his brother-in-law. Chunk's planning to go with them back to New Mexico an effort to set things straight. Bottom line is, he's out for at least a week.

"Kirk is leaving Thursday with his family, driving to Hurlburt Field in the panhandle of Florida. It's near the beach. He's got 14 days of Air Force Reserve duty, augmenting Active Duty personnel in the 306th Security Police Detachment. They're making sort of a vacation out of it. That's a 1,000-mile drive each way, so he'll be out about three weeks.

"You're next but we'll get to you in a moment.

"Gillespie doesn't know this yet, so keep it on the down low. Sheriff Waters over in Alpine called me and said his mother, Gillespie's grandma, is in bad shape. Said she was circling the drain. That's how bad it is. Gillespie doesn't know yet that it's this near to the end. Her mother isn't handling it very well. Leland said he would call me first before he calls Gillespie that she needs to come home. He wanted me to pre-approve her leave. That could be any day now, and I'd expect her to be out for a week or so.

"Randy's next, but I'll get back to him in a minute.

"Dewey's next in line. It's never happened before that both he and Kirk were on annual training at the same time, but it has now. He's got a three-week stint as a guest instructor at the Army's Finance Corps training facility in Fort Benjamin Harrison in Indianapolis. It's a huge deal for him. You may not know it, but he's up for sergeant major. He's flying instead of driving. Praise the Lord. Means he won't have so much time in travel status.

"Slick's last but certainly not least. Sheriff Will Shive over in Val Verde County called. He needs a seasoned cowboy deputy for an undercover assignment in a cattle rustling case. He thought about Slick as a result of our sheep rustling case here. Slick wants to do it, and I owe Sheriff Shive a favor for what they did for us when Cordell got shot. Not sure how long this will take, but it could be a couple of weeks. This is hush hush just like our rustling case was.

"Now, that leaves Randy and you and me. Randy's graciously agreed to work mids for two or three weeks, however long I need for him to do it. As soon as Nick is out of our hair, Randy'll go to mids and you'll be on afternoon shift. Loretta and I will still be on days. She can handle most of the telephone calls and walk-in traffic. I'll also overlap some on afternoons and assist you, especially if anything dicey pops up. I'm not even taking off my uniform when I do go home until I go to bed. I expect you to call me as soon as you get something out of the ordinary. In fact that's an order. Savvy?"

"Savvy."

"Good. Here's the payback. I know you and my goddaughter are planning a trip to Bisbee to visit your sister next month. Take up to two weeks on me. No chargeable leave. I owe you more, but that's the best I can do.

"Last thing on the agenda is perhaps the most sensitive and important. Chief Alex doesn't even know this. You've probably noticed that the number of calls we receive has increased substantially. That's a win-win for cops who are eager for adventure and love to serve the public. At the same time, it means deputies have to work more unpaid overtime.

"I went to see Archie now that he's on the Board of Supervisors to see if I could hire a 10th deputy. Archie said revenue has been down and that the county doesn't have the money right now. He even said if somebody quit or went to another agency, he's not sure he could even get another vote to fill the vacancy. He said the county is going to have to raise property taxes if they want to keep the status quo on services. Even talking about raising taxes is a non-starter for most Quayle County residents. Nevertheless, the board will have to call an emergency town hall meeting soon to lay out the financial problems we're facing. Either they vote to raise taxes, or some services will have to be reduced. No way around it."

"What about the surplus the county had at the end of 1971?"

"All gone. We needed to replace a grader and some other highway equipment. Keep this to yourself. Everything will all come out in *The Trail's End* pretty soon."

"Look, we'll make this work. Archie said they only had two deputies most of the time he was here and the population was roughly the same. They didn't even have a midnight deputy until 1965. I remember that well. No one is in danger of losing his job."

"Will do. Mum's the word. Listen, I just want to say that the two best things that ever happened to me was getting hired here by you and meeting Sarah. I will do whatever it takes to help you or the office out. In fact that's one and the same thing to me. If I have to work 16 hours a day, so be it. Thanks for the comp time next month. We are in serious need of a vacation before school starts. Just have two more semesters to go. Sarah will be thrilled."

"Okay. Get back to work. Chief will be here any minute."

*****

Nick's initial appearance, arraignment, and guilty plea went off without a hitch. Chief later said that Judge Sweeney spent 20 minutes questioning Nick under oath, trying to decide if he fully understood the ramifications of pleading guilty. Nick stood his ground.

Judge Sweeney found him guilty on all three counts. Then he did something out of the ordinary for him. Instead of sentencing Nick right then, Judge Sweeney scheduled it for Tuesday morning. He said he wanted Constance Garrett and her children in court to give them an opportunity to speak their piece. Ditto for Nick's mother and grandmother. He was not compelling anyone to speak, just giving them the opportunity before he sentences Nick. Then he told Sheriff Sol to call Webb County and advise them to have a transport unit standing by, ready to take immediate custody of Nick. If for some reason they cannot do that, he would have a DOC unit take him to Huntsville forthwith.

Monday (in actuality early Tuesday morning) would be Nick's last night in Mosby. Barlow found out at 11:45 p.m. when he reported to duty. That meant he'd have a short-change and report for his next shift at 3:45 Tuesday afternoon. So be it. Hot diggity dog!

CHAPTER 27

The Perfect Storm

Thursday, July 12, 1973

Rocky and Bug Eye stopped for the night in Alpine, en route to The Big Easy (New Orleans.) They had been enjoying the trip in Rocky's cherry, GTO muscle car, with its souped up engine, low, pleasing rumble due to its glass packed mufflers, Hurst four-speed transmission, deep, high gloss, midnight blue finish, sparkling chrome, wide track mag wheels, and snow white, rolled and tucked leather interior, not to mention the envious looks from guys and chicks alike. Nearly everyone who saw it fell in lust. They secured lodging at the Best Western. After dinner, they repaired back to the room and drank icy cold, Coors beer to the point of oblivion. Wednesday night slipped into Thursday morning completely unnoticed. They didn't wake up until 1 o'clock, Thursday afternoon. They both felt like angry bees were swarming in their heads. Their mouths were sour and dry like they had been shoveling hot, steamy piles of baby shit into their pie holes with a wooden spatula.

They checked out late and had to pay extra. They gobbled up an afternoon breakfast of pancakes and greasy sausage links with a bucket of black coffee at the Pancake House down the street. Tasty! They returned to the car feeling almost human. They had just pulled out of the parking lot headed eastbound when they were jumped by a Brewster County mountie (Deputy Ambrose Collins) in a marked unit with his overhead, oscillating, blue light flashing. He had just finished calling in the license plate number for a wanted and registration check. It was a good thing he did, because he'd never get another opportunity.

Bug Eye said, "I wonder what the Hell he wants."

Rocky replied, "I don't know, but I ain't sticking around to find out. Buckle up and hang on. I'm gonna blow his fucking doors off." Then he goosed it. The county mountie flipped on his screaming, high-pitched Federal siren which was mounted on his hood, and the chase was on. The siren was so loud, if you happened to be standing next to it, your eardrums would burst. Instead of fox and hounds, it was cops and robbers. Within two minutes, a second Brewster County unit driven by Deputy Enos Garvey joined in the chase, but he had a lot of distance to cover and was never going to catch up with the GTO unless it crashed or ran out of gas. Basically, Deputy Ambrose Collins was all on his own.

At 142 miles per hour, Rocky's hotrod easily outdistanced Deputy Collins' 1973 Ford LTD, with a 460 cubic-inch V-8 engine, and a California Highway Patrol high speed shift kit with positraction, which topped out at 137 miles per hour. He never gave up. He knew the GTO had no place to run except for east, deeper into the vast, empty, Chihuahuan desert. No place to hide. No good place to make a stand. The GTO was already caught unless the fugitives managed to disable Deputy Collin's police cruiser.

They tried. The passenger leaned out his window and tried twice to shoot out Deputy Collins' tires or ventilate his radiator, each time with a full cylinder of six .357 rounds, but Deputy Collins was too far back. Lucky for him the asswipe didn't have a rifle. After 30 miles of hot pursuit, Deputy Collins asked the dispatcher to call Quayle County and to tell them they were headed their direction. By then, the wanted and registration checks had been conducted and both deputies knew they were in pursuit of a car owned by Bruce K. Givens, a fugitive wanted for bank robbery in Quayle County, in addition to other charges. He was reported to be in the company of Rodney A. Tinsley, also a fugitive, for the same charges. Both were considered armed and dangerous. No shit? Deputy Collins had quickly figured that out. He confirmed that a second man was riding in the front passenger seat and that the passenger had been shooting at him.

Sheriff Sol had taken a domestic disturbance call on the northeast outskirts in Mosby. At the time, Barlow was at the do-it-yourself car wash cleaning up their newest marked unit. Sheriff Sol told Barlow he would call if he needed assistance. He didn't think he would because he knew the two antagonists, Mr. and Mrs. Jethro and Arlene Vogel, very well. They were good people. Jethro worked as a track inspector for the Santa Fe Railway. He had been with them for 19 years. Arlene was the produce supervisor at the IGA grocery. They had three school age children.

Sheriff Sol was off the air the whole time he was at the Vogel residence. He was out for more than an hour because besides being a lawman, he was also doing his very best to be a marriage counselor.

Jethro was in the second week of a two-week suspension from work because he got caught by his supervisor with a half-empty half-pint bottle of Early Times in the chest pocket of his bib overalls while he was eating his lunch in a company utility truck, the type with train wheels that can be lowered so it could be driven on the rails. The company had a zero tolerance policy for alcohol on the job. The loss of wages was having a very serious impact on family finances.

Jethro was sitting on the living room couch, drunk as a skunk, but he was quiet and passive. He was not belligerent or loud. Arlene was in her work clothes, pissed off to the big max. When Sheriff Sol arrived, she pointed at Jethro and yelled, "Look at him! He's completely shitfaced! I'm going to be late for work and I can't leave the kids with him in this condition! Now I'm probably going to lose my job because of him." She burst into tears and plopped down in an easy chair sobbing uncontrollably, hands knotted into fists when she covered her eyes. Then she shouted, "Sol, I want you to take him to jail! It would serve him right. Get him out of my sight."

Sol replied softly, "Arlene, I can't take anybody to jail for being drunk in his own home. There's no law against that." (The very last thing Sheriff Sol wanted to do was arrest someone and put him in jail while they were so shorthanded. He uttered a silent prayer that he wouldn't be forced to make an arrest.)

She said, "Well, there damn well should be if it means the person is going to put his family in the poor house! What am I supposed to do? I'm at my wits end with him! I can't even pay our bills. I don't make enough money." Then she burst into heavy sobbing again.

This went on for ten minutes. Finally, Sol asked, "Arlene, how far are you in arrears?"

"Too far. I got $334 dollars in overdue bills on the counter, my car's almost out of gas, we're nearly out of groceries, and I WORK FOR A FUCKING GROCERY!" She burst into a sobbing fit again.

Sol asked, "What about that, Jethro?"

"It's true, Sol, and it's all my fault. I let my whole family down. I ain't a drunk and I wasn't drinking or drunk when they caught me with that bottle. I had it with me because I was going fishing with a buddy after work. I got drunk today because I'm a sorry piece of shit, excuse my French."

"Where's the bottle you've been nipping on today?"

"She done poured it all down the drain."

"Do you have anymore?"

"Nope."

"What about this? Arlene, you got somebody who could watch the kids today?"

"Well it's nearly 4 o'clock. My sister is probably home by now. I could call and see if it's okay to drop them off over at her house."

"Would you like me to talk to Mr. George (the IGA store manager) for you? I'm pretty sure I can smooth things over with him."

"No. I can call in and let them know I'll be about 20 minutes late. I can make it up, but thanks for asking."

"Okay. This is the last thing. I'm writing you, Arlene, a personal check for $500. Joanna and I have a rainy day fund. You all can start paying me back once Jethro goes back to work. How does $20 a week sound until it's all paid off? You can cash the check at work, buy some groceries, get some gas for your car, and pay your bills."

"Sol, I'm sorely tempted, but I just couldn't. What if folks heard about this? I would be so embarrassed. We're not a charity case."

"It's not charity. You're going to pay me back $20 a week beginning when Jethro gets his next paycheck. Nobody has to know but you and me and Jethro and Joanna. Okay?"

"Okay. Thank you, Sol. You're a lifesaver."

"Jethro, you're going to lay off the sauce. You're a good man and a good husband and a good father. Anyone can slip and fall. You gotta pick yourself up and do what you are more than capable of doing, everyday. Okay? I've known you a long time. Don't let yourself down. Roger that?"

"Roger that. Thanks, Sol."

While Sheriff Sol was otherwise fully engaged as a social worker, peacemaker, friend, marriage counselor, lawman, lender, and several other honorable pursuits, everything on the west side of the county was heating up.

Miss Loretta was all alone in the jail. She answered the phone. It was Miriam Hanson, a dispatcher for the Brewster County Sheriff's Office. She said, "Loretta, our deputies need some help. They're in a high speed pursuit probably less than than 30 miles now from your county line. They're chasing a blue Pontiac GTO, believed to be driven by Bruce Givens. They think Rodney Tinsley is in it, too. The passenger has fired at our unit. I know you all have outstanding felony warrants on both of them, and that you've been looking for them. They've been clocked at more than 140 miles per hour. Can you all set up a roadblock?"

"I think so. We only have two units working right now. I'll give 'em a call and tell 'em to set up on our side of the county line. I'll also have them switch to F-2. Can your deputies switch to F-2 also?"

"Yes."

"Okay. Let's stay connected. Don't hang up. I'm not sure you and I can hear each other over the air. A hundred miles is a stretch even for a base-to-base transmission."

"Will do."

Loretta set the receiver down and pushed the talk button on the desktop radio console. "Quayle 1 and Quayle 6, from Base."

"This is Quayle 6. Go ahead."

"Quayle 6, Brewster SO is in a high speed pursuit on 90 about 30 miles west of the county line. They're chasing a blue GTO registered to Bruce Givens. He has a passenger believed to be Rodney Tinsley. Shots have been fired. They want to know if you can set up a roadblock on our side of the county line. Also, as soon as you respond, switch to F-2."

Base, this is Quayle 6. Will do. Switching to F-2. Give me a radio check."

"Quayle 6, this is Base on F-2. Copy?"

"Lima Charley (loud and clear.)

"Okay, I'll keep checking for Quayle 1 on F-1 until I get him."

"10-4."

Barlow kicked it in the ass and set up just west of the entrance to the little rest stop three miles east of the county line. He didn't encounter any traffic the farther west he drove. Praise the Lord for small miracles! He was in a quandary. How do you set up a one-car roadblock on a flat road with no ditches to intercept a high speed car chase? The suspect vehicle could easily cut around him on either side. What about uninvolved motorists? How do you ensure their safety, prevent them from being hit, or shot, or taken hostage? You can't. Barlow did the only thing he could think of to do. He straddled the middle of the road facing south, with his oscillating blue light flashing. He got on the radio.

"Base, what is the location of the suspect vehicle?"

"Stand by.

(Two minutes pass.)

"Quayle 6, they're approaching the county line. The suspect vehicle is far enough ahead of the lead unit that he no longer has it in sight. Also, I have not been able to reach Quayle 1. What do you want me to do?"

"Keep trying. I'm set up on the highway at the rest stop. I'm getting out of the unit. I'm switching my radio to the external speaker. I may not be able to respond, but I should be able to hear your transmission. 10-4?"

"10-4."

Barlow grabbed his .30-30 Winchester lever action rifle, chambered a 170-grain Winchester Silvertip bullet, and trotted about 50 yards west of his vehicle about 50 feet to the north side of the highway. He took up a comfortable sitting position, shouldered his rifle, aimed at the roadway, and waited. It shouldn't be long now.

He could hear the oncoming GTO screaming towards him when it was only a flyspeck, like a shoulder-fired missile. It slowed down a little as it got closer. Obviously, they had spotted his flashing blue light. Then it picked up speed. Barlow had a straight-on shot, but at about a 30-degree (11 o'clock) angle to the southwest, instead of just due west. It complicated the shot. A lateral shot would necessitate a calculated lead so as not to shoot behind it.

As the GTO continued to approach, it began creeping over into the westbound lane. The driver was planning to bypass the marked unit to its left. When the GTO was about 120 yards out, Barlow fired into the windshield where he thought the driver's head would be. He chambered a second round and continued to aim for the same point. The car slowed, skidded erratically, and swerved towards him out of control. Barlow could see his bullet hole through the windshield. He jumped up and put his second round in the grill to blow a hole in the radiator. It worked, but the car was still skidding out of control. It hit a small boulder and flipped over on its left side, sliding before it came to rest 20 very short feet from Barlow.

Barlow chambered a third round. There was a pregnant pause. Then a perp climbed halfway out the front passenger window with a shiny silver revolver in his hand. The glint from the sun caused the revolver to flash as bright as lightning. The assailant had blood streaming down his forehead. He brought his revolver up shoulder-high, aiming at Barlow, but Barlow shot first, striking him in the chest. Barlow chambered a quick fourth round, and planted a shot smack dab in his face. He slid back down, partially out of sight.

Barlow was 99 percent certain the passenger was dead, but he was taking no chances. Ditto for the driver, whom he could not see. Barlow chambered a fifth round, and circled wide around the GTO from the front driver's side, around the rear, and up towards the front passenger door, ready to shoot again. The passenger was hanging backwards out of the right front window from the small of his back just above his hips, all splayed out. His Colt .357 was laying on the ground. Barlow looked in the window past his body. The driver was piled up on the floorboard under the steering column like a Houdini contortionist. It looked like he died from a headshot but Barlow couldn't tell for sure.

Barlow walked back to his cruiser, loading five more rounds in his rifle (since a round was already chambered) as he walked. He turned his cruiser around, turned off the overhead light, and parked on the westbound shoulder of the road facing west, directly across from the GTO, obscuring it from potential gawkers as best he could. He keyed the mike to call Base just as the first Brewster County cruiser appeared on the scene. Deputy

Ambrose Collins got out of his unit, walked over to the GTO, and looked at the bodies. He asked, "You done all this by your lonesome?"

"We didn't have anyone else. These the assholes who shot at you?"

"The one hanging out the window is."

"Same dude who shot at me in my chase with him a couple of weeks ago."

"He won't shoot at anymore cops now."

"Nope. Can you wait just a sec. I gotta call this in."

"Sure."

While Barlow was on the radio, the second Brewster unit pulled up. Deputy Enos Garvey was driving.

"Quayle Base from Quayle 6."

"Go ahead Quayle 6."

"Situation resolved. Is Quayle 1 still off the air?"

"Go for Quayle 1."

"Quayle 1, I'll wait to talk to you once you get here."

"Roger that. I'm about two minutes out."

Barlow got out of his unit and greeted both deputies. He asked, "Do you all think you could lend us a hand? My sheriff should be here any minute, but we don't have anyone else available today."

"Deputy Collins said, "Hell, yeah! Whatcha need?"

"We need someone to keep any traffic moving, and the sheriff is going to need someone to help him process the crime scene. I would, but since I shot these oxygen thieves, I'm not allowed to."

Deputy Garvey said, "I'll handle traffic. Ambrose, you wanta help Sheriff Sol?"

"It would be my honor."

Sheriff Sol pulled up, took Barlow aside, and asked, "Are you okay?"

"Yes. I handled this the only way I knew how to."

Barlow introduced Sheriff Sol to both deputies. Then he

proceeded to walk Sheriff Sol through the sequence of events while Deputy Collins and Deputy Garvey looked on in awe.

Everyone had an assignment. Barlow handled the traffic, of which they only had two passing motorists, and the Brewster deputies helped Sheriff Sol process the crime scene. It was dusk when they were finally done. Pete Ricketts took the bodies to the medical examiner's office in Del Rio, and Buck Boyd towed the GTO to his secure lot. Sheriff Sol thanked the Brewster deputies. He said he would call Sheriff Waters to express his thanks and appreciation. Then he and Barlow drove back to the jail.

Miss Loretta was still on duty. She ran up and gave Barlow a big hug when he walked through the door. She made sure Sheriff Sol didn't need anything and then she left.

Sheriff Sol and Barlow went back into the sheriff's private office. He sat down at his desk, unlocked his bottom drawer, retrieved a bottle of Wild Turkey 101 and two glasses. He poured them both a snort. They clinked glasses and sipped slowly. Nothing was said. Sol poured them both another one, and they sipped on it too.

Finally, Sol said, "Barlow, I don't know what I would do without you. I really don't. Our offensive line has more than a few holes in it, but you are always there to plug 'em up. Always, without fail. Either trouble has a way of finding you or you seek it out. I'm not sure which. More and more you remind me of our Quayle County patriarch, Ripsnort Sweeney, except you wear a badge and don't have any of his amassed wealth. Someday when I step down from sheriff, I hope you will succeed me. I love you like a son. Suffice it to say, I'm more concerned for your safety than any of the other deputies. You gotta have a rabbit's foot or a four-leaf clover in your pocket. Thank God for that.

"Just think about it. A one-deputy roadblock faced down two killers in a car traveling over 100 miles-per-hour and killed them both with no injury to himself or damage to the police cruiser. It's a marvel. Nothing less."

Sheriff Sol finished his drink, placed the bottle back in the drawer, locked it, scooped up the empty glasses, and walked to the door. He said, "The administrative quagmire can wait 'til morning. No more drama tonight. The Givens Gang is no more. C'est la vie.

"I'm going home. Kiss my wife. Hug my kids. Have another snort. Pray for your wellbeing.

"Soon as Randy shows up, get the flock out of here. Go to bed. Make love to your lovely, precious wife. Pray to God for keeping you safe. Tomorrow will be a new day, full of surprises.

"Come in early, say noon. We'll get some lunch. Look sharp. You know the newsies will be here. I'll put them off until 1:30. You know what to say and how to say it.

"Adiós, Deputy Sheriff Barlow K. Adams, formerly of Arlo, Texas, and now of Mosby, Quayle County, Texas."

"Adiós, Sheriff."

EPILOGUE

Ruminations of a Good Man

Sunday, August 5, 1973

Arthur Baker and his wife returned home from church. Clarice fixed them a fabulous fried chicken dinner, including cherry pie for dessert. Cordell and Darla had gone to Alpine to visit her mother. Hank was back in Austin. Barlow and Sarah were off on a much deserved vacation to visit his sister in Bisbee.

Arthur was feeling out of sorts. He saddled his big bay, Dwight (D. Eisenhower) with the white slash on his face and four white stockings, and rode down to the river. This time he brought his .30-30 Marlin saddle gun and a half-box of shells. He felt like killing a varmint, such as a coyote or a rattlesnake.

It had been 30 years since he had joined the Army Air Force and departed for war. America had been in danger of losing the war against the Germans and the Japs. It was do or die for everyone in America. The U.S. finally whipped them both and freedom ultimately prevailed, but at a tremendous cost in lives and national treasure. Arthur wasn't sure he would make it back home, but he did by the Grace of God. In the hallowed words of Francis Scott Key, America is still "the land of the free and the home of the brave".

Since then, still in the middle of the protracted Cold War with the Soviets, the cease fire of the Korean War, and now what looked like the end of the War in Vietnam, things in America were still in a fine kettle of fish and most likely even worse.

The crooks were in charge and the un-American Americans were gaining control. It looked like President Richard M. Nixon was going to be impeached for covering up the Watergate burglary. Vice President Spiro T. Agnew was staring at prison for extortion and tax evasion from when he was the Governor of Maryland. The federal debt was soaring past $450 billion dollars. Can you imagine? How will we ever pay off that debt? Hippies were protesting the Vietnam War and President Nixon. Free love was turning girls and young women into sluts. Gloria Steinem was leading a man-hating feminist movement. The Black Panthers were spewing out racial hatred. Illegal drugs were stoning our youth. Crime was on the upswing, even in a sleepy burg like Mosby, and on and on and on.

"Ah!" There was a rattlesnake under that creosote bush! Author aimed, fired, and shot it nearly in two. That's what it gets for slithering on the Bar B! He cut off the nine rattles and put them in his shirt pocket.

He found a smooth boulder to sit on, and watched the river slowly undulate to a final destination unknown. Did it stop somewhere in the Gulf of Mexico or did it go all the way to Africa and beyond?

He saw a heretofore undetected roadrunner snatch up a small bird and race away just like the one in the cartoon show.

He watched the few white clouds slowly drift away to the East. Like Black Magic, a vulture had begun its slow circle way up high in the air over the dead snake. How did it spot the carrion so quickly?

A lone tumbleweed bounced across the desert intermittently, solely at the pleasure of the wind.

A bigger lizard chased a smaller one, most likely with intent to consume.

He spotted a little yellow flower on a small cactus.

Before long, Mother Nature had soothed his unsettled nerves. It was time to return to the house and hug his wife.

Life was good. They would be okay. God was in control.

About the Author

Earl Snort is the nom de plumé of a retired law enforcement officer with more than forty years' experience toting a badge and a gun. Before that he served in the armed forces. He and his wife have been married more than fifty years. They reside in the South. They have one son, also a law enforcement officer, and two grandchildren.

This is the author's sixth foray into writing fiction. After a lifetime of writing non-fiction to document investigations of true crime, he decided to try his hand at make believe. He hopes you enjoy the yarn.

April 2023

Making Mountains Out of Molehills

- Author: Earl Snort
- Publisher: TotalRecall Publications
- Paper Back: 9781590954324
- Ebook: 9781590956533
- Number of pages: 320
- Publication Date: 2019

It was 1969. Barlow Adams, age 20, was a recently discharged veteran. He was driving late at night on a lonely stretch of highway in the Trans-Pecos region of Texas. He stopped to render assistance to a motorist with a flat tire. What he stepped into was a vicious attempted rape. He rescued the victim, which catapulted him into an appointment as a deputy sheriff.

Along the way he encounters an enchanting woman who will change his life forever. In addition, he will be confronted by a gang of outlaw bikers who are obsessed with killing him while he is still learning the ropes of becoming a lawman. Will they succeed?

This is the story of a young man in the 1960's, an era which has long been forgotten except for those who lived it.

Barlow Adams Series Book 1

When Dreams Come True ~ Sort Of

- Author: Earl Snort
- Publisher: TotalRecall Publications
- Paper Back: 9781648830006
- Ebook: 9781648830013
- Number of pages: 320
- Publication Date: 2020

The year is 1970. Barlow Adams is a young deputy sheriff in a rural county in the Trans-Pecos region of Texas. He's a rookie still learning the ropes. Up until now, his experience has been limited to working in the jail and performing routine patrol work that is anything but routine when bad men decide to exert themselves in furtherance of their wicked ways.

In recent months, a gang of rustlers had begun to prey on the livestock of unwitting ranchers. The sheriff has decided to stop them cold wherever he finds them. He employs all the limited resources at his disposal to achieve this goal. One of those resources is Deputy Adams, who learns new law enforcement skills in teamwork, criminal investigation, surveillance, and undercover operations.

Barlow also learns something else. The crime may be solved and plans may be hatched to catch the evildoers, but, in the end, there's usually a joker in the woodpile who upsets the applecart and then suddenly Life becomes a free for all.

Barlow Adams Series Book 11

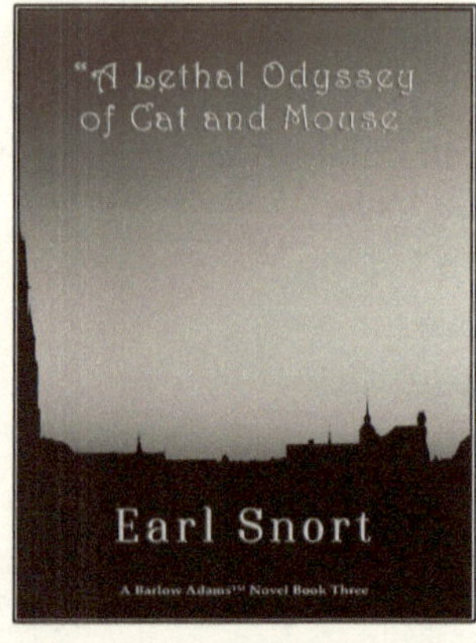

A Lethal Odyssey of Cat and Mouse

- Author: Earl Snort
- Publisher: TotalRecall Publications
- Paper Back: 9781648830785
- Ebook: 9781648830792
- Number of pages: 320
- Publication Date: 2021

The year is 1971. Barlow Adams is a young deputy sheriff in a rural county in the Trans-Pecos region of Texas. After two years of instruction, he completed the Texas Police Officers Standard Training Course, and now he is fully certified as a law enforcement officer. As important as that is, something even more important is about to take place.

Barlow and Sarah, his fiancée, are about to be married.
They don't know it yet, but a depraved outlaw biker Barlow arrested two years ago has decided to stalk and murder Barlow and Sarah while they are on their honeymoon. The outlaw biker isn't operating on his own. He recruits criminals as savage as he is to pull off his barbarous scheme.

By the time law enforcement learns of the plot, the newlyweds have already departed. Until, and unless, they call home, there is no way to warn them.
Tick tock.

Barlow Adams Series Book III

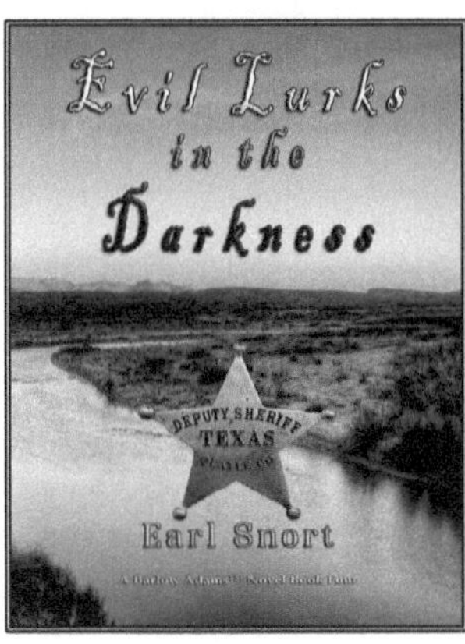

Evil Lurks in the Darkness
Even When Strong Men Stand Watch

- Author: Earl Snort
- Publisher: TotalRecall Publications
- Paper Back: 9781648831782
- eBook: 9781648831799
- Number of pages: 306
- Publication Date: 2022

The year is 1972. Quayle County, located in the Trans-Pecos region of Texas, has seen an uptick of illegal alien smuggling from across the Rio Grande. The alien smugglers are determined and violent. The Border Patrol is overwhelmed with greater numbers of human trafficking cases in other areas, and therefore is unable to assist. Illegal aliens and Americans are dying alike. The small sheriff's office and the local population are left to their own devices to resolve this crisis.

Once again, Sheriff Solomon Pratt, Deputy Barlow Adams, Deputy Slick Oldman, retired Deputy Archie Willis, plus the new rookie, Deputy E.M. Gillespie, and the rest of the staff on the Quayle County Sheriff's Office rise to the occasion to vanquish the threat.

Barlow Adams Series Book IV

Thicker Than Blood
Murder, Hide, & Go Seek Texas Style
- Author: Earl Snort
- Publisher: TotalRecall Publications
- Paper Back: 9781648832567
- eBook: 9781648832574
- Number of pages: 312
- Publication Date: 2023

The year is 1973. A four-man crew of stick-up artists has been on a rampage in South Texas along the Rio Grande corridor from El Paso to Laredo.

One day they stick up the bank and liquor store in Mosby in Quayle County, killing one person and severely wounding another. Mosby is a small town in a large county, with only 3,000 souls and very little crime.

The chase is on. No quarter asked or taken by either side. Sheriff Solomon Pratt and his eight-man, two-woman department are committed to bringing the culprits to justice. Deputy Barlow Adams is doubly committed because one of the victims is his brother-in-law. Barlow's bond with his brother-in-law is thicker than blood.

Barlow Adams Series Book V

The Lawrence County Moonshine War

- Author: Earl Snort
- Publisher: TotalRecall Publications
- Paper Back: 9781648831782
- eBook: 9781648831256
- Number of pages: 200
- Publication Date: 2022

This is a tale of a changeling shortly after these powers were bestowed upon him. Jack, who began life as a rabbit, fell asleep in arid West Texas shortly after wishing he had a home someplace else in a more temperate climate. When he awoke, he was a young man in a forest glen in such a place. He got exactly what he wished for! The problem was, he was wearing an Army uniform and he did not know his location. He didn't even know which century it was! Jack was suffering from a serious case of amnesia.

He soon learned that the year was 1920 and that he had been slumbering on his own property in Eastern Kentucky. He was re-introduced to his cousin, Gerard, whom he did not recognize, yet with whom he had maintained a best-friend relationship since childhood. Gerard also introduced Jack into his moonshine business during these, the early days of Prohibition. Before long, Jack found himself situated between big city gangsters and state investigators.
Lead was flying in the hills of Eastern Kentucky and Jack was in the thick of it.

A Jack Rabbit Novel